I0727361

Once Upon a Genie

DEMELZA CARLTON

Three tales in the Romance a Medieval Fairy Tale series

Return:
Hansel and Gretel Retold

DEMELZA CARLTON

A tale in the Romance a Medieval Fairy Tale series

"What about that plant? Can you tell me its properties?" Mother asked, pointing.

Rhona eyed the yellow flowers. "Tansy. Useful to combat gout or help a woman lose an unwanted child. We use it in tansy cakes and to scent the rushes on the floor on feast days."

"It can also be used to dye cloth in shades of yellow and green," Mother said.

Rhona sighed. "I will never remember them

all."

Mother turned and smiled. "Of course you will. One day. It takes practice, is all. There are books at home full of this, but your head needs to be full of it, too, for you won't have the book in the woods with you." She pointed at a plant with downy leaves. "What of that one?"

Rhona glared at the plant. "A stinging nettle. The young plants can be boiled and eaten, and the older ones can be soaked and the fibres woven into cloth. Best to wear gloves when you pick it, though." She had made that mistake once, and had no intention of doing so again. Nettles hurt.

"And that – " Mother gave a cry as her horse stumbled, and she tumbled from the saddle.

"Mother!"

Rhona slid from her horse and dashed to Mother. She lay face down, with a spreading pool of blood beneath her.

Rhona shook Mother's shoulder, and she'd never been so relieved to hear a groan in her life. "What should I do, Mother?" Rhona asked urgently.

"Use your magic, and get me home," Mother whispered.

"But you said…" Rhona snapped her mouth shut. She was old enough to know that her mother changed her mind when circumstances required it. "Very well."

Rhona took a deep breath, then bit her lip. The breeze came the instant she summoned it, plucking her clothing as it passed, but saving most of its power for Mother. She let the air currents lift Mother back onto her horse, but the animal shied as soon as it smelled blood. The frightened horse bolted, and Mother fell a second time.

This time, she didn't move.

Rhona sent another gust of wind, stronger this time, to pick Mother up and bring her to Rhona's own horse. Rhona's gelding was an old warhorse who shied at nothing, even as he was made to carry two women instead of one.

"Mother, should I go slowly, so I don't hurt you more, or should I hurry, to get you home faster?" Rhona asked.

No response.

That meant Mother wouldn't feel the jolting if they galloped, and they would arrive sooner. Rhona kneed her horse into flight, and the gelding willingly obeyed.

It was both the longest and the shortest ride of her life. Rhona shouted for help as she arrived at her father's house. Her arms ached from holding tight to her mother, but she refused to let go until Mother was in better hands than hers. Healer's hands, hopefully. Someone who knew how to stop the bleeding, for all Rhona's knowledge of herbs had fled when her mother fell.

"Rhona needs a healer, too!" someone shouted. Her oldest sister, Nuala.

Rhona shook her head irritably. "I'm fine. It's Mother who needs help."

"Why are you all covered in blood, then?" Nuala demanded with all the force of a twelve-year-old demanding to be considered a capable adult.

Rhona glanced down. The front of her dress was stained red. "Mother," she choked out, and ran for Mother's bedchamber. Nuala was hot on her heels.

Mother's eyes fluttered open. "Go get the other children, and your father," she said.

Rhona moved to obey, but Mother caught her sleeve. "No. Nuala, not you."

"I am sorry, mistress, but there is nothing more I can do. We can only wait," the healer said.

Mother nodded and waved the man out.

"I'm sorry. I should have gotten you here faster. I should have – " Rhona began.

Mother hushed her. "I do not have much time, he says. I lost too much blood. No one could save me, not even you. To think I'd hoped to give your father a son…but now I never will, and the babe will die with me. Just like my sister."

"Aunt Brigid – "

"Was no aunt to you, though she was my sister. She protected me as only she could, and so when she died, I swore to protect you. Now…it is your turn." Mother winced, then went on, "You must protect your sisters from whatever comes, but especially from Alban invaders. But you cannot use your powers, or they will know."

Rhona almost didn't want to ask, but she had to know. "Know what?"

"That I am not your mother. Brigid was."

"And my father…?"

"Is still your father. When the Albans attacked our home, I was already betrothed to him, his virgin bride, but the Albans…they…" Mother swallowed. "Brigid found me, too late to stop them. She swore she would protect me after that, but when it came to my own husband…the man I loved, I could not stand to have a man touch me. So she…pretended to be me, in the dark. We hid her pregnancy from your father and I told him you were mine. He does not know, and if he were ever to find out…I fear it would break his heart. He can never know you are a witch like Brigid. Never. But you must protect your sisters, like I protected you. Promise me!"

"Mother, I – "

"Promise me!"

Rhona fought to hold back her tears. "I swear on my father's life that I will protect my sisters."

Mother – no, Aunt Blanid – subsided.

"Thank you."

Then Sive, Maeve and Father arrived with Nuala, and all Blanid had time for were whispered words of love and farewell for her family before she left this world.

Then Rhona wept with her half-sisters, for they had all lost a mother that day, and life would never be the same again.

Two

"Tell us a story!" Sive demanded.

Nuala rolled her eyes at her youngest sister, but Rhona fought back tears. Blanid would have told her daughters a story to help them sleep, and Rhona had promised to take care of them.

Rhona moistened her lips. "How about the tale of the Three Little Pigs?"

Nuala gave the smallest nod, but Rhona caught it. This had always been Nuala's favourite.

"Once upon a time, there were three girls,"

Rhona began. "As alike as piglets, all born together, and none could tell them apart. Their mother had died when they were but babies, so a nurse cared for them. One day, when their father and all his household were busy preparing for a feast, the three sisters escaped into the woods, unseen. The nurse searched high and low, but could not find them anywhere. The girls had found a pond, hidden deep in the woods, where they began to play, not hearing the calls of their nurse or the other searchers. But it was a hot day, and a young wolf, separated from his pack, was thirsty, so he, too, was drawn to the pond to drink. And he found the three girls, playing in the mud. He snapped at one of them, but she was so covered in mud, she slipped free of his grasp, pulling her sisters deeper into the water where the wolf could not go. So the wolf, hungry and angry that his dinner had run away to where he could not reach it, set up such a howling that soon all those around heard it. Including the nurse, up at their father's house. When she heard that terrible sound, so close to the house, she thought of the girls. She took up a branch from one of the bonfires, and set off into the woods. She reached the pond, and when she saw the wolf on the edge, she beat him until she drove him off. Then she called the girls out of the water, but the frightened children wouldn't come. Finally, their father came, and the girls were dragged from the mud, looking more like pigs than human children, and forever after, they were known as the Three Little Pigs. Their father made them promise never to run away again, and the younger two agreed, but to this very day, the eldest has refused to give him her promise, and 'tis said that one day she will succeed her father as Lord of the Isles."

Maeve snorted. "That's not true. Girls can't be lords. She'll be a lady, and her husband will be the lord."

"She's already a lady. She doesn't need a husband for that," Nuala said, her eyes shining. This was why she loved the story so much, Rhona thought. Nuala had the true heart of a woman of the Isles, who would never be her husband's inferior. If she chose to marry at all.

"All girls must have husbands, Mother says.

To protect them," Sive said. Then her lip wobbled and her eyes filled with tears. "Mother!"

All three girls took up the wail, for they would never forget. Tonight the loss was fresh in their minds, and no story could soften that loss.

As Rhona's much longer arms wrapped around her sisters, she thought again of the Three Little Pigs. Three sisters, like the girls in her arms. Which made her the nurse with the stick, in accordance with Aunt Blanid's dying wish.

Rhona swore she would wield a mighty stick indeed, should any wolf seek to hurt her family. A blazing brand to set his fur on fire.

Three

The moment Grieve saw her, he knew he was in love.

Bedelia, Lord Calum's only daughter, a dark-haired girl ripe with curves in the all the right places. She blushed rosily as she offered a curtsey to Grieve and his older brother, Mahon.

Lord Lewis, their father, talked of marriage alliances and taking the girl on a tour of the island. Both brothers had heartily agreed to take Bedelia on the tour, and so it was settled.

Yet they had scarcely set out before a rider

came galloping up to speak to Mahon on an urgent matter that simply would not wait. With a curse and an apology to Bedelia, Mahon turned his horse around and headed to where he was needed most. One day, he would succeed Lord Lewis as the lord of Myroy Isle, and he shouldered many of his father's duties in the meantime.

But that left Bedelia to Grieve, who thanked fate profusely, as he proceeded to show the girl the beauties of the northernmost of the Southern Isles. None of the views he presented to her compared to his own view, though – of the rosy cheeked maiden smiling at all she surveyed.

She spoke of her brothers, and how different life was at Langroy Isle, far to the south, so close to Alba you could see it across the water on a clear day. If Grieve sometimes lost track of her words, he blamed the lovely lilt of her voice, that turned his mind into a blissful fog of possibilities.

If he could persuade this girl to fall in love with him as readily as he'd fallen for her, the marriage alliance Father had spoken of would be more than just talk.

And he would have all those lovely curves in his bed…

Grieve daydreamed until dusk, when they returned home again, for the welcome feast Father had promised Bedelia.

She had the place of honour at Father's side, displacing Mahon, who sat between Bedelia and Grieve.

Grieve comforted himself with the thought that the next day, he would have her all to himself again, as they toured the western shores of Myroy, for Mahon would surely be called away for more important things again, leaving Bedelia and Grieve alone for love to blossom.

Father must have planned it this way, Grieve was certain of it.

Mahon was at least five years her senior, while Grieve was only a few months younger than Bedelia. Young for marriage, but not too young.

And Bedelia liked him, while she scarcely said a word to Mahon. Why, she could not even look at him for more than a moment.

Whereas she'd shared plenty of smiles with Grieve while they rode together.

Yes, Grieve thought as he looked at her. Bedelia was his happily ever after, and nothing fate could do would change that.

Four

"Girls, I'd like you to meet my new wife and your new stepmother, Doireann. She has sworn to be a good mother to you girls, after your own was so cruelly taken from us." Father pushed the diminutive dark-haired woman forward. "Say hello."

Nuala, Sive and Maeve chorused their greetings, but Rhona merely nodded. She and her father had discussed the woman before he'd agreed to marry her. Doireann was a widow from Scitis Isle, whose husband had died defending their holding from Alban raiders. A fitting stepmother for her sisters, Father had said and Rhona had agreed, but Rhona had not realised she would be so young. Why, Doireann was only a few years older than Rhona herself.

Perhaps Father hoped to sire a son on the girl. As though she would want another child to care for while she was still busy with Nuala, Maeve and Sive. Sive was scarcely out of swaddling clothes, or so it seemed to Rhona.

"Perhaps you can all go berry picking in the woods tomorrow," Father suggested.

"They aren't ripe enough yet. In a week, would be better," Rhona said.

Father nodded sagely. "In a week, then. Doireann will be settled then, won't you?"

Doireann nodded obediently.

Overwhelmed by so much at once, Rhona guessed. She would be the same, if she married a lord who already had children.

Hope blossomed. Perhaps that was what Father had in mind. Giving the girls a stepmother, so that he might free Rhona herself for marriage. Not that she'd met a man she wanted yet, and Father would not press her into a marriage she did not want. No matter who her mother had been, Rhona was still a woman of the Southern Isles, a woman who chose her own fate and who she might marry.

Doireann was given chambers adjacent to the one Sive and Maeve shared. Not Blanid's room beside Father. She raised no complaint, and meekly did as she was bid. In fact, she said little or nothing, hardly daring to raise her eyes from the floor.

Maybe she was in mourning as much as Father was.

Rhona left her stepmother to her own devices and returned to her embroidery. She hated sewing with a passion, but someone had to teach Maeve, and Nuala would not. Nuala had claimed the dairy as her domain, for churning butter and cheesemaking were her favourite chores. Blanid had approved, and Rhona saw no need to interfere. She liked fresh butter and cheese as much as the next girl, though perhaps not as much as Sive liked drinking fresh cream. A habit Rhona had not yet managed to cure her of, though her stepmother might have more success.

Five

"You may go," Doireann said grandly to Ciara and Siobhan.

The two maids looked at each other, then Rhona.

"Return to your duties at the house, but leave the pony and the baskets," Doireann continued, growing impatient.

Berry picking was something the whole household did, from the lowest servant to the highest lady, or it had been for as long as Rhona could remember. They all ate their fill while filling their baskets, for berries were a summer treat that didn't last for long.

Remembering her father's admonition to make her stepmother feel welcome, Rhona forced a reassuring smile for the two girls. "I'll leave some for you to pick on the morrow, I promise. We shall manage. The girls are much bigger now, so they can carry a basket each." It would have to be a very small basket for Sive, or a very empty one, Rhona thought as she watched Maeve take Sive's hand to show her which berries to pick.

Nuala headed off on her own, swinging a large basket by her side as she selected the best looking bush.

Ciara and Siobhan mumbled something and headed home. Only then did Doireann take up a basket of her own. Ignoring the others, she proceeded to strip a bush on the far side of the clearing.

Rhona sighed and followed suit, only to find Doireann deliberately moving away from her, deeper into the forest, leaving her bushes half-picked. A quick glance told Rhona that her sisters were doing fine without her, so she followed Doireann. Deeper and deeper, until they were surrounded by trees and there wasn't a berry bush in sight.

"The berries are all back there," Rhona said, pointing.

Doireann waved away her words. "Let the children pick berries. I must find the holy spring. I know it's here. They say it was blessed by Saint Columba himself, and sprang up at his touch, and one cup will make any woman fertile, no matter how barren she may be. I heard Lady Catriona of Isla drank the miraculous waters of it on her wedding night, and that was the reason she gave birth to triplets."

Rhona shook her head. "I've never heard of such a spring. And Saint Columba didn't like women, so it does not seem likely he would work that sort of miracle. Especially not here. He feared the witch women of Nimbanmore."

Doireann scoffed, "There are no witches left in the world, least of all here. The faithful wiped such wicked creatures out centuries ago!"

Rhona wondered what the woman would say if she told her stepmother that magic was alive and well, coursing through her blood in readiness for when it was wanted, but she held her tongue. Blanid had told her to hide it, and hide it she would. No one must ever know.

"But the miraculous spring is real. It must be. I shall find it, and drink from it, so that I might bear Lord Ronin a son!" Doireann ducked between two trees, then trotted down a slope.

Rhona glanced back at her sisters. They were already out of sight. If she followed her stepmother, the girls would not know where they had gone. "Doireann, wait. The girls…"

"Go back to the children! I will find this spring on my own. It's not like you need it. You have no husband yet! Wait for me in the clearing. I shall not be long," Doireann called back before she disappeared from sight.

Rhona was torn. If something happened to her stepmother, her father would never forgive her. But if anything happened to her sisters…alone in the woods…Rhona would not forgive herself, and nor would Blanid. Wishing she didn't have to, Rhona said, "Very well. We shall wait."

Her dread-filled heart weighed more than her empty berry basket as Rhona returned to her sisters.

"Where is she?" Nuala asked, popping berries into her already stained mouth.

"Doireann has gone for a walk in the woods by herself. She wants us to wait here for her," Rhona said.

"More berries for us!" Sive cheered. Her hands and face were so covered in berry juice, she looked like she'd slaughtered a pig. Or a piglet, perhaps.

Rhona managed a smile for her sisters. "Let's see who can pick the most before she comes back."

Twilight came, with no sign of Doireann. Rhona had spread a blanket upon the ground, and Sive lay on it, snoring softly. Maeve looked like she wanted to join her, and even Rhona longed for her bed. Nuala was determined to pick berries until the last of the light was gone, but that time was fast approaching.

Finally, Nuala plopped herself down beside Sive. "I wish I'd brought a cloak. I'm cold," she announced.

"I'd prefer a fire," Maeve said. "Much warmer."

Rhona could not magic a cloak into being, but she could build a fire. The warm day meant there was some tinder and a few sticks, but not much. A fallen tree held plenty of timber to burn in its broken branches, but Rhona had not thought to bring anything with which to light the fire.

Nevertheless, she piled up a collection of fuel, then crouched over it so she hid it from her sisters' sight. Only then did she dare bite her lip and unleash the most powerful part of her magic.

The log blazed to life, as though Rhona had added it to a roaring fireplace and not a cold nest of sticks.

Maeve clapped her hands. "Thank you, Rhona!" She stretched out her fingers to the blaze.

Darkness descended, leaving the four of them alone in the woods. Luckily the biggest beasts on Rum Isle were its cows — they would not have wolves to worry about, or bears. "We should probably huddle up together with the blanket by the fire to keep warm, while we wait for Doireann to return," she said. "I'm sure she'll see the light of it, if she is lost, and come back soon." This last was a lie, but her sisters did not need to know this. It was just another burden she would carry alone.

On the morrow, they would return home, and tell Father his wife was missing. He would send men out to search, and they would find her. Rum Isle was too small to hide her for long.

Rhona set several logs beside the campfire, so that she might add fuel through the night if she needed to, before joining her sisters in their blanket bower.

Nuala's eyes drooped, and she soon added her snores to Sive's. Maeve was still awake, though, and her watchful eyes regarded Rhona.

"Is she coming back?" Maeve whispered.

Rhona wet her lips. She didn't want to lie, but... "I hope so. Father would be heartbroken to lose another wife so soon after Mother's death."

An owl screeched in the distance, and Maeve squeaked like she'd been the owl's prey. "What is THAT?"

"Just an owl. You are too big for it to carry,

so it is nothing to worry about. It is catching mice."

Maeve shuffled closer to Rhona. "There are mice in the woods?" Her eyes were wide with terror.

Rhona smiled in the dark. She would never understand her sister's fear of the small creatures. "Not while the owls are out hunting. They are running to hide – probably in our barn."

"Good. Then the cat will get them. She has six kittens, you know." Maeve snuggled closer to Rhona. "Mother said you will protect us. It's true, isn't it? You will keep us safe?"

"As long as I draw breath, I will let nothing and no one hurt you, or any of my sisters," Rhona promised her, and every word rang with truth.

Using any means necessary, Rhona added in her head, as she threw another log on the fire. Even magical ones. No one hurt her family.

Seven

"The pony's gone!" Maeve cried.

Rhona winced at the rude awakening, wishing she could sleep a little longer in some place more comfortable. But she had to put on a brave face for her sisters. "I'm sure he's just gone to find some breakfast," she soothed. But there was plenty of grass in the clearing – grass he'd eagerly devoured yesterday. "Or he was thirsty."

That made more sense. "We should go down to the river for a wash and a drink, too, before we head home. Perhaps we shall find him there, and Doireann, too," Rhona continued, clambering to her feet.

The pony was indeed nowhere to be seen, along with the panniers of berries he'd been carrying. True to her word, Rhona had left some berries on the bushes, so there was enough for breakfast.

She helped Sive wash her breakfast berry juice from her face and hands, but when they still found no sign of the pony or Doireann, she had to admit defeat. "Fill your pockets with berries for on the way. Time to go home," Rhona said.

Eight

Rhona staggered up to the house, her arms aching from carrying Sive. What she wouldn't give to have the pony who'd carried Sive into the forest, but they'd seen no sign of the creature since last night. She tucked Sive into her bed, figuring the girl could wash when she woke in the morning. Maeve and Nuala had washed in the water butt outside, and were no doubt raiding the kitchen for dinner.

Rhona debated whether to join her sisters and grab a bite to eat, or head straight to bed and break her fast in the morning. Her stomach had churned with worry too much to allow her to eat today, and even now she wasn't sure if she could keep any food down. Not without knowing if Doireann was all right. Her father would never forgive her for losing his wife.

Though the hour was late, she should probably wake him to tell him the ill news. She padded softly to her father's chamber, and raised her fist to knock.

A distressed cry came from Sive's chamber. "Mama?"

Rhona's heart broke anew, and she turned to go to her sister.

"Rhona?"

Her father stood in the open doorway, looking distinctly displeased.

"I must see to Sive," Rhona said.

Father seized her arm. "Let Doireann do it."

To Rhona's surprise and relief, her stepmother emerged from her father's chamber, squeezed past them, and headed for Sive's room.

"So she made it back?" Rhona choked out.

Her father's brows lowered further. "No

thanks to you. What possessed you to take off like that, and with your sisters?"

Rhona was lost for words for a moment. Finally, she said, "I thought it would be safer…"

"Then you are a fool. A foolish child, who I thought was past such things. Really, Rhona? A miraculous spring blessed by Saint Columba himself? Where did you hear such nonsense?"

Rhona glanced at Sive's chamber, but Doireann had closed the door.

She did not want to make trouble for Doireann. "I do not remember, but I thought it strange that such a spring should exist so close to home, when I had not heard of it."

"Keeping your sisters out all night in search of this nonsense! What were you thinking?" Father demanded.

She hung her head. "I am sorry, Father. I lost track of the time. We should have returned before dark, but Sive was tired, and – "

"Enough! You are too young to take care of your sisters, no matter how mature your mother thought you might be. They are Doireann's responsibility, not yours. She told me she tried to dissuade you from finding this imaginary spring, especially when your sisters insisted upon following you, but you refused to listen and left without another word. What if one of you had been hurt, hmm? Doireann arrived after dark last night, quite distraught that you had not returned, though you had promised to be but a moment. You were gone hours, leaving her alone in woods she did not know!"

Rhona struggled to make sense of her father's words. No, it was Doireann who had set off to find the spring, who had told HER to wait, not the other way around. And her sisters had never left the clearing, except to wash by the river, and that was hardly but a step away from where they'd camped in the clearing.

"But, Father, I – " she began, not sure how to continue.

"I do not want to hear excuses, for nothing will excuse such reckless behaviour. Do you think any man will want a wife who puts the children under her care in danger, just to satisfy her own curiosity? Go to bed. On the morrow, you will beg your stepmother's forgiveness, and you will submit to whatever punishment she gives you. She is the lady of this house, and whatever she asks you to do, you will obey. Is that understood?"

Rhona swallowed back her fury. "Yes, Father," she lied.

"Good. We will not speak of this again, and hopefully the matter will be forgotten before rumours can spread outside our household. If Lord Lewis were to hear…but he shall not. Both Doireann and I will watch your behaviour carefully from now on, Rhona. So soon after losing your mother…I will not lose you girls as well!"

Seething, she made her way to her chamber and closed the door. She had not been sent to bed without dinner since before Nuala was born, and certainly never before when she had nothing wrong!

How had her father gotten the idea that she had gone searching for the stupid saint's spring? Rhona had not heard a whisper of the place until Doireann mentioned it.

Realisation dawned. Of course, Doireann

had reached home before her. Perhaps Doireann had expected them to have arrived already, and she'd been shocked to find the girls missing. Had she spun a story for her father, painting herself in a good light and placing the blame on Rhona?

Maeve might have made up such a story, but Rhona would never. Father had called Rhona childish, when it was his wife he should have been looking at. Why, the woman was not much older than Rhona, and if her father asked for the marriage to be annulled…perhaps the widow had nothing left, after the Alban raiders had taken everything from her.

Rhona's fury eased the tiniest bit. If she was faced with such a future, perhaps Rhona might lie. Perhaps. But that did not excuse Doireann. On the morrow, Rhona would not apologise to her stepmother. Instead, she would make sure the woman understood she knew what her stepmother was doing, and while she would forgive her the once, if Doireann ever blamed Rhona for her own faults again, Rhona would not be so lenient.

With that firm resolution uppermost in her mind, Rhona prepared for bed. It wasn't until she was tucked up in her blankets that her belly reminded her that she'd barely eaten all day. She rolled over onto her side, hoping to silence the grumbling sounds. She could eat her fill on the morrow, and every day thereafter. Rum Isle might not be the wealthiest of the isles, but they would never run short of food. Not while her father ruled the island.

Nine

After a week spent cleaning every inch of Blanid's former chamber twice, as Rhona's first effort hadn't met with her stepmother's approval, Rhona was ready to stuff the scrubbing brush down Doireann's throat and drown her with the bucket of dirty water.

One good thing had come of all this cleaning. Rhona had moved all of Blanid's things into her own chamber, though the haphazard jumble of chests made it difficult to reach her bed at the end of each exhausting day. Rhona promised herself she would go through everything and keep it safe for her sisters, but for now, she had to drag the mattress back to the bed from where she'd left it airing by the window.

Her arms ached as she made up the bed again, but Rhona had to admit a certain satisfaction at a job well done. The room was no longer Blanid's – if her spirit had lingered, it would not stay here. Even Blanid's favourite candlestick now sat on the table beside Rhona's bed – Doireann would not have it. But she would surely want some light, so Rhona headed down to the kitchen to see if a spare one could be found that was suitable for the new lady of the house.

It took some rummaging until she found a brass one so tarnished she barely recognised it for what it was, but when she carried it to the kitchen table, the cook exclaimed, "Why, I have not seen that since your grandmother died! 'Twas her favourite. Well I remember her coming down here when young Ronin could not sleep. She would sit the candle on that very table, cradle the boy in her arms, and sing him to sleep in that very chair. More often than not, I'd find her still there in the morning, fast asleep, when I came to light the morning fires. I was in my first year of service then."

Rhona blinked, trying to imagine Belen as a young maid, perhaps the same age as Nuala, and not the woman she'd known all her life. "I was looking for something suitable for Doireann." The old candleholder would not do for her stepmother, Rhona knew. Doireann would want the best, shiniest one in the house.

"And it will be, once it's had a polish," Belen said. "I'll get one of the girls to do it. Ciara!"

Ciara looked up from peeling the carrots. "Yes?"

"Polish that, will you? It's for her ladyship upstairs." Belen rolled her eyes heavenward.

Ciara didn't make the mistake of thinking that meant Rhona. "At least I can spit on that."

Rhona laughed. "I should probably clean that, too. She said I was to prepare the room myself, with no help from anyone else."

"You've done the work of two maids this week, and given both Ciara and Siobhan quite the holiday. 'Tis only fitting that she do this for you now, as is proper. The lady of the house should not rub her hands raw polishing some old brass." Belen gestured toward the chair where she'd said her father had fallen asleep in his mother's arms. "Rest a little, Lady Rhona."

Rhona smiled at the title. "I am no lady. Just my father's daughter on a good day, or a drudge on a bad one, like today."

"Not to us. Not to any of us. That slip of a girl might have married your father, but she is not Lady Blanid, or your lovely self. Lady Blanid ran this house, and indeed the whole isle, as smooth as the sea on a summer's day. She never came into the kitchen without a kind word for what was cooking, and a helping hand where it was needed. She never needed no titles to command respect. She was a lady, and so are you. That Doireann…she's as common as muck, and meddlesome besides. Why, she finds fault with every dish that comes out of this kitchen, though 'tis exactly what she ordered. She asks for less salt, so I spare the salt, and she complains 'tis too bland. I add more, and she complains 'tis inedible and sends the whole mess back to the kitchen. Well, let me tell you, that stew most certainly was not inedible. I had two helpings myself!" Belen grinned.

Resting while everyone else worked was not in Rhona's nature, so she picked up Ciara's knife and set to work on the carrots.

"You should hear her hold forth about the only way to chop carrots!" Belen continued.

Rhona faltered. "What way is that?"

"Never mind. I'm sure whatever you do will be good enough for everyone else, and more than good enough for her."

Rhona resumed peeling. Working with a knife was calming, much like preparing herbs in the stillroom, for the repetitive task allowed her mind to wander. But never far. Her thoughts turned to Blanid, or Brigid, or Doireann, and none of them were comforting right now.

Rhona said, "Belen, would you tell me a story, please? One of the folktales where the wicked are properly punished, and the ending is happy."

Belen tapped the spoon on the side of the stewpot. "My lady wishes for a tale? Lady Blanid was one for tales. We could swap them for hours – she knew more than me, for her family collected tales along with the plants they grew. Let me see…she used to tell this chilling tale of a brother and sister, lost in the woods.

"Once upon a time, there was a poor woodcutter and his wife who had two children, a boy and a girl, but they did not have the wherewithal to feed them. So one day, the father took the children into the woods with all the food they had, and left them there, hoping someone might take pity on the mites…"

Parents too poor to feed their children. That was something Rhona would never allow to happen on Rum Isle, she reflected, as she listened to the tale. Poor Hansel and Gretel would not have needed to take shelter with a wicked witch here.

By the time Belen's tale ended, the carrots were cut and Ciara stood beside Rhona, with her mouth open and the polished candlestick in her hand.

"Her ladyship will want the best beeswax candle for that. No tallow for her," Belen said, fitting a candle into the stick before handing it to Rhona. "When you're finished taking that up to her room, come back. I have a treat for you, and your sisters, if you choose to share it. One of the beekeepers brought some honey today, and he was so thankful for the poultice you made for his knee – which is quite healed, by the way – he brought you some honeycomb."

Now it was Rhona's turn to grin. "I will fly up those stairs, and back. You'll see!"

Up she went, but she slowed her steps as she heard voices. Specifically, her father's and Doireann's.

"I said no!" Her father sounded weary.

"But I need you in my bed, for 'tis not a proper marriage if it not consummated. You do want me, don't you, Ronin?" Doireann wheedled.

"I need you to take care of my daughters. My poor motherless girls."

"I could give you sons, if you but lie with me. Much better than girls."

"Watch your words, woman. I love my daughters, and if it were not for them, I would have left you to the charity of Scitis Isle. They need a mother, a woman to take care of them.

Rhona is too young, no matter what she may think. Besides, she will one day leave us to have her own children, and then what? Nay, take care of the children you have, woman, and leave me alone!" Father threw the door of Doireann's chamber open and stormed out.

Rhona ducked into the shadows, where no one would see her.

"But anything could happen to them. Like my family, taken from me in a single raid, and you will go from four girls to none. If you had more children, at least some would survive..." Doireann continued, reaching for Father. "Lie with me, Ronin. I promise I will bring you pleasure, and perhaps one day a son..."

"Lie with yourself!" He shook her off and shut the door to his chamber. Shutting her out.

Rhona felt a perverse pleasure at seeing her stepmother humiliated so, but if Doireann knew she had overheard...

"Anything could happen to them, Ronin. And when it does, then you will come to me. I swear it." Doireann's eyes glittered.

Rhona shivered, hugging the shadows even more fervently. If Doireann meant her and her sisters ill, then she would protect them any way she could. Doireann would not harm them. This Rhona swore, hoping the fire in her soul would hold her oath stronger than her stepmother's. For only one of them could win, and Rhona could not lose her sisters. Not now, not ever. And as for marriage? There was no way she'd leave her sisters at the mercy of her stepmother for some man.

Ten

Lord Lewis rose and the hall fell silent. "It is with great pleasure that I announce the betrothal of Lord Calum's daughter, the Lady Bedelia, to my son, Mahon."

What? Grieve tried to shout the word, but somehow before it left his throat his voice died.

Bedelia was to marry his brother? How?

The hall erupted in cheers and calls for more ale, so that they might drink to the health of the happy couple. Grieve drained his own wine cup, but his voice wasn't at the bottom of the cup, either.

He forced a smile as the toasts went on and on, until he finally found a chance to escape from the hell that the hall had become.

The moment he reached the yard outside, Grieve leaned against the wall, ready to throw up every bite he'd eaten. She was marrying Mahon? Why?

"Grieve!"

He thought he'd imagined her voice calling his name, but when he raised his head, there she was, haloed in the golden light spilling out of the hall. No, not a halo – hellfire, for that's what she was to him. Terrible temptation that would damn him forever.

He turned away.

"Why are you not happy for us? As my only friend here, I thought you would be the first to congratulate us, and wish us well."

Grieve moistened his lips. He prayed his voice had returned. "I thought we were friends, and maybe even more. But I was mistaken. We spent every day together, talking, laughing, as I showed you Myroy Isle, while my brother was too busy to spare even a moment for you. Yet you choose him, the brother you barely know, over me."

She drew herself up, dark eyes flashing. "I know he is the man I love, and the man I shall marry."

Grieve couldn't believe what he was hearing. "How can you love him? You've barely spent more than a moment in his company. It is those fairy stories you told me about – you have read too many of those, where a pair meet and fall in love in less than a moment. Such stories are not real!"

"I knew it the moment he kissed me," Bedelia insisted. "There was magic in his kiss. I felt it from my lips right down to the tips of my toes."

"You haven't been alone long enough with him for a kiss!" Grieve protested. "You've been with me every day! If I'd been forward enough…forgotten common courtesy…and stolen a kiss, would you have chosen me instead?"

He'd considered it, many times, but he'd always stopped himself. Now he regretted it more than ever.

"On my first night here, he asked if he might kiss me good night, to apologise for being absent from my side all day. His lips touched mine and…my heart was his." She stamped her foot. "He stole nothing I did not freely give. Not that first kiss, or anything after." A rosy blush coloured her cheeks.

Realisation dawned. Last night, Grieve thought he'd heard a woman's voice in Mahon's chambers. A maid or one of the girls from the village, he'd thought, and dismissed it. But it had been no maid. His brother had bedded the wanton Bedelia.

Grieve wasn't sure what came over him. Anger and bitterness and longing all collided and he couldn't think any more. He seized Bedelia's shoulders and pressed his lips to hers, desperate to show her how much he loved her.

She shoved him away, swiping a hand across her mouth.

"Your brother has more honour than you'll ever know," she snapped.

"Honour? What honour is there in taking you to his bed before you are married, treating you like a whore?"

Her hand landed on his cheek, a sharp sting from such a small hand. "I came to his chamber, to give him my answer to his proposal. I asked him to prove that he would be a good husband to me. This is still the Southern Isles, not Alba. A woman is free to choose, and I have. I chose well." She spat at his feet and stormed off.

"Bedelia, wait – "

Bedelia strode past a man whose face was in shadow. A man Grieve could not afford to ignore.

"Good night, Father," he said as he attempted to follow her.

Father caught his arm. "No, leave the girl. She will be your brother's wife soon enough, and you'll only make trouble for them. It seems you leave me no choice but to take you to the Council meeting with me, for I cannot leave you here."

Grieve hung his head. "She played me for a fool, Father."

The grip on Grieve's arm tightened. "No, you made a fool of yourself, son. Better men than you have made fools of themselves over women, and I'm sure you will not be the last. Better to learn wisdom, and not follow those who do not want you. Perhaps one day, a woman will invite you to her bed as readily as Bedelia did your brother. But until that day comes, stay away from your brother and his wife. Or I've no doubt she'll bruise your other cheek to match the one you'll have in the morning." Father laughed. "Pack your things. We leave on the morrow. Better to be early to this meeting, for I fear the Albans are preparing for war, and we must be ready when they come."

"I'll take war over women any day," Grieve muttered. Maybe he wouldn't need to marry at all. Not with Mahon and Bedelia rutting like rabbits. Why, they'd have a litter of heirs in no time.

Father only laughed. "Spoken like a man who knows little of either. But that will change."

Eleven

Father frowned over the message a breathless courier had just delivered. He'd run all the way from the harbour. "I must leave now – the Council meeting has been called early. The Alban king is looking at the Southern Isles again, and the raids are getting more and more brazen. Lord Angus and Lord Lewis believe it means war, which we must plan for." He seized Rhona's shoulders. "If you see boats coming, take Doireann and your sisters and hide. The caves will be well stocked, so you may hide there until my return."

Doireann hurried up. "What is this? What are you hiding?" She addressed Rhona, not Father, but it was Father who answered.

"Doireann, I must go to a Council meeting. If Alban raiders come as Lord Lewis says they will, you all must hide. Rhona knows the way." Father turned to go.

Doireann dug her claws into his arm. "You cannot leave me here with raiders on the way!" she screeched. "They will kill us all! I demand you take me to this hiding place at once!"

With difficulty, Father pried her off. "I do not have time. I must sail with the tide. Rhona will take you there, if it becomes necessary." He headed upstairs to pack.

Doireann followed him, her loud protests and pleadings audible to everyone in the household. Rhona pitied the woman, who had every right to fear a raid, for she had lost everything in one before. But Scitis was a barren rock, nothing like Rum Isle. Rum Isle protected its own.

Finally, Father departed, riding off at a gallop before Doireann got the idea in her head to go after him.

Doireann fumed for a moment, before she turned her fury on Rhona. "Take me to this safe place. Now!" She dug her fingers into Rhona's arm, much like she'd done with Father.

Rhona looked deep into the crazed woman's eyes, and saw something other than fear. Desperation, perhaps? She did not know. But she would not stand for being manhandled by this woman. Fury burned deep within her, and it was almost like Doireann felt it, for she released Rhona with a hiss of pain.

"If you insist, I will take you to Sanctuary in the morning. It is a day's journey, for we can only ride so far, before we must proceed on foot. But we will never find it in the dark." Rhona turned and headed back to the stillroom.

To her relief, Doireann did not follow.

Twelve

Grieve stayed on the shore of Loch Findlugan among the other lords' sons and retainers. Servants busied themselves with preparing tents and food for their lords, but like the other sons, Grieve had little to do.

Not for the first time, he wondered why his father had bothered to bring him to the meeting, if there was nothing for him to do. Only the lords of the isles were allowed on Council Island.

Father should have left him at home. Bedelia had been sent back to her father's house to prepare dresses and such things for her wedding to Mahon, so it wasn't like Grieve would have been in the way at home. Maybe Grieve shouldn't have mentioned his desire to challenge Mahon for Bedelia. But what else did a man do when his brother had stolen the affections of the woman he loved?

The familiar thwack of metal finding its mark roused Grieve from his dark thoughts. He'd always enjoyed archery – so much so that his father had allowed him to train some of the other local men to hit a target. If the Albans invaded, it would be by sea, and every arrow that found its mark before the Albans reached shore meant one less man to fight.

Laughter greeted Grieve as he joined the men assembled in front of the target. He soon saw why.

"Has a witch cast a spell on the target so that no one can hit it?" he asked.

More laughter. Someone handed the bow to Grieve. "Let's see if you can do better."

They backed up, allowing him space to line up his shot. An unfamiliar bow, when he'd been too busy riding with Bedelia or sailing to practice…Grieve would be lucky to hit the target at all. Yet he refused to back down from the challenge. Notch, draw, breathe…release.

His arrow thwacked into the target, slightly left of the centre.

A smattering of applause broke out.

"Who's next?" Grieve asked, holding out the bow.

Someone snatched it from his hand, muttering that they could do better.

The man beside Grieve stuck out his hand. "I'm Damhan. Lord Roe's son."

Grieve shook his hand. "Grieve. I'm Lord Lewis's."

"Are you the one Bedelia's going to marry? She's fallen hard for you. Singing and hugging herself and talking of nothing but going home to Myroy," another man said, eyeing Grieve with interest. "I'm Dermot. Lord Calum's my father."

Grieve hung his head. "No, she's to marry my older brother."

Dermot grinned. "Lucky escape for you, then. She's Father's little princess, leading him around like he had a ring through his nose.

She'll do the same for your poor brother, I've no doubt. You're better off finding a girl more biddable, or one who has no brothers, and a claim to an island that'll come to you when you marry. They say one of Lord Angus's three daughters will inherit Isla."

"You mean the Three Little Pigs?" Grieve blurted out. Everyone had heard the tales of the girls, who must be homely as hell to have kept such a terrible name.

Damhan waved his hand, as if dispelling an unwelcome odour. "Ah, they only got called that for the day they played in the mud. Comely girls, all three of them, with their mother's red hair. Though with a dowry like Isla, none of them need to be more than tolerable. I'd court any of them, if they looked my way."

"My father says Isla had best be held by a Viken after Angus, and he's keeping the oldest girl for an alliance with the Viken king."

The bow had come back to Grieve, and he took his turn. His second shot was better than the first — and much better than any of the others.

"She's still a woman of the Southern Isles, or she will be, if she's too young to be a woman yet. No Viken will have Lord Angus' daughter against her will while a single Islander draws breath. If she falls in love with an Islander, she'll marry where she pleases. Much like her mother did, to my father's endless sorrow," Dermot said, drawing back the bow. His shot landed in the dirt three feet in front of the target.

"Try again," Grieve urged him. "Only this time, aim a yard higher. The arrow will naturally fall to earth, so you need to let it soar more first."

Dermot nodded, and did as Grieve suggested. A moment later, his arrow thwacked solidly into the centre circle of the target.

More applause and a couple of cheers.

"Who's next?" Dermot asked, lifting the bow up in invitation.

"Me," said a boy. "But only if Grieve here can offer me some coaching. So that next time I shoot an Alban, I hit him right between the eyes instead of between the legs."

Laughter erupted, and cries of, "There's nothing to hit between an Alban's legs, anyway!"

Grieve grinned. Maybe Father had been right to bring him along after all.

<h1 style="text-align:center">Thirteen</h1>

Rhona did not sleep well, so she slipped into the stillroom for some willow bark to ease her headache on her way to breakfast. Dealing with Doireann and a headache was more than any saint could be expected to endure, and Rhona was certainly no saint.

Yet as she entered, she had the distinct feeling that something was wrong. The drawers were not all closed properly, and she made a particular point of shutting her jars away from all light so that the herbs might keep for longer. The books were out of order, too – Blanid's carefully drawn herbals, listing every plant she'd ever heard of, and quite a few that Rhona knew would never grow on Rum Isle. Rhona knew them by heart, of course, but occasionally she still checked some of the more exotic ones before administering them to anyone. She didn't know how her grandparents had procured some of the plants they possessed, but they'd made sure Blanid's stillroom held everything their own garden could supply.

"Lady Rhona, her ladyship demands to know when you are ready," Ciara said.

After Belen took up the title, they'd all started doing it, and Rhona could not bring herself to tell them to stop. They didn't look at her differently, nor curtsey at her like she was some princess, but now they came to her as they must have once come to Blanid. The message was clear – the staff saw Rhona as the lady of the house, not Doireann. It earned her more of Doireann's dark looks, even as it lessened the weight of her father's disappointment, just a little, but not enough to make her feel safe in her own home again.

And now someone had been through her herbs – since she'd left the stillroom last night.

"Ciara, did you or any of the others come in here last night, or this morning? Perhaps to get some willow bark, or herbs for cooking?"

Ciara shook her head. "Not me, mistress. I wouldn't know one herb from the other."

"But the herbs are all in my books, and I was still abed. You or one of the others might have opened one of the herbals to read..." Rhona stopped when she realised Ciara has trying to smother a laugh. "What is it?"

"You forget, Lady Rhona, that the only ladies who can read in the house are you and your sisters. Unless it was a matter of life or death, we would all let you sleep, and ask you for what was needed when you woke."

Of course. No wonder the girl laughed. Her sisters would wake her if they wanted something, knowing they would have it faster from her than from a lot of tiresome reading. "What of Doireann?" Rhona asked urgently.

Ciara shrugged. "I do not know. But surely she would summon you if she wanted something..."

Unless Doireann wanted something she did not want Rhona to know about. Medicines could be poisons if used in the wrong dosage, as Rhona knew well.

"Have my sisters come down for breakfast?" Rhona asked.

"Yes. Her ladyship insisted. Then she asked for some small cups so that they could all drink a special cordial…"

Rhona swore. Whether by design or mistake, Doireann might have poisoned the girls already. "Tell her I'm coming." She rummaged through the bottles, but she couldn't be sure which one Doireann had taken. Unlike the cupboards, the bottles appeared untouched. Everything seemed to be there, unless Doireann had poured the contents of one into a bottle of her own. And Rhona wouldn't know which bottle to check — it wasn't like she kept track of how much was in each one. Blanid might have known, but she wasn't here now.

Rhona paused to grab a cloak before heading outside, where Doireann sat on the box seat of a cart. A cart full of chests and casks, which were occupied by her bleary-eyed sisters. Sleepy from being woken too early, or because they'd been drugged?

Please, don't let it be the second, Rhona prayed silently as she approached the cart. "It will take longer by cart," Rhona said.

"I am not leaving my things here to be stolen by raiders. Show me to the place where we will be safe!" Doireann insisted.

Reluctantly, Rhona climbed onto the cart beside her sisters and they set off down the road, or what passed for one on Rum Isle.

"Which way?" Doireann demanded every time they reached a fork where the cart tracks went more than one way.

Rhona would respond with right or left or to continue straight, until she felt as drowsy as her sisters in the summer heat. She'd brought a cloak, but perhaps she should have thought to bring a hat.

"I'm thirsty," Sive announced.

Before Rhona could stop her, Maeve uncorked a flask and held it to her sister's lips. Sive gulped the liquid down, her eyelids drooping, before she slid off her box and lay down on the bottom of the cart, sound asleep. Beside Nuala, Rhona realised in horror. Then Maeve picked up the flask and drained the contents. She toppled to the floor, too.

Rhona snatched the flask from Maeve's slack fingers. "What did you give them?" She inhaled deeply at the lip of the bottle, trying to discern the contents. Strong spirits burned the inside of her nostrils, softened by the scent of lavender. That couldn't be all she'd given them. Some poisons had no odour, but one could taste them…

"Just a draught to put them to sleep, so that they will stay quiet. Now, tell me where Rum Isle hides its riches, and nothing worse will happen to them," Doireann said, her eyes flashing.

"Rum Isle's secrets are known only to its own. You may have married my father, but you will never be one of us," Rhona spat. She tipped up the flask and let a drop of the treacherous liquor fall onto her tongue. Spirit burn and lavender sweetness, without the one thing Rhona dreaded – the bitter gall of opium from the Holy Land. Perhaps Doireann had not found it yet. As it was, the liquor was a strong sleeping potion, no more, that would leave the user with a hangover and headache when they awoke, at worst. She let the flask slip from her fingers.

Just in time to see something dark blot out the sun before it collided with her head, and all the lights went out.

Fourteen

It seemed almost no time at all before the final feast was over and the Council dispersed to go home. Grieve rode with Dermot, Damhan and the boy whose name was Brian, while his father lagged behind, discussing serious matters with Lord Ronin. At least, they looked serious – Father could be discussing a chess match with the man, for all Grieve knew.

Ships lined up in the harbour, waiting for the tide to take them all home.

Grieve made to follow Father to their vessel, but Father shook his head. "You're to go with Lord Ronin. He needs an archery instructor for his men, as he has no sons of his own. Albans will strike at Rum Isle before they make it to Myroy, you may be sure, so it behoves the lords of the inner isles to keep up their defences to give the rest of us warning in the event they send more than a raiding party."

Lord Ronin inclined his head. "Your father tells me you have the makings of a good master-at-arms, young Grieve, and some skills with a bow."

Grieve lifted his chin proudly. "I have trained my father's men since I came to manhood, Lord Ronin, and I was easily the best archer among the boys on shore today. But with practice, they might be able to match my skill."

Father laughed. "He'll never be good at chess, like I told you. Too forthright for playing at politics. But I hope he will be just the man you need, Ronin." He gave the command for his crew to raise the sail and was soon out in the bay, out of earshot.

No word of farewell, or when Grieve might be allowed to come home. Maybe never.

Lord Ronin eyed Grieve. "We shall see. Come, boy. You're too old to be a proper page or fosterling, but still young enough that I can call you my squire. Master-at-arms and other such offices can wait until you've had time to prove yourself."

"Yes, my lord. And I will," Grieve swore.

Lord Ronin smiled. "Good man. Climb aboard." He gestured toward his boat.

For a moment, Grieve was lost. An unproven boy, a new squire, a good man…what was he really? He had no home, and no family around him any more.

Time to choose his own fate. Grieve strode aboard the ship bound for Rum Isle, vowing to show Lord Ronin, his father and any other man with eyes to see that he would prove he was every bit as good as his brother. Better, maybe. And Bedelia? She could be miserable with Mahon, for Grieve would not give the girl another thought.

Fifteen

The bright summer's day had given way to miserable weather, but the rain pattering on the ground was nothing to the drumming inside Rhona's head. Rhona groaned, sat up, then groaned again.

"Where are we?" Nuala asked.

Rhona blinked. Her sisters huddled together under a pine tree. Of course, they hadn't thought to drag her under shelter, too. Then again, if they'd drunk enough strong spirits to send them to sleep, they wouldn't feel much better than she did right now. In no shape to be dragging anyone's body.

"Not at home, where we should be," Rhona grumbled. She shuffled under the tree with her sisters. Only now did she realise fog had crept over the island, as it did on days like this. They could be spitting distance from home, and she would not be able to see it.

Rhona bit her lip, hoping to stir up a breeze to improve visibility.

"I'm cold!" Sive moaned, climbing into Nuala's lap.

Rhona let the breeze swirl away into the woods. Yes, the fog lifted just enough to show the tree trunks before it was all whiteness once more. They could not be far from the edge, if Doireann had dumped them from the cart. She would not have had the strength to drag Rhona far from the road, unless she'd had help.

But who on Rum Isle would help Doireann against Lord Ronin's children? No one Rhona knew. And as the mistress of Blanid's stillroom, she knew everyone on the island.

"We must wait for the fog to clear, and then we will find shelter from the rain. I'm sure there is a cottage or croft quite close, but we might miss it in the mist. Once we know where we are, we can go home," Rhona promised.

"Can you tell us a story to pass the time?" Maeve asked.

"The Three Little Pigs?"

Maeve shook her head. "Something else. Something new. We have heard that tale too many times."

And there would be no nurse come to save them today, Rhona knew. It would be up to her and her sisters to find their way home. She thought of the tale Belen had told her, the first night she'd called her Lady Rhona. That might do. "Have you heard the tale of Hansel and Gretel?"

The girls shook their heads.

Rhona drew in a deep breath. "Once upon a time…"

Sixteen

Grieve eyed the huddle of buildings on the clifftop as they approached Rum Island. "You'll need better fortifications than that," he observed. "Plus a barracks hall or two to accommodate your people if you are invaded. Father had me build a new hall at the beginning of this year, so we'd be able to house the women and children, not just the menfolk."

Lord Ronin laughed. "Rum Isle may be closer to Alba, but we are not as numerous as the people of Myroy or Isla. I think you'll find we have shelter enough for all of us, but the fortifications are not a bad idea. When we get the island men assembled, we can discuss it then." He nodded at the house. "First, I must greet my family, for they'll have missed me."

Butterflies rioted in Grieve's belly. Lord Ronin had spoken affectionately of his wife and daughters, but meeting them was another thing entirely. What if they did not like him? He managed with strange men and boys just fine, but girls? Bedelia was the only one he'd shared a house with since his mother had died, and he didn't want to remember how badly that had gone.

"This is Doireann, my wife," Lord Ronin said, wrapping an arm around a woman who resembled Bedelia. Well, small and dark, at least — she was thinner, without the luscious curves that had attracted him to Bedelia. And Doireann did not smile.

"Where are the girls?" Lord Ronin asked her.

Doireann's frown deepened. "I must speak to you about them. The oldest one, she turns the others against me. Not three days ago, they disappeared, and I could find no trace of them. I have not seen…"

"Father!" The same word cried by three different voices, as three girls raced along the path to embrace Lord Ronin.

The three girls looked like they'd been playing in the woods, judging by their muddied clothing and the twigs and leaves that clung to them.

Their mother looked like she was building up to give them a good scolding. One Grieve did not intend to witness.

"I'll go see about some timber to start those fortifications, shall I?" he said to no one in particular, and headed off in search of an axe.

Seventeen

They'd seen Father's ship arrive in the harbour, and hurried to get to the house before he did. Alas, they'd been too slow.

Doireann and Father stood outside the house, at a distance where no one could stand close enough to overhear them without being seen.

At least, no one who did not have magical means of hearing.

Rhona bit her lip, letting a little of her magic out to create a breeze that brought back the sound of Father's conversation with Doireann.

As she suspected, the woman was telling lies again.

"You girls run ahead. Father is home," she said to her sisters.

Nuala and Maeve seized Sive's hands and took off up the hill, shouting Father's name.

Rhona longed to run with them, but it was more important to make sure Candace arrived safely. The old woman had grown an alarming shade of pink as she huffed and puffed her way up the hill. Still, she waved away Rhona's offer of assistance.

"If I cannot walk up this hill under my own power, how will I ever run around after those three little fillies? Nay, if you are as spry when you are my age, girl, then you will thank the heavens yourself." Candace grinned and continued ambling, ever upward.

"You must not let them eat or drink anything she has touched. Nor let her touch them, either," Rhona said. "She tried to poison us once. There is no knowing what else that witch will try next."

"It's been a long time since there's been a witch at Rum Isle, or any of the Southern

Isles," Candace said, shooting a sideways glance at Rhona. "Not since your aunt, Brigid, died. But she was a good witch, always willing to help. Perhaps this one is not as experienced, and gave the children the wrong dose or the wrong herb. She is young, you said, not much older than you."

Rhona tossed her head. "I would not make such a mistake. Mother taught me better than that." No, Aunt Blanid, she corrected in her head.

When they reached the house, Doireann had left, and Father stood alone.

"Widow Candace," Father greeted her, before offering Rhona a kiss. "It is a long walk from your cottage. What brings you here?"

"Doireann poisoned us, then left us in the woods," Rhona snapped. "I managed to get the girls to Candace's cottage, but Maeve took a chill, so we stayed a little until she recovered enough to walk home. Candace has agreed to come and help take care of the girls, as their nurse."

Father blinked. "I'm sure it is all a mistake. She's such a sweet girl, she would never..." He shook his head. "I apologise, Widow Candace, for the stories my daughter has been filling your head with. I shall send you home on horseback, with gifts from my cellar to repay you for your time."

"My cottage is cold now my daughters are all married. Seems I could be useful here, if your daughters are giving you trouble," Candace said.

Rhona opened her mouth to protest, but a hard look from Candace silenced her.

"Your new wife is just finding her feet, after all. I'm sure I shall be a great help to her. I am used to work, and the lady of Rum Isle has enough cares resting on her shoulders." Candace moved toward the house. "I shall start by seeing those girls wash up. They look a fright, after walking in the woods. You'll see. I'll take good care of them." This last earned Rhona another look from Candace before she vanished inside.

Whatever Candace believed, at least she would watch over her sisters. Rhona couldn't ask for much more than that.

"I must speak to Doireann," Father said.

When Rhona stepped forward to follow him, he held up his hand. "Alone, Rhona. I will speak to you later."

Damn right, he would. And she'd have just as much to say. In the meantime, Candace would keep an eye on the girls, while Rhona changed out of her soiled gown. Something brighter and cleaner was needed, as befitted a dinner that would double as her father's welcome home after the Council meeting. Ugh, and a clean shift. One that didn't have leaves in it, or mudstains in places where no mud should be.

Rhona marched toward her chamber, intent on making herself presentable once more.

There was still some water in the jug, so she stripped off and washed. The fresh shift clung to her still-damp skin, letting off a faint whiff of lavender. The shift had not lain in the chest long, then – those in the bottom would smell much stronger.

She reached for the blue gown she'd worn at the last feast day, when Mother – Blanid – had presided over the feast with all the joy of a woman who'd had no idea it would be her last celebration. Blanid had clucked over the gown that day, telling Rhona she needed to wear more womanly things, for the hem of the gown that had been suitable for the girl Rhona had been was far too high for the woman she had now become.

The dress fell from Rhona's nerveless fingers back into the chest. She should give it to Nuala, but then what would Rhona wear? Blanid had promised to make her new gowns that fit her better, but she'd died before she could even cut the cloth, and Rhona was no seamstress.

The only womanly gowns Blanid had left had been her own. Gowns that would be wasted on Doireann, who had no right to wear them, either, Rhona fumed.

For the first time since Blanid had died, Rhona knelt beside the chests she'd moved from Blanid's chamber to her own. She opened the first, and breathed in the rose scent that Blanid had made wholly her own. Not least because her precious roses, which were carefully tended in the sheltered southern herb garden, had come with her to the island when she'd married Father. Other women had dowries of cloth and jewels, lands and houses, but Blanid and Brigid's parents had been renowned for their glorious garden, modelled on the one where Rhona's grandmother had grown up. So it was no surprise that Blanid had arrived with as many medicinal plants as her parents could provide.

Or had that been Brigid's doing?

Rhona would never know, now, for the two women who might have told her were now dead, silenced forever.

But with them both gone, she had a responsibility to remind her father who ruled here. And it wasn't Doireann, the conniving widow from Scitis.

Rhona dug through the dresses, looking for the sky-blue gown Blanid had worn which matched her own. Instead, she found one of yellow-gold silk, so soft to the touch she'd lifted it out of the chest before she knew what she was doing. It was lined with cream lambswool, as soft inside as out. Rhona had never seen Blanid wear this gown, yet when Rhona pressed her face to the fabric, she smelled an unfamiliar scent – sharp and fresh, tingling her nostrils as though it was something she should remember, but had forgotten. Citron, was that was this was called? No, the word was lemon. A kind of fruit that grew in warmer climes than here.

In her grandparents' garden, most likely.

Rhona slipped the gown over her head, letting the lambswool embrace her like it had been made for her. Only her waist was narrower, so she tightened the laces a little before tying them again. Blanid's bronze mirror stood in the corner, polished to a high sheen so that Rhona might see how well she looked. Or how well she might look, if she picked the bird's nest remnants out of her hair.

Swearing, Rhona unbound her hair and found a comb. It would take some time to get all the twigs and leaves out, but she would need to if she wanted to remind Father that she was a woman grown, and every bit as worthy as Doireann of being believed.

When she had finally freed her hair of snarls, tangles and twigs, she had to decide whether to pin it up, or leave it loose. Loose would attract more leaves the moment she ventured into the woods again, but that's how Blanid had worn hers at every feast day. A few pins, or a headband fashioned from a pair of narrow braids, were all that restrained the golden mane Blanid had proudly worn loose as she presided over the people of Rum Island.

The thwack of an axe hitting wood reached Rhona's ears. She peered out the window, wondering why anyone would be chopping wood so late in the day. They had cut turf enough to feed the house fires well into next month – no one should be cutting precious timber.

But there was no one at the chopping block, and besides, the sound was coming from down by the river. The only timber by the river was the willow trees, bred from the one that had been part of Blanid's dowry. The only source of willow bark on the island. If anyone was cutting into those trees, they'd have her to answer to. Especially if they wasted any of that precious bark.

Rhona slid a pair of boots onto her feet and marched out for confrontation.

Eighteen

"What in heaven's name are you doing?"

The voice was feminine, but authoritative. Accustomed to being obeyed. It could only belong to Lord Ronin's wife, Lady Doireann. Grieve let the axe hang by his side, no threat to the lady. "My lady, Lord Ronin wishes to build better fortifications to protect your house and all those who live there." He lifted the axe for another swing.

"Touch that tree again, and I promise you shall regret it. Even more so when I refused to give you any willow bark for the pain."

Grieve whirled, shocked. Lady Doireann had looked so small and docile – not the sort of woman who would threaten him with pain for touching a tree, of all things. "M-my lady?" he stammered.

He glimpsed the tall figure coming toward him, before the sun chose its own moment to enter the fray. The rays blinded him, and appeared to set fire to her. One moment a woman, the next a golden pillar of flame, heading inexorably for him. The axe dropped from his nerveless fingers. Grieve wanted to run, but at the same time, he didn't dare take his eyes off the terrifying spectre before him.

"What is wrong with you, boy?" she demanded.

As if to make his mortification complete, the sun hid its face behind a cloud once more. The fiery goddess transformed into a woman. A woman who didn't look a bit like Lady Doireann. Wheat coloured curls hung to her waist. The breeze played with some of the outer tendrils, the movement reminiscent of tongues of fire. Add that to the butter-coloured dress she wore, and it was easy to see how his overactive imagination had turned a girl into a goddess, with just a bit of sunlight.

He laughed shakily. "For a moment, I thought you were on fire," he admitted. He traced the shape of her body in the air. "Sunlight in your hair and in your dress. It looked like you were wreathed in flames. I thought I was going to die, and that you were going to burn me to death, without the flames touching you at all."

She backed up a step, her eyes widening in horror. She almost tripped over the hem of her gown, which was a little long for her, he'd only just noticed. She cast her eyes down. "My mother told me many times not to play with fire."

Grieve managed a smile. "My mother told me the same thing," he said. "But I did not listen. I once burned down a whole hay shed. My brother told me the cat had had a litter of kittens and that I could see them in the morning, but I was impatient, and took a candle in there at night..." Now it was Grieve's turn to bow his head. "I earned a sound thrashing from my father for that, and as a punishment he made me rebuild the hay shed. After that, I preferred to build with wood, not set fire to it."

Her eyes was still wide. "And what of the kittens?" Her voice trembled. She might look like a woman but she could not be much older than Grieve himself.

Now Grieve grinned. "They were never in the hay shed. The cat had her kittens in the barn, where the dairy cows slept." He held out a tentative hand for her to shake. "I am Grieve Lewisson, from Myroy Isle. I am to be Lord Ronin's squire."

She eyed his hand suspiciously for a moment, then took it in her own. "Rhona." Her eyes dared him to ask for more than just her name.

All Grieve's instincts screamed that this would be a trap, though what sort, he did not know. "It is a pleasure to meet you, Lady Rhona, guardian of this tree. I have heard tales of naiads, but this is my first time meeting one." He closed his mouth, giving her a challenge of his own.

Her narrowed eyes made him worry that

he'd made a mistake. Perhaps he should have just complimented her on her name the way he had when he'd met Bedelia. Then again, look how well that had turned out.

Then Rhona gave a tiny smile. "I think you mean a dryad, not a naiad. Dryads live in trees. Naiads are river spirits. But both are myths. They don't exist. At least, not outside of stories. And we are both too old for such things."

Grieve recognise the regret in her tone, for he shared it. Life was much simpler as a child, believing all his mother's tales to be true. "Then why protect this tree so passionately?"

"Because it belonged to my mother," she said. "She brought the trees, and many other medicinal plants, when she came to… When she came to live with my father."

"And your father is…?"

She gave him a look of deep disgust. "Not stupid enough to build a fortification out of willows, or anything that burns so easily. Here on Rum Isle, timber is too precious. We build with sod and stone, so our kittens are safe from boys who like to play with fire, and our people sleep safer in their beds, knowing that when Alban raiders come, and they will, they will not be burned alive, for it would take powerful magic indeed to burn down a sod house." A girl she might be, but the hard look at her eyes said she knew as much about war as Grieve himself, or perhaps more. For a moment, she looked like his own father, telling Mahon how to prepare for war. She seized his arm, her touch searing through the cloth as though the flames Grieve had seen earlier were not as imaginary as he thought. "Come. We shall both go to see my father together, and if his witch of a wife is behind this… I will make her rue the day she was born."

Grieve let the girl pulled him into Lord Ronin's house, all the while musing that if one of the two women he'd met today was a witch he would place his wager on Lady Rhona and not the mousey Doireann. But he kept this thought to himself, lest Rhona turn her fury on him again.

Nineteen

"Brigid," Father breathed, his eyes wide.

Rhona glanced down. Had this gown belonged to her mother – her birth mother, not Blanid? That would explain why she'd never seen Blanid wear it. She rubbed her fingers down the silk. She'd treasure it now she knew.

But now she had more important matters to attend to. "Father, why was this boy cutting down trees by the river?"

"Ah, you've met Grieve, your new foster brother," Father said. "He is Lord Lewis' son, and to be treated with every courtesy. As you are not needed here, will you show him around the island and introduce him to everyone? Lord Lewis sent him to help with our defences, so show him everything."

He meant Sanctuary, Rhona knew. Strange that he did not mention its name before Doireann. Did he not trust her either? Rhona could only hope. She moistened her lips. "Yes, Father." She headed upstairs to pack some things to take. A horseback tour of the island could be done in a day, but if she was to show this stranger Sanctuary…she wanted to take her time, to find out if he could be trusted. Unlike Doireann.

Three days, she decided, if they left this afternoon.

She would need riding clothes, not this beautiful gown. The only thing she had left from her mother. Not to mention another cloak, for hers was still covered in mud from when Doireann left her in the woods. Candace had offered to clean it, but Rhona had wanted to show it to her father as proof of his new wife's perfidy. But it could wait until she returned.

As long as Candace took care of the girls.

Rhona headed for her sisters' room, where she could hear giggling.

Candace sat with the three of them, reciting a rhyme that named each of Sive's toes before tickling the small girl.

"Did you tell Father what she did?" Nuala demanded.

Rhona hung her head. "I tried, but he still does not believe me. Mistress Candace, I swear to you that every word I spoke to you and my father is the truth. She has drugged my sisters once, and next time, she might give them more than a simple sleeping potion. She said as much to me before she knocked me out." She rubbed the lump on the back of her head, still tender after almost a week. Who would have thought Doireann could muster so much power in a single blow? "Please, whatever you do, do not let the girls eat or drink anything that Doireann has touched. I trust the staff, for they are all loyal to my father, but they still must obey her. They will tell you if she touches anything in the kitchen, though she hardly goes in there. But if she does – "

"Hush, girl. I will keep them safe. Your mother nursed my girls through a winter fever when I thought I would lose them. Lady Blanid should have sent word when she was taken ill. I would have been here directly to help." Candace smiled.

"But I must go away for a few days. Will you…"

Candace bowed her head. "I will care for the Lady Blanid's girls like they were my own. By the time you return, Lord Ronin will have accepted me into his household as a nurse again. You may not remember your wet nurse, but Lord Ronin remembers me well. I will make sure of it, if he tries to forget."

Did that mean Candace knew who Rhona's real mother was? Rhona opened her mouth to ask.

"Where are you going?" Maeve demanded.

Her sisters could never know. "Father has a new squire, and he wishes me to show him the island. When we return, I will introduce him to you."

"Will he have new stories?" Sive asked, her

eyes shining.

Always, it was stories. If only fairytales were true, and some handsome prince or knight in shining armour would come to save them from Doireann and this war with the Albans.

Rhona managed a smile. "I shall ask him while we ride, and let you know the answer when we return." She made a private wager with herself that the answer would be yes – Grieve had seemed to like telling stories. Perhaps he would have some even she had not heard yet, that he could tell to amuse her on their journey.

Smiling to herself, Rhona headed for her room.

Off came the beautiful golden gown, to be carefully placed in the chest with Blanid's things. She would need a thicker shift – wool instead of linen. She loosened the laces and let the shift slip to the floor.

A male voice swore.

Rhona whirled in panic, and met the eyes of a red-faced Grieve, who turned around as though his life depended on it.

"What are you doing in my chamber?" she

demanded, clutching her shift to her chest.

"I'm not in your chamber, just on the threshold," he said. "Your father told me to follow you, so I did. I waited for you to speak to your sisters, before following you here. How was I to know you intended to undress?"

It sounded reasonable enough. It wasn't like he'd tried to hide.

But…

"Why didn't you say something when I took off my gown? Before I removed my shift?" Rhona demanded. She tugged the woollen shift over her head, so she wouldn't feel so exposed.

"Because I was mesmerised, my lady. It wasn't until I regained my senses that I realised what I should have done. I froze. I could not help myself. I've never seen…" He swallowed, seemingly unable to continue.

"A naked woman before?" she finished for him, feeling her fury build. Oh, if only she could use her magic to blast him out the window. She'd never felt so humiliated in her life.

He managed a watery smile. "Oh, no, I've

seen one of those. A few, actually. Just…never one as beautiful as you. One glimpse and…I lost my mind, my lady. I could no longer think or speak. I could only stare." He ducked his head. "Please accept my forgiveness. I did not mean to offend you. I swear it will not happen again."

Beautiful. He'd called her beautiful. No one ever said that. Well, except her father, and he didn't count. Maybe she would forgive him. After all, she'd never seen a naked man before. She'd probably stare, too.

Instead of the brown overdress she'd intended to wear, Rhona chose the rose-coloured one Blanid had once favoured for festival days, until Maeve was born and her waist thickened too much to tie the laces. Blanid's wine-coloured riding cloak went perfectly with it. Oh, but her hair…

Rhona pulled out the pins and set to work, braiding it in earnest. When she had her hair as firmly under control as the blush that had briefly coloured her cheeks, she turned and said, "Shall we go, Grieve Lewisson?"

Twenty

If he'd known she was about to undress, he would have turned his back on her. That would have been the honourable thing to do. But his breath had caught in his throat as the gown came off, and then her shift…

Yes, he'd seen naked women before. But none of them had such perfect breasts. And nipples as pink as…well, the dress she now wore to hide them. As if anything could hide the swell of her breasts now he'd seen them — they were permanently burned into his brain. He would dream of them for the rest of his days, Grieve was certain of it.

Still he waited for her to slap him like Bedelia had, but she did not.

Then she stood before him, only a breath away, her eyes level with his. Gazing at him expectantly.

"What did you say?" he asked, feeling even more stupid.

She gave him a mischievous smile, as though she'd plucked the thought from his mind and it amused her. "I said, shall we go, Grieve Lewisson?"

He'd never heard his own name sound so…seductive. "Anything you wish, my lady," he managed to say.

"We will not return for a couple of nights, so bring whatever you'll need," she said, bundling a few things together. She tucked the bundle under her arm.

Grieve held out his hand. "Allow me to carry that for you." He might have forgotten his courtesies earlier, but that meant all the more reason to remember them now.

Rhona laughed. "You've seen quite enough of my underthings, Lewisson. You see to your own. I shall meet you in the kitchen."

Feeling his cheeks grow hot all over again — she'd been the one caught naked and unaware, so why was he so much more embarrassed? — he headed for the room he'd been told would be his. A comb, some spare clothes, his cloak…what else did he need? His mind refused to work properly. All he could see was her pale skin, curves he ached to touch…and those breasts!

He gritted his teeth and forced the image out of his head as he descended the stairs two at a time to where his nose told him the kitchen lay.

"I do not know what your father is thinking, Lady Rhona, truly I don't. First her ladyship and now young Lewisson…but you may rest assured that Candace and I will keep an eye on them for you. We are old friends, us two, though the friendship soured a little when she married. We both wanted young Paddy, you see, but he had eyes only for her…"

Grieve stepped inside the room, inhaling the scent of roasting meat and fresh baked bread. He wanted to eat it all.

"He looks like the younger one, not Lewis's heir at all," the woman continued. The cook, Grieve assumed. "Your father and Lewis can't be serious about this."

"Lord Angus himself was a younger son, and now he's Lord of Isla and High Lord of us all. Stranger things have happened in tales as well as in truth. Who can say what will come to pass?" Rhona said. She bit into a crust of bread.

"Who indeed?" Grieve said, reaching for the loaf.

The women's eyes widened – evidently they had not seen him enter.

He tore off a chunk and chewed with relish. No matter what this cook thought of him, at least she would feed him well. "This is the best bread I've tasted in weeks." He swallowed and continued, "I am my father's second surviving son. My brother Mahon will be lord after Father. He will also marry Lord Calum's daughter. Father has not told me about his plans for me, though he sent me here. What do you know that I do not?"

"He expects you to marry one of Father's

daughters and succeed him as Lord of Rum Isle. As I'm the only one old enough, it seems Father has set his sights on giving me to you. Hence this farce about defence and a tour of the island."

Lady Rhona? His? Desire burned deep within him at the thought. If only. But the look in her eyes dispelled that idea as quickly as it had come. Lady Rhona would never accept him as a husband, especially not if her father pushed her to do so.

"Defence against Alban raiders is never a farce. They are a very real threat to us..." Grieve began.

"The boy's right about that. Lewis always was a strategist, and his son must be the same. It can't hurt to have his help defending the place. I will give you as many provisions as the horses can carry, just in case." The cook pulled two loaves from the oven, wrapped them well, then handed them to a maid who carried them outside.

"Come, Lewisson. We may still manage a few miles before dark," Rhona said, leading the way outside.

Two horses stood in the yard, saddled and ready to go. The bread-bearing maid fastened the nearest one's saddlebags. "Safe journey, Lady Rhona," she said with a respectful bow of her head. She glanced at Grieve, but said nothing as she went past.

Bemused, Grieve stared after her. First the cook, now the maids. At home, all would have at least bobbed a curtsey to him, though they'd known him since childhood. Here, things were very different indeed, if the servants had little respect for their betters.

"Wipe that look off your face, Lewisson," Rhona advised him from her perch atop a horse. "Siobhan is betrothed to the first mate on Father's ship. She's not for you."

"No, but you are," he said without thinking. He swung up onto his horse, only to find himself face to face with the furious girl.

"I belong to no man. Not my father, not you, and definitely no one who even thinks a woman can be owned. No self-respecting Islander woman would allow such a thing. I choose to take you on a tour of Rum Isle because my knowledge of the island is second only to my father's, and you might be able to help us defend our home against all enemies."

Now it was Grieve's turn to bow his head. "I am your servant, as I am your father's squire, Lady Rhona. I am indebted to you for your kindness, I'm sure. All enemies of such a lovely lady are, of course, my enemies as well."

She almost smiled at that, but when he looked again, the smile was gone as though he'd imagined it. "Pretty words, Lewisson. You'll need more than words if it comes to war." She set off at a fast trot, and it took Grieve a moment before he could persuade his horse to follow, by which time she was several lengths ahead of him.

He feared she always would be, but that didn't stop him from striving to catch up. Lady Rhona was a woman he wanted to catch, but only if she allowed it.

Twenty-One

Rhona headed for the eastern watchtower, reasoning that it was the only suitable place to take him that was an easy ride before dark. Sanctuary could be reached just as easily, for they didn't have a cart, but she wasn't sure she was ready to show that to him yet. Better to take him on a full tour of the island and see what kind of man he truly was before revealing any secrets. Lord Lewis was no fool – if he'd sent his son to help Father, then Grieve could help. But if he was a strategist like his father…he might use Rum Isle as a pawn in a much larger game with higher stakes than Rhona could see. Rum Isle might not be important to Lord Lewis and his son, but it was everything to those who lived there.

"Are you planning on pitching me off a cliff, my lady?" Grieve asked after some time.

Rhona smiled. To someone who didn't know what to look for, the clifftop watchtowers looked like ordinary crags. "Maybe later. You have not yet vexed me enough for that. Perhaps on the third offence I will not be as forgiving."

She dismounted, and glanced over her shoulder to see what Grieve had made of her half-joking response.

"I shall endeavour not to cut down any trees, or look at you, without your permission. Is there anything else you'd care to warn me about, so I do not offend you again?" He lifted his hand. "Wait, I already know I must be kind to kittens."

"It is always wise to be kind to kittens," Rhona said. She headed for the standing stone that marked the entrance, then slipped into the rock crevice behind it. It was a tight squeeze, but grown men used this passage every day, so she knew she would fit. When she was through, she extended a hand. "Come, Lewisson, if you wish to see Rum Isle's first line of defence against invaders."

He grumbled as he squeezed through the gap, then stood beside her. "A cave." He did not sound impressed.

Rhona laughed. "Rum Isle is full of caves, some on the land, and some on the cliffs, and some you can only reach at high or low tide, for the ocean hides a veritable army of rocks to keep Rum Isle safe. The ancient peoples of the isles found this one, and improved upon it." She led him deeper into the shadows to the steps. Twisted and winding, worn by the tread of generations of boots, the steps led up into the tower, or at least that's what they called the top of the crag. The roof of the top cavern had caved in, leaving it open to the elements, but with a clear view all the way to Alba on a clear day. Today, like most days, it was hidden in mist, but she could still see for miles. As could tonight's watchman.

"Good evening, Lady Rhona," he said.

"Good evening indeed, Ximeno," she said. "This is Grieve Lewisson, my father's new squire from Myroy Isle. My father wants him to see all our defences. Where is Nuno?"

"He said he would go get our dinner from Mother. Did you not see him?" When Rhona shook her head, Ximeno continued, "Then he must have met a pretty girl, who distracted him."

Grieve burst out laughing, then stopped when he realised he was the only one.

"What's funny?" Rhona asked coolly.

Grieve was still grinning. "Why, doesn't he mean you? But we saw no one on the way here…"

"Nuno is sweet on Ciara, though I am not sure if she is as sweet on him. He makes frequent visits to his mother, though, hoping to see her, so Belen encourages him, even if Ciara gives him no hope." Rhona sniffed. If she wanted a man, she would not toy with his affections like Ciara. Though it seemed to drive Nuno wild, so perhaps she knew her man better than Rhona thought. Still… "Ximeno, can you tell him how we run things here? I'll unsaddle the horses for the night."

Without another word, she hurried down the steps and away from the only man on Rum Isle who thought she was worth looking at.

Twenty-Two

Grieve watched her go, too bewildered to ask why. Ximeno just shrugged, then began to point out the features of their clifftop eyrie, including what Grieve had taken for an eagle's nest but was actually a watchfire which could be seen from the other three towers when it was lit. He stroked the smooth stone, shaped into a natural tower with only a little help from men. The other towers Ximeno pointed out looked almost identical to this one – natural formations that no one would look twice at, approaching the island for the first time.

Unlike the wooden watchtowers at Isla and Myroy, which stood out for what they were.

When Ximeno's spiel seemed to wind down, the man took Grieve's arm and looked around before dropping to a whisper. "A word of advice, if I may. Lady Rhona might not be the prettiest girl on the island, but it is cruel to mock her for it. She is the best healer on Rum Isle, perhaps in all of the Southern Isles, and it does not matter if a man must look upon her face instead of his sweetheart's when the lady's help is needed. And she's still the Lady of the Isle – when she marries, her husband will be Lord Ronin's successor, for his claim will go to her. If you intend to stay here, it is not wise to offend Lady Rhona."

"She's already talked about throwing me off a cliff," Grieve admitted, but his thoughts were more on Ximeno's words than his own. Not the prettiest girl on the island? Had Ximeno even looked at the girl? Even clothed, she was lovely. Tall and fair as a Viken, perhaps taller than any other woman he'd seen on Rum Isle, but far from ugly.

"Then you had best guard your tongue most

carefully. You must have offered Lady Rhona a grievous insult to offend her so," Ximeno said. "She will be a true lady when her father passes, much like her mother was. Nothing like the new one. They say she throws screeching tantrums if her whims are not acted upon, and never does a thing for anyone. Why, we found her with a cart bogged in the mud the other day, partway home. She beat Nuno with a stick when he didn't get the cart wheel free fast enough. If you ask me, Lord Ronin should get that one pregnant as quickly as possible, and hope the childbed fever takes her like it did his first wife. Poor Lady Blanid. Lady Rhona must be heartbroken even her healing arts could not save her."

"I…thank you," Grieve said. "I should probably help Lady Rhona with…the horses." He stumbled down the uneven steps, wondering how the watchman managed not to break his neck each time he had to race down them to report a raiding party.

"So, do you still think we're defenceless?" Rhona greeted him.

"There's a saying on Myroy that as long as a

man still has his wits, he will never be defenceless," Grieve said, stretching his frozen fingers out toward the fire. "I never said Rum Isle was without defences, just that it would benefit from stronger ones." He drew in a deep breath, hoping to inhale courage with the air. Something to stop his knees from shaking, as he added, "And when your watchman spoke of a pretty girl, of course I thought he meant it as a compliment to you. Why would he not? Why, just look at you."

"I believe you already did that, this afternoon," Rhona said dryly.

As if on command, Grieve's cheeks reddened. "I said I was sorry for staring, but I'll never be sorry for seeing what I saw. A vision of loveliness no man would want to forget. And I'll challenge any man who dares say otherwise."

She shook her head, but there was a smile on her lips. "Pretty words, Lewisson, no more. I am not so vain as to wish I were the most beautiful girl in the Southern Isles – I know my own reflection, and I am content. I'm sure your flattery is well meant, though unnecessary. I've already set out our bedrolls, and you may share my bed tonight." She gestured at a stone alcove, where Grieve saw his things beside hers.

His mouth dropped open, but he couldn't think of a word to say. He stared, yet he could detect no hint of laughter in her expression. She expected him to share her bed?

"I…I thought it was customary to start with a kiss," he said.

Uncertainty flared in her eyes. For all her forwardness, she was as nervous as he was.

Grieve grew bolder, stepping forward so that he could embrace her. He lifted a tentative hand to her cheek, which was as soft as he'd imagined it to be. "So beautiful," he murmured.

Her lips parted, but no sound came out.

Gently, oh so carefully, he touched his lips to hers. Her slight gasp dared him to do more, as her fingers tangled in his hair, holding him close. Only then did he dare to tease her tongue with his, and the taste of her, the softness of the woman in his arms, was enough for him to lose his mind. Once he'd started, he could not stop kissing her – no, not even to draw a breath that had not caressed her breast first with its airy fingers.

By the time Rhona pushed him away, her eyes blazed with the same desire coursing through his veins. With trembling hands, he unfastened his cloak and dropped it on the stone floor. Then he seized the hem of his tunic…

Her hand covered his, pulling the hem down. "Keep your clothes on, Myroy boy. I said you may lie with me – to keep warm, for 'tis cold in this cave, even with the fire going. If I want you to be my lover, I'll tell you so, but not tonight. Though that was a fine kiss. If I do choose you for a lover, I'd hope for many more such kisses."

He stepped away and straightened his tunic. "My apologies, my lady. Your beauty bewitched me again. If you desire another kiss, you have only to ask."

She laid a hand on his chest. "Rhona. You are a lord's son, and I am a lord's daughter. After sharing a kiss like that…we should at least be friends."

"Only if you call me Grieve, the name my mother gave me. And accept that when I say you are beautiful, I mean every word. If other men cannot see it, then they are fools."

She took a deep breath, looking as enervated by the exchange as he felt. "Very well, though it is strange to think every man I have ever known is a fool. Doesn't it seem more likely that the one man who sees things differently is more foolish than the rest? Grieve?"

It was strange yet lovely to her his name on her lips once more. He wanted to hear her gasp it, moan it, maybe even scream it for joy. One day, he promised himself.

"If I am a fool, then I do not know it. How would I know? Ah, I have heard some kings keep fools in their courts, who amuse them by telling tales. Shall I share some of the stories I know, and see if they amuse you?"

Rhona sat beside the fire and broke a loaf in two, before handing him half. "Tell all the tales you want. If you tell me one I have not heard, then I will open a bottle of my father's best wine. Belen slipped one into the saddlebags."

A challenge, the likes of which no Myroy man could refuse. Grieve took the bread and began, "Once upon a time..."

Twenty-Three

Shuffling footsteps woke Grieve. A man tiptoed through the cave, taking exaggerated care to make as little noise as possible as he ascended the steps. Nuno, he assumed, for the man looked like last night's watchman, his brother.

Grieve took a deep breath, and inhaled an unfamiliar floral scent. He glanced down. He'd shared Rhona's bed, just as she'd promised, but he had not expected to share tales with her half the night until he'd fallen asleep with her warm weight in his arms. Now, the fully clothed girl was pressed against his side, one arm flung across his belly as if to claim him. Her hand was dangerously close to where he dreamed she'd caressed him. Where he wished she'd touch him now, for he stood to attention for her in anticipation of a more intimate embrace than the one they were in now.

If his father and Lord Ronin sought to matchmake him with Rhona, then he would embrace their plan with all his strength.

"Marry me, Rhona," he whispered into her hair.

He snorted softly. He'd known the woman for a day, but he knew he'd never get her out of his head.

Rhona shifted, and her hand drifted lower, then fastened around him. By all that was holy, how could he feel the heat of her touch through his tunic? Whatever she touched, she burned.

"Well, you're a big one, aren't you? Dreaming about some girl back home?" she asked, giving him an agonisingly good squeeze before letting go.

Grieve swallowed. "Thinking about the girl

in my arms right now," he said. "The beautiful Lady Rhona."

She shifted away from him and sat up. "No good morning kisses for you, then. You go take care of that, for we have a long ride ahead of us. I must show you the rest of the island, and tonight, we'll sleep in Sanctuary. The island's biggest secret of all."

Already his arms felt empty without her, but Grieve did as she said. Riding with a raging hard-on for the woman beside him would make for a hell of a day.

Twenty-Four

Perhaps it had been the wine, or all those well-told tales, but as she'd cuddled up to Grieve's warm body in her bedroll that night, Rhona knew she'd made her decision. She would show him Sanctuary. But not because her father had ordered it. No, she'd show him because she wanted him to stay and become one of them.

She'd known him for a day, and yet it felt like she'd known him forever. An easy familiarity had sprung between them last night, like they were a long-lost brother and sister.

Yet that kiss…no, that had not been brotherly at all. While her lips were locked with his, she'd seriously considered taking things further, perhaps even letting him make love to her. She'd never thought much about marriage, but she did know one thing – she'd not go to her marriage bed as some virgin maiden who'd never known a man's touch. No, when she took a husband, she'd already know he was a skilled lover.

If Grieve could set her body aflame with a single kiss, imagine what he could do with the rest of his body…and hers…

She dreamed he'd asked her to marry him, but before she could answer, she awoke. Perhaps that was for the best, for she'd found him pitching a tent in his tunic with a look of panic on his face lest she notice. She'd have to be blind indeed not to notice he carried a mighty sword beneath his belt as well as the one that hung from it.

Idly, she wondered what it would feel like to have that length of hot, hard flesh slide inside her, as his hands caressed her and he told her over and over again how beautiful she was.

Rhona almost laughed aloud. A daydream, that's what it was, conjured out of the silly stories they'd told last night. Knights and princess, genies and sultans, courtesans and princesses…all living happily ever after, with no thoughts of war or what might happen in the future. If only life were like the stories.

If it were, then she and Grieve could lie abed, making love to each other so that every moment was happy ever after. But not today, for Nuno had returned, and that meant Ximeno would want their cave to sleep in after standing watch all night. So she freshened up and broke her fast, while Grieve readied himself for the ride along the western side of the island, before they headed to Sanctuary.

The prettier side of the island, some said, because it was the side furthest from Alba. But it was also the least sheltered part of the island, for there was nothing to stop the waves from rolling in and smashing against the cliffs. The spray flew so high Rhona tasted salt on her lips more than once.

If she were to kiss Grieve again, would his lips be salty, too? Her eyes met his and a smile lifted her lips almost of its own volition. Her heart raced as though she'd galloped along the clifftop, instead of keeping to the slow pace such uneven terrain demanded. Grieve was several yards away, yet he'd stolen her breath somehow.

Perhaps…

"What do you think of the plot between my father and yours?" she asked him.

"Which one?"

"The one to make us marry."

Grieve reined his horse to a stop, and Rhona's mount almost collided with his. Close enough to touch, and he did, capturing her hand in his own. "I know nothing of any plot, for the gossip in your kitchen was the first I had heard of it. But the more I think on it, every moment I spend with you, the less I care whether there is a plot at all." He pressed his lips to her hand, a chaste kiss compared to the one they'd shared last night. "I would like to kiss you again, Lady Rhona, and with you in my thoughts, there is no space for anyone else." For a moment, his eyes were dark and full of feeling, before he turned away to gaze toward the horizon. "But you must show me all of Rum Isle's defences. I must make sure…the island…is protected."

The love that had blossomed in her breast as she anticipated another delightful kiss shrivelled in the summer sun as Grieve put more distance between them.

Rhona sighed. She dreamed too much, she knew, for there were too many stories in her head. Grieve was right to be practical about these things, for love could not stop a war.

Twenty-Five

Grieve cursed his clumsiness with words, and with women. For a moment there, it seemed they'd shared the same thoughts, and then it had all gone wrong. Was he supposed to say he heartily approved of their fathers' plot? That couldn't be right – she had made it very clear that she would follow her own heart, not her father's plans.

He scarcely paid attention as she showed him the other three watchtowers and the harbour, introducing him to everyone they met. He smiled and nodded and shook hands, accepting more cups of ale than was good for him.

More than once, he'd had to take a trip into the bushes, to Rhona's amusement.

On the third such detour, she'd waited until he'd climbed back onto his horse before she said, "At least you gave me a show of your own this time. 'Tis a fine arse you have, Lewisson. A mite pale, but I don't suppose it sees much sun."

She'd been watching him piss? Grieve's face grew so hot he feared his skin would crisp off. And then…he smiled, at the knowledge that she'd been watching him. Maybe she was not as cold to him as he'd thought.

He hurried to catch up to her. "Are there any other parts of me you consider fine?" he called.

She tossed her head. "I'm sure I'd have to see more of such parts before I could make a judgement like that."

He drew even with her. "And what parts of me would you like to see more of, my lady?"

She darted a glance at him, then looked away. "I'm sure I don't know. But you have seen all of me, so it seems only fitting that I should see all of you. And I thought we agreed to use first names, not…anything else."

"So we did. And if my lady wishes to see all of me, she has only to ask."

She closed her eyes. "Grieve…"

"Yes, Rhona?"

"Stop. We have arrived."

Grieve looked around. "This is no sanctuary. A sheltered depression, out of the wind, with the river running alongside, but it is too open. The enemy would only need to follow your trail here, and there would be no escape. You'd be slaughtered."

"And yet no enemy has ever taken Rum Isle," Rhona said softly. "You see that waterfall?"

Grieve's gazed followed her pointing finger. "It's pretty," he said cautiously.

Rhona laughed. She slid down and began to unfasten her saddle. She gave her horse a slap on the rump in dismissal and carried her things toward the waterfall.

Grieve hurried to do the same. But the buckles refused to unfasten, so by the time he'd freed his horse, Rhona was nowhere to be seen.

"Rhona?" he called, feeling like a fool. He set off for the waterfall, wondering if he would see her from there.

The waterfall turned pink, before she emerged from behind it, brushing water droplets from her cloak. "Are you coming, or are you waiting for an enemy army to appear?"

It was another natural watchtower, Grieve guessed, as he scrambled up the damp rocks to where Rhona stood.

"Come and see," she said, turning to lead the way.

He was surprised to find the entrance was big enough to walk through without ducking his head or turning sideways – unlike the watchtowers she'd shown him. The passage beyond narrowed as it led upward, and he left his saddle beside hers, shouldering his bags so they wouldn't catch on the walls. The combination of slippery stone and the sharp incline made it a challenge to keep his footing, but Grieve managed to follow Rhona without actually falling, though he slipped twice. He noticed several passages that led to the left and right, but Rhona did not turn, and he had no choice but to follow where she led.

Then she stopped so suddenly that he slammed into her, wrapping his arms around her to keep from knocking her over.

"Welcome to Sanctuary," she said, glancing over her shoulder at him. "And if that's your saddlebags I can feel digging into my shoulder, I think you've just squashed the bread."

Grieve realised he still held her, and reluctantly relinquished the woman he only wanted to pull closer. He mumbled an apology.

"This is Rum Island's stronghold. None have ever taken it, and none shall while Islanders hold it," Rhona said.

Grieve could see why. The place was like one of the legendary ancient fortresses – in fact, it probably was one. The cavern was huge – his father's great hall would fit in here twice over, with space to spare. Why, you could fit most of Myroy Island's people in here. A stream ran along one side of the cavern, presumably an offshoot of the river that fed the waterfall at the door.

In the light of the flames of the firepit, which was already lit, though Rhona could not have been here long enough to light such a fire, Grieve could just discern steps at the opposite end of the cavern, spiralling upwards.

"Is there a watchtower atop here, too?" he asked.

She nodded. "Two, actually, though they are not so much towers as higher caverns through which the river used to flow. The island is riddled with caves, but these are the highest and the biggest. From the east spire, you can see clear to the sea, and with men in both east and west, two men can keep watch over the whole island, while our people live comfortably in the cavern below. There are smaller caverns, branching off. Some are store rooms, while others belong to particular families who have lived on Rum Isle for generations. There used to be a cavern where we kept our horses, but the roof collapsed and no one has yet shifted the rubble. The main cavern is a meeting place, an underground village square, where the cook fire is kept burning while anyone resides here."

"Ah, so that's why the fire is lit! Here I thought you must have some magical means of making a blaze so quickly, but the watchmen here must keep the fire burning instead." Grieve grinned at his own joke.

Rhona didn't seem to find it funny. Instead, she seemed lost for words.

"Are you going to introduce me to the watchmen of Sanctuary? Which spire first, east or west?" he prompted.

"There is no one here but us. The watchmen of the cliff towers retreat to Sanctuary when their families are here, but in summer it is empty but for the harvest, stored for when we need it in winter." She blinked, then seemed to regain a little of her earlier enthusiasm. "Would you like to see my family's cavern? It's called the Lady's Chamber, because it's usually the Lady of Rum Isle who leads her people here, while the lord and his men defend the island long enough for their families to reach safety."

She led the way along the stream, then crossed a set of stepping stones to the far bank. Behind a rock pillar was a third set of steps Grieve hadn't seen before, and light glimmered at the top.

"Do the men of the isles make it to Sanctuary, or is it a fight to the death?" Grieve asked. Not that any Islander would run from a fight — they were not cowards. But Alba had many more men than the Islanders could muster, and anything Grieve could do to make sure the Islanders lived to fight another day, he must.

"Sometimes," Rhona said. "The cliffs are a natural defence, and every man on Rum Isle must keep a bow with a number of arrows. They are supposed to practice archery every day, too, but I fear they have been lax of late. It has been a long time since Albans last raided our shores. Most of the heroic tales of this place are about the courage of ladies, not men, though. And some include commanding the army of archers, when our men are away."

She reached the top of the steps, and edged to the side so that Grieve might enter the cavern beside her.

Light streaked down from a hole in the

roof, sparkling through the waterfall that splashed down into a pool which overflowed into a second cascade that undoubtedly fed the stream below.

Grieve laughed. "Are you sure it's not called the Lady's Chamber because it has a bath in it?"

Rhona smiled. "It's not a bath I'd enter by choice. The water is icy cold, so it's better to take a bucket of it and set it by the fire to warm before you wash." She cupped some in her hands and drank. "Freezing, but as pure as anything you'll find on Rum Isle. Taste it yourself."

Grieve knelt beside the pool and cupped his hands.

Rhona made a sound between a squeak and a scream.

Grieve jumped to his feet, his hand flying to the hilt of his sword.

But there was no enemy to fight, or at least none that would take damage from a sword.

Rhona stood in the middle of a puddle of water that must have come from the roof, which had soaked her to the skin on its way down. "Can you get me some dry clothes, please?" she asked.

"Of course." Grieve hurried down to the main cavern, grabbed her saddle bags and raced back up the steps.

When he reached the chamber, the bags dropped from his hands and he lost the ability to speak.

Twenty-Six

The moment Grieve left, Rhona stripped off her wet clothes and used the dry parts to mop the water from her skin. After the long day's ride, she needed a wash, though this wasn't how she'd imagined it.

What was taking Grieve so long? Could he not find her bags? Rhona scanned the cavern, looking for the chests her family kept here. The clothes and blankets would certainly be in need of an airing, but a musty tunic was better than nothing.

Ah, there they were – stacked by the

sleeping alcoves. She pried open the catch on the topmost one and lifted out blanket after blanket, looking for the clothing she knew had to be here somewhere. It wasn't until she reached the bottom of the chest that she encountered what felt like a sleeping fur, but when she pulled it out, it turned out to be a winter cloak made of sealskin. She rubbed the velvety fur against her cheek, remembering when this cloak had belonged to her grandmother and she used to bury her face in it.

Something fell to the floor behind her.

Rhona swung the cloak around her shoulders, holding it closed with one hand as she whirled to face the intruder.

"By all that's holy…" She marched up to Grieve. "You're making a habit of catching me with my clothes off. A vainer lady than I might think you like what you see so much, you wish to see it again."

"I do." The words had no sooner left his lips than he turned as pale as mist. "I mean – "

Rhona held her cloak open. "There, then. Look your fill, and may your eyes burn out of

your head after the devil is done with you, for
— "

"My God, you're beautiful."

Now Rhona was the one lost for words. Grieve stepped forward and kissed her, drawing her body against his warmth, and cocooning the rest of her in the cloak. This man could kiss her forever, if he wished, but Rhona became increasingly aware of something hard pressed against her hip. She glanced down, and forced herself to break that irresistible kiss.

"Stop poking me with your sword," she said.

Grieve turned red as he glanced down, too. "I'm sorry, my lady, but like I said, you're beautiful…"

"No, not that sword. Take it off!" Before she could think the idea through, she unbuckled his belt and let it drop to the floor, sword and all. "Better. Now, kiss me again."

"I think it would be best if I obeyed your earlier order, my lady. The one where you asked me to get your clothes. Because if I kiss you again, while you are like this…" Grieve gestured at her body, the longing clear in his eyes as he looked at her. "I fear I will forget all thoughts of chivalry and honour, as though the devil himself sat on my shoulder, whispering in my ear. I will already pay a painful penance for the thoughts in my head right now."

But Rhona's blood was afire, and so was his. She was certain of it. "It is me you owe penance to, staring at my body so. It seems only right that I should get to do the same." She reached for the hem of his tunic, and tugged it up over his head.

"Lady Rhona, I think if I were naked, too, it would only make things all the harder."

Her breathing came fast now. "Then you should take off your hose, so we can do something about that."

Despite his half-hearted protests, Grieve soon stood naked before her, wearing nothing but his cloak. Now it was Rhona's turn to look her fill, at the lean, muscled man before her. Yes, oh yes. He was everything she could want in a man. In a lover.

She threw herself at him, twining her arms around his neck as she kissed him deeply. As her breasts met his hard chest, her body seemed to flame to life, just as she knew it should. She reached around to cup his butt cheeks, which were every bit as firm as they'd looked. But that only pressed other parts of him harder, more insistently into her belly, demanding more.

More that she wanted to give.

Rhona drew him down to the pile of blankets, letting out a contented sigh as his weight settled atop her. Then his lips descended to her breasts, kissing, sucking, setting off currents deep inside.

"Yes, oh yes…" She scarcely recognised her own voice, so breathless with need.

She wrapped her legs around his hips, wanting to feel him everywhere. She reached down to stroke him, guiding him to where she wanted him.

She cried out as she felt something hot slide inside of her, but it was too small to be what she wanted. His fingers, she realised. "I want you, Grieve. All of you."

"I'm your first. I can feel it. I don't want to hurt you."

Yet his fingers stroked her, driving her mad

with desire for what she really wanted. Taunting, tempting, tantalising...tipping her over a cliff she'd never seen, into bliss. For the first time in her life, she soared in a man's hands. This was better than her dreams.

"Grieve, I need you. Please." It came out as a joyful sob in a voice Rhona still didn't recognise as her own.

His eyes darkened with desire as he lifted his head to meet her eyes. "Rhona, are you sure?"

She'd never been so sure of anything in her life. "Make love to me, Grieve."

He grasped her hips, the hard heat of him replacing where his fingers had stroked her only moments before. He thrust what felt like a burning brand inside her, searing her insides until he filled her completely. And it felt so good.

Breathlessly, she urged him on, moaning as the molten heat that was him moved inside her. Again and again and again. Until she could no longer control the bliss she felt, and screamed his name.

Dimly, she heard her own name on his lips, before he leaned forward to kiss her.

She looked up, lost in his eyes, as she clenched around the part of him still inside her. This was what she wanted. "Marry me, Grieve," she said.

He stared at her, then began to laugh. As he sat up, he withdrew from her, leaving her emptier than she'd ever felt before. He headed for the pool to clean himself up. Only when he was done splashing, did he stop laughing.

Rhona wrapped herself in her cloak, wanting to relive the memory of his touch, branding it into her skin for every moment they were apart. "What's funny?" she asked.

"I thought a lady expected a marriage proposal before she shared her bed, not after," he said.

Rhona shrugged. "I can't imagine why any woman would agree to marry a man before knowing what sort of lover he was. When I agree to share my bed with one man for the rest of my life, it will not be a stranger who I have not touched."

He brought a dripping cloth to where she lay, and held it out. "I fear I am a messy lover. I scarcely know what possessed me, just that I wanted to possess you. I hope I did not hurt you. There is a little blood..." He pressed the cloth to her thigh, and steam rose up into the air. The cold water was chilly against her burning skin, but Rhona relished it, even more as Grieve stroked her thighs with the wet cloth in an intimate caress that promised she would know no better lover than him.

She covered his hand with hers. "You didn't hurt me. That was...wonderful. I want you to share my bed again tonight."

He swallowed. "For warmth, like last night? For I give you fair warning, my lady. I will do my best to honour you as you deserve while I am awake, but I fear my dreams. After knowing the joy of your beautiful body, I know my dreams will be filled with you. And if my hands stray onto your body as I sleep, it is because I long to make love to you all over again."

Again? Twice in one night? Never had she heard of a man visiting his wife's bed more than once in a night. The thought was thrilling...tantalising...too much for her to resist.

"Then I insist we sleep naked. I long to feel you inside me again."

"As my lady commands."

Twenty-Seven

Three times he'd made love to her, each time more delightful than the last. If he'd had the stamina, Grieve would have loved her all night, until the dawn light kissed her cheeks, for he'd never met a girl so eager, or so angelic when she cried out his name for the joy he'd brought her.

But would it be enough? Doubt gnawed at him, after what she'd said last night. That she wouldn't marry a man unless he was the sort of lover she wanted in her bed for the rest of her life.

He slipped out of the bed they'd made of the blankets on the floor, and headed for the pool to wash himself once more. He dressed, then headed to the cavern to see to breakfast. Perhaps he could bring it to her, so that she might break her fast in bed.

He found the bread he'd squashed last night, along with some hard cheese. If she still slept, then he could offer her a hot breakfast. Grieve set about coaxing the fire into life from the embers. When he had a decent blaze going, he set about melting the cheese and toasting the bread.

"Grieve?"

He'd taken so long, Rhona was not only awake, but dressed for the day, her fingers working to braid her hair so quickly it seemed to require no thought on her part at all.

"I'm making breakfast." He waved at the toast, which had started to burn. Hastily, he pulled the bread out of the fire and blew the flames out. "I was going to bring it to you."

"It was cold without you." Her eyes said so much more.

Grieve's mouth grew drier than the toast in

his hands. He set the cheese on it and held it out. "Careful, it's hot."

She took the offering with both hands, smiling. "I like things hot." She lifted her lips for a kiss.

Grieve wiped the worst of the crumbs off his hands, then carefully cupped her face. So beautiful, and that fire in her eyes... He touched his lips to hers, and for that moment, they shared the passion of their night together. He wanted to unlace her gown and do it all over again, but he wasn't sure how long it would take to return to her father's house. Where Grieve fully intended to ask Lord Ronin for her hand, and every other bit connected to it, too.

"You must be a witch, for you have cast a spell over me," he said.

Rhona stiffened in his arms. "I have done no such thing." She pulled away, putting several yards between them before sitting down to break her fast.

Curse his clumsy tongue. Grieve concentrated on making his own breakfast, while he tried to work out what to say to make things right.

Finally, he settled for: "Lady Rhona, if anything I have done has offended you, then I am deeply sorry. I only meant that I am so in love I cannot think straight any more, for all my thoughts are of you. If you are willing..." He turned, hoping to meet her eyes before he dropped to his knees, as custom demanded.

But Rhona was gone. She hadn't heard a word.

Grieve swore, then bit into his bread and cheese, burned his tongue, and swore some more.

He fell silent when the scrape of booted feet at the entrance alerted him that he was not alone any more.

"Rhona?" he asked tentatively, hoping she had returned.

Instead, a child emerged from the passage, followed by another, then an older woman holding the hand of a third. "Good thing you have the fire going, young man, for we'll need it. The Albans picked a cold, clear day to attack, thinking we'd be huddled around our fires and not watching for them. More fool them, I say."

"Albans? Where?" Rhona appeared on the stepping stones, concern wrinkling her forehead. "Candace, where is my father?"

The woman looked grim. "He set off yesterday for Isla. Something about a declaration of war from Alba. This is the start of it, I'm sure."

Rhona nodded, watching more people enter the cave – some of them the women Grieve had met in her father's kitchens. The whole household was here.

"Where is Lady Doireann?" Candace asked.

The cook shook her head. "She threw a mighty fit, saying she would not leave a scrap for the Albans to steal. We left her trying to put more things in a cart than it could carry. When one of the men told her so, she ordered him away, saying she would drive the cart here herself."

Rhona swore, using words Grieve had rarely heard from a lady. "Then she's even more of a fool than I thought, for she does not even know the way. I'll go fetch her."

The cook seized her arm. "Lady Rhona,

don't. If the Albans capture you, your father will never forgive us."

"He will also not forgive us if we leave Doireann to die, or worse," Rhona said grimly. "Stay here. I shall go alone."

Grieve jumped to his feet. "No you shall not! I should be the one to go."

Rhona glared at him, then subsided. "Fine. You may come with me." She trotted up the steps and returned with her cloak around her shoulders, and a bundle of cloth that she shoved into Grieve's arms. "Put this on. You'll need it."

The sweet girl who'd shared his bed was gone. In her place stood a cold-hearted warrior, like the Vikens she resembled. Grieve had never been frightened of a woman before, but right now, Rhona was terrifying.

He buckled on his sword belt, but decided to wait until they got outside to don his cloak. He wished he'd brought armour with him, but what he had was back at Lord Ronin's house, along with his other weapons. The sooner they got there, the better.

Twenty-Eight

Rhona only glanced behind her once to make sure Grieve was following her before she set off at a gallop for home. She'd be there by noon – she only hoped it would be soon enough to get Doireann to safety. Doireann had lost everything to raiders once – it would be needlessly cruel to allow it to happen again. Rhona might not like the woman, but she couldn't bring herself to hate her that much.

Her thoughts were occupied with a far more important question: was she willing to reveal her magic to save Doireann, if that's what it took? For to do so would be to reveal that she wasn't Father's legitimate daughter, but the result of a union between him and a witch. As her father's bastard, she had no claim over Rum Isle, and neither Grieve or his father would want such a union. If she had to use magic to save Doireann, then she would lose Grieve.

But if she let the Albans harm Doireann, then her father would probably disown her, no matter who her husband was. And she couldn't live with herself, knowing she'd sacrificed another woman for her own happiness.

But if her father found out she was a bastard, he'd probably disown her anyway, so no matter what she did, Rhona would lose her home here.

Tears blurred her vision, but Rhona wiped them away. This was not a time for self-pity. She had to do what was right, and damn the consequences. She might not like Doireann, but the woman was still family, albeit by marriage, and no one hurt her family. Least of all a bunch of Alban scum.

She wove through the woods, trusting

Grieve to keep up, as they neared her home. As they reached the last of the trees, Rhona dismounted, and tied her horse where it would be out of view of the house. She gestured for Grieve to do the same.

"We'll be too high if we climb the ridge on horseback. On foot, we can creep up on the house unseen. If the raiders have already arrived and we are too late…I do not want to give them any warning of our arrival," she said.

"My weapons are in the house. If I can get them, I will be more use to you than I am now with just a sword," Grieve whispered.

Rhona nodded, not wanting to voice her thoughts. If the Albans had not yet arrived, Grieve would have no need of his weapons, and all that would matter was the speed with which they got Doireann away. If the Albans had arrived before them…then Grieve's weapons were as good as lost, and nothing would save Doireann but a powerful show of magic. And that would cost her everything she held dear.

They crept up the slope, keeping low until they reached the shelter of the stones at the top. As a child, she'd traced the carvings on them and wondered what they meant, but now all her attention was on the beach at the base of the cliffs.

Her heart sank. The Alban boats had already beached themselves on the sand, and aside from a pair of boys they'd left on guard, the men were nowhere to be seen.

They might have gone inland, attacking farms and crofts. But the biggest house closest to the beach was her father's, on the cliffs overlooking the beach. They'd be fools not to go there first.

"They might already be at the house," she told Grieve. "Best we use the cover by the river to get closer."

He nodded, and followed her down the hill to the river. Grieve was quieter on his feet than she thought he'd be – she had to glance behind her more than once to make sure he was still there, but he was, as intent as she was on making this rescue work.

If only they weren't too late.

If Doireann was dead…

Then none of the Albans would leave here

alive, Rhona swore.

They'd raped Aunt Blanid, sentenced her mother Brigid to a lifetime taking care of her sister with no chance of marriage, and destroyed Doireann's home and family. She'd be damned before she allowed them to take any more from her family.

Grieve reached the willow trees first, crouching behind a trunk that still bore the marks from his axe. "We're too late," he whispered.

No. They couldn't be. Rhona dropped to her knees and peered through the forked trunk of what had been the first willow on Rum Isle.

In the yard that had always been the heart of her father's household stood perhaps a dozen Albans, clearly recognisable in their piss-yellow tunics. They'd be pissing themselves in fear by the time she was done with them. Rhona rose, careful to keep hidden behind the seaward tree trunk. She bit her lip until she tasted blood, taking her time choosing her target.

"Bring her to me!"

The shouted command had their attention, and Rhona's, too.

Doireann appeared, marched between two men who each had a hold of one of her arms.

Rhona changed her mind about the spell, swapping fire for air, as she sent a breeze through the yard that carried Doireann's words to her.

"Please don't hurt me. I did as I was bid!" she insisted. "All the riches of Rum Isle. I know where they are!"

Maybe a fire spell was called for, after all. A fire spell that turned that treacherous bitch into a ball of flame.

"Where?" A man with fancy armour over his yellow tunic stepped up to her.

"A cave in the woods. They're all there. I can show you…if you promise to let me go." Doireann fell to her knees. "Please, sir. You spared me on Scitis so that I could come here to find out what you wish to know."

The man laughed. "You would betray your new husband so easily?"

Doireann spat on the ground. "Lord Ronin is no husband to me, if he's even a man at all. He would not share my bed, not even on our wedding night. There's no marriage between us, and no love either. He forces me to run after his unruly brats like a servant, but won't give me a child of my own. You can have his island, and all that's on it. All I ask is that you let me go so that I might find a real man to be my husband."

"After you have shown us this cave, woman. Then we shall see."

"Let me…let me get the cart, so it will be easier to bring everything back." Doireann clambered to her feet, then took a tentative step toward the pony cart.

Rhona bit her lip, readying a fireball. The moment Doireann climbed atop that cart, Rhona would set it ablaze.

"Ooh, look, a Viken spy," a voice said behind Rhona. Then something crashed into the back of her head and darkness descended.

Twenty-Nine

Grieve had only a moment to reach for his sword, but he was too slow. One blow felled Rhona, and the second sent him half-stunned to the ground. He tried to fight, but his attacker shouted to his comrades, and soon there were a dozen Albans upon him.

"Tie them up. We always need more slaves," the Alban leader ordered, and Grieve soon found his hands bound to his feet. Another man tied Rhona's hands behind her back, then threw her over his shoulder and carried her off.

"Hey. Hey! You can't take her away. That's Lord Ronin's daughter!" he shouted.

The leather-clad leader strode up to him, leaning down so that he might look Grieve in the eye. "She looks too old to be one of his brats to me. Bring the other one."

Doireann was dragged over and thrown to the ground in front of Grieve.

"Who are these two?" the man demanded.

Doireann glared at Grieve. "The boy is the son of Lord Lewis of Myroy. She's Lord Ronin's eldest, and the most unruly of the lot. Good for ransom and not much else."

Grieve met the woman's eye. "At least I still have some honour. I'm not selling out the only people who would take me in to the enemy who killed my family!"

Doireann's eyes burned. "You're a man. You'd never understand." She jerked her head at Rhona. "She will. You'll see. Once all the Albans have had her, stolen her maidenhead and her virtue, she'll agree to anything to make them stop."

"Enough. A lord's maiden daughter is worth more intact. Nobody touches the girl. Not yet." The leader pointed at Doireann. "Get her up, and follow her to this cave. If she cannot show you, kill her."

Two men seized Doireann, ignoring her screaming protests, and took her away.

The leader turned to Grieve and the man still carrying Rhona. "These two…should be held somewhere they cannot escape from. One of the deserted isles we saw on the way. We can return for them later."

"Don't you hurt her!" Grieve shouted.

"And shut that one up," the leader said wearily.

A boot came out of nowhere, colliding with Grieve's head, and blackness embraced him.

Thirty

Rhona's head hadn't hurt this much since she drank a whole jug of wine at Sive's christening. Only she couldn't remember drinking anything this time. Instead, her mouth tasted of blood. She rolled over, and encountered another warm body, but this one didn't move.

She'd fallen asleep with Grieve after making love, and everything afterwards was a bad dream, she told herself, but even she couldn't believe the lie.

"Grieve, where are we?" she asked.

He did not respond, and only then did she

dare to open her eyes. A swollen lump adorned his forehead, crusted with dark blood. But his breathing was even, and his heartbeat felt strong under her hands. Alive, but unconscious. What she wouldn't give for some willow bark now.

Rhona sat up, wincing as her head gave a warning throb. She ignored it. Better to take stock of her surroundings. The light was dim, but still enough to see. They were in a cave, but not of the same stone as Sanctuary. Rhona knew every habitable cave on Rum Isle, and this wasn't one of them. The entrance to this cavern was blocked by a latticework of thin branches, with holes too small for her to fit more than her hand through, yet large enough to see to the larger cavern beyond.

It might not be Sanctuary, but someone called this place home. A pallet in the corner for a bed, and a fire burning peat that smelled like home. A pot bubbled over the fire, but Rhona could not smell what it contained over the smoke from the fire itself.

Her gaze swept the chamber, landing on the light source. It was no candle or lamp, but something else entirely. A swirling blue mist, trapped in what appeared to be a giant platter set against the wall. The thing glowed faintly, and Rhona fancied she saw her own face in the mist before it vanished. Whatever it was, it was magical, which meant that whoever lived here was a powerful witch.

But Rhona was the only witch in the Southern Isles. If there had been another, surely she'd have heard of her. For magic called to magic, and she would know if someone cast a spell near her. For a witch to hide herself and a powerful magical object like this one, she must be a formidable witch indeed. One Rhona did not dare to challenge by magical means.

"Please let us out. I must go home," Rhona said, drawing herself up to her full height.

"We all want to go home, but not everyone gets what they want. The sea wanted to take you from the beach where I found you, but I rescued you from the waves and brought you here. I must keep you two together. The mirror insists." The woman who stepped into view was nothing like Rhona expected. Young and dark-haired, her eyes seemed to contain the night sky.

Rhona shivered. She buried her magic deep inside, where she hoped the woman would never find it.

"Who are you?" the woman asked.

Lost in the woods and taken prisoner by a witch. It was so like one of the tales she and Grieve had swapped that Rhona answered automatically: "I am Gretel, and that's my brother, Hansel. If you don't let us go, our father, Lord Lewis, will not be pleased. Who are you?"

"Once a queen, now a slave, loved by two men, one of whom is now dead and the other is dead to me. I am Briska, now queen of a rock that boasts little more than fearless deer and this horrible stuff called snow."

She sounded mad, though she did not look it. Maybe the magic had made her so.

"You must let us go," Rhona insisted.

"I must do nothing of the sort. The mirror says...the mirror says you must be together. But if you are brother and sister, as you say...then I am cursed!" Briska's eyes glowed blue, the same as the misty platter on the wall. "Bah, I should have known escape was an illusion. You shall not leave here until you break the curse!"

She stormed out, and no amount of calling brought her back.

Rhona slumped to the floor beside Grieve, wishing he would wake up.

Thirty-One

The first thing Grieve became aware of was something cold and wet touching his forehead. Not cold enough to numb the pain, though.

He reached for his sword, but the scabbard was empty. They must have stolen it from him, along with everything else. And Rhona.

Grieve sat up, and saw the most beautiful sight he could have imagined. Rhona's startled face as the wet cloth dangled from her hand, forgotten.

"Are you all right? Did the Albans…did they hurt you?" he asked. He prayed that the leader's promise could be trusted. Who knew with Albans?

"Someone hit me over the back of the head. But nothing else," she said. "You have a bump on your head, too – much worse than mine. Do you know where we are?"

Grieve looked around. "A cave? They didn't say where they were taking us. Somewhere we could not escape from, waiting for a ransom from my father and yours."

Rhona dropped her voice to a whisper. "I told her our father is one and the same, and that we are brother and sister. Hansel and Gretel. They were the first names I could think of. She's a witch, and names are powerful in spells. If she does not know ours, perhaps she will not be able to cast curses at us."

Grieve laughed, then winced as that made his head throb more. "Held captive by a witch, just like a story. Do you have any clever ideas for escape?"

Rhona shook her head. "She keeps saying things about a mirror, and how she is cursed, and we cannot leave until we break the curse. But I know nothing about curses. What about you?"

"I'm no witch, and nor are you. I can shoot a bow, build a house, and lift a sword to defend what is mine. If she's living in a place like this, perhaps I could make a bargain with her. It's worth a try."

He began shouting for the witch.

Rhona tried to hush him, but Grieve only shouted louder.

"Silence, boy!" the dark-haired woman hissed, stalking into the cave like a cat hunting prey. "Or I shall cast a spell on your tongue that will render it unfit for speech, though it may do other things." She smiled, and her hands glowed blue.

Grieve swallowed back the swear words that leaped to his tongue. So the woman was a witch. He would have to be careful, was all, he told himself. "What will it take for you to let my sister and me go?"

This only seemed to anger her further. "Brother and sister. The mirror lies. It will take an abomination before I can release you, and for the mirror to release me from my curse and my exile here."

None of this made any sense to Grieve, but she evidently believed it. He only knew that curses were not his area of expertise. "How would you like to live somewhere better than this cave? If I can't break your curse, maybe I can make your exile more comfortable."

She sniffed. "I do not need a lover, least of all some boy who is supposed to…never mind. I will not do it!" This last was addressed to what appeared to be a mirror on the wall. An image of Grieve and Rhona's faces appeared on it for a moment, before all it showed was the witch's reflection.

A magic mirror. Just like something in a story. And just like in a story, he must somehow trick the witch into letting them go free.

"The men of Myroy have a reputation for our skill with wood. I can build you a beautiful house where you can live. Walls where you can hang your mirror. A bed to sleep on, instead of a pallet on the floor." Grieve had her attention. Now he needed to sweeten the deal. "Much warmer than this cold cave, I promise. Just ask my sister about the other places I have built."

"Oh, he's quite good with wood," Rhona said. "You should have seen the first barn he built by himself when he was just a boy."

Grieve winced. That first barn had been a disaster. But if the witch did not know that...

"What sort of house?" the witch demanded.

Grieve spread his hands wide. "Whatever you like. Point me at the wood, and I shall build you a palace fit for a queen."

Her eyes narrowed. He had her, Grieve was certain.

"A wooden palace. If that is the best I can hope for now...then I accept. You shall build me a palace, and when I am satisfied, you shall go free." The witch nodded, then pointed at Rhona. "But she stays. I will not have...abomination...here."

"No." Grieve folded his arms across his chest. "When the palace is complete, both of us go free."

She eyed him thoughtfully for a long time. "Very well. I shall set you both free, if you give me your solemn vow that you shall never kiss your sister, nor share her bed."

Grieve wanted to laugh, but he did not dare.

"I swear by all I hold dear, by my sister's own life, that I will never kiss my sister, and I will never share her bed." An empty promise, for the only sisters he had died in infancy, and he would not share their grave, nor kiss a corpse if he could help it.

"Good. Then you may start work." The witch unlocked the door, opening it just wide enough for one person to slip through. "But she stays until your work is done."

Grieve squeezed through the gap, then heard it close behind him. "If any harm comes to her, the deal is off."

The witch inclined her head. "Agreed."

"Grieve, I don't trust her," Rhona said behind him.

Grieve didn't trust her, either, but he didn't dare say it. Instead, he ignored Rhona and followed the witch outside to plan out her new palace.

Thirty-Two

Rhona spat out a mouthful of the strange food that burned her mouth. "You are trying to poison me!"

The witch looked affronted. "I feed you the same as I eat. It is not my fault your delicate stomach will not tolerate it." As if to demonstrate, she snatched Rhona's bowl and began to spoon the contents into her own mouth with evident signs of approval. "It is perfectly good venison. I don't know what you are talking about."

Between the burning food, strange flat

sheets of what the witch called bread and the gritty white liquid that the woman called milk but didn't taste like it had come from any kind of cow Rhona had ever met, Rhona wasn't sure how long she would last as the witch's captive. Forcing down every bite of food and then forcing it to stay down was a daily struggle, exacerbated by her need to hide her magic deep inside, too, lest the witch sense it.

Yet the more Rhona saw of this witch, the more she thought the woman was mad. She spent hours talking to the misty platter that looked nothing like the bronze mirrors on the islands, yet the witch insisted on calling a mirror.

More than once, Rhona had seen her own face in the mist, and Grieve's, too. She fancied she'd seen the mirror show that blissful night she and Grieve had spent together in Sanctuary, once or twice, but the witch shouted at it that such things were an abomination before storming out. Without the witch present, all the mist did was swirl, without showing pictures.

Rhona barely saw Grieve, who wasn't even

allowed to sleep in the same cavern as her any more. Only when the witch was fast asleep did Grieve dare to approach the door to Rhona's prison. His hands were too big to fit through the bars, so she had to shove her fingers through to feel his touch again.

"Kill her in her sleep, and let's leave together," Rhona begged on the first night.

But Grieve had shaken his head. "I gave my word, and I will not break it. If she dishonours our deal, then I will have no mercy, but for now, stay here where you will be safe. There is no way off this island — there are no boats at all. Unless I can build one or persuade one to land here, the witch is our best chance of finding a way home. I'm working as fast as I can, but I cannot build a house in a day, so you must have patience. I swear to you, I will get you home."

The witch had awoken then, putting an end to any further conversation. "Get away from her!" she'd shouted, swatting at Grieve with a broom.

So Rhona fought her frustration, finding reserves of patience she didn't know she had.

Most of her days, she spent sitting in the corner of her cell, wondering what her sisters were doing at home. Whether her father had arrived home yet. And what had happened to Doireann.

Finally, one night Grieve came in so exhausted, he flopped right down on his pallet and didn't seem to want to get up again. "Tomorrow, I shall finish my work, and you can move your things from here to your new home," he told the witch. Lifting his head so that he might meet Rhona's eyes, he added, "And then tomorrow, we shall go free."

"Yes. Good," the witch said, intent on stirring the pot over the fire. It undoubtedly contained something intended to burn through the roof of Rhona's mouth. What she wouldn't give for some normal bread, or a piece of roast pork, but the only animals the witch had were deer, or at least that's all the meat she used.

The next morning, Rhona washed with the small bucket of water in her cell, and attempted to re-braid her hair. Today, she would be free.

The witch wandered in and out of the cave,

as usual, muttering to herself or the misty mirror. Rhona paid her little attention until the woman dropped the pot she'd been holding with a clang.

"It will not happen! Incest is against nature!" she shouted at the mirror.

Rhona peered through the bars of her prison. The mirror showed her and Grieve, locked in a lovers' embrace. The image brought a blush to her cheeks as she watched her own image arch her back and cry out in joy. What she wouldn't give to do that with Grieve again. When they were home, and wed, she promised herself.

"Better to kill them than let him defile her so. Now, before it is too late!" The witch seized a knife and raced out of the cave.

Rhona shouted for the witch to come back, but the woman never heard.

She was headed out to kill Grieve.

She would have to get through Rhona first.

Rhona threw her weight against the bars, trying to pry them apart wide enough to let her through. To no avail — the latticework was too firmly fixed to come apart in her hands.

But it was wood, and wood burned.

Would it matter if the witch knew about Rhona's magic? By day's end, one of them would be dead. As long as the witch didn't get to Grieve before Rhona could warn him.

Her hands were already bleeding from her fruitless attack on the door, so the spell was barely a thought away. She pressed her bloodied hands to the wood, leaving two handprints as she backed away.

Rhona pressed her back against the wall, as far from the door as she could get, and commanded the wood to burn.

The handprints ignited, leaving blackened holes in the lattice, as flames licked hungrily at the edges. Within moments, the whole door was ablaze, and it only took a few minutes before the whole thing was reduced to ashes.

Rhona hitched up her skirts above the embers, and marched through the still-smoking remains of her prison.

"I'm coming for you, bitch," she said.

And if the witch had hurt Grieve, her death was going to be slow and painful.

Thirty-Three

Grieve heard the approaching footsteps, but he didn't look up until he'd finished hammering the shingle into place.

"Almost done!" he called. "Three more to go, and then I'll climb down to show you around!"

He'd be done already if one of the shingles hadn't split overnight, bringing down part of the roof. But that was the thing about wood. It might look perfect at first, and fit just fine with all the rest, but weeks or months or sometimes even years later, the fault deep inside would start to show, and it would crack, to the detriment of all around it. Much like people, really.

He shot a furtive glance at the witch. She was barely more than a girl herself, of an age with Rhona and Bedelia, which meant he had to tread carefully lest his clumsy tongue land him in trouble again. His care seemed to have paid off, for the witch appeared pleased with his progress on her house. Well, she had, until now. The frown on her face sent out silent alarm bells, warning him to rethink his every word before he spoke.

He hammered the last shingle into place. "Would you like to see inside your new palace, mistress?" he called from his perch on the roof. Out of reach, he thought, then wondered just how far she could cast a spell. If it was like an archer firing arrows, then he was well in range, and nowhere he stood would be safe.

Grieve climbed down the ladder and rounded the cottage. She stood in the same spot, her frown even deeper.

Grieve strode past her and opened the door. He bowed extravagantly. "Your new palace,

Your Majesty."

She almost smiled, lifting her head regally as she stepped forward.

"Get away from her! She means to kill you!"

Rhona raced into view, shouting at him and the witch.

"What?" Grieve stared at the witch, as she stared at him. He took a step back, just in case.

Rhona slowed to a halt, panting. "She said she was going to kill you." Her eyes widened in panic. "Oh, no, you don't!"

A gust of wind blew Grieve almost off his feet, it was so powerful. The same gale had pinned the witch against the door, though she struggled against it. In her hand was a curved knife with a green stone blade, like nothing Grieve had ever seen before.

The witch's hands glowed blue.

"Don't you dare touch him, you bitch!" For a moment, it looked like Rhona held a handful of flames, before she drew her hand back and threw the missile. Whatever it was, it splashed at the witch's feet, engulfing her boots in roaring flame.

She screamed and ran inside the house,

slamming the door behind her.

Rhona followed, raising her arms.

"Move, Grieve," she said. She waved her hand in his direction, and this time it seemed the very air lifted him up and deposited him at her feet. "Now, burn, bitch," she said, gritting her teeth. She turned her hands palm up, lifting them as though raising an imaginary host to heaven. But what she raised was more hellish than divine, as the house he'd painstakingly built went up in a whoosh of flame.

"Rhona!" He couldn't seem to say anything else. Couldn't think. Rhona, a witch? How?

A burst of blue light erupted from the house as the roof collapsed, so blinding they both had to turn away. It took a moment for Grieve to regain his sight, and when he did, half the house was gone, collapsed in on itself and the witch's body, no doubt, for the woman's screaming had stopped.

Rhona's breast heaved. She bent down to pick up the knife, which had magically landed at her feet.

Grieve's blood ran cold. Magically, indeed. She'd just killed a woman. What else could

Rhona do?

Perhaps the witch wasn't the one he had to fear after all.

He rose onto unsteady feet. If he'd been frightened of her before…she terrified him now. A woman who could command fire didn't need him to protect her. She didn't need anyone's protection – she was a force of nature all by herself.

Rhona threw her arms around his neck and kissed him. It took him a stunned moment before he could force his mouth open to return her kiss.

It wasn't enough. She sensed that something was wrong, and pulled away.

Tears glimmered in her eyes. "I'm sorry. I couldn't let her kill you."

Grieve didn't know what to say. It didn't seem right to accept her apology, not when she was sorry for saving his life, but thanking her didn't seem right, either. Instead, he said, "How will we get home now?"

She turned and surveyed the water. "We'll need a boat." She closed her eyes and bit her lip.

Grieve felt a breeze spring up, nowhere near as powerful as the one that had carried him, but he knew it came from the same source. Rhona. A witch so powerful she commanded the elements.

Fire, air…would she part the sea so that they might walk home? Anything seemed possible.

Never in his life had he felt so small, so insignificant. Not even when Bedelia rejected him.

He was nothing next to Rhona. No one. For she deserved some great hero, a man of power and wealth and courage, while what was he? Some lord's younger son, who owned little more than his clothes and weapons, which he was competent with, but no more than that. He worked wood, but she could turn a week's work into ash with a wave of her hand.

Grieve fancied he heard voices.

"We should try in the lee of Nimbanmore. Good fishing there."

Fishermen? He glanced around, but saw no one but themselves.

"There's a curse on Nimbanmore, my

grandmother says. No one who goes there ever comes back."

This voice was softer, as though whispered on the wind.

"We're not going to land there, just fish offshore. Hey, what's that smoke? Seems there's someone on the island."

That's how she was doing it, Grieve realised. Stealing the sound of their words somehow.

"Where are they?" Grieve asked.

Rhona opened her eyes and pointed. "In the lee of this island. Nimbanmore, which explains why we are the only ones here. There is a curse here, an ancient one, laid on the lake at the top of the mountain. I can feel it faintly now, but it won't hurt us. Not if we can get off this island soon." She waved her hand. "They will have no choice but to come to us. The wind in every other direction will send them onto the rocks."

Grieve couldn't believe what he was hearing. "You're going to kill some innocent fishermen?"

She tilted her head to the side and smiled.

"They are hardly innocent. What man is? But no, I do not intend to kill them. If they cannot sail in this wind, they may wreck their boat, but they are Islanders and fisherman. The fishermen of Rum Isle survive gales far worse than this. They will come to the beach here, and take us home. You'll see."

It seemed to take forever before the boat landed on the beach, and the men aboard hailed them. Rhona explained who they were and how they needed a ride home, for which she would happily pay the men to make up for their lost catch.

This was Lady Rhona, Ronin's daughter, not the frightened girl she'd been for the last week in the witch's prison. How much of that had been real, and how much a pretence? Grieve truly didn't know the woman at his side at all. Witch, woman, wonder…but she could never be his wife. He wanted to worship her, not ask her what was for dinner.

Exactly as Rhona had foretold, Grieve found himself beside her on the fishing boat, headed home to Rum Isle. Standing beside the woman who held his heart, when he would never have hers.

Thirty-Four

Lord Ronin wept when he saw Rhona, and he couldn't seem to stop thanking Grieve for bringing her home. He either didn't hear or chose to ignore Grieve's protestations that he'd done nothing, and embraced him like a son.

Doireann was dead, murdered by the Albans, and Ronin had feared Rhona had suffered a similar fate.

"If not for you, I would have lost everything," Lord Ronin said with an enormous sniffle.

He still had his house, all the supplies in

Sanctuary, and three of his daughters unharmed because of their early retreat to the caves, Grieve thought but didn't say as the three girls lined up to hug Rhona and drop an awkward curtsey each in his direction, at their father's command.

Grieve wanted to turn and run right out of the house, then maybe take up an axe and vent his frustration on a dozen trees, but Rhona would not approve. So he stayed and tried his best to look the part of the hero, though he felt like the opposite.

"And I would like to say that Rum Isle will always be home to the man who saved my daughter. May you always be here to keep her safe, for I am sure Rhona will want to marry you as soon as possible, and I give my hearty blessing to you both!" Ronin said with a watery smile.

"Father…" The warning in her tone made Grieve want to run more than ever.

The one woman he wanted for his wife, who could never be his.

"There's my boy! They say you've saved one girl, and I could ask no less than a hero for the quest I have in mind." Father entered the hall, arms spread wide to embrace his son.

"Father, I need to speak to you," Grieve muttered as his father hugged him.

Lord Lewis clapped him on the back. "Let's leave them to their family reunion, so we can have one of our own." He led the way into the yard.

Grieve went further, walking all the way down to the river. He knew Rhona would hear him if she wished it, but perhaps her father might not.

"Father, I saved no one. Lady Rhona saved herself. She is…" Grieve lowered his voice to a whisper. "She is a witch. She has power over the elements of fire and air. I saw her reduce a house to ashes in minutes. Surely her father must know, for how could she keep that hidden from her own family? Yet he seems to believe I saved her, instead of the other way around!"

Father scratched his chin. "It always was a mystery that Lady Blanid fell pregnant so quickly after her wedding, for she was not one to take her husband to bed earlier than needs must. Especially after…well, Lord Ronin nearly lost her to Alban raiders, too. Her sister saved her, or so 'tis said. I always wondered how a slip of a girl could take on a whole party of raiders like that. If what you say is true, then your girl must be the sister's daughter. But still Ronin's, for he would not have acknowledged her if she were not."

"I don't care whose daughter she is!" Grieve exploded, struggling to keep his voice quiet. "She's a witch. A sorceress. A woman who can burn me where I stand with a wave of her hand. I cannot marry her!"

Father stared. "She seems a lovely enough girl. If you can but keep from provoking her, there is little to worry about on that account."

"I'm not worried for me! I'm worried for her! What do I have to give her? I'm not fit to lick the ash from her boots! I'm no hero – I'm no one. She deserves far more than anything I can give her." Grieve gazed at his father, begging him to understand. "You should have sent me to war first, not here, so I might be a war hero, at least. Someone with something to offer her."

"So you like the girl, but she thinks you're not good enough, hmm?"

Grieve shook his head. "I do not know what she thinks. I…she…when she kissed me, it seemed like she liked me…but I…"

"You will not be the first man who did not feel ready for marriage. Even I hesitated once…but the right lady will have her own way of making her heart known. Perhaps it is best to take you away from here for a while, until you are ready." Lord Lewis held Grieve's gaze, so he could not look away. "The Alban king has sent a letter that is tantamount to a declaration of war. He demands Lord Angus' eldest daughter and heir, Lady Portia, as bride to one of his sons."

Grieve spluttered. "We can't give her to Alba. Handing over Isla to them is tantamount to giving them all the Southern Isles."

Father grinned. "So you do understand a bit of strategy, after all. Yes. Giving them the girl is to give them everything. But there's more. The Council sent an envoy to the Viken king, asking for him to honour our alliance and send troops to fight the Albans when they come.

Lady Portia...will be the price of that alliance. A marriage bargain between her and the Viken prince, when he lands on our shores." He cleared his throat. "But she must be kept safe, never be without a bodyguard at all times. Lady Portia is no witch. She needs protection, and the Council agrees. That's why we all had to send a member of our family to form her bodyguard. I need Mahon on Myroy, so I must send you."

Leave Rhona? The very thought cleaved Grieve's heart in two. "Father..."

"Fools like Calum are sending suitors for her hand, seeing this as a chance to take Isla for their own. But any man who marries her is doomed to die, if he is not either the Alban prince or the Viken one. The alliance will be written in her maiden's blood, or her husband's lifeblood. I need one man among them who can lead them, forge them into the bodyguard the girl needs. Before she shoots the lot of them. She's a keen archer, I've heard." Once again, Father's eyes captured Grieve's. "You are the only man I trust. That is why I sent you here first. If your heart is here, then there is no way you will lose it to Lady Portia. And when you return, you will be a war hero – Lady Portia's valiant protector. Surely Lady Rhona cannot turn her nose up at that."

Grieve closed his eyes. "What sort of girl is Lady Portia?"

"She is her father's daughter, and her mother's, too. Passionate to a fault, but she knows her duty. Catriona married for love, but she also married the only man who could lead us. Angus says Portia will do the same. Your job is to make sure she gets a choice, though my money's on her picking the Viken prince."

"Very well, Father. I shall go to Isla. For how long?"

Father shrugged. "Until the war is over, and the girl marries her prince. War is a messy business. No one can be sure how long it will last."

Grieve bowed his head. "Then we must tell Lord Ronin, and Rhona."

Father grinned. "Want me to bring a bucket of water to put the fire out?"

Grieve wished he could laugh, but there was nothing funny about deserting Rhona now.

She might not need him, but that didn't change how much he cared about her. If war was coming to the isles, the Albans would return in even greater numbers, and she could be caught unawares again. But he'd been as good as useless, anyway. Better to go to Lady Portia, and be useless among a dozen other men, hoping they would be enough to protect the girl.

Grieve took a deep breath and marched up to the house. This would not go well.

Thirty-Five

"Rhona, wait!" Grieve called, but Rhona didn't.

She intended to set fire to something and watch it burn to ashes before she'd do anything for Grieve again. One moment he was ready to marry her, and the next he intended to head off to guard some girl on a faraway island? Who was this Lady Portia to him, anyway?

She wanted to run into the woods and hide where he'd never find her, but the sea was closer. Something on the beach would surely burn. But the tide was in, licking at the sand,

and the rock the seals liked to sun themselves on was now surrounded by dark water. Rhona didn't care. She summoned a gust of wind to carry her to that rock, where no one could reach her until she willed it.

"Rhona, come back! Please," Grieve said, as he slowed at the water's edge. "I have to do this."

"You have to protect Portia, do you? And why is she so special?" Rhona reached for the beach, for the tiny specks of dried seaweed and sawdust between the sand, and ignited them. The shore lit up like a grassfire.

Grieve jumped back onto a rock. "She's Lord Angus's daughter. His eldest. The heir to Isla."

The fire died for lack of fuel. Rhona cursed. "So? What's Isla to you? Why kiss me, make love to me if you intend to go off and marry this other woman so you can be lord of her island instead? Is Rum Isle not good enough for you? Or is it me? I am not good enough for you, now you know I am a witch and a bastard."

Grieve shook his head. "It is I who is not

good enough for Rum Isle, or you. You are…a powerful sorceress, who will one day be the lady of prosperous Rum Isle, able to protect this place without needing a husband. As for Angus' daughter…Lady Portia and the lordship of all the isles is as far beyond me as the very heavens above. The Albans want her as a wife to one of their princes, and I have no doubt the Vikens will offer for her as well."

"Women are not prizes to be carried away like the spoils of war," Rhona snapped.

Grieve sobered. "No, you are not. And nor is she, which is why I must go. Alba will not have her without a fight."

Rhona swallowed. "Is she more important to you than I am?"

"No," he admitted. "She is perhaps the most important woman in the isles right now, because with her claim to Isla comes a chance at kingship, or so the Council says. I should want to defend her with my life because if Alba gets her, then they will conquer us all, and no one will be safe. I would give anything to stay here and marry you like I promised. But war is coming, and I am honour bound to fight and defend what is ours, as is every man of the isles. And you…you are not mine. Not yet. I don't deserve you. You saved us both on that island, and you have no need of me as your defender. When war comes to Rum Isle, as it will to Isla, I know you will save your family without me. My place is where I am most needed, and my father says it is on Isla, guarding the last of the Three Little Pigs."

It was Rhona's turn to laugh. "You mean THAT Lady Portia of the little pigs tale? She cannot be much to look at, if she is likened to a pig. I imagine she is kept cloistered like some princess in a tower, waiting for her prince to come and claim her."

"Perhaps. I do not know, for I have never seen the girl. My father says that she has inherited her father's instinct for politics, and that she is fond of archery. Perhaps he is sending me to her to be her bowyer and archery instructor, more than her bodyguard. I will not be alone, either – all the lords are sending men to guard her. It will not be forever. Only until the war against the Albans is over, or the girl chooses a husband."

Rhona jumped off her rock, splashing through the shallows to shore. She was too tired to use magic, and too tired to argue any more. Grieve was right, though it pained her to admit it. "Fight with honour, and don't let the Albans touch her. And when your duty is done, come home to me. I will wait for you."

Grieve ventured onto the sand, crossing the distance between them without hesitation. "Truly, I do not deserve you. But I will do as you command, for I live in hope." He kissed her, the moment stretching as Rhona tasted longing, desire and duty in that kiss. Longing and desire wanted to continue, but it was duty that ended it. "Farewell, my lady. If it is our fate to meet again on these shores, then I will marry you."

Then he turned and was gone. Rhona waited until he was out of sight before she sank to her knees and let the tears flow. If fate didn't bring him back to her, she'd burn that bitch's bones to ash. Just like the witch. And every Alban who thought to stand between her and vengeance.

Thirty-Six

Rhona didn't return to the house until she knew they'd sailed away. Her eyes were probably red from crying, but no one would notice if she kept her head down. If her father asked, she could say they were tears of grief for Doireann.

She entered the Great Hall, expecting to find it empty.

Of course, it wasn't.

Lord Lewis lifted his cup to her. "My son tells me you are a witch, Lady Rhona. We haven't had one here on the isles in many years. We may need your help to drive off the Albans if it comes to war."

Father slammed his cup down. "No, man, you may send your sons to war, but leave my daughter be. Women protect their homes, with force if need be, but they do not go to war. We need her here at home."

"You're holding her here, just like you did to Brigid. I don't know what you did, but no matter how much she wanted to marry me, she stayed here with you! You had a wife. You didn't need her!" Lewis said, pouring himself another cup.

"Lady Brigid loved her sister, not me. Maybe not even you, either. I could not have kept her here against her will. The woman took on Alban raiders thrice, with not a survivor among them. If she were here, Doireann would not have died." Father peered into his cup.

"Doireann was a traitorous bitch who deserved to die. The Albans only spared her on Scitis because she promised to tell them the location of the riches of Rum Isle. They killed her here because she could not lead them to

Sanctuary." Rhona folded her arms across her chest. "I would have killed her, had they not knocked me unconscious before I could. I heard enough to damn her before they did. My mother would not have protected her."

Father peered blearily at her. "Did Blanid tell you? She was the only one who knew, except Brigid and me. I was too drunk on my wedding night to know the difference – drunk because I couldn't bear to see the bride I loved flinch every time I touched her, after what those bastards did to her. The second time, I knew she wasn't my wife, but, God forgive me, I lay with her anyway. She said she would do what her sister couldn't…to pretend…and I did. Blanid claimed you as hers, and I knew you were mine. Brigid wanted to give me a son, though, so we tried again…and again, but the babies did not live long enough, and then, nor did she. And Blanid…it took years before she would tolerate my touch, but she promised her sister she'd try…but we never had a son. When she died, I swore I'd never lie with another woman, and be grateful for the children I had. Doireann was a widow, I wanted her to be a nurse to my girls, but she refused to live under my roof unless we were married. So I took another vow, but she was never a wife to me. My daughters are enough."

"You mean you knew I was a bastard?" Rhona asked.

"You are my daughter, the heir to Rum Isle, until I say otherwise, and there are no bastards under this roof. I swore to Brigid on her deathbed, and I keep my oaths." Father rose. "I will hear no more of this matter. As the Lady of Rum Isle, you will protect it as your mother would."

Rhona slumped into a seat and poured herself a cup of wine. "Yes, Father."

Father nodded, took his leave of Lord Lewis, and left.

"Now how did he know you were thinking of running away to Isla, and Grieve?" Lord Lewis asked.

Rhona glared at him. "I most certainly was not!" she lied.

Lord Lewis sipped from his cup, then set it down. "My son tells me you are fond of stories. May I tell you one? One I do not think even my son knows, though he will, in time."

Rhona inclined her head. "Go on."

"Have you heard the story of the Three Little Pigs?" At Rhona's nod, he continued, "And do you remember who saves the little girls?"

"Their nurse," Rhona said slowly. "Like Candace saved my sisters."

"What if I told you it was the wolf?"

Rhona eyed him. "Then I would think you a fool, Lord Lewis, which my father tells me is not true. But if you have had as much to drink as my father, perhaps it is the wine talking."

Lewis laughed. "Wine does not talk, but it does make men talk. Too much, sometimes. Like the day Lord Angus told me about his little wolf, the prince we have all pinned our hopes on." His shrewd eyes peered at her over the rim of his cup. Lord Lewis was as sober as Rhona herself.

"What if I told you Lord Angus took a Viken fosterling, a young prince, his blood as royal as both the king's and the crown prince, as a favour to his father? And on the day of the feast meant to welcome the boy, Lord

Angus's own daughters went missing. Little Portia, the leader of the three, wanted to go swimming, she said, but her nurse said no. So when the nurse wasn't looking, she led the girls out of their father's house and down to a pool she'd heard the boys speak of… And when no one could find the girls, the young prince went searching. He found the girls in the mud, and raised the alarm so the nurse came running. Two girls came when the nurse called, but little Portia refused. He waded into the middle of that mud in his best clothes, heedless of the damage he did to them, and coaxed her out. A different man might have thrown the little girl over his shoulder and carried her out, but that boy offered her his hand and they walked out of the woods together, hand in hand."

"Why are you telling me this?" Rhona demanded.

Lewis smiled. "My son adores you, Lady Rhona, and I know he will return to Rum Isle for you. Much like I know the Viken Wolf Prince is in love with Lady Portia, and he will return to claim her. My son will do his duty, for he is honour-bound to uphold his oath. I knew your mother, and she would never desert her family, not for love or her own happiness. She would fight to the death to protect those she loved. Including you."

Rhona's eyes blazed. "Are you telling me to stay home, like a good little girl?"

To Lord Lewis' credit, he did not back down. "No, Lady Rhona. I am suggesting you do everything within your power to protect Rum Isle and its people, including yourself. For the only man who can end the war against Alba is that Viken prince, and until he arrives, you are the best Rum Isle has. Just as I am all Myroy has, and Grieve must keep Portia safe for the Viken. We all must endure until our allies arrive. But that doesn't mean we won't fight. On the contrary. We will be defending our homes, more fiercely than any Alban raider can imagine." Lord Lewis rose from his seat and bowed. "Lady Rhona, I would hope you burn every Alban you see, before he even reaches the shore of your lovely isle. I have no doubt you will make your mother proud." He headed off.

Rhona sipped from her cup, deep in

thought. She wasn't sure what to think, or to do. Too many revelations in too short a time. And yet…somehow, she thought it would all turn out all right in the end. How, she did not know, but all the best stories did, and hers…would be the best she could make it. Making her mother proud did have a lovely ring to it.

Thirty-Seven

When war came to Rum Isle, her people came to Sanctuary. So it was, and so it always would be. After the initial attack, though, the Albans had left no garrison on Rum Isle, so most of her people had returned to their homes. All except Lord Ronin's family, for their home had been burned along with the Albans and their boats. Rhona had learned her lesson – after the first attack, she'd burned the boats at sea. No Alban would set foot on her shore while she lived.

There had been whispers at first, until her

father insisted that his daughter had Lady Brigid's blood in her veins and the magic that ran with it, and she would defend the island alongside its men. After watching what she could do, the men heartily embraced this idea, and the whispers ceased.

So Sanctuary echoed with emptiness, until a boat was spotted approaching Rum Isle.

The watchmen reported this to Rhona, while the people of Rum Isle filled Sanctuary again.

"We have visitors," Rhona announced to her family. Her sisters huddled closer together, looking fearful. "Don't worry, I shall see them off shortly."

Father caught her arm. "Don't go out there alone. I shall come with you. Remember what happened to Doireann."

Rhona gently pulled out of his grasp. "Doireann got what she deserved, luring Albans to our home. As will our latest intruders. Don't worry, Father. They will tell no tales once I am finished with them."

But Father would not be dissuaded. He buckled on his sword and shouldered his crossbow. "Once we both are finished with them. I am not so old that I cannot defend Rum Isle."

Blowing out a frustrated breath, she waited for him to lead the way out of the cave and onto the ridge, where he took up his accustomed spot behind a boulder that was just the right height to rest his crossbow on.

Two figures beached a coracle, before one climbed the rocks above the beach and started shouting. Shouting her name.

Rhona swore. "It's Lord Lewis. With another man."

Her heart leaped. Was it finally time to stop hiding, and start fighting?

"I have a proposition for you!" Lord Lewis bellowed.

Rhona squinted at the second man. Only one man had a proposition she might want to hear, and Lord Lewis' companion did not look like Grieve.

"Stay here and defend the girls, Father. I will speak to him."

Bless the man, he looked like he wanted to argue. As though two men would be any match for Rhona and her magic.

She bit her lip. Sparks erupted from her fingers. "I will be fine, Father."

He nodded. "And I will keep them in my sights."

She let the wind carry away the sound of her footsteps, so that the men would not hear her approach. Lord Lewis's companion dressed like a man of Isla, with a coracle to match, but no Islander ever wore a sealskin so fine over Isla wool, except perhaps Lord Angus. Lord Angus was closer to her father's age than this man, who could not be older than thirty. And Lord Angus had no sons, least of all this giant.

Lord Lewis shouted his offer again.

"I'm already betrothed, and not to that beast of a man." Rhona stepped out of hiding.

She'd surprised the Viken, for that's what he must be. Was this the man Lewis had promised would come to their aid?

Lewis' impassive face told her nothing. Instead, he gestured for the Viken to speak.

He inclined his head with what appeared to be genuine courtesy. "I am no beast, lady." The rumble of his delightfully deep voice said otherwise, as he continued, "I am Rudolf Vargssen, Prince of Viken. I have come from my cousin, King Reidar, to cast the Albans out of the Southern Isles." His eyes flashed with something like battle-fire.

One man's fire would only go so far.

Rhona dismissed him with a flick of her fingers. "Just you and old Lewis here? You have no chance, Prince of Viken. Not without an army that can match the Albans."

A faint smile curved his lips. The Viken liked a challenge. "I have three ships." Rudolf pointed.

Still Lewis said nothing. Did he think she was a politician like Lady Portia, able to read men and their true intentions before they knew themselves? Lady Portia dealt in subtleties. Rhona did not.

"Is this the wolf we are waiting for?" Rhona demanded.

Lewis inclined his head. "He is."

She wanted to breathe out a sigh of relief, but the Viken had his eyes on her. Instead, she inspected him right back. "What is your stake, Prince of Viken? What do you get out of saving the Southern Isles?"

For just a moment, Rudolf looked lost, like a boy looked out through his eyes. Then the moment was gone and he stood as stoic as before, almost as though she'd imagined it. But she hadn't.

"He wants Lady Portia," Lewis supplied.

Good luck, Viken. If Grieve was to be believed, and he usually was, Lady Portia would be no easy conquest. She might not be a witch, but she had her own weapons. If this man sought to bully Lady Portia into a marriage she did not desire, Rhona would defend her alongside Grieve and the others. "Lady Portia is no prize, like the women of other lands. She is the Lady of Isla, and if she does not like you, may heaven help you, for no one else will."

She expected him to defend his title, his suitability as a suitor. His right to conquer a woman.

What she didn't expect was his laughter.

He wiped his eyes and shrugged. "Portia liked me well enough before I left. If she likes me still...well, I guess we shall see. As long as the lady is safe, I will be satisfied."

She stared at him for a long moment. He spoke the truth, she was sure of it. And that look in his eyes…yearning, that's what it was. But for Portia or her claim?

Slowly, Rhona said, "She is safe enough. My betrothed guards her with his life."

Rudolf relaxed just the slightest bit. Relieved. Rhona bridled. If he dismissed Grieve and his men so easily, she would give him a piece of her mind.

"My son has sent word?" Lewis asked eagerly, interrupting her train of thought.

Rudolf would keep, Rhona swore, as she answered, "When he can. His letters are carried in secret and left in a place only he and I know. The lady lives, and so does he."

Lewis' grin was positively devilish. "How goes the hiding, Lady Rhona? Are your sisters sick of fish yet?"

Rhona turned her glare on Lewis. "They complain constantly. The sooner this war ends, the better." If she could play a part in it, it would be over much sooner.

The two men exchanged a glance.

"Would you like to help with the war, Lady Rhona?" Rudolf ventured. He almost sounded like he wanted her to refuse.

Fat chance of that. "My father will not approve."

Lewis laughed. "Old fool. He thinks my son should save you, for what man would follow a hero who got himself saved by a maiden?"

No, her father worried about her. Needlessly. "Something of that sort." It was Grieve she worried about. If she went to war…Grieve agreed with her father. He would not forgive her for going to war, when it was his place to fight.

Lewis jerked his head at Rudolf. "We can blame the victory on the Viken. I'm sure he won't mind."

The Viken looked affronted. A proud prince, this one. "I prefer to fight my own battles, but I am not such a fool as to refuse the help of an ally. There are shieldmaidens among my people, Lord Lewis's late mother among them, who fight alongside their men. If you can assist my army..."

He didn't believe she could. Then he was a

fool.

Rhona bit her lip, and the bush behind Lewis burst into flame.

He yelped and ran down to the water, but she sent the fire racing after him, blistering the very sands to glass until the sea steamed around him. "I told you! This witch can burn anything! With her on your side, you can't help but win!"

Witch. Rhona didn't like that word. She fought to find more that would burn in the sand at Lewis's feet, but all she found was a clump of seaweed that sent up a satisfying cloud of steam. She would not help this man conquer her countrywoman. They were Islanders, not Vikens or Albans who used women like slaves. And Lewis was a traitor who deserved to die with them.

There was a whump as Rudolf fell to his knees on the sand. "Lady Rhona, I beg you to help me free the Southern Isles from the invaders. I will give you anything you ask."

It was so easy to say no, but then she would be as much a fool as Lewis. If this man with his three ships prevailed, he would face Grieve.

And Grieve would die to protect Portia.

Rhona took a deep breath. "I want all I've ever wanted. My husband. Free him from his oath to Portia, so that he can come home and marry me."

The Viken bowed his head. Understanding lit his eyes. This man had known love, too. Time would tell if it was for Lady Portia, and whether she shared his love. And Rhona would be at his side when it did, to protect her own people if it came to it. Damn Grieve and his stupid pride. It was time for this war to end, and this wolfish Viken had the power to do it. With her help.

Rhona took a deep breath. "What would you have me burn first?"

"Myroy Isle, and every other island where Albans seek to hide," Lewis said, splashing out of the sea. He shrugged. "What? I'm the Lord of Myroy. I can burn it if I want to." Lewis produced a jug from under his cloak and lifted it in a toast: "To winning this damned war!" He drank deeply.

Rudolf held out his hand. "Do we have an accord?"

If Rudolf was to live up to his name, he would have to win this war. Perhaps Grieve need never know the part she'd played. Rhona placed her hand in his. "We do, Wolf Prince."

His fingers closed around hers with a delicacy she had not expected. If it weren't for Grieve, she might actually like this Viken. Perhaps Portia would, too.

But it was too early to think of such things. First, she had a war to fight, and win.

Thirty-Eight

Rhona had seen death and destruction enough for a dozen lifetimes. She'd seen men die screaming, burning, and she'd enjoyed it. Prince Rudolf was the only man who dared stand at her side, or anywhere near her, and he did his best to arrange his face into an expression of battle-hardened watchfulness. But he was still a man, and sometimes he'd feared, sometimes he'd despaired, but more often he cheered in triumph as their growing army won yet another victory over the diminishing Alban army.

For he might be a Viken, but the Islanders treated him like one of their own. What Lord Lewis had told her was true – Rudolf had grown up on the Isles, Rhona had learned, fostered by Lord Angus, though none had known he was a prince then. And he'd fought alongside many of them as a boy, which even Rhona had to admit made him one of them. For who but an Islander fought to defend the Southern Isles?

Albans ran at the sight of him, for his reputation flew faster than an eagle. He slaughtered and burned everything in his path, they screamed, little knowing it wasn't Rudolf at all they feared, but Rhona herself. And she didn't slaughter and burn everything. Just Albans. But she let the stories spread, as stories always did. She laughed when her own people called her the Viken witch, thinking she had arrived with Rudolf. Better that they believe a lie than that she was one of their own. The men of Rum Isle knew the truth, but they kept their lady's secrets. As did Rudolf.

Twice Rhona had seen Rudolf's spirits rise at the sight of a red-haired woman on Isla, only for them to be dashed the moment the women opened their mouths. They were Lady Portia's sisters, identical in all but name and disposition. Rudolf had two of the Little Pigs, but he really wanted Number Three. Who was kept captive in a castle the Albans had dared to build on Council Isle.

When he'd heard that, he'd ordered them to ride without rest until they arrived at the loch. No one had dared argue with the hard Viken. Not even Rhona. This war had gone on too long – they all wanted it to be over.

The sisters rode with Rhona all the way to Loch Findlugan, which made the men keep their distance. They needn't have – the pregnant one, Arlie, spent most of the journey describing the gowns she wanted to make for Rhona. If it hadn't been raining, Rhona didn't doubt the woman would have had a needle in hand, making a start on the first gown while she rode. Rhona had half a mind to take her up on the offer. It would be nice to have a new gown again.

Lina had little to say, except when answering her sister's questions about the cloth bales in Lord Angus' storerooms. But Rhona could feel her eyes everywhere, sizing up the army and the land and everything they encountered. No doubt taking stock so that she might report to her husband, Lord Angus' steward.

Rudolf stayed away when the women were with her, which suited Rhona fine. Every time he looked at them, his eyes burned with a desire that forced him to look away. He burned for Lady Portia, hotter than any blaze Rhona had kindled. If Portia refused him…Rhona wasn't sure what he'd do. That's why she would see this through to the end. Prince Rudolf, the Wolf Prince of Viken, as he was now known, had fought too long and too hard to just give up, and with an army at his back, Rhona might be all that stood between him and Portia, if the girl refused him.

But Rhona would stand, for this war would be all for naught if Portia was forced into a marriage against her will. For the women of the Southern Isles fought for freedom as much as their men, and Rhona would not yield.

When Rudolf sent his envoys across the

loch, against Rhona's advice, she considered returning to her tent, not wanting to see if the Albans opened fire on the two helpless women in the tiny boat. But something within her could not turn away, so she stayed. A whisper of magic sent a breeze behind the boat, speeding it to the castle, then swirling back to her, carrying the voices of those inside.

But not the words she wanted to hear.

For the first time in years, she heard Grieve's voice again: "I don't care if they're her sisters or not. If they are soldiers in disguise, then they die on our swords, but if they truly are Lady Portia's sisters, then we'll send them up to the tower with her, where they'll be safe. God knows she could do with the company of a woman again. Keeping her amused is more than I have the wit or energy for, I fear."

Grieve's loyalties had shifted, as Rhona had known they would. He served Lady Portia now. He'd forgotten Rhona had ever existed.

Rhona bowed her head, wiping away a tear before anyone could see it.

"What is it? What's wrong? Is it Portia?" Rudolf seized her shoulders, forgetting in his panic who she was.

Rhona eyed him coldly. "Your Lady Portia is in the tower, soon to be joined by her sisters. So safe her guards have little to do but amuse her."

Rudolf's breath whooshed out of him. "Thank the heavens for that. For a moment, I thought…"

He remembered himself and released her.

"Forgive me, Lady Rhona." The Wolf Prince bowed regally. "By this time tomorrow, our alliance will be over, and the war will be won."

Rhona wiggled her fingers. "I could set fire to the castle from here, if you want it to be sooner. The walls are stone, but there is enough timber in there to burn."

His eyes widened in horror. "You cannot! Portia is in there, you said. Safe. You can't risk…and what of your man? The bargain we made? If he is dead, then he is freed of his vows, and I release you from yours."

Oh, the bitter gall, that both Portia and Grieve lived, and neither she nor Rudolf would be reunited with the ones they loved, for the pair no longer loved them. She had killed plenty of men, but she would not be the one to rip Rudolf's beating heart from his chest.

"He lives, too," Rhona said shortly. "Until tomorrow, then, Wolf Prince."

Thirty-Nine

It was strange to have a tent to herself again, but Rhona lingered there as long as she dared the next morning. She toyed with the idea of avoiding the noon peace council, but in her heart she knew she could not.

The Wolf Prince believed the cowardly Albans would surrender Portia. If she was lucky, Grieve would be among the girl's honour guard. Rhona could remain in the background and watch unseen as she saw how things played out between Portia, Grieve and Rudolf.

But when the boat landed, there were three armoured men aboard – no women.

Rudolf appeared as impassive as ever, not showing the surprise Rhona knew he must feel at not seeing Portia with them.

They came ashore, removing their helms as Rudolf did. That's when Rhona clapped both hands to her mouth to stifle her cry. The cowardly Albans had sent Grieve to treat with Rudolf in their place, without Portia. They'd sent him to his death.

Rhona had chosen a place where she could not hear them, and no magical breeze would carry their words across the whispering of half an army. She began to shove her way through the men, intent on hearing what was said. Grieve's last words, if that's what they were.

She would not let them be, she vowed. Even if he now loved Portia instead of her, she would not let him die.

A sword scraped out of its scabbard and Rhona lost patience. She sank her teeth into her lip, and magic blew a path for her to the lakeshore.

"Sheath that thing, you bloody fool!" she

shouted, running toward Grieve.

His eyes widened. "Rhona?" Down came the sword, and his eyes lit up.

Rhona could feel the fire inside her, ready to burn the world twice over in Grieve's defence. Thrice, if he loved her still.

"You lay one finger on this man, Wolf Prince, and our alliance is over!" She marched past Rudolf and took her place at Grieve's side. No man in Rudolf's army would rise in his defence against her.

Even Rudolf hesitated. He looked at Grieve for what was likely the first time. "Who are you?"

Before Grieve could speak, Rhona snapped, "He's Grieve Lewisson, my betrothed, and the head of Lady Portia's personal guard." She half expected him to wince at her words, but Grieve merely nodded. Rhona turned to Grieve. "Why have the Albans sent you to negotiate?"

The men behind Grieve burst out laughing. "What Albans? They've all fled, like the cowards they are. Even Mason, when we shut him out. Council Island and the castle belong to Lady Portia."

"No. It belongs to my husband."

Everyone turned to stare at the newcomer. Her red hair was a banner of flame brighter than anything Rhona could conjure, marking her as the lady herself. But as she approached, Rhona found it hard not to laugh. The third Little Pig indeed, for Lady Portia's gown was caked in mud to the knees.

Then Rudolf's eyes lit up, brighter than her hair. He mustn't have noticed the soiled gown as his oh-so-majestic lady made her muddy way along the lakeshore. He'd gone to war for her. Men had died for her. More men would die for her, if this war went on. One muddy girl.

A girl who hid behind her guards, and Grieve. No longer. Rhona fixed her gaze on the girl, willing her to show some sign of why they had all fought so long and so hard.

"My husband." When Portia repeated the words, she laid her hand on Rudolf's arm. She'd placed herself opposite Rhona, so that their eyes met.

Rhona expected curiosity, or

hostility…something that told her Portia had no idea who she was facing.

But Portia's face lit with a friendly smile. "Lady Rhona." Then she offered her cheek.

But she did not leave Rudolf's side or take her hand from his arm, all the while her gaze held Rhona's. In order to give Portia the kiss of peace custom demanded, Rhona would have to approach and bow her head to kiss the shorter girl.

Portia knew nothing about Rhona. Not her power or her rank or…anything. Every man present feared her, holding their breath as they waited to see Rhona's response, yet Portia smiled on, oblivious.

"It is a pleasure. I have heard so much about you," Portia said, glancing at Grieve.

Or not oblivious.

With one glance, she said it all. She knew all about Rhona's magic, for Grieve had told her, but she was Lord Angus's daughter. A politician, like her father before her. In her father's absence, Portia stood as ruler of the Isles, but she recognised Rhona's power over Rudolf's army. Between them, they held the power to end this war, unite everyone present, and bring peace.

Rhona would drop to her knees and kiss a pig for that. But Portia was no pig. She was a lady who outranked Rhona. A lady who winked, the moment Rhona's lips left her cheek, as though they were the best of friends sharing a secret.

They had done what countless fighting men could not do. Two women had ended a war with a kiss.

"I look forward to your wedding. You must sit beside me at the feast to celebrate mine. Of course, you and Grieve must sit with us at the high table. I insist." Portia's eyes were on Grieve as she said this. Either she enjoyed his pain or…was there nothing between her and Grieve, after all?

Rhona dared to hope.

"My lady," Grieve breathed. It wasn't clear which lady he was speaking to, as his eyes darted from one to the other.

Portia lifted her eyebrows. "I hope you mean Rhona, for I'm not yours any more. Protecting me is Prince Rudolf's job now."

Of course. Her marriage released him from his vows. Grieve was free.

Portia lifted her and Rudolf's linked arms, raising her voice in a warcry that would have made any general proud. "Isla is ours!"

The army – her army – echoed her words, over and over until the valley rang with a woman's warcry. As it should be.

Rhona felt a timid tap on her shoulder.

Grieve stood there, the only man among them not cheering. "I am no longer needed. Is there any chance…would you still be willing…I mean…"

"You'll marry me today, or not at all, Grieve Lewisson. I've waited long enough, and there's a priest hereabouts who will say the words for us, or I'll light his boots on fire," Rhona said.

"But what will your father say?" Grieve asked.

"Who cares, as long as you say yes?"

Of all the men present, Grieve alone had the power to crush Rhona entirely.

She moistened her lips. "If you don't say yes, I give you fair warning I'll light your boots on fire. I'm getting really good at that."

Grieve laughed. "You need no magic to light me on fire, my lady. But you have always known that. If you wish to be married today, then I will do everything in my power to grant your wish. The war is over. It is past time that you are wed."

"You're telling me." Rhona would have said more, but Grieve caught her in his arms, and her mouth was soon too busy for anything as dull as words.

Forty

Father Fintan was only too happy to perform the ceremony, boasting that he'd officiated in the prince's wedding to Portia, only last night. When Rhona finally said the words that she'd dreamed about for so long, she wasn't sure who was happier – her or Grieve. The priest pronounced them husband and wife, then dropped his voice to a whisper to tell Rhona he would happily counsel her on the duties of marriage at any time, especially after the wedding night.

Rhona just laughed. "If my husband has

forgotten how to please me in bed, I'm not the one you'll hear it from, Father. I'm not sure Grieve will confess it to you, either." She seized Grieve's hand. "Come, husband, we have a wedding feast to attend."

The camp was strangely empty, though the tents crouched like ghosts in the moonlight. Everyone else was in the castle, and the sounds of merry feasting carried across the water without the help of a breeze, magical or otherwise.

"The only feast I want is you." Grieve's words hung in the air, tantalising, tempting. Too much to refuse.

He tugged her into his arms. His embrace and the kiss that followed felt as natural as breathing – all things she wanted to do for the rest of her life.

"To my tent, then," she said, leading the way. She entered, waving her hand to light the braziers that turned the tent from chilly to bearable. She heard a clink behind her. Grieve's sword belt, most likely. He would not need it here.

"I have some wine here somewhere. It is

not a bottle of Father's best, but..."

"Perhaps after, my lady. I am drunk on you already."

No one spoke to her as sweetly as Grieve. Oh, how she'd missed that. Rhona whirled, wanting to see the love in his eyes as he looked at her.

He tugged off his hose and stood naked in the firelight. Her husband. War had only improved him, turning lean, boyish muscle into the harder, muscled man before her. Everything she could ever want.

Grieve laughed. "I seem to remember I was the one lost for words, seeing you naked. Have the tables turned?"

"I..." The fire began in her belly, coursing through her veins until it flamed in her cheeks. She'd never needed a man more than she wanted Grieve now. "I need to feel you inside me, Grieve. Now."

"Then let's get you out of this gown, for I've dreamed of you every night since the day I left." His hands didn't fumble as he unlaced her gown and had her out of it before he'd finished kissing her. Her shift vanished, and now she was naked before him. He carried her to the bed, fingers caressing her even as he kissed her. There was none of the boyish nervousness from before. Now, he played her body with the deft strokes of a masterful man.

Rhona arched her back as she cried out for joy, begging for more. Grieve had anticipated her, once again, thrusting deep into her before her first blissful orgasm had finished. On the second thrust, her hips rose to meet him, ever equal to anything he was willing to give.

They moved together, one body in more than mere words, until they uttered twin cries of joy as they reached their peak together, too.

It wasn't until they lay tangled in each other's arms later, that Rhona thought to say, "Remember that witch on Nimbanmore Isle? She would be horrified at what we've just done. She thought we were brother and sister, remember."

Grieve traced a circles around her nipples, grinning as she shivered at his touch. "There's only one witch whose opinion I care for. My lovely Lady Rhona, you never did tell me...what sort of lover am I?"

Her hands slid down his belly, stroking him into readiness. Only then did Rhona flash him a wicked smile. "I'm sure I've forgotten. But I'd love to be reminded."

Grieve rolled over, settling between her thighs. "What sort?" he demanded.

"One who likes to tease me," she grumbled, reaching for him.

He leaned forward and kissed her breasts. "If you will not say, then I will tell you. I am the sort of lover who will love you with every breath until the day I die. The sort who wants to hear my name on your lips as you cry out for pleasure, over and over again." He thrust into her, as if to punctuate his words. "And what sort of lover are you?"

She couldn't think, too intent on the pleasure of feeling the heat of him inside her again. Deep inside, where he belonged. "I'm yours," she said simply. "And as long as we're together, we get to live happily ever af....oh, Grieve!"

Grieve chuckled. "As my lady wishes, of course."

Forty-One

Briska stamped out of her boots, but the blazing leather had already set the floor alight. Swearing, she bit down hard and fought to cast the only spell that could save her. The circle of blue light flared and died, once, twice…but on the third time it seemed to stay, wavering a little, but enough. She stepped through the portal, which collapsed behind her. She peeled off her singed stockings, to find her feet red and blistered with burns. She stuck her feet in the water bucket, moaning as the icy water numbed the pain.

The mirror unclouded for a moment and a face appeared. "Well done," the woman said.

"What do you mean, well done? That brother and sister almost killed me!" Briska snapped.

The woman laughed. "Brother and sister? You are too easily persuaded. That's what got you into this mess in the first place, but I will help you. This pair are matched, and so you will move onto your next quest. Your new assignment is in the icy north, I'm afraid. You will need warmer things."

Ice and snow? Perfect for burned feet.

Briska lifted her arms. "I am ready when you are, Mistress." The last word came hard for a woman who had once been a queen, but she had little choice now. Slavery to the mirror and its mistress was all her life held now.

A portal opened before her, and Briska stepped through. The mirror, her chest of belongings, and her precious sack of spices landed in the snow behind her.

Another day, another couple. Though she shook her head when she thought of Hansel and Gretel. That pair would not have an easy time of it, she was certain. She might have made a match of them, however unwillingly, but they had a lot of work for even a hope of happily ever after.

Her mistress's face appeared in the mirror. "Next, you must match Kai and Gerda," she said.

Briska sighed as she saw the picture of the pair. At least these two had clothes on, unlike the fornicating brother and sister. Thank the heavens for small mercies. And snow to cool her feet.

From queen of a kingdom to queen of the snow, Briska's work was never done.

But first, she would need a place to live, for her new palace was gone. And all the ice and snow gave her an idea...

Wish:
Aladdin Retold

DEMELZA CARLTON

A tale in the Romance a Medieval Fairy Tale series

One

Maram wasn't sure she could think of any creature she disliked quite as much as a camel. They smelled like a carpet some drunkard had mistaken for a toilet, were about as comfortable to ride on as a bag of rocks, and they made noises reminiscent of a rutting man in the throes of the most violent lust imaginable. Actually, they were exactly like a lust-crazed man. The same hard muscle, the same sounds, and after a particularly energetic night, they didn't smell much better than a camel.

But the camel's look of disgust and habit of spitting in front of her made it less attractive than a well-muscled, naked man, who would give her some pleasure, while the camel only made her backside ache. And the matted carpet of fur upon its back seemed to drink the desert sands and rub it into her clothing when she wasn't watching. Thank the heavens it was a short journey from the port to the city, where her father's palace was waiting.

And a bath, an unheard-of luxury in some of the places she'd visited this trip. Oh, they'd had tubs and water and knew how to wash, but a bathhouse where a lady might immerse her whole body, or share that space with her lover? They'd looked at her like she was mad.

Perhaps she was, Maram reflected. Normal princesses stayed in their fathers' palaces until they reached an age to marry, when they meekly accepted the husband their fathers chose for them. They spent most of the rest of their lives on their backs, conceiving or giving birth to children to ensure the succession of their husband's line. A life spent in bed, their every need seen to by a host of servants. No need to travel or sit on a camel. Or even lift an eyebrow to seduce their husbands, who came to their beds every night without fail.

A small smile found its way onto Maram's face. Well, most nights they went to their wives. Some nights, they fell under the spell of a foreign princess and spent a glorious night trying to please the princess instead. Skills they could then use on their wives, or at least Maram hoped they would. Just because those married princesses lived an easy life, didn't mean they shouldn't enjoy their husbands' attentions. Childbirth wasn't an easy matter, or so she'd heard, never having experienced it for herself. So if she borrowed their husbands for a night – willingly, always willingly, for men were weak, and weaker still when subject to the strength of her seductive magic – she returned them with improvements she hoped their wives appreciated.

An enchantment of her own design, that ensured they gave pleasure to any woman they bedded. She had not yet worked out how to eliminate the faint blue glow that enveloped their man parts while the spell was active, but perhaps it did not matter, for surely their wives had seen enough of them not to need to look too closely. Maram had certainly not heard any complaints from her lovers, or their wives.

And her father reaped the benefits, in strategic trade agreements, alliances and other political favours his ambassadors asked for, but she ensured. She lifted her hood so that she could see Elcin, the ambassador she'd accompanied on this trip. He rode at the front of the camel train, of course, proud of his successful mission. Maram didn't begrudge him his pride, even if his success was mostly due to her. Other ambassadors had made her job more difficult – Hasan, the first ambassador she'd accompanied, had tried to force himself on her more than once, refusing to allow her to do what her father had sent her to do. Elcin had been a delight in comparison, and she would tell her father so.

Desert dust smudged the horizon now, and she knew she was close to home and the end of this interminable camel ride.

Sure enough, the city gates soon rose out of the golden brown sand, sentinels standing straight and tall to welcome her home.

Maram passed between them without glancing to either side, though she inclined her head to the bowing guards and peasants who lined the road to her father's palace. Even veiled and hooded as she was, covered in travel dust, her clothing marked her as the Sultan's daughter.

The Sultan who would demand her report before she could take that much-needed bath. She sighed as she glimpsed her favourite bathhouse, but she could not stop. Later, she promised herself. Along with all of Elcin's good news, she brought urgent tidings her father needed to know more than she needed to bathe. Even if she did smell of camel.

Her father was in his audience chamber, waiting for them, when they arrived. Elcin prostrated himself, but Maram merely stood back, inclining her head to the Sultan when he turned his enquiring gaze on her.

"So, tell me what new alliances you have made for me," the Sultan said to Elcin.

Not for the first time, Maram was glad for the veil that hid her face and her boredom from her father's court as Elcin recounted her political victories.

"And what of Beacon Isle?" Father asked.

Here Elcin hesitated. Not because his news was bad, but how close it had come to being so. "Beacon Isle is ruled by a woman, who calls herself a queen. Most unusual."

Elcin had not understood Queen Margareta's power until it was almost too late. Instead, he'd addressed his proposals to the queen's young grandson, Vardan, until Maram had intervened. The boy…nay, young man, for he'd proved himself more than capable in the bedchamber, had happily surrendered to her charms and left the great hall to his grandmother and Elcin.

Maram had whispered a warning to Elcin

that if he did not show the grandmother proper respect, her not-quite-of-age grandson would never be allowed to accept her father's proposals. Elcin had showed the woman more than respect, judging by his blushes the following morning. The newly widowed Queen Margareta had required Elcin to show her some favours, too, before she granted him any.

Politics was a game best played in bedchambers, Maram reflected. Or bathhouses.

"But do we have access to their harbour?" the Sultan rumbled.

Elcin bowed so low his forehead pressed against the floor. "Yes, Your Majesty. Queen Margareta was most insistent about that. She would have us forsake all other ports in the region to trade solely with Beacon Isle."

Maram's veil hid her broad smile. Margareta knew a good bargain when she saw one; she'd toyed with Elcin until she had what she wanted. Only then had she conceded to the trade agreement with the Sultan. In her place,

Maram might have done the same. Instead, she'd educated the prince who would one day make some girl a charming husband.

Something Maram herself would probably never have. Ah, but what did she need a husband for? She was a princess, and her father or his heirs would provide for her until the day she died. If she needed a man for anything, she could take a lover. Someone she chose for her own pleasure, and not just to satisfy her father's political aspirations.

"Maram?"

Maram jolted out of her reverie. "Yes, Your Majesty?" she asked.

"Do you need to rest after your journey, or will you share the evening meal with me?" Father asked.

Maram bowed. "My father does me great honour. I am quite refreshed at the thought of sharing a meal with our esteemed Sultan."

Father made a sound deep in his throat that told her he saw through her flattery, but he knew what she really meant – that she had news to share that she could not repeat in front of his court. News that would not wait, or she would not have appeared in court so travel-worn.

Her father's attendants dismissed the court, while the Sultan himself led the way to his private chambers. Chambers that overlooked the harem gardens, where his wives spent most of their lives.

As Maram herself might have, if it weren't for her mother's treason. Her mother's crime gave her a freedom she was grateful for, every day, though it had cost her mother everything.

"I keep thinking I might see your mother among them, but then I must remind myself that she is gone," Father said, settling beside a well-laid table.

"You can't blame yourself," Maram said quickly. "Yours was a political marriage. You were not to know that Mother's heart lay elsewhere. Perhaps she and her lover are now reunited in the afterlife."

Father spat out his wine. "There will be no afterlife for either of them. They are not dead, Maram, no matter what you may have been told. An enchantress or enchanter who commits treason is not put to death. They face a worse fate — a lifetime of enslavement, apart."

Maram's mouth dropped open. "You mean Mother is alive?"

Father nodded. "Alive, but enslaved to a magical object. She must do the bidding of its owner until she is freed. As long as she is enslaved, she cannot age or die."

"What of her lover?" Maram asked. She remembered Amani, a kind man who had conjured flowers and sweet treats for her. It wasn't until much later that she'd realised the man was her mother's lover.

Father shrugged. "Enslaved to an old lamp I once owned. He was supposed to do my bidding, but I grew tired of seeing his face, so I got rid of it."

Poor Amani, condemned to an eternity of slavery for the crime of falling in love with the wrong woman.

"But I do not want to think of that man, and I try not to think of your mother. Though

I believe you are more beautiful now than she ever was," Father said. "We are alone now. No need to cover your face."

Finally. She'd grown so used to baring her face while they travelled that wearing a veil once more was irritating, though it had kept the worst of the sand out while they trekked through the desert. Maram peeled off the layers of linen and dropped them in a dusty heap on the floor. She shook out her hair, and gritted her teeth as it released a small cloud of sand. "The desert will not let me rest until I have told you my news," she said. "Word in the port and at every oasis between there and the city is that Sheikh Basit wants to expand his territory. He has attacked several camps, sending slaves to market through the port. From what I can gather, the camps may have been in your territory at the time. That makes the slaves he's taken your people. If it is true, we cannot afford to ignore this."

Father pounded his fist on the table. "That grasping fool keeps sending envoys here, asking for one of my daughters to be his bride.

His ambition knows no bounds. That son of a camel herder!" He let out a stream of less polite insults that were enough to make Maram's ears burn.

"Perhaps you should send him a bride, Father," she said, selecting a slice of melon. She'd missed the fruit of home while travelling.

"Let that camel dung soil one of my daughters?" Father demanded.

Maram smiled. "I was thinking of Anahita."

Father's eyes narrowed. "Do you truly think so?"

Maram nodded. "I think it is the only way to protect your people from him." Her half-sister Anahita liked to play politics as much as Maram, though her style was more direct.

"Very well." Father bowed his head. "Was there anything else of importance that Elcin missed in his report?"

"Not really. Except that I believe he has fallen for the charms of the Mistress of Beacon Isle, Queen Margareta. Either you should send him to the isle regularly to keep the woman sweet, or you should keep him away from her altogether, and see that he finds a bride who will replace that woman in his affections."

"Should I doubt his loyalty?"

Maram thought for a moment, then said, "No, not yet. But she is a powerful enchantress, a fact she keeps hidden from many of her people, though not from me. Perhaps you should keep him away from her, after all. He is a good man. It would be a shame to lose him."

"Who do you recommend?"

"Someone sweet and shy, younger than he is. The opposite of the powerful queen. Perhaps one of my cousins. Hold a celebration feast for his return and see which of the girls cannot keep her eyes off him. A love match would suit him, I think." Maram sipped her tea, feeling the heat sink into her very bones. Oh, she had missed the tastes of home.

"It sounds like you really like this man," Father mused, not meeting her eyes. "Why not you?"

Maram laughed. "Because I am not some doe-eyed innocent who will adore him as he deserves. Besides, what would I do with a husband? I can't imagine he would allow me to travel to foreign countries, negotiating trade agreements for you. Face it, Father. I am no use to you as some man's wife. But as a jewelled courtesan, I can bring the world to your feet."

"You are still my daughter, and you deserve a reward. You have done more than my ambassador, I have no doubt, yet you ask for so little in reward. If you ever wished for a husband, Maram, I would grant your wish."

Maram moistened her lips. "You do not think I would cheat on him as my mother did to you?"

Sadness clouded Father's expression. "You are not Briska. There is too much of me in you. She pursued her passions with no care for the future, but you see as far as I do, and plan for the future you desire. Maram, I swear to you, if you wish for a husband, I will consent to any match you desire."

It was a lie, and they both knew it. Her father would only marry her off for an alliance that brought him more benefit than she did currently as his unofficial ambassador. But her life suited Maram, so she did not say so.

"Father, I promise you, the only man I want is one who will build me a palace that has its own bathhouse, an edifice to rival the grandest bathhouse in the city, but for my very own. And not even you can give me that." Maram smiled sadly. Her father's palace had been built on a plentiful water supply, but her favourite bathhouse had a spring which fed the pools inside, and no other water in the city could compare to it.

Father waved her away. "Of course, you must bathe. You are a dutiful daughter indeed to come to me before you have properly washed away the dust from your journey. I shall see to it that the Firdaus Bathhouse is closed to all but you and your attendants for as long as you like."

Maram inclined her head. "Thank you, Father. It is too late in the day now, so I shall bathe in my chambers tonight, but tomorrow…tomorrow I will accept your offer.

A bathhouse to myself for the day is reward enough, I think."

It wasn't, but for now it would do.

What man would want her for a wife, anyway? Most men wanted a virginal bride, the sort Maram wanted for Elcin. They would not want a woman who had taken dozens of lovers to her bed. Lovers who had given her pleasure but nothing else, for her healing skills were sufficient to stave off disease or pregnancy, but still. To most men, that made her unclean and not a fit bride.

Of course, if they met her and fell under her spell, no man could resist her, but she did not want a man by magical means. As a lover, maybe, but not as her life's partner.

Maram sighed. She was destined to go through life alone, taking a series of lovers, but never to truly love. At least she had the freedom to choose her lovers. Not even Anahita could claim that.

And a bath. On the morrow, she would have a bath.

Maram clapped her hands to summon a

servant to help her wash in what the palace could provide. Tomorrow she could soak, but today she could at least be clean.

Two

"I can make you rich beyond your wildest dreams. The Sultan's daughters will mistake you for a prince, you will be so wealthy, and you may have your pick of them!" the well-dressed man boasted. "I am Gwandoya, and if you come to work for me, you will never go hungry again!"

"That's because everyone who does, dies," Berk muttered.

"Really?" Aladdin asked.

Berk shrugged. "Well, whoever does believe

him enough to go work for him, never comes back."

Aladdin laughed. "Well, if I went to work for him, amassed a fortune and married some princess, I wouldn't come back, either. Who wants to sit around all day in an alley that stinks of piss?"

"That's because they stable the camels here. I worked there once. Evil things, camels. They bite and spit and stand on your feet until they break all the bones, but if you fight back, you're the one who gets thrown out," Bugra piped up. The boy was not yet a man, but Aladdin had been younger than Bugra when he started coming here looking for whatever work he could find.

"What about you, boy?" Gwandoya asked, pointing at Bugra. "What do you think of my offer?"

"What offer's that?" Bugra asked.

"Riches untold, and a princess for a bride!" Gwandoya said, his eyes lighting with unholy fire.

It was far too early in the morning for that

sort of zealotry.

"Sounds better than shovelling camel shit," Bugra said, stepping forward. "Will she be pretty?"

"Far more beauteous than any woman you have ever beheld!" Gwandoya promised.

"Hey, you don't want to do that," Aladdin said, reaching for Bugra's shoulder. "He might be taking you to sell you as a slave in the market."

Bugra shrugged off Aladdin's hand. "He promised me a princess, he did. And gold. You're just jealous you didn't accept first. When I'm a prince, I'll come back and throw you a copper coin so you can use the baths. Meanwhile, I'll have a palace of my own. You'll see." Bugra headed off with Gwandoya, leaving the other men staring in their wake.

"Think we'll ever see him again?" Aladdin asked.

"Nope," Berk drawled. Other men shook their heads.

"No one who goes with Gwandoya is ever seen again," an old man said, sadly.

"Should we tell his family where he's gone?" Aladdin ventured.

The old man shrugged. "No one to tell. His mother died last year. No one will miss him." He sighed. "Much like the rest of us. If we cannot work to keep our families fed, what use are we? We should all go with Gwandoya, for it is only a matter of time before we die unmourned by anyone who matters, for our families will starve long before us."

Some of the other men nodded in agreement, but none had the energy to argue. Perhaps none of them had anyone left to lose.

Except Aladdin, who rose from his crouch to stare down at the hopeless humanity who were the closest thing he had to friends. "Speak for yourself. My mother would mourn me. I'm not staying here, waiting to die with the rest of you. A caravan came into town last night. I heard it. I'll head down to the bazaar and see if anyone needs some extra hands to help unload the goods." Anything was better than wallowing in misery, waiting for work that would not come.

So he strode out of the alley and down the main street, toward the markets, but with no idea what to do. Such was the story of his life. His father had insisted he learn to read and write, and assess the quality of goods for when Aladdin followed in his father's footsteps as a merchant. But his father had died before Aladdin was old enough to take over the business, and his mother had sold all their goods just to survive, leaving them with nothing. Not even a trade Aladdin could follow to earn a living, for he was too old to apprentice and besides, no tradesman would take him without money to pay for his board. Money his mother no longer had.

So Aladdin walked through the market, seeing good silk and bad, brass polished to look like gold and gold so dirty it looked like cheap brass, food fit for the Sultan's table and stuff even a starving goat would turn its nose up at, but he could afford none of it. He was a merchant's son turned street rat, and his mother earned more money with her spinning than he did waiting all day to be hired for a day's labour that he was never offered.

He made it to the other end of the market without realising, only to find the street full of guards. "Make way for the princess!" one shouted, shoving a camel driver under the feet of his own lead beast.

Guards who would happily let a merchant be trampled wouldn't care if they killed some street rat, Aladdin knew, so he ducked into the nearest building – the city's oldest bathhouse. He ignored the sign that said the place was closed, and shouldered open the door. The shadows inside were cooler than the street, and he could hide here until the guards went past.

It wasn't as though a princess would enter a public bathhouse. The Sultan's precious daughters undoubtedly bathed in the confines of the harem, where no man could gaze upon their virgin beauty.

One of the guards must have seen him, though, because the door was thrown open. Aladdin hurried to find some deeper shadows to hide in. He found an alcove where the staff kept the towels, and ducked behind a towering pile of cloth. Surely no one would look for him there.

"You may go," a deep feminine voice said grandly. A voice Aladdin heard in his very soul.

Booted footsteps trooped outside at her command.

A princess who used a public bathhouse? This he had to see. Unable to resist, Aladdin peeped around the towels.

A veiled woman stood beside the pool while her female servants busied themselves fetching cloths and bowls of water to bathe their mistress before she immersed herself in the mineral bath.

One came into his alcove, and Aladdin had to dive behind the towels again, though he doubted the serving girl saw him in the dark. But if the princess was going to bathe, he'd best get out before someone saw him. He couldn't have picked a worse hiding place if he'd tried. Aladdin pressed his eye to a crack in the shutters, hoping the streets would be clear enough to allow him to escape.

No such luck. The street was filled with the

princess's guards, who would capture him the moment they saw him. Peeping at the princess, however unintentionally, carried a death penalty they wouldn't hesitate to carry out.

So he had to stay put, and wait the woman out. Once everyone left, then he could leave.

He settled on the tile floor. It was more comfortable than the alley where he'd spent more days than he could count.

"There. Leave me. I will summon you when I have need of you." The princess's voice echoed through the bathhouse, amplified by some sort of magic so that it seemed she spoke beside him.

Aladdin crept to the entrance of his alcove again, curious.

Four veiled women bowed, then left, and Aladdin's heart stopped as he beheld the most beautiful woman he'd ever seen. The curve of her shoulders, enticing his eyes to travel down the crease of her spine to her peach-shaped bottom. His hands itched to touch her, to see if her skin was as soft as a peach. He'd eaten the fruit in his childhood, but it had been many years since he'd done more than look at them longingly in the market.

But never as longingly as he looked at this woman now. A princess he had no right to stare at, though he could not drag his eyes away as she descended the shallow steps into the pool. She ducked under the surface of the water, then came up and flipped onto her back, stealing Aladdin's breath as he caught sight of her breasts. Fruit from heaven, surely, so round and perfect. This princess's body was a priceless treasure none but the highest of men deserved to possess. Maybe not even then.

Aladdin buried his face in his hands. He deserved to die for what he'd seen. But if he did, he would die happy.

"Step out of the shadows, where I can see you," the princess commanded.

One of her attendants had stayed, Aladdin guessed. He ducked back behind his towels, where the woman would not see him.

"Do you really want me to summon my guards to drag you out? Come, now, man. You have seen your fill of me, so it is only fair that you let me at least see your face."

Aladdin risked a peek around the towels, to find the princess's dark eyes fixed on his hiding place.

She spread her arms wide. "I am unarmed, as you see. I will not harm you."

Just looking at her condemned him to death, but Aladdin knew he'd already sealed his fate. Fixing his gaze on her face, he took three tentative steps into the space before he fell to his knees, pressing his forehead to the floor. "Your Highness, my humblest apologies for my disrespect. I sought to clear the road to let your entourage pass, only to find myself trapped in here. Why does one of the Sultan's daughters do such honour to a common bathhouse?"

Her laughter was low and musical, bouncing off the walls and straight into Aladdin's heart. He never reacted this way to anyone.

"This is no common bathhouse. This is the first bathhouse built in the city by one of my ancestors. Better than anything in the palace, I assure you."

It was Aladdin's turn to laugh, and the walls boomed the sound back at him. He clapped a hand over his mouth, but it was too late. Anyone outside had surely heard him.

The princess did not sound worried. "They won't come in unless I call. They are my attendants, and they serve me."

"What kind of princess are you?" he burst out.

"The sort who entertains men alone if it pleases her, who prefers this bathhouse to the shallow pools in the harem. The Sultan has many daughters, and we have our own talents. Some of us are not destined for marriage alliances." She sounded almost bitter at this.

"Any man who saw you would be a fool not to beg for your hand," Aladdin said.

"Most men prefer other parts of my body to my hands," the princess said drily.

Aladdin lifted his startled gaze to her face. "But...I thought..."

Pain appeared in her eyes. "I am Princess Maram, a courtesan from the Sultan's court, who accompanies our ambassadors to far off countries. Sometimes I persuade the men of other royal houses to look favourably on my father's proposals. Most men find my body hard to resist, though you don't seem to struggle. Why is that? Do you prefer men?"

Aladdin's face reddened. "Your Highness, your beauty is irresistible indeed, but I am a humble spinner's son. I have grown used to not having things I desire, however ardently." As if to remind him that he had not eaten since the previous day, his stomach gave an alarming rumble.

Princess Maram's eyes narrowed. "Yasmeen, have food and refreshments brought for two," she called.

"Yes, Your Highness," came a voice from the entrance hall, but the girl did not appear.

Aladdin allowed himself to breathe again. "You are too magnanimous, Your Highness."

She smiled. "No, I'm quite selfish, actually. I am accustomed to having men stare at me hungrily because they desire me, not because they are starving, therefore your hunger must be satisfied. What is your name, spinner's son?"

"Aladdin," he choked out.

"Aladdin, which means excellence and faith. A name you share with the sultan who commanded that this bathhouse be built. I think there is more to you than being a simple spinner's son." Maram's eyes seemed to see into his very soul, and Aladdin was helpless to stop her.

For the first time, he forced himself to meet her gaze squarely. "Forgive my impertinence, Princess, but I am no more and no less than my mother's son."

She smiled. "And I am my mother's daughter, which defines me more than you know. I will forgive you, if you will forgive my poor choice of words."

Aladdin bowed his head to the floor once more. "There is nothing to forgive, Your Highness."

Three

Maram saw the boy duck into the bathhouse, and when she entered the cool space, she sent out her magic to search for him. She hid her smile when she found the boy hiding behind the towels. She would lure him out soon enough. First, she wanted her bath.

She let her attendants wash her, for the four of them made faster work of it than she could. Another time, she might have asked one to stay, to read or sing or converse with her while she soaked in the bath, but something about the boy's presence changed her mind, so she sent them away instead. Let them think she was meeting a lover. It would not be the first time.

She bit her lip, tasting blood as she cast a seduction spell on herself. The spell spread out like mist, swirling around the columns until it reached the alcove where her quarry concealed himself. She sensed his resistance, and wondered if he was younger than she'd thought. A child who did not yet know a man's urges would not respond to her spell the way a man would.

She called to him, first with her spell and then with her voice, until the combination of command and threat brought him out of hiding.

She was surprised to find not a boy at all, but a man grown, though a young one who was not much taller than her. Painfully thin, too, as though he did not eat enough. A thought that he confirmed early in their conversation, when his empty belly gave him away.

His gaze kept drifting away from her in a way she'd never seen happen before. No man could take his eyes off her when she cast a seduction spell, especially not when she stood naked before him. Yet he resisted, this Aladdin. A prophetic name for a man met in this place, built by his namesake so many centuries before.

Yasmeen brought the midday meal and Aladdin disappeared back into the alcove, not venturing out until Maram dismissed Yasmeen. In the servant's absence, Maram was forced to serve the food herself, but Aladdin thanked her so profusely for every bite that she found she did not mind.

He ate like a man who had been brought up in court, not some starving spinner's son, as he said. When he had finished, he bowed deeply before her again and said, "You have my gratitude, kind Princess. How may I repay your kindness?"

"Satisfy my curiosity," she said. "Tell me what you know of magic."

"I know nothing, except that it killed my

father, and my mother sold everything we owned to prevent it from killing me, too," Aladdin said.

"How?" Maram demanded.

"She paid a witch to cast a spell on me, one that would shield me from magic." Aladdin's lip curled. "I told my mother she was wasting her money, for even if magic did exist, there was no proof that the witch could cast such a spell, or that it would work."

"How long ago was this?" Maram pressed.

"Ten years or more."

She inhaled sharply. "A powerful spell indeed, to last so long and still work."

He did not look convinced.

Maram took a deep breath, bit her lip, and cast a second seduction spell, more powerful than the first. The last time she had done such a thing, it had taken an entire troop of eunuch guardsmen to keep the three men she'd targeted from taking her by force.

Yet all Aladdin did was raise his head to look at her. No, to look at her face, an oddity in itself. "Did you cast a spell?" he asked.

"Yes. Do you feel any different?" she asked. If necessary, her guards would be here in moments, but she didn't think it would come to that.

"Your Highness has treated me with kindness, allowing me to share your meal and see beauty most men only dream about. I feel as though if I were to die today, I would die happy." He frowned. "Though my mother would not be so happy."

"Not as though you wished to…do things to me?" For the first time in years, Maram felt a blush colour her cheeks.

"Your Highness, the moment I saw you, I dreamed of more than any man deserves. What I wish is of less importance than I am, and I am nothing."

His dark eyes told her he spoke the truth as he believed it, impossible though it seemed. How could a man consider himself nothing?

She reached out. "Please, rise."

His hand enveloped hers, but he was too chivalrous to do more than grasp her hand as he rose uncertainly to his feet.

Maram moistened her lips. "Kiss me, Aladdin."

"Your Highness, I am not worthy." He stood as tall as she did, yet he bowed his head.

"What if I told you less worthy men than you have kissed me, when I did not ask them to, nor wish it?"

Now he met her gaze and anger flared in his eyes. "Then I hope your guards cut those men down, as they deserve. As they will no doubt do to me when you are done with me."

"No!" Maram burst out. "I swear they will not touch you. But…but I would like you to touch me." She shrugged out of her robe, so she stood naked before him once more.

Aladdin laughed bitterly. "Your Highness, I have done many things I am not proud of, but I have yet to sell my body, and I will not. I promised my mother when I was a boy that I would not take coin from the brothel keepers, who were very interested in me when I was younger and prettier, and I am a man of my word, even if my word is all I have left."

"Then I am not worthy of you, Aladdin,

man of your word. Because I have sold my body countless times to secure concessions for the Sultan, and I have no doubt I will be called upon to do so many times more." Maram fought back tears. With his simple statement, the man had shamed her, yet he had done nothing wrong.

"Princess…"

"Kiss me. Please." Even as the words left her lips, she knew they had no power over him. He was immune to her magic, for all his pretty words.

Aladdin's hand cupped her cheek. The rough skin of a man who worked for a living touched her for the first time, but she relished it. This was real.

His face loomed close and she fought to slow her breathing as her heart fluttered like a bird within her ribcage.

His lips were gentle as they brushed hers, tentative and light like the touch of a bird's wings. His eyes were wide with something like panic, undoubtedly mirroring her own.

He'd never kissed a woman before, Maram

realised.

She seized his face in both hands, and pressed her lips against his. He tasted of honey and spiced almond milk, as if the last drop from his cup still lingered on his tongue. She wanted more than a taste. Heavens help her, but kissing this man was like her need for air itself. Her head spun and her heart raced as never before. No man had ever had this effect on her.

And he was not as immune to her spell as she'd thought. His tongue rose to dance with hers, his lips moving with her like music itself. He made a sound of satisfaction, deep in his throat, as his free hand came to rest in the small of her back. Still he kissed her, stealing her breath as he breathed life into her love-starved body.

No man had ever…

"No, Princess. I gave my word." He stepped back from her, peeling her fingers gently from the hem of his tunic.

She'd almost managed to tug it up and over his head. Who was he to resist her?

"But I want you to make love to me," Maram insisted. Making love wasn't what other men had done to her, but with Aladdin it would be different, she was certain.

"I want to free you from your slavery, selling your body for the good of our country," Aladdin replied.

Maram snorted, an unladylike sound that no other man had ever heard from her. "A princess's body is always used for the good of her country. Even the ones who form marriage alliances are brood mares for their husbands, living proof of the alliance between my father's kingdom and their husband's."

"So to free you, I would need to find you a husband who would love you, yet who has a kingdom to rival your father's, so that you could marry the man?" He raised his eyebrows.

Maram laughed. "Wealth to rival my father's, now, I think. He has all the alliances he needs, thanks to me, but he would marry me to a wealthy man if he thought the man's wealth outweighed my value to my father as an ambassador." She shook her head. No such man existed, she was certain. And if he did, he wouldn't love her. He'd want a virgin princess, not a well-used courtesan.

Yet Aladdin's eyes lit up at her words, as if they'd given him hope. "So if I were to amass a fortune, your father might be willing to bestow your hand on me? Then we could both have what we desire. You would be free, and I would be honour-bound to make love to you."

Her mouth was dry. "I wish it could be so."

Aladdin bowed low. "As do I, Princess. But you are a princess, so beautiful you put the sun and moon to shame, and I am a humble spinner's son, with not even the coin to pay you for the meal you have so kindly given me."

Maram waved away his compliments. "It is not necessary. Consider it fair payment for your refreshing conversation and company and…that kiss." She licked her lips, wanting another.

Aladdin seemed to read her thoughts and he backed away, toward the shadows from whence he had come. "My first, Princess, and I am honoured that it pleased you. I fear it will also be my last. Farewell." He disappeared into the darkness, and reluctantly she let him go.

He was just a man, and a lowborn one, at that. So why did she feel so bereft with him gone?

Maram summoned her servants to help her dress, but her thoughts were on Aladdin, the one man who could resist her spell.

Four

His thoughts filled with Princess Maram, Aladdin had to force himself to sneak out the back of the bathhouse instead of returning to her, like he wanted to.

She was a princess and he was nothing. He repeated this to himself, hoping that if he said it often enough, he would believe it. Because for that hour he'd spent in her company, he'd dreamed of more. More kisses like the one they'd shared, more such meals, maybe joining her in the bath, and…

No. She was a princess and he was nothing.

A princess who wished to be free. A beautiful caged bird who would soar, if only her father would let her.

"Did you find work today?"

Aladdin glanced up to meet his mother's enquiring gaze. He'd walked home without realising it, he'd been so deep in thought. "No, Maman. I'm sorry."

She sighed. "There must be something for you. Perhaps tomorrow you will have better luck. I have spent all day spinning, so if I take this thread to the tailor's, perhaps I will have enough coin to buy bread for your supper."

His unusually full stomach ached at the thought that he'd eaten, but he hadn't thought to bring anything home for his mother. "I'm not hungry, Maman. Save it for tomorrow, or for yourself. I will just go to bed."

But even lying on his thin straw pallet, Aladdin could not sleep. Maram and her melancholy haunted him. The perfect princess, whose kiss had awoken a longing he'd never known before.

When day dawned, Aladdin was no closer to getting the girl out of his mind. He trudged to the alley where he and the other labourers waited for work that never came. Day after day, he made the journey there, then home, in a dreamy haze that wouldn't lift. Hunger gnawed at his insides, but he ignored it.

"I can make you rich beyond your wildest dreams. The Sultan's daughters will mistake you for a prince, you will be so wealthy, and you may have your pick of them!"

Gwandoya's boasting burst through the haze in Aladdin's mind, as though he heard it for the first time.

Aladdin rose to his feet. Yes, he wanted to pick one of the Sultan's daughters. Because he dreamed of nothing else but Princess Maram.

"What about Bugra? Did you make him rich, so he married some princess?" Berk asked. "Is that why you need someone new?"

Gwandoya shrugged. "The boy made his fortune so quickly, he now has more gold than he can carry. He has no desire to work for me any more. Will you be next?"

Berk spat on the ground at Gwandoya's feet. "Not me. I'm not crazy."

"What about you?" Gwandoya looked Aladdin up and down, no doubt seeing what the other men did – that Aladdin was not strong enough for hard labour. Too many years with too little to eat had seen to that. "You will be able to eat like a king for the rest of your life if you come and work for me."

Aladdin would settle for sharing his meals with Maram. "What would you have me do?"

"Come with me and I will show you," Gwandoya said.

Berk caught Aladdin's shoulder. "Don't, man. Bugra's likely dead in the gutter somewhere, and if you go with him, you will be next."

If he didn't find work soon, Aladdin knew he'd be dead in a gutter anyway. He hadn't eaten in two days, and his mother was too tired to spin. A quick death was better than starving to death, and if there was a chance he might be able to free Maram…

"So be it. I shall take my chances," Aladdin

said. He dropped his voice to a whisper that he hoped only Berk would hear. "If I survive, I swear I will return here, if only to tell you the truth of what happened to Bugra and the others. If I do not…please tell my mother that I love her, and my last thoughts were of her." Whatever happened, he would no longer be a burden on his mother, for her spinning was enough to support her alone without him.

Berk looked like he wanted to say more, but he pressed his lips together and nodded. "May you have better fortune than the rest of us."

Gwandoya clapped Aladdin on the shoulder. "Good boy! You will be rich, you shall see!"

Aladdin wanted to believe him, so he hoped, but in his heart, he dreaded what would come next. Anything that made a starving boy rich had to be unpleasant. Otherwise, why would Gwandoya share such riches with anyone?

<h1 style="text-align:center;">Five</h1>

Maram trudged back to her apartment, vowing not to return to the bathhouse unless he was there. Somehow that one encounter with Aladdin had left the place empty of all joy for her. She had returned every day, yet he had not. She wanted, no she needed to see him again. She'd been touched by so many men, but that one kiss from him had burned through her memories of all of them so that only he remained.

Who was Aladdin? More than some simple

spinner's son. More than any man she'd ever known…they'd shared one moment, but that moment was everything.

"Did you put him up to it?"

Maram blinked. Two hulking shadows bracketed her favourite couch and the dark-clad figure who reclined upon the cushions.

"I'm still in mourning, you know," Anahita said, throwing herself down in a picture of despair.

Maram smothered a laugh. "In mourning for which husband? Do you even remember his name?"

Anahita sat up indignantly. "Of course I do. It was…um, Abd-something-or-other. I think. Oh, what does it matter? He never wanted me to address him by his name. I was supposed to call him Master, like I was a slave. Me! It is not fitting to speak ill of the dead, but that man…"

"Is not mourned by anyone, least of all you," Maram finished for her. "Father has a problem with Sheikh Basit. He is attacking the outlying towns and camps, taking our people as slaves."

Anahita frowned. "Then he is a fool, and Father does him too much honour, giving me to him as a bride. Is he at least a handsome fool?"

Maram shrugged. "I do not know. I have never seen the man. What do you care? All of your husbands meet untimely ends. One might think you drive your husbands to suicide."

"Oh, hush." Anahita flapped her hand at the nearest guard. For all that her sister never went anywhere without them, Maram had never learned their names. "Get us something to drink."

The man bowed and left without a word, while his twin folded his arms across his chest to appear even more formidable.

Anahita didn't even seem to notice. Maram would never understand why her sister favoured these two enormous men as her personal guards. They'd been a gift from her first husband, a man Maram knew deserved his untimely death ten times over.

"He cannot be handsome, or you would have kept this sheikh for yourself," Anahita said. "The gossip in the palace is that you have a new lover in the city. One you meet in the old bathhouse near the city gates." Anahita's eyes sparkled. "Who is he?"

Maram's heart ached at the mention of Aladdin. "No one." She wet her lips. "And he is not my lover. I met a man there once. I have not seen him since." But she would give everything she owned to see him again. Or for more than a kiss.

Anahita whistled. "A man who can resist you! A superior creature indeed. You must introduce me to this paragon. Perhaps he can keep me company when you go travelling again. A widow always needs so much consolation!"

"No!" Maram snapped, more sharply than she'd intended. She softened her tone as she continued, "You'll be living in marital bliss with that sheikh, I'm sure."

"Marital bliss is not for the likes of me, or you," Anahita said. "Why else would Father allow us to have apartments outside the protection of the harem?"

Maram shot a pointed glance at her sister's remaining bodyguard. Either one of them would be quite the temptation to her father's wives, some of whom had not spent a night with their husband since their wedding night. Someone who hadn't grown up in a harem might think it a place full of secrets, and it was, but secrets were the currency of the place, and they flowed as freely as coins in the marketplace. For a politician like Maram who was known to have her father's ear, nothing stayed a secret for long.

"Fate is fickle. You don't know what she might have in store for either of us. Perhaps you will find a handsome prince of a husband who will outlive you. And I..." She might meet Aladdin again, a man of vastly changed fortunes, who could marry her the way he wished to.

"You might find some prince who doesn't know the difference between a virgin and a courtesan, a man so stupid he allows you to rule in his stead," Anahita finished for her with a smile. "I know you. You would never be content to be anything less than a queen. I think you like the power you have over men when you travel to foreign lands. There are tales of queens who rule like men, I am told."

Maram thought of Queen Margareta, a world-weary widow who was lonely without her husband. "There are a few such women, and their lives are not easy. I would not aim so high. But sometimes it would be pleasant to be loved."

Anahita laughed. "As opposed to just being desired? You speak of that thing all the crusader knights long for. What do they call it? Some sort of divine cup? Or is it a bowl?"

"The holy grail," Maram said. "And no one knows what it truly is. They speak of a story about a knight named Perceval, or Gawain…ah, I forget. It is a favourite among foreign courts. The object is a myth, no more."

"Ah, there is always some truth in old tales, even if it is hidden deep. There are men who love their wives above all else." Now Anahita looked wistful.

"Those men are not princes, or men with

power of any kind, then," Maram said gently.

Anahita grinned. "Not powerless at all. He must have the power to please you, surely?" She pumped her hips like a rutting man might, making them both blush.

"Enough about men. They are poor gamblers, for they never bet anything of value. I have new jewels and trinkets from my travels and I'm sure you have gifts from your latest husband that you haven't yet lost in a game of chance. What say you to dice, or a round of chess?"

"It has been a long time since I have played chess. I suspect you are after that necklace...or is it the jewelled dagger?" Anahita asked. "I must teach my men to play, so that I might stay in practice while I am with this new sheikh."

"Dice, then, for a fair match. You will like some of my new jewels, and I always did like that dagger." Maram clapped her hands, and one of her serving women fetched her dice box.

"Now you are home, we should go hunting.

I have a splendid new falcon, Merlin, who has a taste for frogs above all else." Anahita grinned as she selected a die made of green glass.

"Frogs? She sounds like a very strange bird. Has she never tasted a fat pigeon?" Maram asked, choosing a die of rose-coloured wood.

"Plenty, but if she hears a frog, she will abandon the hunt to dive for the frog. Why, I've seen her skim through the bathhouse, making all the harem girls scream." Anahita's smile turned wicked. "They screamed even louder when they saw the size of the frog Merlin had plucked from their bath."

Maram tucked her feet up under her and shivered. "I'm sure I would scream, too. I do not like frogs. Slimy creatures."

"I'm told the crusaders eat them as a delicacy at home," Anahita added. "Perhaps Merlin was a crusader's falcon."

Maram felt sick at the thought of a frog anywhere near her mouth. "Enough talk of your crazy bird. Before you cast the dice, what do you hazard?"

"What would you like best, the necklace or the dagger?"

"The dagger, for it will defend me better against frogs," Maram said.

Anahita pulled the jewelled dagger from a fold in her robes, its sheath glittering with more jewels than the blade itself. "The dagger it is, then, though I doubt you will ever use it. A blade is not your style, sister. You are far more subtle than that."

"When men have had too much to drink, subtlety is lost on them, and a woman has need of a dagger," Maram said.

Anahita nodded. "You should train with me and my men one day, so that you might better defend yourself, dagger or no. For the times when a guard is not close enough to call."

Anahita's eyes met Maram's in shared pain. Both had known the violence of men, and neither wished to be a victim again.

Maram broke the silence. "So you bet the dagger, sheath and fighting lessons with your men. I will counter with an amber comb, gifted to me by the king of Kasmirus."

"Just a comb? My dagger is worth more than that," Anahita scoffed.

Maram pulled the comb from her hair and laid it on the table. "Ah, but this comb is immune to dragonfire. A dragon roasted the princess wearing it, crisping her hair to ash before it ate her, but the comb is untouched."

Anahita's eyes widened. "Did you see the dragon?"

Maram flashed an enigmatic smile. "If you want to trade for tales of foreign lands, you must increase your bet."

And so the game began.

Six

Gwandoya led Aladdin out of the city, to where he had tethered a couple of camels. Aladdin glanced apprehensively at the large beasts with hooves as big as his head.

"Have you ever ridden a camel before, boy?" Gwandoya asked.

Aladdin shook his head, not trusting his voice. He might emit an unmanly squeak.

Gwandoya barked a command at the beasts, and they both knelt down on the sand. "Climb on here, and hang on here," Gwandoya said, pointing. He waited for Aladdin to obey before he nodded slowly. "Good." He climbed aboard his own animal, then barked another order that made the animals rise to their full height once more.

Aladdin grabbed for the hairy hump in front of him to stay on the beast. "Maybe we could walk instead?" he asked weakly.

Gwandoya laughed. "And how will we carry anything back, hmm? These camels can carry very heavy loads – more than you, I think, boy. And we will reach our destination faster with them, oh yes."

"Where is our destination?" Aladdin asked, but Gwandoya didn't seem to hear him. Instead he urged his camel into motion and Aladdin had to hang on for dear life. How could something so huge move so fast? Surely its teeth were rattling in its head, like Aladdin's own.

An eternity later, when Gwandoya slowed to a halt beside an oasis, Aladdin pried his cramped arms off the camel's hump. When the animal lowered itself to the ground, Aladdin slid off into the sand. He staggered toward the water. "Is this our destination?" he croaked.

"Of course not, silly boy. This is where we stop to drink," Gwandoya snapped, before hitching his smile back up. "Drink your fill, for we have far to go until nightfall."

Aladdin's heart sank. "On the camels?" He swallowed and nodded. "Of course, on the camels. As you said, we will get there faster."

Gwandoya eyed him. "You learn fast. Maybe you will do better than the others."

The others who had died, Aladdin thought before he could stop himself. He forced a smile. "So I will get so much gold the Sultan will give me two of his daughters as wives?"

Gwandoya seized Aladdin by the shoulders and shook him. "Not the gold. Don't touch the gold." He released Aladdin. "There are other kind of wealth, things far more valuable than gold."

Aladdin opened his mouth to ask what, but then he closed it again. Gwandoya had talked about Bugra having more gold than he could carry…and now Aladdin couldn't touch it? Did that mean gold had killed Bugra, or something else? Something that owned the gold, perhaps? Aladdin had heard tales of dragons, but he'd never seen one. He wasn't sure he wanted to, either. Not if it would be the last thing he saw.

Gwandoya took out a parcel of food and proceeded to eat his fill. Aladdin watched him with his belly growling, wishing he had the courage to ask for some from his new employer, but he didn't dare. What the man had unwrapped didn't look edible at all. If Aladdin wasn't mistaken, Gwandoya was happily crunching through a handful of large bugs. Aladdin might be hungry, but he wasn't that hungry.

"Didn't you bring food, boy? Here, have one," Gwandoya held out his hand.

A closer look only confirmed that they were indeed beetles and what looked like the most enormous crickets Aladdin had ever seen, mixed with salt and spices.

"I'm not hungry," Aladdin lied, waving the creatures away. "I am eager to start work." And finish riding this benighted camel, he thought but didn't say.

Gwandoya brightened. "Good. Then we shall go, arrive by sundown, yes?"

Aladdin swallowed. "Yes."

Seven

By the time Gwandoya called a halt again, Aladdin was ready to leap off the camel with the sincere wish never to ride one again. Whatever flesh he'd had on his backside had been bounced off by the crazy animal's gait between the oasis and what looked like a pile of boulders.

Aladdin would have no trouble when he tried to obey Gwandoya's order not to touch the gold, because who would leave anything of value in such a desolate place? There wasn't even any water here to justify stopping.

Gwandoya grinned, his teeth surprisingly white in the afternoon light. "We are here, yes?"

Aladdin wasn't sure how to answer, so he didn't bother.

Gwandoya led Aladdin to a rock that didn't appear any different to the others, then knelt beside an old fire pit. He took a leather flask from his belt and poured the contents over the half-charred timbers. Then Gwandoya pulled out a tinderbox and set about rekindling the fire.

Aladdin considered telling the man it was pointless to attempt such a thing with damp wood, but nothing this man did would surprise him any more, so Aladdin sat down on a nearby stone instead.

The fire flared to life faster than any Aladdin had seen before. The liquid must have been lamp oil, Aladdin realised. Gwandoya spread his arms wide and began to chant in a language Aladdin didn't recognise as he danced about the fire.

For a moment, Aladdin thought he saw wisps of smoke rising from the man's hands, but he shook his head. He must be imagining it. Except the smoke was thickening until he couldn't deny it was real. Sparks jumped between the smoke clouds, like nothing he'd ever seen before. And still Gwandoya chanted.

The man was a magician, Aladdin realised, dread clenching at his stomach. Aladdin had heard stories about dark magicians who used blood to cast spells. Was that why he needed Aladdin – to provide the blood in this unholy ritual? Is this how the other men had died?

The smoke cloud surrounding Gwandoya streamed toward the stone, taking the vague shape of a man, though a giant man. The smoky figure grabbed the stone and pushed it to the side, revealing the dark entrance to…what? The underworld?

Gwandoya didn't look surprised. He had done this many times, Aladdin guessed. But not enough to succeed in his dark purpose, which was why he needed Aladdin.

"We're going in there?" Aladdin asked.

"No, we are not."

Aladdin breathed a sigh of relief.

Gwandoya continued, "You are entering alone. You will journey through the underground city to the treasury. Touch nothing on the way. Once you reach the treasury, and this is very important, tuck your robes up around you so that not even the hem touches the gold in there, for if you touch it, you will surely die."

Like Bugra.

"You are looking for a lamp. An old, brass lamp that will appear out of place amid such treasure."

"So why is it there, then?" Aladdin asked before he could stop himself.

Gwandoya glared at him. "It has great personal value to me."

Aladdin didn't believe a word. He might be a street rat, but he'd been raised to be a merchant, who had to know the difference between truth and lies as much as he needed to be able to sort brass from gold. "So I find this old lamp of yours, and then what? Where's the wealth you said I'd find?" Aladdin asked.

Gwandoya lifted his chin proudly. "Bring the lamp to me, and I shall richly reward you."

Another lie. But Aladdin merely lowered his eyes and nodded.

Gwandoya pulled a ring from his finger and held it out. "You will need this. This magic ring will allow you to open doors in the city."

Aladdin took the ring gingerly. It seemed real enough, the blackened silver speaking of its great age. "Do I have to do the dancing and chanting thing like you did?"

"The inner doors are not as stubborn as the city gates. You will only need to command them to open, and they will."

No chanting, then.

"Do I get a torch?" Aladdin asked hopefully. The city gates really did look like the gates to the underworld.

"There are torches inside. They will allow you to reach the treasury," Gwandoya said. "Find the lamp, and it will light your way back to me."

The lamp that wasn't his, but Gwandoya

wanted so badly he was willing to kill as many men as it took to bring the thing to him. But not enough to venture into the city himself.

"Right. Here I go, then," Aladdin said with forced cheer.

Wishing he'd stayed in his own city, where he belonged, Aladdin stepped into the dark.

Eight

"Isn't she beautiful?" Anahita marvelled as her eyes followed the falcon's flight.

"I've never seen a bird fly so fast," Maram admitted. She didn't want to watch the bird make a kill – she didn't share her half-sister's thirst for blood – but she couldn't deny she envied the bird her freedom of flight. Maram might travel the world with her father's ambassadors, but right now, she would give anything to fly, to be able to see everything in the city. Every man, too, with the sharp eyes to recognise the one she wanted. So she might ask Aladdin why he avoided her.

Maram sighed deeply. The one man she wanted, who apparently had no desire for her. Fate was laughing at her, she was certain of it.

Anahita bumped her hip against Maram's as she took a seat on Maram's stone perch. "Where does he live, your bathhouse lover?" Anahita asked, peering out over the city. "Only Merlin has a better view of the city than we do from this ridge. Why, I can see the bathhouse. Is he waiting there for you now?"

Maram shook her head. "There is no one waiting for me. Not there, not anywhere."

"Men the world over pine for you, just as you are doing now. Perhaps this lover of yours is simply fate turning the tables on you," Anahita said. She let out a piercing whistle, summoning her falcon back.

The bird circled, swooped, then circled again, not seeming to want to land yet.

Maram didn't blame her. Why would she give up the freedom of flight when she hadn't found what she sought?

But she wasn't a bird. She was a princess, a daughter of the Sultan, who did not search the alleyways of the city for a man who appeared to be a street rat, yet had higher morals than any royal prince she'd ever known. She would send a servant in search of him, Maram decided. Aladdin wasn't that common a name – she'd never known another man called that – and he lived alone with his mother, she thought he'd said. If Aladdin avoided her, his mother could not. She would send the servant with an invitation for Aladdin's mother to present herself at the palace. Maram would share a meal with the woman and ask her why Aladdin had not returned. His mother would know – mothers always did. Her own mother…Maram shut that thought down before it could fully flower in her mind. Her own mother knew nothing of her life now – such was the fate of a treasonous former Sultana.

"Oh, you stupid bird! Not another frog!" Anahita cried in dismay as the bird dived into a well.

Maram couldn't suppress a smile. Evidently she wasn't the only one who loved what she shouldn't.

Nine

For the first time, Aladdin found Gwandoya had not lied. Inside the door sat a stack of torches. He seized one and carried it back to what remained of Gwandoya's fire. It was enough to light the torch, which was all Aladdin needed. He stepped back inside the cave and set off down the tunnel into the depths.

After several turns, Aladdin found himself at a crossroads of sorts, with two paths to choose from. Gwandoya and the doorway were out of sight, so there was no one he could ask for directions. Swearing, Aladdin peered down both tunnels, but neither dusty stone passage seemed more inviting than the other.

This cave ran deeper than he'd thought. Deep enough for a man to get lost in, maybe. Was that how Bugra had died? Aladdin moistened his suddenly dry mouth. Other men might have died here, but he would not. He backtracked to where he found another unlit torch in a bracket on the wall, and lit that, too, before he headed down the right hand passage. Any torch he saw, he lit, so he'd know he'd passed this way before.

Pretty soon, the warm light of all the torches behind him made Aladdin comfortable enough to start looking around him, at what wasn't a cave at all. The tunnels had been carved by tools, not nature, and he could see the marks of axes where they'd been opened out. Some tunnels came to dead ends that looked more like rooms where people had lived and worked. But where were the people?

They'd left tools and clothing behind, even bedding, but everything was covered in a thick layer of dust. As though the people who lived here had left in a hurry, intending to return, but they had not. What had driven them out, and what had prevented them from returning? Aladdin wasn't sure he wanted to know the answer to either question.

Especially not if the answer was somewhere in the city with him. Someone or something had killed Bugra, and Aladdin had no desire to be next.

He entered, then backed out of a prayer room. Perhaps he should take a moment and pray, he thought, then decided not to bother. Who knew which direction to face, anyway, so deep underground? No one would hear his prayer from here.

The next corridor ended in a dead end, blocked off by a boulder that looked like a smaller version of the one at the entrance. A door, Aladdin guessed, eyeing it. "Please open?" he suggested.

The round stone rolled smoothly aside,

revealing a new passage. Aladdin breathed a sigh of relief, and stepped through.

More passages, more rooms, more torches, and more doors that opened at his request. Aladdin knew he descended deeper into the earth at each step, but he'd seen no sign of treasure, lamps or otherwise.

If he wanted to hide a pile of untouchable gold in this maze of a city, where would he put it? Aladdin considered this for a moment, before he had his answer. He'd put it either in the very centre of the city, or in the furthest depths from the entrance. Whichever was easier to defend if the city were attacked.

Aladdin laughed, the sound echoing through the empty tunnels. What would he know about defending or attacking a city? He should be safely home in his. All he had to do was find the benighted lamp, hand it to the madman outside, and he could go home.

Deeper he went, taking the tunnels that led down until he could go no further, for his way was barred by a bigger door than any he'd seen yet. This was the one, he was certain of it.

"Open, please," he breathed.

The door rolled open. Aladdin took a deep breath and thrust his torch inside.

At first, it didn't look too different from the store rooms he'd passed, with dusty casks, boxes and sacks piled up on either side of a narrow aisle. But something glowed at the end, as though he'd arrived at the surface and not the depths of the city.

Aladdin crept forward, suddenly glad he was so thin, for a bigger man wouldn't have fitted so easily between the chests piled up to the ceiling. The hem of his tunic dragged along the top of a chest, revealing costly polished wood under the dust. This was the treasury, all right. What had Gwandoya told him to watch out for? Not to touch the gold, or let his clothing touch it. Pulling his tunic tight around him, Aladdin proceeded forward into…the light.

The second chamber didn't look any different from the first, at first, for whoever owned the contents of this place preferred to keep it safely locked in chests, instead of piled up all over the floor, as Aladdin might have expected. Someone with countless wealth would surely be careless with their coins. But the first glimpse he got of gold was in a chest that someone had pried open so roughly it no longer closed. Bugra would not have had the strength to do this – and nor did Aladdin. How many men had Gwandoya brought here? And why had they all failed?

Aladdin rounded the corner and found his answer. A lit lamp sat in an alcove on the wall, so blackened from use it was hard to tell it was brass. But the flame was as bright as ever, illuminating a chest full of riches that surely belonged to a king or a sultan. Gold jewellery snaked around a collection of gold lamps, so shiny they hurt his eyes. Aladdin squinted, and looked again. The chest was not full – it was barely half full, and some rings and a necklace lay on the ground in front of it, as if dropped by someone in a hurry to cram as much treasure as they could into a sack to take with them.

Automatically, Aladdin stooped to return the treasures to their chest.

"I thought you were brighter than the others," a strange voice said.

Aladdin jerked upright. "Who said that?"

A blue glow appeared on Aladdin's right, atop a barrel. The light grew until it took the shape of a man. A man who was as lanky as Aladdin himself, though his clothes were far finer than anything Aladdin owned. "That would be me," the bluish man drawled, snapping his fingers. The blue light vanished, leaving the magic man looking as normal as Aladdin, or as normal as any man who hadn't appeared from a ball of light.

"Who are you?"

The man bent double without rising from the barrel. "Kaveh, servant of the ring you wear on your finger." He nodded at Aladdin's hand. "And you?

"Aladdin." He didn't know what else to say. Unemployed street rat? Minion to the madman outside? Son of a spinner? His heart lurched at the thought of what would happen to his mother if he died here. It would break her heart. "I need to grab that lamp and get it out of here." He reached for the alcove.

Kaveh whistled. "So you are brighter than the others. You're the first one who went for the right lamp."

Aladdin's hand closed around it, a moment before he realised that a lit lamp would be hot to the touch. To his surprise, the metal was as cold as the stone underfoot. "Must be magic," he muttered.

"Sure is. Why do you think that madman wants it so much?"

Aladdin hefted the lamp in his hand. It was such a small thing – his mother had two such at home, both in much better state than this. "What does it do?"

Kaveh grinned. "Give it a rub and find out."

Aladdin almost obeyed, then stopped himself. Something had killed the other men Gwandoya had sent here. He'd survived this long, but who knew what Kaveh's motives were? Perhaps he'd killed them, or tricked them into doing something that had.

"No," Aladdin said. "I have a job to do. I must fetch this lamp from the city and bring it back to Gwandoya. Then I get paid." Not enough to let him see Maram again, though, Aladdin realised with a sinking heart. A man who ate bugs wouldn't have a princess's bride price to spare. Why hadn't Aladdin thought of that before?

"The only repayment he'll give you is a slit throat. He can't risk you telling anyone what you found in here," Kaveh said, as though reading Aladdin's thoughts.

Aladdin sank onto a chest, his head in his hands. "What will I do? I have to get home. I need that money." Funny, Gwandoya had never mentioned just how much Aladdin's payment would be. Now he knew why.

"In debt, are you?"

Aladdin shook his head. "Who would lend money to someone like me? Even I know I'll never be able to repay them. No, it's…there's this girl…"

Kaveh's eyes lit up with an unearthly glow. "A girl? Is she as glorious as the moon?"

Aladdin's mind cast up a vision of Maram bathing naked in the bathhouse. The image from his dreams. "The moon herself would weep to see her, she is so beautiful."

"So you want a gift to win her affections?"

Aladdin laughed. "I would need a whole kingdom before I had a chance of that. She's the Sultan's daughter, you see, and I am no prince."

Kaveh nodded thoughtfully. "So you need a gift fit for a princess. You know, I think I can help you."

Help never came for free. "What will you want in return?" Aladdin asked.

"Don't give the madman back his ring, and I'll show you the perfect thing to win your princess's heart, and her father's, too."

Aladdin stared at Kaveh for a moment. "What do you want me to do with the ring?"

Kaveh shrugged. "Keep it. I'd like to meet this princess of yours."

"She's not mine, and she never will be," Aladdin said steadily.

Kaveh grinned. "Never say never. Women fall in love with their heart's desire, not with whoever their father wants them to marry."

Aladdin didn't bother arguing this time. Judging by his clothes, Kaveh was highborn, maybe even as highborn as Maram herself. He had no idea what it was not to be able to remember when he'd last eaten – or wonder when he might eat again.

"We'd better get this lamp up to the surface. I said I would, and my word is all I have left." Aladdin rose.

"You're a fool," Kaveh said.

Aladdin knew he was right. "Perhaps, but an honest fool."

Kaveh shook his head. "I don't have to watch this." He dissolved into sparkling blue light, which streamed into the ring before the light winked out.

Aladdin peered at his hand. It looked like an ordinary silver ring, but he knew he hadn't imagined Kaveh.

Aladdin tucked the lamp inside his tunic, before tightening his sash to make sure it didn't fall out. He'd come too far to lose it now.

The hike back through the tunnels seemed a

lot shorter now. Maybe it was because he was headed for the surface, or he knew where he was going, Aladdin wasn't sure, but there was a spring in his step as he glimpsed the yawning entrance to the cavern he'd dreaded when he first saw it. How wrong he was.

"Do you have it?" Gwandoya asked eagerly, his shadow blocking the light coming from the entrance.

Aladdin dug into his tunic and produced the sorry-looking lamp. "Yes."

Gwandoya beckoned him closer. "Give it to me!"

He wasn't just eager, he seemed…rabid, Aladdin thought uneasily.

"Where is the payment you promised me?" Aladdin demanded.

Gwandoya wet his lips. "It is back in the city. I will pay you on our return."

Back went the lamp into the depths of his clothes. "Then I will keep it a while longer."

"I said give it to me!"

His instincts screamed at him to obey, but Aladdin ignored them. "And I said pay me."

The two men stared at one another, Gwandoya's chest heaving as though it cost him a great deal not to kill Aladdin on the spot.

All the more reason to hang onto the thing the madman wanted, Aladdin told himself.

Gwandoya forced out a smile that didn't touch his eyes. "As you wish, boy. But return my ring."

"Don't do it!" Kaveh's voice whispered.

The smile died. "What did you say?"

Aladdin swallowed. "Of...of course." With shaking hands, he pulled the ring from his finger. "Come and get it."

Gwandoya's eyes blazed. "I will not set foot in that cursed city! Anyone who steals from it is turned to – "

A great rush of wind came from behind Aladdin, so powerful that it pushed the boulder door shut, leaving Gwandoya outside. The man could be heard shouting and hammering outside, but the rock didn't move.

"What in heaven's name..." Aladdin began, risking a glance over his shoulder.

"I said not to give it to him," Kaveh said calmly, pressing his back to the boulder and folding his arms.

Realisation dawned. "You opened all the doors. Even that one. No man could move that stone. Not even Gwandoya, now you're in here with me. What are you?"

"I told you. I'm the servant of the ring," Kaveh said smugly. After a moment, he relented and added, "My previous owner charged me with protecting the city. Only one who wears my ring can open the door from the outside when it is closed, and no outsider may pass through the city gates with gold from the city that does not belong to him."

Dread curdled in Aladdin's belly. "What happened to the ones who tried?"

Kaveh waved his hand behind him. "They made a generous contribution to the city's wealth."

Aladdin approached what appeared to be a line of dusty statues. He lifted his torch and reached to brush the dust off the nearest one's face.

"By all that's holy!" Aladdin jumped back. Bugra's horrified face stared back at him, above a tunic that bulged with the treasures he'd tried to steal. Too heavy for him to carry, Aladdin realised, for they'd cursed him into a gold statue. He swallowed. "What have you done to him?"

Kaveh shrugged. "My master wanted me to just kill them, but who wanted decaying corpses stinking up the city gates? Especially if no one was home. So I thought gold statues might be better. When the prince returns, he can melt them down for the treasury."

"Will that hurt them?" Aladdin asked.

"Of course not. They're dead. Does a chicken feel when you roast its corpse?"

Unbidden, Aladdin's stomach growled even louder this time. "I would much prefer a chicken to a statue," he admitted.

Kaveh clapped his hands. "I can help you there. I know where the prince's store rooms are, where he keeps a lifetime supply of honeyed dates, among other delicacies."

Though he was now trapped in an

underground city with a strange man who glowed blue, while another madman hammered on the gates, for the first time since he'd left home, Aladdin began to feel the tiniest bit better about his future. Any future that held honeyed dates had to be good, he was sure of it.

Ten

"Your Highness, the woman is here," the maid said, bowing low. There was a slight emphasis on the word 'woman' that made it sound like an insult.

Maram set down her sewing, already inclined to be grateful to Aladdin's mother. She'd never much liked sewing, but she'd needed to do something with her hands to still her impatience. Now the search was over, she could stop. "Is she alone?"

"Yes, Princess."

Maram fought to hide her disappointment. "See that she is served refreshments while she waits. I will be there directly."

Maram chose her favourite gown, a jewelled thing that impressed even the richest kings, for this audience, and struggled not to tap her foot with impatience as her maids dressed her. Her reflection was quite dazzling to behold, Maram fancied, turning this way and that in front of her mirror. Too dazzling for a woman Aladdin had described as a simple spinner?

Of course it was.

She ordered her maids to bring her the plainest gown she owned. Maram should have known better. They brought her a gown of a purple so deep, it appeared black, with a matching veil. Tiny glass beads sewn onto it only helped complete the illusion, for they were invisible against the black. To the casual observer, she appeared to be in deep mourning, but once light hit the fabric, it glimmered like the starry sky over the desert. It was far from plain, but it would have to do.

When her maids had made sure the veil

covered all but her eyes, as befitted a princess at a public audience, Maram headed out of her apartment into the palace proper.

As she approached the room where she'd asked Aladdin's mother to be shown to, she heard raised voices. No, one raised voice – a wailing woman, rising over the softer male voices in the room.

Maram's heart constricted in her chest. Had something happened to Aladdin? No, surely not. She stepped into the room, unnoticed.

A woman in black rose up onto her knees, clutching the hem of a guard's tunic in her white-knuckled hands. "Please, tell me what you have done with my son. He's a good boy, he would not do anything to offend the Sultan. Take me instead!" She collapsed on the floor, sobbing, before she accosted the other guard with a similar plea.

Neither guard seemed to know what to do with the woman, and they both looked relieved to see Maram.

"You may go," Maram said, then surveyed the room. "Where are the refreshments I asked for? See that they are brought here immediately."

"Yes, Your Highness." The two men bowed and hurried out.

The woman threw herself full length on the floor before Maram. "Your Highness, please have mercy on a poor mother. Tell me why you have imprisoned my son."

"Aladdin is in prison?"

The woman let out a wail. "It is a mistake, a misunderstanding! My son would never do anything to offend the Sultan!"

Maram shook her head. "Mistress, please, get up. Tell me what has happened to Aladdin."

The woman rose to her knees, wiping her eyes with her veil. Hers was black, though so threadbare Maram could see through it. "I do not know. He left to find work, as he does every morning, but he did not return. No one has seen him. Then some guards came to my humble house and told me to come with them to answer questions about my son. Please, Your Highness, tell me what he has done!"

Maram beckoned one of the guards back into the room. He stood in the doorway, reluctant to enter any further. "Send a man to the prisons, to see if a man named Aladdin is held there, and if he is, find out what his crime may be."

The man bowed deeply. "I will, Your Highness, but we already checked there. There is no prisoner of that name anywhere in the city. The only Aladdin we could find is reputed to be this woman's son, so we brought her. As she said, the man has not been seen for days."

Maram nodded and dismissed him. "Mistress...please, can you tell me your name?"

"This humble mother is called Sadaf, Your Highness."

"Mistress Sadaf, please, sit with me." Maram gestured to the table where – finally! – the food and drink had been laid out. She gestured for one of the maids to shut the door behind her and Maram was alone with Aladdin's mother. Only then did she unwind her veil so that Aladdin's mother might see her face.

Sadaf crept timidly to the cushion Maram indicated, still not raising her eyes to Maram's face.

Maram settled on her own cushion. "Mistress Sadaf, I have invited you here to…" What could she say? She wanted to ask where Aladdin had been since that day in the bathhouse, but if she had no idea where he was… "I wish to ask about your son," Maram said finally. "Is it possible that he has left the city?"

Sadaf shook her head. "Aladdin has never stepped out of the city gates, Your Highness. He was born here, and he has never left. So when he did not come home, I thought…" She covered her mouth, but not fast enough to hold in a sob.

"We will find him," Maram said, though she had no idea how. If her father's men hadn't found him inside the city by now, it stood to reason that he was either not in the city or he was dead. No, surely not dead.

Sadaf burst into noisy tears. "Thank you, Your Highness. I do not know what we have done to earn such kindness, but if there is anything I can do to repay you, tell me, and it is yours."

"If he returns…when he returns," Maram corrected herself, "Send him to the palace to see me."

"Who should he ask for, Your Highness? If my son came to the palace, asking to see a princess, he would surely be turned away," Sadaf said.

She was right. No one would see Aladdin the way Maram did. "Tell him to ask for Princess Maram. No, he is to tell the guards that Princess Maram commanded him to present himself at the palace." They would believe that.

"As you command, Your Highness." Sadaf bowed low.

"No, I don't. I ask…" Maram stopped, lost. "Mistress Sadaf, please understand me. It is not a command. That is only what he must tell the guards. Tell Aladdin…tell Aladdin that I wish to see him, and if he wishes to see me, what to say to the guards." There, that sounded better.

Sadaf's knowing eyes were upon her, and Maram didn't know where to look.

"My son is as charming as his father. I do not know how you came to meet him, Your Highness, but if my son is in prison, then it is because he is accused of being a thief," Sadaf said.

"Aladdin is a thief?" She didn't want to believe it. If he was a thief, surely he would have stolen something from her in the bathhouse. He hadn't touched her jewels, her clothes…nothing.

Sadaf smiled faintly. "My son has never stolen anything in his life, or so I had thought, but a princess's heart is something so precious, so priceless, perhaps he could not resist." She bowed low once more. "I will do as you ask, Your Highness, if I am lucky enough to see my son alive again."

Without waiting to be dismissed, Sadaf backed out of the room, and left.

Maram couldn't seem to close her mouth. Were her feelings for Aladdin that obvious?

Surely she did not look as hopelessly enamoured of him as the royalty of the northern lands were of her. Surely not.

She shook the silly thought out of her head. What she looked like and what Sadaf thought didn't matter. Aladdin was missing, and if he'd been missing long enough for his mother to despair of his return…he must be found.

Eleven

Aladdin woke to find his head pounding, as though he'd drunk too much wine. As if he could afford to drink wine. "Where in heaven's name am I?" he asked the inky darkness.

"Tasnim, the forgotten city," a familiar voice replied, as a glimmering blue ball appeared and expanded to become a man. Kaveh.

"And why does it feel like a camel stomped on my head?"

"That would be the cask of Prince Firdaus' private reserve you drank." Kavek sounded amused. "It's powerful stuff, or it was a century ago, when he first bought it. Now it must be strong enough to kill an ox. I told you to drink sparingly, but you told me you were too thirsty."

Aladdin lurched to his feet. "Well, now I don't want wine. I want water. I'm sure I saw a well around here somewhere."

"You won't find any water in it. Why do you think all the people left? Without water, the city would die."

Kaveh began to tell a story about a ruling prince who vanished when the water did, and the fate of his people, but Aladdin shut him out and concentrated on looking for water. His mouth tasted like rats had nested in it and used his throat for a privy. He never wanted to drink wine again.

In the faint blue light from Kaveh following him, Aladdin came to one of the wells he remembered. A dusty bucket lay on the ground beside the well, so he hooked it up to the rope and lowered it into the depths, praying for the splash.

He'd almost lost hope when he heard it —
though the sound was faint and deep. Aladdin
let the bucket drop lower, then began hauling
it up again, hand over hand. It was heavier
than before, he was certain of it.

When the bucket rose into sight, the blue
reflection on the surface of the liquid of the
brimming pail was enough for him to let out a
hoarse cheer.

"I wouldn't drink that if I were you," Kaveh
said.

Aladdin ignored him again. He lifted the
bucket to his lips and only then did the stench
reach him. Aladdin coughed. "What is that? It
can't be water."

Kaveh grinned. "Well, it was once water.
Before some bastard pissed it out, maybe, and
threw it down the well before he left the city.
Where it's been festering ever since."

Aladdin gagged and tipped the bucket's
contents back where they'd come from. "Is
there no water in the city at all?"

Kaveh shook his head. "That's what I've
been trying to tell you. There's no water here.

The only liquid to drink in this city is wine."

Aladdin had drunk enough wine to last him a lifetime. "So where's the nearest source of water?"

"Half a day's ride, back the way we came."

Of course it was. The oasis where Gwandoya had first called a halt, Aladdin would wager.

"How long would it take to walk?"

Kaveh eyed him critically. "Forever. You wouldn't last the distance, not as starved as you are. You'd need to stay here for a month at least, emptying the royal larders, before you had sufficient strength."

"There isn't enough water here to last a month."

Kaveh brightened. "But there is more than enough wine, even after seeing the way you drink it. You'll need a flask or two for the journey, for it is at least a full night's march to the oasis."

"A month? My mother will go mad with worry over me. I must set out as soon as night falls."

Kaveh shook his head. "And I thought you were a bright one. You will not survive, you fool. And what of the treasure you wanted to take back to win your princess? Even if you had the strength to make it to the oasis before the sun rises, you would not be able to carry anything of value back with you. If you return home, it will be poorer than when you left."

The princess? Maram was the least of Aladdin's concerns now. But taking something home as payment seemed like a good idea. At least he'd have something to show for this foolishness. "What of the curse that prevents thieves leaving with their ill-gotten goods?" Aladdin asked suspiciously. "Are you trying to get me turned into a statue like the others, so that I can enrich the city, too?"

"I'll carry it out," Kaveh said. "The curse doesn't apply to me. Why, I could proclaim you as the new Prince of Tasnim, rightful owner of the city and all its riches, and no one would contradict me!"

"A prince?" Aladdin tried to sound sceptical, but the tantalising thought of walking into the

Sultan's palace, being announced as a prince, before asking for Maram's hand in marriage, was too strong to resist.

Kaveh smiled. "A fitting husband for a princess, if you carry a suitable gift for her and for her father."

For even just the chance of seeing Maram again, it was worth the risk. "A week, then. In seven days, when the sun sets, I will set out for the oasis."

"And while we wait, I shall show you all the secrets of Tasnim, and its treasures." Kaveh's grin broadened. "Treasures fit for a princess, as you shall see. What the prince kept in his harem was vastly superior to what he locked in his treasury."

"I thought you said everyone was gone. Do you mean to say the women are still here?" Aladdin asked, horrified. "We have to save them!"

"The prince's concubines were the first to leave, taking all their jewels with them. I am sure they are as far from the city as they can get." Kaveh's eyes glowed brighter. "No, it is what they did not take that I must show you."

Aladdin nodded. "Then let me find a flagon of wine, if there is nothing else to drink in this place, so that I may break my fast and drink to the vanished prince's health, before I steal his most precious treasures." This did not sit well with Aladdin, but what other choice did he have?

"As the Prince of Tasnim, you cannot steal your own things. They are yours, as is everything in the city. You shall see." Kaveh said. "I have proclaimed it, therefore it must be so!"

Aladdin sighed. He'd gone from one madman's clutches to another, and still he had none of the promised wealth either had lured him with. Oh, he still had the blackened lamp, tucked into his tunic, but what use was such a thing here? Still, this madman had the only light in the city, and he was the only man who could open the doors, so Aladdin followed him deeper into the labyrinth. It seemed the most sensible thing to do.

For the moment.

Twelve

Kaveh pushed open the city gates, then peered outside. "There's no one here," he reported. "Just like I told you."

Aladdin breathed out a sigh of relief. If Gwandoya wasn't waiting for him, then perhaps he would be able to make it home alive. He still had a desert to cross, a daunting thought even with Kaveh's help.

"Do you have the wineskins?" Aladdin asked. He would drink the contents tonight, and refill them with water when they reached the oasis. After he had drunk his fill of water for the first time in a week.

"I have the wineskins, and everything else you wanted. I may not be a particularly powerful djinn, but I do have some talents," Kaveh said with a sniff.

Talents such as carrying enormously heavy loads, or moving heavy things, Aladdin knew now. And to be visible or not, as he chose, along with whatever he was touching. A week with the man had given him a greater understanding of both Kaveh and the city of Tasnim. But there was still one question he hadn't answered…

"Why are you helping me again?" Aladdin asked.

"To see this princess of yours," Kaveh replied. "I told you that."

Aladdin sighed. Kaveh could keep his secrets. Aladdin had enough to worry about. "Let's go, then, or we will never reach the city where she lives."

The sun might have sunk behind the desert dunes, but the sand still held its heat, which bit at Aladdin's boots. Boots Kaveh had insisted he take from the prince's things, along with suitable clothing for braving the desert. So now Aladdin wore fabric finer than even Kaveh, and leather so soft he wanted to stroke it. So if he died in the desert, at least his corpse would be well-dressed, Aladdin consoled himself, then snorted. Small consolation for failure. He did not intend to fail. He intended to live, and return home to his mother, and maybe, just maybe, see Maram again.

It was hope that kept him trudging through the desert dunes until the sun rose high in the sky, following Kaveh's directions even as the heat shimmered off the sand and blinded him. Every valley seemed an oasis, but when he reached it, there was no water to be found.

It was nearly noon when Aladdin reached the oasis, and he threw himself face down in the water, gulping his fill. He would have drowned there, perhaps, if not for Kaveh, who dragged him into the shade formed by a stand of palm trees. Aladdin fell into an uneasy doze, which turned into sleep as the sun sank once more.

Kaveh woke him at dawn. "Time to move, or you will be roasted alive," he said.

Aladdin managed to make it to the makeshift shelter Kaveh had constructed while he slept. Fallen palm fronds and some coarse sacking made a bower out of the hastily dug hole in the ground, but Aladdin was nevertheless grateful for it. Kaveh produced some nuts – Aladdin didn't dare ask where from – and a filled water skin, then told Aladdin to rest.

Despite spending all night asleep, Aladdin had no trouble obeying the djinn. He'd never walked so far in his life, and as soon as night fell, he had the other half of his journey to finish. If he survived the day.

To Aladdin's surprise, Kaveh woke him at sunset, and he almost felt optimistic about his chances of reaching home.

The oasis was scarcely out of sight by the time Aladdin disabused himself of that notion. The blisters he'd barely noticed on the first day had swelled to carbuncles in his boots, and the sun had found him inside his little shelter while he slept, burning his skin as surely as boiling water would. Yet on he slogged, for Aladdin knew he was headed home.

One foot in front of the other, until he could go no further. Aladdin fell to his knees. "I can't," he wheezed.

"I'm not going to let you die out here, so some corpse robber can pick me up. Get up!" Kaveh slid an arm under Aladdin's shoulders and heaved him to his feet. "If I have to carry you the rest of the way, we're going to reach the city!"

So Aladdin staggered on, while Kaveh helped him, until Aladdin saw what looked like the city gates looming before him, lit with the fierce light of a desert dawn. "I'm home," Aladdin mumbled.

"Not yet you're not. Where do you live?" Kaveh asked grimly, his grip tightening around Aladdin.

Aladdin pointed and mumbled something he hoped made sense. He was moving again, so Kaveh must have understood some of it, at least.

"Do you recognise this place?" Kaveh asked impatiently.

Aladdin peered blearily at the worn door he'd opened and closed a thousand times. "Home."

"Good." Kaveh shoved the door open.

Aladdin staggered inside, then pitched forward into oblivion.

Kaveh cursed. "Hello, lady of the house! Is this your son?" he called.

A woman emerged from the dimness, hastily wrapping a veil around her hair. "I…Aladdin?"

Aladdin was beyond responding.

"I found him outside the city walls," Kaveh said. "He said he lived here."

"He does! Oh, how can I ever thank you? Or repay you?" the woman asked, falling to her knees beside Aladdin. "You have answered a mother's prayer."

Kaveh smiled. "Granting wishes, who'd have thought?" While Aladdin's mother was distracted, Kaveh disappeared. For the moment, his job was done.

Thirteen

"Have you heard anything?" Maram asked fretfully.

The guardsman shook his head. "No, Your Highness. I have told the prison guards to send word if they see a man with that name but no one has seen him. Are you sure he exists?"

"Of course he does! And so does his mother!" Maram snapped.

The guard bowed deeply. "My apologies, Princess, if I have offended you."

If this man knew half the things she'd seen and done in foreign courts, he would not worry about offending her. Maram hid her smile. "You are forgiven. I am...frustrated. I do not understand how a man can vanish in this city and not be found."

"Perhaps he is not in the city, Your Highness."

She'd thought the same thing, but Sadaf had insisted Aladdin never left the city. Sadaf...perhaps she should send for the woman again?

Maram considered for a moment, then shook her head. No, Sadaf had promised to send word if her son returned. If she had half the honour of her son, then she would notify the palace the instant Aladdin returned.

Unless he did not want to see her...

Maram swallowed. If Aladdin did not want to see her again, would Sadaf tell her? Or would she worry about offending a princess, too?

"If you have not heard anything by the end of the week, summon Sadaf the spinner to the palace," Maram said.

Another bow. "As you wish, Your Highness."

No, what she wished was to see Aladdin now, at this very moment, but Maram knew as well as anyone that wishes were seldom granted, and when they were, they would rarely be what one wants.

So she sighed and forced herself to find some distraction to keep her mind busy until she received the word she wanted, or the week ended. Whatever came first.

Fourteen

Aladdin was certain he had to be dreaming, for he distinctly heard his mother's voice, and his mother never left the city. Even if Berk had told her where her son had gone, there was no way she would venture out alone to search for him, and she did not have the money to hire men to help her.

So he took his time opening his eyes, for surely he had collapsed in the desert, and the sun above would be drinking the last drops of water from his body before it killed him. At least the last thing he heard would be his mother's voice and not Gwandoya's mad laughter. And dying of thirst was faster, kinder than a slow death by starvation. He almost felt like he was lying on a bed, instead of in the unforgiving sand. Still, the sand at the oasis had been soft…

But someone would find his body, and the ring, and Kaveh would be angry that some corpse robber had him. So Aladdin had to get up, and struggle on, or Kaveh would roll a boulder across him…

Aladdin forced his eyes open and sat up. His head hurt like he'd drunk too much wine again, but he'd grown used to that in Tasnim. He blinked away the blurriness, waiting to see either the desert or the rock walls of Tasnim. What he did not expect to see were the whitewashed walls of his mother's house.

"Maman?" he croaked. If this truly was her house, she must be here, for he'd heard her voice.

He heard something crash to the floor. "Aladdin?" A moment later, she emerged from the gloom.

"How did I get here?" he asked. "And do you have any water?"

"Of course!" She reached down and only now did Aladdin see the jug and cup on the floor beside him. She filled the cup and handed it to him.

Aladdin drained it, then refilled it himself and drank a second cup before his parched throat felt moistened enough to speak. "How did I get here?"

Maman shot a dark glance over her shoulder. "Your friend, Kaveh, carried you in here, half dead from exposure and thirst. He comes every day, bringing food and other things, but he refuses to take any money or thanks for it. And he disappears, like he has done again. It is as though he does not wish to be seen here."

Something tightened around Aladdin's finger, before the pressure eased as quickly as it had come. Kaveh's ring. He was not gone, the pressure reminded him.

"I will settle everything with him, Maman,"

Aladdin promised. "You don't need to worry about it."

"I do not trust him. Yes, he saved your life, but he has secrets that he does not say." His mother frowned.

"Let the man keep his secrets. He is allowed to them."

"We still must pay him. Did you bring any money back from whatever you were doing? I searched your clothes, but all I found was this thing." She held up the blackened lamp. "Perhaps we can get a coin or two for it. It is heavy brass. If I can polish it well, perhaps enough to pay him back a small amount..."

Before Aladdin could stop her, she spat on the lamp and began to rub at it furiously with a handful of her skirt.

Blue smoke erupted from the spout of the lamp, pouring out until it filled the room from floor to ceiling. Just like with the ring, the smoke took the form of a man, a man so enormous he had to bend double to fit in the room.

"I am the servant of the lamp," the smoky

man boomed. "What do you wish of me?"

Maman's eyes widened in terror, and she whimpered as she tried to back away from the djinn, for surely this was another of Kaveh's kind. Then she overbalanced, falling backward and striking her head against the wall.

"Maman! Are you all right?" Aladdin asked, rushing to check. The back of her head was bleeding from where it had hit the wall, but she still drew breath. He carried her to the bed, not sure what else to do.

"I said: what do you wish of me?"

Aladdin whirled to face the djinn. The lamp had fallen to the floor, so he picked it up. "You frightened my mother and now she is hurt. I wish you would fix the mess you have made."

"I cannot undo what has been done, but I can heal her," the djinn said.

Aladdin blinked in surprise. It took him a moment before he had the presence of mind to say, "Then do it."

He watched in fascination as the djinn bent over his mother, holding out his hands. Blue light arced from his hands to her, until her head was enveloped in a blue cloud. Then he waved his hand and the light died. "It is done," the djinn said. "When she wakes, it will be as though she was never injured. What else do you wish of me?"

Aladdin wet his lips. "Answers. What are you?"

"I am the servant of the lamp, and my master is whoever holds it in his hands."

"So you are a djinn?"

"Yes."

"You can perform magic? What sort of magic can you do?"

The djinn swelled to fill half the room. "I can make you the richest man alive. Transport you to the farthest reaches of the Earth and back again in the blink of an eye. Build you a palace so magnificent even the Sultan will beg to see inside."

Aladdin sucked in a breath. He wanted all of those things, but he knew nothing came without a cost. Before he wished for anything, he needed to talk to Kaveh. He knew Kaveh, whereas this djinn was a stranger.

"What would you wish me to do first, master?" the genie rumbled.

Aladdin thought for a moment. His belly rumbled, reminding him that it had been a long time since he'd eaten. Kaveh had provided him with food, and there had been no ill consequences from that. Finally, he said, "I am hungry. Bring me something to eat."

The djinn bowed low, then vanished.

"Show off," Kaveh muttered, emerging like a wraith from the ring. "Mister high and mighty, all powerful master of everything."

"Do you know him?"

Kaveh glared at the lamp. "I have seen him before, yes. Prince Philemon was master of the lamp for a time, before he disappeared, and he had no need for me when he had him. He handed me to one of his servants, who sold me to buy bread after he left the city. To the madman I'd rather not return to."

"Would you rather I'd asked you to fetch my food?"

Kaveh looked affronted. "You had no need

to ask him for anything. I gave you the contents of the royal larder! I still have some of it, too. If I can remember where I hid it. Must be here somewhere, the house isn't that big..." He wandered about the room, waving his arms as though he expected to touch something unseen. "Ah, here! You liked the prince's almonds, so I brought two barrels."

"I liked them because they were the only thing that didn't require cooking, or taste so sweet they made me terribly thirsty," Aladdin replied. He'd eaten so many almonds in the last week, he'd happily live the rest of his life without eating another.

"Oh," Kaveh seemed crestfallen, but not for long. "I brought the prince's garden, too. That will impress your princess, you'll see."

"The entire garden?" Aladdin had briefly wandered through what Kaveh had called the harem gardens, a large, high-ceilinged cavern filled with artificial trees made of metal and gemstones. Every jewelled leaf, flower and fruit had been lovingly crafted so each was unique, but under all the dust Aladdin had found it hard to be impressed. It had looked so forlorn, a world that had once glittered with magic but was now brown and dull with dust.

"Just the trees. Most of the shrubs. And all the flowers."

The entire garden, then.

"Where did you put it all?"

Kaveh opened his mouth. "Ah – "

A cloud of blue smoke exploded into the room, then parted to reveal a host of golden dishes bearing a banquet of more food than Aladdin had ever seen in his life. Things that could only have come from the palace kitchen, or one like it.

"Your meal, master," the huge djinn boomed.

Maman screwed up her face, moving restlessly in the bed as though she were about to wake. She would not be happy to see the giant djinn in the house still.

"Now, go hide in the lamp, or wherever it is you go, until I summon you again," Aladdin said.

The djinn set the dishes down and

disappeared.

Just in time, for Maman sat up. "What was that thing?"

"Nothing, Maman. I have food for us. What would you like to eat?"

Maman looked around in bewilderment. "Where did you get the money for so much food, or such dishes?"

Kaveh had disappeared again, leaving Aladdin to explain on his own. "I fear you would not believe me, Maman. It is a story for another time. But I did not steal them, and they belong to us now. Of that I am certain. Now, let us eat, and when we are done, perhaps we can sell the dishes to a goldsmith so we can buy you some new clothes."

Maman nodded. "Very well. We can talk after we have eaten."

For the first time in longer than he could remember, Aladdin sat down to a meal with his mother, where they both ate their fill. For once, he'd done something right.

Fifteen

"You wished to see me, Father?" Maram asked as she stepped into the Sultan's lavish apartments. She did not want to go on another diplomatic mission until she knew what had happened to Aladdin, but she could hardly refuse. "Which part of the world would you like me to conquer next?"

He laughed, for he knew as well as Maram did that she spoke only partly in jest. "No, I am happy to have you home, daughter, at least for now. It is your future I am thinking of, and all the conquests you have already made. You deserve a reward."

Maram clapped her hands. "Then you will build a bigger bathhouse on the palace grounds? I know just the place…"

Father shook his head. "No, we have all the bathhouses we need. And you will not be here to use it when it is built, so where would the point be in that?"

Maram's heart turned cold. "Where will I be, Father?" This news did not bode well.

He waved for her to sit down. Maram selected a fat cushion and took her seat.

"You know that my Vizier, Ali, has been a good and faithful adviser to me since I ascended to my father's throne. As deserving of reward as you, in fact," the Sultan began.

Maram nodded slowly. Yes, Ali was a good adviser to her father. He had an astute mind and while she did not always agree with him on international relations, she still respected his experience in matters of local politics. "He has had several wives, and many children by them. A new, young wife would be a burden to him,

I am sure."

"Indeed, and so he has told me. In fact, when I asked him what reward he would want from me in return for his loyal service, his thoughts were for his children."

Maram waited, her dread building. She had no intention of training some poor girl to be a courtesan. She might have chosen this path for herself, but she would not recommend it for anyone, and she would fight her father if he tried to force one of the Vizier's daughters to become her replacement.

"His oldest son, Hasan, who he hopes will succeed him as Vizier one day, has never married. Ali says it is because he wishes to have only one wife, the most perfect of all. It seems he has been madly in love with you since your first diplomatic mission together." Father smiled indulgently.

"Hasan can go fuck a camel, for I'll never let him touch me," Maram wanted to say, but those were not the right words to say to the Sultan. They weren't entirely true, either. She'd prefer the camel to do the fucking, forcing itself on Hasan as the man had tried to do to her.

"Hasan is not the husband I would have chosen," Maram said instead. It would be a good match for him, and also a politically astute one for her, as she and her children would never have a strong claim on the throne, so Hasan could not usurp the place of her father or, upon his death, one of her brothers.

"I had not thought to ask you to choose a husband yet, but Anahita tells me it is time," Father continued.

Maram's blood boiled. Why, that little sneak. Avenging herself on Maram for suggesting Anahita marry again. If Anahita hadn't already left the palace to seek her new husband, Maram would slap her silly. She still would, when she saw Anahita again, for the girl never stayed married for long.

Maram forced herself to swallow down her ire. She was a politician, she knew how to negotiate better than anyone. "Perhaps it is time for me to marry, before I am too old for motherhood. But I would not want to marry a man who is unworthy, or who could not provide for me and my children. I am comfortable here in the palace, Father, and I would not wish to live anywhere less comfortable. Before I consent to marry this man, I would like to see him build me a palace fit for a princess." With a bathhouse, she thought but did not say. Because when he failed to include a bathhouse that pleased her, she could delay further by insisting that it be built.

Father nodded thoughtfully. "Yes, you are right. He must have a house deserving of his bride. So we will announce your engagement tomorrow, as I had planned, but the wedding must wait until Hasan has provided a suitable place for you to live."

Maram allowed herself to breathe again. Construction was slow, so she would have time to locate Aladdin in that time. Perhaps even persuade him to change his mind about becoming her lover.

In the meantime, she had to find a way to stop this marriage to horrible Hasan. She should have shoved a knife in his guts when she'd had the chance, all those years ago, instead of holding it to his manhood and threatening to amputate his crown jewels if he did not leave her alone. Now…if all else failed, she would find an assassin to do the job for her.

Sixteen

"And so, that is where I have been. Exploring an underground city, getting left behind, and having to trek through the desert to get home," Aladdin finished. He'd managed to tell his mother the truth without mentioning djinn once.

"A truly alarming tale, my son. But what does this have to do with the princess?" Maman asked gravely.

Aladdin choked on his water, briefly becoming a fountain before his coughing fit eased. "What princess?"

"Her Highness Princess Maram, who summoned me to the palace to give you a message," Maman said.

"What message?" he asked faintly.

Maman scrutinised his face. "You do not seem surprised that one of the Sultan's daughters would summon me, or leave a message for you."

Now he'd done it. "I met her once in the marketplace. She was very gracious."

"What was a princess doing in the bazaar?"

He could answer this without incriminating himself too much. "She had just returned from a long journey abroad, and she was on her way to the bathhouse."

"Princesses do not..." Maman's eyes widened. "Most princesses do not. Only one does. The Traitor Queen's daughter, the witch the Sultan sends abroad to enchant foreign princes." Maman shook her head. "No wonder she is so beautiful and yet unmarried. What man would want a wife who has known more men than she can count – and foreigners, at that? Unwashed, uncouth, unmannered, with no idea of proper behaviour...and they eat the strangest things!"

No stranger than Gwandoya, though he was a foreigner, too, from southern lands instead of those in the north from whence the crusaders came. But Aladdin didn't want to think about the madman. His thoughts were of Maram, and his mother's slight to the lovely woman.

"What man would deserve her," he corrected. "Beautiful, enchanting, gracious, and the Sultan's daughter. Every man desires her, whether she wills it or no. But it is her father who will not allow her to marry. She is too valuable as an envoy to ever be free."

"Careful, my son. It sounds like you are under her spell, too. If she is forbidden to marry as you say, then you risk heartbreak even thinking about her. Forget her."

Aladdin shook his head. "I cannot. And if she gave you a message for me, then she has not forgotten me, either. Maman, please tell me...what did Princess Maram say?"

She sighed. "She wanted me to tell you to present yourself at the palace, saying she commanded you to do so. But I fear that if you do, it will only result in your doom. If you are lucky, the palace guards will turn you away. If you are not lucky…it is only a matter of time before the princess tires of you, and she will have you killed or imprisoned without hesitation. Please, I beg you, do not do as she asks."

Aladdin nodded slowly. "You are wiser than you know, Maman. The palace guards will never admit a street rat into the Sultan's palace. But you have been allowed in. You have dined with the princess herself. You must go to the palace, and present a gift to the Sultan for me. If he likes my gift, then you will ask the Sultan to summon me, so that I might beg for the hand of his daughter."

"No, I cannot. The Sultan will not see me…and what gift can you possibly offer that he will accept?"

Aladdin held out a cloth-shrouded bundle, peeling the layers away to reveal the treasure beneath. A small, jewelled shrub, perhaps two handspans in diameter, glittered in the lamplight. Each berry was made up of a cluster of amethysts so dark they almost seemed black, a stark contrast to the mother-of-pearl petalled blossoms. Together with the green agate leaves, the whole thing weighed far more than a shrub should, but Aladdin thought his mother could manage it. "Give this to the Sultan as my gift, and tell him that if he allows me to make Princess Maram my bride, I will give him a whole garden of trees and bushes such as this."

"I will take it to the Sultan, and we shall see what he says," she said doubtfully. "As long as you are sure this is what you want."

Aladdin laughed. "Maman, I have never been so sure of anything. This will work. I am certain of it."

Seventeen

Father had assembled what looked like his entire court, Maram reflected as she surveyed the crowded audience chamber. Ali the Vizier and horrible Hasan stood triumphantly on the dais at what would be her father's right hand, which was why she stood as far to the left as she could. But she wasn't hiding – even if she could in such a garish dress. The rose coloured gown and matching veil were richly embroidered in silver and gold. A diamond necklace matched the jewelled fillet that held her veil in place. Despite their magnificence, her diamonds were a calculated insult. She'd inherited them from her mother and they were well known, for the former Sultana had worn them to court as often as she attended.

Maram felt Hasan's eyes on her as her father's herald announced the Sultan's arrival.

Her father had a smile for her that she happily returned. Never mind that he wanted her to marry the wrong man – he had her happiness in mind, however misplaced his plans for it might be. No matter. Maram would make plans of her own.

The Sultan reached the dais and commanded the court to rise. This took a moment, as many had prostrated themselves and clothing had to be straightened. When the susurrus of silk-smoothing had died down, Father cleared his throat. "My subjects, before I hear today's petitions, I have happy news to share with you. My daughter, Princess Maram, is engaged to marry Vizier Ali's son, Hasan. The wedding will take place once Hasan has finished building a palace suitable to house my favourite daughter."

Hasan's grin died as he stared at the Sultan in horror. Ah, Father had not warned him earlier, it seemed. Maram made no effort to hide her triumphant smile as she surveyed the cheering crowd. A royal wedding meant a feast, and an excuse to show off their finery, with perhaps the opportunity to win favours from the celebrating Sultan or the newlyweds.

Only one pair of eyes appeared as shocked as Hasan's — that of Aladdin's mother, Sadaf. She stood at the back of the crowd, barely visible behind the more pushy petitioners, but she met Maram's gaze as squarely as though the two women were equals, so great was her shock.

When the cheering died down, Maram excused herself and made her way through the crowd to where she'd seen Sadaf. She needed to speak to the woman, to ask if her son had returned.

Yet when she reached the back of the audience chamber, Sadaf was nowhere in sight. Maram hurried outside, hoping to catch the woman before she left.

"You arrogant bitch. When you are my wife, I will see that you learn your place," a voice behind her snarled.

Ah, Hasan. He'd followed her out here.

"If I become your wife. You forget you have a palace to build first," Maram returned. There were a dozen guardsmen within hearing distance – if Hasan so much as touched her, they would arrest him in an instant at her command. But if she married him…he'd probably try to beat her to death. Try, and succeed.

"I'll build a brothel for the likes of you. That should be good enough for the whore to foreign pigs."

More than ever, Maram regretted letting this man live. Not for long. She'd find an assassin before sunset.

Maram smiled sweetly. "Build as many brothels as you wish. I'm sure you will need all the money you can muster to build a palace that meets my expectations. Oh, did my father not tell you? When he said you must build a palace fit for a princess, it is this very princess who will judge its quality. My place will be a palace as befits my high station. Whether it is my father's palace or yours will be up to you." She scanned the square, but it seemed that Sadaf had disappeared.

Cursing Hasan for distracting her, she headed back to her apartments. Her only consolation was that she left him cursing just as colourfully behind her.

Eighteen

Aladdin didn't bother to greet his mother when she returned. "What did the Sultan say?" he asked eagerly.

Maman set her cloth-wrapped bundle down. "The Sultan said the princess is to marry the Vizier's son, and he is building a magnificent palace for her. You are too late, my son. I told you she would only bring hurt and heartbreak."

A magnificent palace…where had Aladdin heard those words before? Not from his mother, surely.

It wasn't until he sat down to the noon meal with his mother, the remains of the royal repast the djinn had brought for them the previous night, that he remembered it was the djinn who'd mentioned palaces. And how he could build them.

"Maman, I need you to go back to court, and speak to the Sultan."

She stared at him. "Did you not hear what I said? She is marrying someone else, as soon as the palace is finished! Did you lose your wits out in the desert, and bring back madness in its place?"

Aladdin laughed. He did feel a little giddy, but only because he could feel happiness in his grasp. Maram had a chance at freedom — marriage to the Vizier's son would grant her that. All she needed was a suitable palace — a palace he now had the power to provide, thanks to Gwandoya. "No, Maman. I brought something far more valuable with me. Do you recall the lamp you tried to clean last night? It is no ordinary lamp. It contains a djinn."

She shuddered. "Djinn are unholy creatures, traitorous magicians who deserved to die for their crimes, but the sultan they pretended to serve was merciful and let them live on in slavery instead. If that lamp contains a djinn, you had better throw it into a deep well, where it can no longer harm you. I shall do it myself." She rose and looked about her.

Aladdin was doubly glad he'd hidden the lamp. "No, Maman. I shall deal with the lamp. I need you to speak to the Sultan. Do you still have the gift?"

Maman waved irritably at the bundle. "I wish I did not, for it is a cumbersome thing."

"Give it to the Sultan, as I asked you to this morning. Beg him to grant me a private audience tomorrow morning, when I will bring another gift, more sizeable than the first." Silently, he prayed that the djinn had not lied about his abilities. If he had, then at least Aladdin would have the garden. That was something, at least.

Maman pushed her dish away. "I am no longer hungry. I will go now, for the sooner we put an end to this folly, the better. I ask only one thing. If the Sultan refuses to see you, will you forget about the princess, and pursue more sensible things? There are plenty of merchants' daughters in the city who would happily agree to marry a handsome boy like you. I would like grandchildren."

No merchant's daughter would spare him a second glance, Aladdin knew, and nor should any princess, either. If the Sultan did grant him an audience, Aladdin would need to dress like he belonged in the palace. More to ask for. He hoped it would not be too much.

His mother departed for the palace, grumbling as long as she was in sight.

Aladdin slipped back into the house and shut the door. "Kaveh, is my mother correct? Are all djinn evil?"

Kaveh burst from the ring in a flash of blinding blue light. "What have I ever done to you that you call me evil?" he demanded.

Aladdin cast his mind back, trying to recall his mother's exact words. "Maybe not evil. Just traitorous. Are you a traitor?"

Kaveh's dark eyes burned. "There was once a sultan who called me that. Now he was evil, in the worst sense of the word. Half the kingdom wanted him dead, me included. I led the rebellion that brought the palace down on his head, crushing him beneath the stone. His successor, a man who had fanned the flames of our rebellion to white-hot heat, only to reap more benefits from it than anyone else, was my judge. He could not risk another rebellion, he said, so all traitors must be punished. Many of my men were executed, and my family had perished at the old sultan's hands, so I stood alone, the last of all of them. I expected death, but he saw fit to grant me life. A lifetime of servitude, as a servant to the ring, a punishment reserved for magic-wielders who betray their rulers. I believe he meant it as a gift to me, but a warning to everyone else that he would not tolerate treachery, for I had pledged my loyalty to the Sultan before him."

"Who or what do you serve?"

Kaveh let out a weary sigh. "I am the servant of the ring you wear, remember? As long as you wear it, I serve you."

"At what cost to me?"

A new respect dawned in Kaveh's eyes. "You must wear it always, for I will pass to the ring's new owner should you lose it. But other than that…no, I bear the cost of my servitude. The spells I cast come from the magic in my blood, blood I am bound to shed in your service and anyone else who wears the ring."

"What about the djinn of the lamp?"

Kaveh shrugged. "He is bound as I am. If you wish to know his crimes, you must ask him, for I do not know. Both of us are bound to use our magic to serve our masters, and perform whatever magic they wish of us, if we can."

"What can you do?"

"I can move things with magic, or make things unseen. I could carry you through the desert, if you commanded it, or make you invisible, but if you were to ask me to enchant this princess so that she falls deeply in love with you, that is something I cannot do. I have no aptitude for seduction magic."

"And the other djinn?"

Kaveh glared at something over Aladdin's shoulder. "Why don't you ask him? He's been listening to every word we say, but only now does he make an appearance. You should probably consider yourself honoured, for his previous master had to polish his lamp before he'd deign to help him, and even then, his gifts were tainted."

Aladdin turned, and found the second djinn standing behind him. He still towered over them both, but he evidently didn't feel the need to be as impressive as he had yesterday. Did Aladdin imagine it, or was there some sadness behind the djinn's otherwise impassive expression?

"Servant of the lamp, you said you can build me a palace. In the blink of an eye, you said. Is it true?" Aladdin demanded.

"I did not. A palace I can build, but it will take at least a night to truly be worthy of being called a palace."

Aladdin nodded. "Then I wish you to build a palace beside the one where the Sultan resides, yet more magnificent than the Sultan's. It must have…it must have…" He struggled to think of anything he knew a palace should have. He'd never been inside one before. "A bathhouse befitting a princess. Like the ancient one near the city gates. So that Princess Maram may bathe whenever she wishes without having to leave home."

The djinn's eyes widened. "The palace is not for you?"

"I wish that it could be, but no. This palace will be my gift to Princess Maram, to celebrate her marriage."

The djinn bowed low. "It shall be done, master. By dawn, you shall have your palace." He vanished.

"If I didn't know better, I'd say the man is half in love with your princess, too," Kaveh said. "He had a strange look in his eye. I wouldn't trust him if I were you."

"Says one traitor of another," Aladdin returned. Too hastily, perhaps, for he agreed with Kaveh. The nameless djinn had many secrets he had not yet shared to be trusted fully yet, if ever.

Kaveh bowed his head. "I betrayed an evil man, and I do not regret it. I would do it again. But I have served many sultans and princes since, and I have never been tempted to turn traitor again. Sometimes a man must break his own vows to do what is honourable. But the servant of the lamp…I do not know his crime, or who he betrayed. Some traitors dishonour their liege with every breath."

Aladdin nodded. Sage words from a man who by the sound of things had lived far longer than a normal man. Tomorrow, he would have his answer. But in the meantime…

"Can you make sure the palace includes a place for your garden? I would like to see it in all its glory, laid out for the princess."

Kaveh bowed and attempted to imitate the other djinn's tone: "It shall be done, master." He laughed. "Those jewels never looked right underground. By the time I am done, your garden shall sparkle in the sun like the treasure it is. You deserve it, and this princess, too."

Aladdin wanted to believe him, but he didn't dare. Not yet.

Nineteen

"The Sultan, Your Highness," a maid announced.

Maram dropped her embroidery and rose to her feet. "Father. What an unexpected surprise."

He smiled. "I have something that will surprise even you, I think, for I find it so unbelievable I must show you to be certain I have not imagined it all." He pulled off his jewelled turban and scratched his head, a sure sign that this was no official visit.

Maram ordered refreshments and settled her father in the place of honour before taking her place across from him. "I feel like a child, waiting for a bedtime story," she admitted. "Will you tell your tale, Father?"

He sipped from his cup, then set it down. "I hardly know where to begin. After you left this morning, I held my usual audience. The petitions were so dull I found myself falling into a doze. If it weren't for Ali at my side, I suspect I might have snored. But he is a loyal vizier who would never let me do such a thing. An hour ago, I decided I wanted to retire, and opened my mouth to say so. Yet as I raised my eyes, they met the gaze of a woman who refused to look away. I fancied those dark eyes seemed to accuse me of something, though I knew not what. Instead of signalling an end to the audience, I told Ali I would see one last petitioner – her.

"When the guards brought her forward, at first, I thought they were mistaken. She threw herself face down before the dais, barely daring to say a word for some time. Long enough for me to see she wore mourning black, but both her veil and gown were so well-worn it had faded to grey. Cheap stuff, too, like she was one of the poorest in the city. What could one such as her wish to accuse me of? Curiosity baited me, so I commanded her to speak."

Father drained his cup and indicated he wanted it refilled.

"She raised herself onto her knees, and I found myself staring into those same eyes, but perhaps I had imagined the accusation I thought I'd seen before. Instead, now she seemed resigned. She laid a bundle at my feet and begged me to accept her son's gift."

Father waved a servant forward. The gift, if indeed that was what she carried, filled her arms, and she seemed relieved to set it down beside Maram.

"Is this it?" Maram asked, her hand hovering over the coarse cloth wrapping the item.

Father nodded.

Maram twitched back a corner of the cloth, then gasped in surprise. She peeled away the wrappings until she had revealed the whole thing, though she didn't dare touch it. To touch it would be to spoil its magnificence.

The jewelled thing looked like a blackberry bush from the cold climates far to the north, with ripe fruit begging to be picked and flowers promising more for tomorrow. And so lifelike – whoever had crafted this knew the real thing. Why, she could almost taste the delicious sweetness on her tongue, a delight she had not known for far too long. She reached out to touch a berry, the reassuringly cold jewel reminding her that this cunning creation was not real.

"Who made this?"

"I do not know, for she did not say. All she said was that it was a gift from her son."

Maram's eyes met her father's. "Who is her son, who can afford to part with such a priceless gift? And why does his mother wear cheap widow's weeds when he has the coin for such magnificence?"

"I will find out on the morrow, for I have invited the man to a private audience with me."

Maram blew out her breath in a rush. Disappointment clouded her face. "Is that all you have to tell me?"

Father laughed. "Indeed it is. Like the audiences of the legendary storytellers of old, you must wait another day to find out what happens next." He rose to depart.

"Wait, Father, you forgot your shrub." She cradled the treasure in her arms, and offered it up to him.

He smiled. "You keep it. I see in your eyes you appreciate its beauty truly, like your mother would have. Consider it a wedding gift, for something tells me it should be."

He left, but Maram scarcely noticed, so busy was she in examining her new work of art. For that's what it was. A precious thing — why would anyone part with it, unless they needed to sell it to live?

What kind of man gave such a gift?

She wished she'd thought to ask her father to be present at tomorrow's audience, so that she might see the man for herself. But Father would have asked her to be there if he'd wanted her presence. He valued her opinion, and if he meant to keep this man at his court, she would meet him soon enough.

And when she did, Maram resolved to ask him who his jeweller was, so that she might give the jeweller's name to Hasan and insist he create a garden of such things in her palace. One such shrub would bankrupt him for sure.

Best not to have Hasan assassinated yet, then. First he had to build her a ruinously expensive palace. With emphasis on the ruin.

Twenty

"Master, your palace is complete," Aladdin heard the djinn say.

He wrenched his eyes open and wished he hadn't. The predawn light told him it was far too early an hour for anyone to be about. But he remembered Kaveh's warning, so he rose and dressed. "Show it to me, then," he said.

The djinn waved his arm and a portal opened up in the east wall through which he could see the darkness of some other place entirely, instead of the rising sun he knew would be hitting that wall. The djinn bowed. "After you, master."

Reluctantly, Aladdin stepped through the wall, from his mother's tiny house to a cool, spacious hall. Oh, this was exactly the sort of place where Maram belonged. Mosaic tiles stretched up the walls and across the ceiling, mirroring the night sky over the desert. Even the tiles underfoot were the exact colour of the desert sands.

The djinn said nothing as Aladdin crept from room to room, unable to keep himself from staring. Having never seen the Sultan's palace, he hoped this would be good enough. It was certainly better than anything he'd seen in the prince's apartments in Tasnim. The bathhouse was an exact replica of the one where he'd first met Maram, including the towel storage alcove where he'd hidden. The djinn had not forgotten towels, either – the soft cloths were piled high, waiting for their royal mistress.

Aladdin took a deep breath, and lost himself in memories of that day. He'd spent one perfect day with her, and it would have to be enough. She would live here with her new husband, and be so happy she never thought of Aladdin again.

"You must see your audience chamber, master," the djinn said.

Aladdin opened his mouth to say that no part of this palace was his, but there would be time for that later. Instead, he followed the djinn up a curving flight of stairs to the level above.

The djinn had timed his entrance perfectly. As Aladdin stepped out of the archway into the hall, the morning sun hit the windows in a blaze of magnificence. For unlike the other windows in the city, these were closed in panes of glass and translucent gemstones. A veritable rainbow of colours cascaded down the walls to the floor, before dancing up to the ceiling from cleverly placed mosaic tiles that reflected light everywhere. A room designed to dazzle, which indeed it did.

Aladdin lifted a hand to his eyes, lest he be blinded by so much brightness. "Now show me the garden."

"Allow me," Kaveh said, leading Aladdin down the stairs again and into a courtyard in the heart of the palace. At first glance, he'd created what appeared to be a real garden, but when the morning sun touched the trees, it shattered that illusion into a thousand beams of light. Each berry and flower seemed to take on its own glow, glittering in harmony with each leaf and trunk, but it was nowhere near as blinding as the audience hall above. This place held a welcoming glow, inviting him to linger a little longer. Oh, if only he could, but this place was not for the likes of him. It would house Maram and her new husband.

"It's perfect," Aladdin said, and was surprised to see both djinn swell with pride at the compliment. "I have another request. Is there any way I can see Maram's betrothed?" Seeing the man who had won the heart of the lovely princess would remind Aladdin why he would never be good enough for her, or this palace.

"I shall bring him here directly," the djinn

said, opening a hole in the wall.

"No! I don't want him to know I'm there. I want to see him in his home, where I imagine he'd be asleep now," Aladdin clarified.

Kaveh bowed. "I'd be honoured to help you. Invisibility is my speciality."

Leaving the other djinn behind with his handiwork, Kaveh and Aladdin made their way through the near-empty streets to the Vizier's house, where the princess's soon-to-be husband lived. They entered the house and dodged between servants readying the house for the day. No one spared them a glance, buoying Aladdin's hopes that Kaveh had made them truly invisible.

"The best bedchamber is this way," Kaveh said softly, leading Aladdin upstairs. "Don't worry, they can't hear us."

"How do you know where it is? Have you been here before?" Aladdin asked.

"This house has belonged to a long line of viziers. The man in office may change but the house does not."

One day, Aladdin would ask Kaveh how old

he was. Today was not that day, though, as he fought to catch his breath while they hurried up the stairs.

Aladdin heard quiet sobbing, then a smack of flesh on flesh followed by a pained cry, like a child being spanked. Curiosity made him follow the sound into a grand bedchamber, but the scene he found made him wish he hadn't.

A semi-naked slave girl, judging by what remained of her torn clothes, squirmed under a naked man who evidently took great pleasure in her tears and cries of pain as he bedded her. He clenched his fingers around her breast, squeezing until she let out a little scream, then backhanded her across the face, adding what would be another bruise to match her two blooming black eyes.

"You like that, don't you, slut of a sultan's daughter? Answer me!" the man demanded. He hit her again, twice, eliciting more cries of pain. "Answer me!"

Finally, the weeping girl whimpered, "Yes, master. Your touch honours me."

"Louder!" he insisted, slapping her face

again.

Her voice rose to a shriek as she repeated the words, over and over, at his command, each sentence punctuated by another blow from the brute.

Aladdin wanted to help the girl, but what could he do? He was half the man's size, and there were dozens of servants who would come to his assistance. Why weren't they coming to help the girl? For surely they could hear her…

He stuck his head out of the open doorway. Sure enough, a steady stream of servants filed past, intent on their tasks for the day.

The girl screamed, and Aladdin saw a serving girl flinch. She stumbled, then caught herself and continued past, hugging her arms to her chest. Arms bruised almost black in places, Aladdin noticed, matching her own fading black eyes.

All the female servants bore the marks of this monster, he realised. All were young and pretty, or would be if not for the bruises. No older women worked here.

"Is that the Vizier?" Aladdin asked. Even as the words left his lips, he knew they could not be true. The brute had not looked old enough to be the father of an adult son, old enough to marry Maram. Dread curled a cold tendril around his heart.

"No, that is his son, Hasan, who will soon marry the princess," Kaveh said sadly.

Aladdin swore. "Not while I live, he won't. If he lays so much as a finger on her perfect skin, I will kill him myself."

How did a humble spinner's son stop the daughter of the Sultan from marrying whoever she wished? The Sultan would not listen to him. Perhaps if he was the Vizier's equal, or a prince…

A bubble of inspiration burst in Aladdin's head, brighter than dawn in his own audience chamber. For it would be.

"Kaveh, go to the alley behind the entrance to the marketplace. There you will find a number of men waiting to be offered work. Labourers, all of them. Tell them you come from me, and you will pay them a week's wages if they meet me at the gates of the city an hour before my audience with the Sultan."

"What will you be doing?"

"Persuading the servant of the lamp to make me look like the richest prince in the world. One who deserves not only that palace, but the princess, too."

Kaveh grinned. "That's the spirit. I still haven't seen this princess of yours yet."

Twenty-One

"Leave me," Maram commanded her attendants, and they did, leaving her alone in the bathhouse.

Except…she wasn't really alone.

"You may approach," she said softly.

A dark-clad figure melted out of the shadows. "I was informed you might have a job for me."

Maram turned a seductive smile on the hooded man. She did not need to see his face as long as he could see hers. "There is no might about it. If you are indeed the best assassin in the city, then I have a job for you."

"There is no assassin better than me," the man said.

Maram knew it was a lie, but this man probably did not. The best assassin she knew was out of the city, with no definite return date, so second best must do.

"Then tell me. If someone paid you to assassinate the Sultan, how would you do it?" she asked.

The man shook his head. "I would not take that job."

"What about the Vizier?"

"He is an old man. Old men are prone to clumsiness. If old age does not carry him off, perhaps he might stumble down some stairs, or trip and hit his head."

The stories Maram had heard about this man were true. He was clever enough to make cold-blooded murder appear like an accident.

"And what about the Vizier's son?"

"He is young and strong, but death lurks in the most unlikely places. One of his servants might slip poison into his wine, for it is well known that he is a hard master."

"What if someone asked you to kill a princess?"

"You toy with me, Your Highness. I could kill you now where you stand, for you carry no weapon. By the time your servants came to your assistance, you would be dead." He bowed his head. "But an assassin with my skills has the freedom to choose which jobs he takes. And I would not wish to rob the world of your beauty, so you are safe from me. I do not kill women."

She had heard this, too.

"What poison would Hasan's servants choose, I wonder?" she said.

The assassin produced a small pouch. "A little will send him to sleep, but enough will make sure he does not wake up."

Maram nodded, satisfied. "Then I will pay you for it now, and on the night before my wedding, I ask you to meet me here once more, to complete the job." She held out a jingling purse.

He exchanged his pouch for the purse, then paused to count his coins. "This is more than my usual fee."

"You will receive the same again when your job is complete."

He bowed deeply. "As Your Highness commands." He melted into the shadows once more.

When she was certain he'd gone, Maram peeped into the pouch. She almost laughed. He'd given her opium, a drug she'd used more often than any other. A waste of good coin, but never mind. She had no doubt Hasan used the stuff, too, so it would be no surprise if anyone found the pouch in his house. Or in hers.

She left the bathhouse deep in thought, only to find her guards on the steps outside, holding back a crowd.

"What's going on?" Maram asked, craning her neck to see past her men.

"There's some sort of procession in the street. Everyone's lined up to see some prince come to visit your father."

She wasn't sure which of her men had spoken, for they were too intent on the street below to turn when they spoke to her. Gross disrespect she could have the man killed for, she knew, but Maram understood men better than most. Curiosity was a powerful thing, and she had no desire to inspire enmity in her father's guards. If she killed Hasan, she would need them to be sympathetic to her, or they might suspect.

"A gold coin to the first man to tell me the prince's name, and where he comes from!" she cried, pulling the coin from her purse.

A shout came from the crowd: "The Prince of Tasnim!"

More shouts followed the first, but none seemed to know more than the name of his principality. It was enough. She handed the coin to one of her guards, who saw it went to its rightful owner.

She need not have bothered. The prince's entourage appeared then, gaudily dressed men who threw fistfuls of coins into the crowd. Maram did not recognise the livery, for that was what it was – these richly dressed men were the prince's servants.

After them came dancers, whirling in unison, so that their veils and skirts spun like tops. Finally, there were ranks of what she thought were porters, if a lowly porter could afford the silks these men wore. On their heads, they carried dishes piled high with gems much like those she'd seen on the jewelled shrub her father had shown her.

Behind the porters rode a man on a horse so pale it appeared white – something no horse could in the desert, for the sands coloured everything they touched. But they could not touch this animal, as fine as any in her father's stable.

The man…no, the prince, for he wore a crown nestled in the folds of his turban, threw coins into the crowd, too, earning a rousing cheer from everyone as he passed. Maram tried to get a glimpse of his face, to see if he was one of the princes she knew, but the cheering, waving townspeople made that impossible.

The prince passed, followed by another

company of coin-throwing servants, and the crowd closed ranks behind him to join the parade to the palace.

Maram cursed inwardly and waited a long time until the road cleared before she commanded her men to clear a path for her to go home. Whoever this prince was, he'd intended to make a spectacle of himself, and she would soon know far more about him than she cared to.

Twenty-Two

When Aladdin prostrated himself before the Sultan, he had a sudden image of the Sultan commanding one of the guards to lop off his head before he could rise.

No, he told himself. The Sultan was a wise and just ruler. He'd wait for Aladdin to speak and say something wrong before he executed him. Some reassurance. More than ever, Aladdin wanted to take to his heels and run home, but he knew he could not. He had to save Maram from that man.

"Rise," the Sultan commanded.

Aladdin rose onto his knees. "You Majesty, in thanks for your kind invitation, I have brought you a gift." He waved Berk and his men forward. They laid their baskets of jewels at the Sultan's feet, then bowed again.

The Sultan's eyes gleamed almost as brightly as the jewels he surveyed. "Such a generous gift demands another in return. What would you ask of me, Prince of Tasnim?"

Kaveh's whispers in the crowd had reached the Sultan's ears, then, as he'd promised.

"I ask for the Princess Maram's hand in marriage."

The Sultan's eyebrows rose. "But she is already betrothed to another."

No, she was betrothed to a beast of a man who did not deserve her. "So I have heard, but I understand there is a condition on the betrothal. Namely, her husband must build her a palace befitting such a priceless princess before the marriage can take place." He saw the Sultan open his mouth to respond, so Aladdin hastily added, "I propose a contest between her betrothed and myself. Whoever can build a palace that meets with her approval first, will win her hand."

If the Vizier or his son were present, they would surely object, but the Sultan had granted Aladdin an audience alone, if the crowd he'd brought in his procession could be considered alone.

The Sultan eyed him. "My daughters are precious to me, especially Princess Maram. I would not bestow them lightly on a man I do not know. I will consider your proposal for a day, and give you my answer on the morrow." He gave a wave of dismissal to signal the end of the brief audience.

"Thank you, Your Majesty. But if I may add one thing...I took the liberty of building a palace beside your own which I had hoped would satisfy the princess. If you are of a mind to accept my proposal, I humbly request that Her Highness tell me how poorly I may have anticipated her wishes on the morrow." Aladdin held his breath. He had little hope that Maram would be present tomorrow, but if the

Sultan denied that part of his request, he might be more inclined to accept the rest.

"We shall see."

Indeed we shall, Aladdin thought, as he and his men backed out of the audience chamber. Tomorrow could not come too soon.

Twenty-Three

Maram stabbed the needle through her embroidery, wishing she'd chosen to attend court today instead of going to the bathhouse to meet with the assassin. Now she'd have to wait until her father retired for the day before she heard what the prince had said.

"Are you thinking of becoming an assassin? I've heard tales of men in the far east who execute traitors by piercing them with a thousand needles."

Maram dropped the needle in surprise.

"Father?"

"I have another gift for you today, but it will not fit in here. You must come with me if you wish to see it."

A squad of guards waited outside, and Maram hastily secured her veil, realising they would be leaving the palace, for neither she nor her father required an escort so large within the palace grounds.

Father filled her in as they walked. The prince had asked for her hand, and promised her a palace, just as she'd asked for from Hasan.

"A palace he tells me he has already built — here," Father said with a flourish as the building came into view.

Maram's breath caught in her throat. How had she missed it this morning? Too intent on her thoughts, she supposed, as her men fought their way through the crush outside the palace.

A second palace sat beside her father's, grand and gleaming in the sun. The open gates beckoned her in, and Maram could not refuse the elegant invitation. The scent of rosewater reached her nostrils — whoever owned the palace had seen fit to perfume the entrance steps, a delightful touch.

As she stepped inside, she expected servants to come rushing forward to greet her and offer refreshments, yet there was no sound but the echo of her and her father's footsteps on the tiles. They were alone in this palace. A palace that easily outshone her father's.

The tiled floors were so perfectly smooth, they seemed to be made of a single piece of stone. Every room had a different ceiling mosaic, so lifelike it seemed she was staring up at the real sky and not a picture of it. And the bathhouse…tears sprang to her eyes to see her dreams made real, in a way no man could have known she wanted, for she hadn't even told her father how much she wanted this. The bathhouse was as opulent as the rest of the palace, but it was also familiar — if the bathhouse she'd visited that very morning were made anew, then surely it would look like this. A copy of the place on the day it opened, all those centuries ago…but no one could know such things!

Shaking her head at the impossibility of what her eyes were telling her, Maram no longer knew what to think.

"Come and look at the garden," her father called.

Only now did Maram realise she stood alone in the bathhouse – her father had ventured into the courtyard without her.

A courtyard or a garden? Maram wasn't certain until she saw the light glint off what she'd taken for grass. No, the ground was covered in grass-coloured tiles, while jewelled shrubs and trees dotted the courtyard like the harem gardens at home. A jewelled replica of the harem gardens…a place no prince had ever visited, for her brothers had been given their own garden for their boisterous play. The only men who had ever visited them were sultans, like her father, or traitors like her mother's lover, Amani. There was magic at work here. Magic meant to delight her, and her alone.

Maram's mouth was unbearably dry. More than ever, she wished for a servant to offer her refreshment, but no one granted her wish.

"Father, whoever this man is…whoever built this…I must meet him," she said. Because if he was even the slightest bit better than Hasan, she would scream her YES to his proposals before he could repeat them to her.

A shape stepped out of the shadows. A shape wearing a crown in the folds of his turban. The prince threw himself face down on the green tiles. "I am honoured by the presence of such a beautiful princess and her father in my humble home."

Maram glanced around, only to find her father nowhere in sight. Had he gone, leaving her alone with this man?

It seemed he had.

Maram took a deep breath. "Rise, Prince of Tasnim, for I am the one who is honoured. Why would a man I barely know offer me such a magnificent gift?"

"Because Hasan does not deserve you." The prince rose stiffly to his feet, only to lose his turban partway up. It clanged to the tiles, crown first, and rolled away.

She couldn't hide her smile. "And you do?"

"No," he said, raising his head to meet her eyes. "But I could think of no other way to free you of both slavery and your betrothal to him."

Maram's breath caught in her throat and she couldn't seem to draw another one. This couldn't be. It couldn't. Yet...

"Aladdin?" she gasped.

Twenty-Four

Aladdin stood invisible by Kaveh's side, watching the Sultan and Princess Maram marvel over the palace the two djinn had built. Now, Aladdin truly believed she was as precious to her father as he'd said. The Sultan spent more time watching his daughter's reactions than looking at the place. She meant more to him than whatever diplomatic assistance she provided to the court.

For a moment, he wished he'd told the Sultan about Hasan instead of creating such an elaborate scheme. He would never give the daughter he loved to that man if he truly knew what Hasan would do to her.

"What? Did you spot a mistake in the tiles?" Kaveh demanded. "Why do you look so miserable?"

"I should have asked the Sultan to call off the engagement, not offered a new one. She will see through this for sure." He waved at his silk clothes. They felt so slippery against his skin he worried they would slip right off and leave him naked. Not that it mattered when he was unseen, but...

"Don't be daft," Kaveh snapped. "Once the Sultan's given his word to the Vizier, he can't break the engagement, unless a better offer comes along. You made him the only offer he could accept. And once he sees the audience chamber, he will."

"But the princess will hate me for trying to deceive her. I'd hate me for making a bargain with her father without knowing I had her consent first. If there was a way I could speak to her before her father..."

Kaveh nodded. "Here she comes. I'll take him up to see the audience chamber, and you take a moment with your princess." He strode across the courtyard and materialised on the steps to the upper levels. He bowed deeply. "Your Majesty, my master bade me to greet you and show you anything you wish to see. I would recommend the audience chamber..."

The Sultan cut him off. "I had begun to think the palace was empty. Let us see this chamber." He headed up with Kaveh.

"Father, whoever this man is...whoever built this...I must meet him," Maram said, stepping into the sun. She blinked, blinded.

Aladdin could not have asked for a better opportunity than this. He threw himself at Maram's feet.

At her command, he rose, taking his time to meet her eyes and the complete lack of recognition he expected to see there. A princess would not remember a poor boy she'd met in the bathhouse.

"Aladdin?" His name was music on her lips.

He wanted to sink to his knees again, and

give thanks to whatever deity had helped him this time. But he forced himself to stay on his feet, for she had ordered it.

"How did you manage to build such a place? So lavish, so perfect, so fast?" she asked. "When I last saw you, you hadn't eaten for days, yet now..." She ran a hand down his tunic.

So that's why royalty wore silk. The feel of her fingers through it was pure bliss. Aladdin wanted to moan in pleasure, but he knew he only had a moment before her father returned. "I cannot tell you, for you would not believe me. I scarcely believe it myself. What I can tell you is that I ventured out into the desert and found a priceless treasure. A treasure that made all this possible, though it nearly killed me to return here. It's for you, Princess. All of it. If there is anything you wish changed, name it, and it shall be done. You don't even need to accept me – the palace is my gift to you. All I ask in return is that you don't marry that brute, Hasan."

Maram's eyes hardened. "Why would I not

want the man who risked his life for me, to give me this, to save me from that brutish fool? I've been to the bathhouse every day, sent men out looking for you…by all that's holy…" She tore the veil from her head and threw it on the tiles. Maram shook her hair off her face – a night-dark river Aladdin longed to stroke – then wrapped her arms around Aladdin and kissed him.

She tasted sweeter than before, more intoxicating than the finest wines in Tasnim, and more arousing than any of the erotic murals in the prince's harem. The softness of her body in his arms made him wonder if he truly had died and gone to paradise after all.

"Maram!"

At the Sultan's exclamation, Aladdin reluctantly released his angel and held his arms out wide in surrender.

Maram waited to finish one last kiss before she unwound her arms from Aladdin. "What, Father? I'm going to marry this man. He'll see more than my face and hair, soon enough." She bent to retrieve her veil, trailing her fingers across Aladdin's groin. "Soon enough," she repeated softly.

Aladdin's cheeks grew as heated as…he could hardly face the Sultan while he had a tent in his accursed silk pants. A normal tunic would have hidden everything, but in this finery…he forced himself to retrieve his turban and hold it before his groin to hide the effect Princess Maram had on him.

She winked as she wound her veil around her hair, leaving her face uncovered. "Prince Aladdin wishes to know if any improvements should be made to his palace. It appears perfect to me, but you have seen more of it than I have."

The Sultan stared from Aladdin to Maram. "What about Hasan?"

She frowned. "What about him, Father? I doubt he has laid so much as a single stone on the palace he promised to build, but if I'm wrong, I will happily compare the two. We already know who will be the victor in any competition."

"What will I tell his father?"

Maram shrugged. "Tell him you received a better offer from a prince. He's your adviser. If he advised you to accept a vizier's son over a prince, he'd be a fool, and out of a job. You needn't tell him right away. I will need at least four weeks before my wedding. You'll have some time."

"Four weeks?" Aladdin blurted out.

Maram smiled mischievously. "Four weeks until the wedding, yes. It will take that long for my dress. A royal wedding is worth celebrating." She winked. "Don't worry, my prince. I shall have my things moved to your palace tonight. From this moment, I am yours."

Oh, how he longed for that to be true. But it was not. "No, you and this palace will not be mine until we are married. Until then, this palace belongs to you alone, Princess. I will stay with my mother but, with your permission, I shall visit you, if you wish."

Maram's shock brightened into a smile. "Oh, I do wish."

The Sultan coughed. "It seems my daughter

has made her decision, and what father would argue with a woman in love? Shall we meet on the morrow, Prince Aladdin, or will you accept my answer now?"

Aladdin bowed. "I will accept whatever Your Majesty is gracious enough to grant me."

The Sultan laughed. "My favourite daughter, it would seem. Just like her mother, I can refuse her nothing. But I will add one thing." His expression darkened. "If you hurt her, if my daughter sheds a single tear because of you, I will have your head severed from your body so fast, you will not have time to blink in surprise before your heart stops beating."

Aladdin met the Sultan's eye now, not a subject to his sovereign, but a future son-in-law to a protective father. "If I ever cause harm to come to Princess Maram, I will offer my head to you myself, for I will deserve such a fate."

He opened his mouth to ask what the Sultan would do to Hasan, but he'd taken his daughter's arm and already started walking away.

Hasan no longer mattered. Maram would marry him, and make Aladdin the happiest of men.

"I'd have risked killing myself, crossing the desert for her, too," Kaveh said fervently. "You are one lucky man."

Yes. Yes, he was.

Twenty-Five

When they returned to the Sultan's palace, Maram knew she would have a lot of questions to answer. But for the first time in longer than she could remember, she did not care. She'd seen him, she'd kissed him and by some incredible change of heart from fate, she'd get to keep him. Aladdin. The only man who'd ever touched her heart.

The only man who kissed her like he cared how he touched her, not wanting to consume her in his own blazing passion. Oh, Aladdin had passion enough, she was certain of it, for she'd seen it in his eyes as he kissed her.

But he didn't want to marry her for himself. Oh, no. He wanted to save her from Hasan. One day she would tell him how she'd planned to save herself, but not until after they were married. She didn't want to frighten him. Then again, Aladdin was not some soft courtier, to be frightened by a woman who took her fate into her own hands. No, he was a man who would risk everything – even his own life – for the woman he loved.

Her mouth became dry. Did he love her? He had not said so, but then he'd hardly had the chance to do so. Yet why else would he risk so much for her, if not for love?

"How do you know this man, and why have I never heard of him?" Father demanded.

Maram blinked. She'd been so lost in thought she hadn't realised they'd arrived in her private apartments, and they were alone. She pulled off her veil and shook out her hair. She would have to be careful, for her father thought Aladdin was a prince, and she had no desire to tell him otherwise.

"I met him once, briefly. I liked him very much then and I believe he liked me, too, but as neither of us were in a position to marry at the time, I thought such a thing would never happen. Evidently I underestimated both his affection and his wealth." She blew out a breath. She would not make that mistake again. Aladdin was not a man to be underestimated at all.

"What about Hasan? Why would you agree to marry Hasan if you loved this man so much?" Father persisted.

Ah, here was the crux of the matter. She was her mother's daughter, after all.

"I never intended to marry Hasan. He is a vicious brute who beats his servants and has wanted to do the same to me since the moment we met. I had hoped to bankrupt him by forcing him to build a palace that I would never be satisfied with. Then, when he was so deeply in debt he could no longer continue, perhaps he would give up his suit, and he'd be forced to release the servants he has abused for so long."

Father's eyebrows rose so high they disappeared into his jewelled turban. "How did I not know this about him?"

Maram lifted her shoulders in a delicate shrug. "Perhaps only women gossip about such things, or perhaps he hides it well from anyone outside his household. But you sent him with me on a trading expedition, where he tried to turn me into his whore. He did not succeed, and has hated me ever since. I had no idea you were unaware of his true nature, Father." Though it didn't surprise her. Vizier Ali must have known, and worked hard to conceal it from the Sultan.

He frowned, evidently deep in thought.

Maram let the silence build. Her father would fill it when he chose to.

Finally, he said, "So you don't wish to marry Hasan, but you do want this other man? This prince? He will make you happy?"

"Yes, Father. Aladdin will make me happy." He already had.

"But he will take you away from me, to his

own kingdom."

Maram had never seen her father pout before, but he looked dangerously close to doing so now. "Father, I will make it my mission to make sure Aladdin likes it so much here in our city, that he never wants to leave his palace. You will have to travel a little further to see me, but not so far as you think."

He nodded. "I'll summon Hasan and his father, and tell them the news. They certainly won't be happy when they hear."

No, they would not. Especially Hasan.

"Can you wait until I have left the palace, Father? I fear Hasan's anger will make him do something…reckless, when he hears the news."

The Sultan smiled fondly. "Of course. I will wait two days – will you be ready then?"

Maram nodded. She was so used to travelling, she and her servants could have her room stripped in an hour, if need be, to catch the tide. But never before had she felt that leaving a room would change her life forever. Now, there would be no returning from a future that was so unknown. Could anyone truly be ready for anything the future held?

"I shall," she vowed.

Twenty-Six

All the way home, Aladdin should have been walking on air, but he couldn't help but worry. The man he'd seen this morning, beating his slave, would not like losing Maram. What man would?

If another man – a real prince, perhaps – were to appear in the palace and persuade the Sultan that HE was a better match than either Aladdin or Hasan, Aladdin would not simply stand by and accept it. Not unless he truly believed someone could make Maram happier than he could.

The moment he got home, he dug out the lamp and summoned the djinn. Without waiting for the djinn to ask for orders, Aladdin said, "I need you to protect the princess in the palace you built. She'll bring her own staff, I'm sure, but she'll need guards and…I don't know what. And you. If all else fails, I need you to protect her."

"As you command, master. If I may suggest…"

Aladdin looked up. The djinn wasn't normally any more helpful than he needed to be. Not like Kaveh. "Yes?"

The djinn ducked his head. "I suggest placing the lamp in the palace treasury, so I will always be close by if Princess Maram needs me."

Something in the djinn's tone made Aladdin suspicious. "You are not to speak to her, interact with her in any way, or permit her to see you, unless her life depends upon it," Aladdin added.

This didn't seem to upset the djinn at all.

"Yes, master."

Aladdin decided he must have imagined it.

"If I may not speak to her…can you tell me if she liked the palace?"

Aladdin hesitated for a moment, but he couldn't see any reason not to answer. "Yes, she did. So much that she agreed to marry me because of it."

"Does she not reside in her father's palace?"

"Of course she does."

"Then why would she want another?"

Aladdin squinted at the djinn. He sure had a lot of questions about Maram. "Something about bankrupting the brute who expected to marry her. Not me, the other guy."

The djinn roared with laughter. "Oh, she is her mother's daughter. So ruled by passion, she would rather ruin a man than kill him outright. I would prefer a clean death, myself."

Feeling he was missing something that the djinn deliberately chose not to share, Aladdin told the djinn to hide in the lamp so that he might take him to his new home in the palace. The princess's palace. In four short weeks, it would be his, too. He'd need to find a more suitable place for his mother, as well. The tiny house they'd moved to after his father died had never felt like home, and he owed his mother more than this place. A palace of her own, perhaps, or an apartment in Maram's. He'd ask her when he saw her.

In the meantime, Aladdin made his way through the city. He'd persuaded Kaveh to find him some more suitable clothes than the embarrassing silk suit he'd worn for his triumphal entry into the city, and Kaveh had provided him with a fine linen tunic with matching turban and trousers. At first glance, they were no different to his normal clothes, but Aladdin could feel the difference. There were coins that jingled in his pockets, too, courtesy of the djinn who'd also filled the treasury in the palace with enough wealth to do him for several lifetimes.

And all because he'd accepted a job from that madman, Gwandoya. Who could still be trying to recruit men to do his dirty work, Aladdin realised. He had to warn Berk and the others.

He made his way to the alley where they would normally be, but the alley was empty. Of course, they'd done their day's work in the procession this morning. He hoped Kaveh had paid them well for it. None of them had recognised him in his finery, and he hadn't dared to climb down off his horse once he was on it so that he might speak to them. The beast had proved just as challenging to ride as a camel. Henceforth, Aladdin swore to walk on his own two feet, wherever he went.

And his feet would lead him back to the alley on the morrow, for Berk deserved to know he'd been right about Gwandoya.

When he arrived at the palace gates, he found a steady stream of servants carrying things from the Sultan's palace to Maram's, before returning for more.

He found her in a set of apartments overlooking the garden. "Why did you not choose the best bedchamber?" he asked as he entered. "Unless your father plans to move into your palace with you, you will be the highest ranking inhabitant of the house."

She laughed. "Not so. You're royalty, too, remember – I left the best apartment for you. Though I hope to be invited in there often. Every night, in fact."

Her kiss didn't take him by surprise, but it seemed to melt things inside him that had no business melting. "Princess, this palace is yours, and you are free to go wherever you wish."

"What about in here?" She slid a hand under his tunic, then frowned as she encountered something hard. "What is this?"

Not what she had hoped for, certainly. Aladdin pried the lamp from her fingers. "It is…a lucky talisman, that has protected my house and now will protect yours. I'll just put it in the entry hall…" He found a suitable alcove high on the wall, and tucked the lamp into the back of it. "There. Now you will be safe." Oh, how fervently he hoped that would be the case.

"Now, you can invite me to your chamber," Maram said.

More than anything, he wanted to do just that. To take this beautiful woman and anything she offered.

"Not yet. It would be dishonourable to do so before we are married," Aladdin said with considerable regret.

She laughed. "I am not some blushing virgin, as you well know. We are promised, and I know you are a man of your word. I promise our nights together will be the greatest pleasure you have ever known."

Aladdin swallowed. Every word was the truth, and yet…

"You may not be a virgin, but I am, and I fear my clumsiness will make you wish to break your promise. I am not worthy of you. Not yet."

Her eyes mesmerised him like never before. "What if I told you I knew a spell that could guarantee when you make love to the woman of your heart's desire, she will know nothing but pleasure at your touch?"

His mouth was too dry to speak. He tried twice before he had to clear his throat to get the words out. "Keep your spell for our wedding night, for you will need it then. Please, Princess."

She stared at him for a long time, then nodded. "All right. If you wish. I have never had to wait for a man before and I find I do not like it. However, I believe you will be worth the wait, so I shall."

If Aladdin looked at her for any longer, he would be lost in her eyes, and he would agree to anything she desired, for he desired it, too. He bade her a hasty farewell and hurried out before he could surrender to her.

It was a long walk home, but he noticed little of it, for his thoughts were filled with Maram, and their future nights together. The desert heat was cold in comparison.

Twenty-Seven

For two days, Aladdin did not visit her, and it drove Maram mad. She'd seen him again, and kissed him. She'd kissed him so many times he heated her blood near to boiling, and still he resisted her. Not even their betrothal was enough to bring him to her bed. If she didn't know better, she'd swear the man had seduction magic of his own, but she'd never met a man so frightened of intimacy before. Clumsy, indeed. She'd known clumsy, and he wasn't. His every kiss was perfect — making love to him would be even more perfect.

Yet still he did not come, and it was her turn to fear. Had she driven him away with her persistence? Or did he have other matters to attend to? For she knew he was no prince, not truly, so his money must come from somewhere. When she saw him next, she would ask about it, and this time, she would not rest until she had her answer.

Darkness crept over the city on the second day, dulling her spirits until Maram had scarcely any appetite for her evening meal.

A cacophony of banging and shouting sounded outside, and Maram sent a maid to find out what was going on.

Another maid came skidding into the room, wide-eyed. "Your Highness, he's here!"

So Aladdin surprised her servants, did he? "Send him in," Maram said, calling for a second place to be set at her table for her soon-to-be husband.

The first one returned, laughing. "There is a madman outside, rattling a great bundle of new lamps all tied together, offering to trade new lamps for old. There is an old lamp in the entrance hall. I found it while I was cleaning. Shall I take it to him and see if he will truly trade it, as he says?"

Maram no longer cared about whatever was going on outside. "Fine, fine," she said vaguely, combing her fingers through her hair. Did she have time to summon a servant with a comb to do a proper job? She had not expected Aladdin to come so late, and she did not want him to find her looking anything but her best.

"What is this I hear that you are to marry some prince? You are promised to me!"

Hasan burst into the room, his eyes as wild as any madman outside.

Maram cautiously rose to her feet, so that she might run if she needed to. "My father, the Sultan, controls my fate, as he rules over us all," she said slowly. There were no guards in her private chambers. Her only weapon was a small eating dagger, and even that lay on the table where she'd left it.

"You're mine! Mine!" Hasan spat, striding forward.

Maram scuttled back, hoping she had judged the entrance to the gardens right. Once she reached the darkness, she could turn and run, and perhaps hide.

Her back hit the wall. Oh, by all that was holy, she had the worst luck. Maram edged to her left, closer to Hasan, but also closer to freedom.

Not close enough. His meaty hands closed around her throat and choked off her air.

"You belong to me, not some foreign prince!"

Colour leached away from Maram's vision as she struggled to breathe. Hasan would kill her after all and she and Aladdin would never…she'd never…

"You dare to steal from me!" a new voice roared.

Hasan threw her to the floor, knocking the remaining breath from her lungs. Maram coughed and gasped and fought to stay conscious. She had to get to the knife…

"She is my bride, and no one else's!" Hasan shouted back, storming back the way he'd come.

Maram dragged herself across the floor and snatched the knife from the table. Thus armed, she subsided on the tiles, too exhausted to move any more just yet.

But she had to. Had to get up, be ready to run or defend herself, because if she didn't, Hasan would kill her for sure.

She drew in a great gulp of air, then another, and the second was somehow tainted with smoke. Fire. Faintly, she could hear her servants screaming, and the sound of running feet as they escaped the blaze now filling her palace with smoke.

She coughed, hard, tears blurring her vision. Maram grabbed the table and hauled herself into a sitting position, still coughing as the smoke grew too thick for her to see.

She must have hit her head, she decided, because she couldn't be seeing what she thought was before her. The smoke coalesced into a giant, blue man, who faced off against Hasan as though the two were about to fight.

"Kill the miserable thief. No one steals from

Gwandoya!" the unfamiliar male voice said.

Maram blinked, her vision clearing just in time to see the blue man clasp his hands together and bring them down on Hasan's head. Hasan's head burst like an overripe melon, bits of flesh splattering on the tiles, before his headless body collapsed amid the gore.

"Oh my God," Maram breathed, then clapped a hand over her mouth to muffle the scream that would not be silenced. The blue man had killed him, squashed him like an insect, all over her floor...

And she was next.

With a squeak, Maram leaped to her feet and bolted into the garden. She sank to her knees behind a shrub and hoped the shadows hid her from the blue man's sight.

Moments passed, and no one gave chase. She dared to breathe again.

"Servant of the lamp, I command you to take this palace and everyone in it, and carry it to my homeland," the unfamiliar man ordered.

"As you wish, master," boomed a voice that

could only belong to the blue giant.

Then the ground shook beneath Maram as though the palace had been hoisted on the back of a giant camel. She lost her balance, slamming her head against a tree, and darkness swallowed her whole.

Twenty-Eight

Getting measured up by another man while wearing little more than a loincloth was a new sensation to Aladdin, and he wasn't sure he particularly liked it, but Maram would expect him to wear nice clothes to their wedding, and probably afterwards, too, so he resigned himself to getting used to spending more time at the tailor shop. Besides, wishing for clothes from the djinn seemed even stranger, for Aladdin had no idea where the clothing came from. He hoped the djinn used magic to create it, but what if he stole it from someone? The Sultan or some other rich man might not notice a few missing tunics, but if he'd taken things from a merchant or tailor, that made Aladdin himself little better than a common thief. The two djinn had given him riches enough that he could afford to buy such things, so he should do so.

Not to mention he was certain the tradesmen and merchants who had been his father's friends before he died had provided charity to himself and his mother – a kindness he needed to repay. So if he'd ordered more tunics than he normally wore in a year…so what? He had the coin, and they wanted the business. He hadn't ordered anything but his wedding clothes made in silk, though, remembering the indecent way it had clung to him, especially when his desire for Maram had made him lose control. It would not happen again on their wedding day, he swore – he would be the picture of modest decorum.

Though he was finding it increasingly hard to stay away from her, in every sense of the word. He might not have shared her bed yet, but she certainly shared his – dominating his dreams every night. Aladdin knew he would pay her a visit today, and this time, he wasn't sure he could refuse her invitation to stay the night. Maram was intoxicating, in all the best ways.

Perhaps he would bring her a gift. He stopped in the bazaar to examine the caged birds, wondering which one she'd like. The jewelled garden would be better with some life in it. He wanted to get her a bird that would sing beautifully, but the only sound any of them seemed to want to make was a distressed peeping right now.

A streak of gold shot between the cages and pounced on a loose thread that hung from the hem of his tunic. A cat – the tiniest he'd ever seen. Aladdin caught the kitten and held it up to better inspect it. The little creature batted at his turban until a fold came loose, then sank its needle-like teeth into the corner.

"How much for this ferocious beast?" Aladdin asked the merchant who owned the menagerie.

"If you can keep the little menace from killing my exotic birds, you may have it as a gift," the man said. "I keep the mother for the mice, but she has so many babies, I fear the city will soon be overrun."

Aladdin tossed him a coin anyway, then tucked the kitten inside his tunic, where it promptly curled up and went to sleep.

Now he had to go to see Maram – before her present woke up and clawed through his clothes. Unable to wipe the grin from his face, Aladdin set off for the palace.

"Stop! Are you Prince Aladdin?" a voice demanded.

It was on the tip of his tongue to tell the truth and deny it, but Aladdin knew he had little to fear from the Sultan's guards now. Why, he would soon marry the man's daughter.

"I am he," he said grandly.

Two guards took his arms. "Then you must come with us. The Sultan commands it." They marched him the shortest way to the Sultan's palace, away from Maram.

Aladdin sighed. She would understand, surely.

The guards released him without warning, dropping him on the tiles of the Sultan's audience chamber. Instead of getting up, Aladdin merely bowed deeply. "How may I serve Your Majesty?"

"You can tell me where my daughter and her palace are!"

Aladdin wanted to laugh, but he restrained himself. "Her palace is beside your own, and no doubt Her Highness Princess Maram is inside it."

The Sultan made an exasperated sound. "Show him!"

Aladdin's guards hauled him to his feet and half carried him out of the hall to the gates of his palace. Or where the gates of his palace should be. Where the palace had stood only yesterday, now there was only bare earth, compressed under the weight of the absent palace.

One of the djinn had turned it invisible,

Aladdin decided, reaching for the gate he knew had to be there. But his fingers closed around nothing but air.

He didn't resist as the guards dragged him back to the Sultan and left him on the floor.

"Her servants tell hysterical tales of giants and magicians and blazes that smoke and do not burn. Complete nonsense, for something has driven them all mad and made them run from my daughter's service. But they all agree on one thing: she was in the palace when they left, and now there is no sign of the princess or her palace. Tell me where they are!" the Sultan demanded.

Aladdin raised his head. "I do not know."

"Tell me, or I shall instruct my guards to cut off your head. Last night, I bade good night to my daughter in that very palace you caused to be built overnight. Today, the palace is gone. My daughter is gone. And so is the Vizier's son, Hasan. No one else can tell my how a palace can appear in a night – and disappear just as quickly. Can you?"

"Magic," Aladdin croaked. He swallowed,

attempting to moisten his suddenly dry throat, then said it again. "No one could do such a thing without magic."

Was Hasan some sort of magician, who'd somehow stolen both the palace and Maram? If he had, Aladdin had to find her. The palace didn't matter, but Maram…she could not be left to the mercies of the man who had none.

"Are you a magician?" the Sultan thundered.

"No," Aladdin admitted.

"Do you know what the punishment is for stealing from your sovereign?"

Aladdin did not, but he was sure he wouldn't like it. "Your Majesty, I have stolen nothing from you. In fact, I am as incensed as you. Someone has stolen my palace and the woman I love. I ask for your leave to hunt down this thief, so that I may bring him to justice. Give me a month, and if I cannot find him, you may do as you wish with me."

"Why should I trust you? If I release you now, what assurance do I have that you will return in a month, or at all?"

Aladdin met the Sultan's eyes steadily.

"Because, Your Majesty, if I do not find her in that time, then I fear Princess Maram will be dead, and I will beg you to die so that I might join her."

The Sultan was silent for a long moment before he finally said, "Very well. But if you fail to return my daughter to me, you will not need to beg. Your death will be painful, I promise you."

"Thank you, Your Majesty." The words came out of his mouth, but Aladdin's thoughts were not in the Sultan's palace at all. Instead, they were with Maram, wherever she might be. He prayed Hasan had not hurt her yet, and that Aladdin would be in time to save her from him.

He had to be.

Twenty-Nine

Maram woke in her own bed, her head throbbing as though she'd attended one of those all-night feasts the northern kingdoms loved so much. The ones where wine flowed like water.

But if she had attended such a feast, there would be a naked man in her bed, and she would be wearing a lot less than she was now. Instead, she was alone, wearing the same clothes she'd worn yesterday. All she was missing was her shoes.

She rose and called for her servants, but received no answer. In fact, the palace was strangely quiet, as though she was alone, yet she could see daylight filtering through the windows. Her staff were never lazy – they would not be abed at this hour. One of her maids should have woken her hours ago.

Something was terribly wrong.

Maram crept out into the garden, which sparkled in the sun as though nothing had changed. She knew otherwise, though, touching her head where it hurt most. She'd hit her head on a tree. This morning, the trunk was marked with a streak of blood that had blackened in the sun. Maram had not imagined the events of last night.

That meant Hasan was…Hasan was…

She swallowed and squared her shoulders. She had to see it again to be sure.

Her feet made almost no sound as she traversed the cool tiles to the entrance hall. Her eyes scanned the floor for the spot where Hasan had fallen.

Where he'd splattered.

Her stomach roiled, but Maram refused to let the nausea rule her. His body had been right there…yet now the tiles were clean of blood and brains and whatever else was supposed to stay inside a man's head when he was alive.

She had not imagined it, Maram told herself. Perhaps that's where the servants were – called to her father's court to bear witness to the body they'd found. She should join them, for she'd seen the blue man kill Hasan with her own eyes.

Not that her father would believe there was such a thing as a giant blue man made of smoke. Maram herself didn't believe it, but if there had been some magic at work, then perhaps such a thing could exist. Such magic was beyond her, though.

She returned to her apartments and dressed carefully, for she had no servants to help her. No matter. She managed, as she always did.

With one final pat to make sure her veil was in place, Maram marched to the gate. She crossed the entrance hall without faltering, maintaining a steady trot as she descended the sunlit stairs into air that seemed distinctly cooler than usual.

Only when she reached the bottom of the stairs did she dare to look up into the street outside the palace gates.

But the street was gone. In its place, endless grassland stretched to the horizon, the straight line broken by a few scrubby trees. This was not the city or the desert she knew – it was somewhere else entirely, a country Maram, even in her extensive travels, had never visited before.

She heard a squeak, which drew her gaze back from the horizon to the gates. Someone's dogs were nosing something in the grass, so she took a step closer to investigate.

One of the dogs heard her, for it lifted its bloodied muzzle and mewed at her. It was the strangest dog she'd ever seen. Why, it sounded almost like…

A loud roar drowned out whatever thought she'd intended to have as a larger creature rose from the grass. This Maram could identify.

The lioness was leaner than the ones she'd seen in menageries across the world, but there was no mistaking the deadly intent in her eyes as she stalked. She appeared to be hunting, and the dogs were not dogs at all, but lion cubs, eating the remains of…Hasan.

If she'd had anything in her belly, Maram would have brought it up then and there.

She had no right to feel faint at the thought of someone killing the man, not when she'd been ready to hire an assassin to do the job for her, Maram told herself, but it was no use. Even she would have seen that the man was given a proper burial, not fed to someone's pet lions.

Except…there was something wild about this lioness that made her take another look. No chains or collars bound them. No fence or walls caged them. The lioness and her cubs were free as the air, which meant there was nothing stopping them from…from…

Maram scrambled up the steps, not daring to take her eyes off the lioness. She backed inside the palace, fingers scrabbling at the door so that she might shut it firmly behind her. Were there bars? Something to keep the lioness out?

"You should not leave the palace, Princess. It is not safe."

Maram whirled, pressing her back to the door. "Who is there?"

A figure stepped out of the shadows, then bowed. "I did not mean to frighten you."

The light coming through the windows hit him, and stole Maram's breath in the same moment.

"Are you going to kill me, too, like you killed Hasan?" she demanded of the blue man.

"He commanded me to protect you," the man said. As she watched, he shrank, until he was almost the size of an ordinary man. "Hasan deserved his fate."

She didn't argue. She, more than anyone, knew what Hasan was capable of. Perhaps the blue man was right.

The blue man swallowed. "You look just like her. Only more beautiful. How is that even possible?"

Maram knew only one woman who looked like her. "How do you know my mother?" she demanded, looking him in the eye for the first time. Only then did she falter, for recognition came as a shock. "Wait, Amani?"

He bowed his head. "I am."

"What are you doing here?"

"I am the slave of the lamp, which your betrothed kindly brought back to the city."

"Aladdin?"

Amani smiled faintly. "So that is his name. We were never properly introduced, and the enslavement spell on me is so strong I'm not sure I could call him anything but my master, anyway. He is a good man, a rare thing in these times, though I hope you will not be disappointed to discover that he is not a prince."

Maram wet her lips. "I already know. I met him before he left the city and found...wait, did you say a lamp?" She lifted her gaze to the alcove where Aladdin had placed his lucky lamp, but now the alcove was empty. "Where is it? He will be terribly disappointed that it is gone."

"Gwandoya the magician carries it with him, close to his heart. He is my master now, not Aladdin, though I wish it were otherwise. Gwandoya's desires run darker than Aladdin's simple tastes, and I fear what dark purpose he will use me for."

"Use you?" Maram ran through what Amani had told her, as well as her father, about his punishment for being the queen's lover. "Wait, you are a djinn, the servant of the lamp. No, the slave of the lamp, and your master is…the man who ordered you to kill Hasan."

Amani nodded. "I let him believe Hasan was your husband. I'm not sure he can tell the difference between him and Aladdin. The man is clearly mad."

"Where are we?"

"I am not sure what country this is, but we are many miles south from your home, far from any city."

Maram slumped. "So there is nowhere to escape to, even if the gates were not guarded by lions."

"The only way you will ever go home is if you persuade Gwandoya to order me to transport you or the palace back to your city." Amani smiled sadly. "If you have any of your mother's wiles to match her beauty, then I am sure you know how to make a man do whatever you wish."

Amani had known her as a child, so he had no idea how many men she'd seduced, all for her father's benefit and the good of the kingdom. What was one more, if it meant going home to Aladdin?

It would be a betrayal of Aladdin, and the freedom he had won for her. She had promised herself to him, and to let any other man touch her...Maram shivered. No, she could not even feign pleasure in any man's touch but his. Aladdin was the only man she wanted now, and she would not betray him with another, even if it meant their wedding would be delayed. She would return to him, somehow. There had to be a way. A way that did not involve seducing a madman.

Thirty

"Have you seen the palace that was here yesterday?" Aladdin asked. "It was here, but now it's gone." When the man shook his head, Aladdin tried another passerby. "Did you see anything here last night?"

People shook their heads and moved away from him, eyeing him suspiciously as they passed on the other side of the road.

Aladdin couldn't really blame them. After all, if he'd been confronted by a desperate man asking if he'd seen his palace, Aladdin might have thought him a madman, too. And it wasn't the palace he cared about as much as Maram. If Hasan had hurt her…he didn't know what he'd do.

He kept his head down as he ambled through the bazaar, not wanting to look at all the things he'd thought about buying for Maram.

"Aladdin? Is it really you?"

It took a moment for the sound of his name being called to penetrate through Aladdin's wretchedness, and it took another long moment before he raised his head to focus on the man calling. "Berk?"

Berk grinned. "We all thought the madman had killed you, like Bugra! Ah, you should have waited, for there was work enough for all of us earlier this week. Some foreign prince came to court one of the Sultan's daughters, and he needed porters to carry his treasures through the city before he made them a gift to the Sultan. Never have you seen such riches! Gold and jewels and all manner of precious things. He paid handsomely, too. So handsomely we hope he leaves soon, and needs our help again. That much coin would feed my family for a year."

"Did you see what happened to his palace?" Aladdin asked, hardly daring to hope.

Berk scratched his head, then righted his turban. "Not me. But one of Rasul's boys might have — they watch the place all day, ready to fetch the prince a porter if he needs one."

"All day? What about all night?"

Berk shrugged. "The boys go home for dinner after dark. Now their father can afford it."

Aladdin's heart sank. The boys wouldn't have seen anything if they weren't there.

"Hey, Rasul! Did your boys see anything strange about the prince's palace yesterday?" Berk shouted.

Rasul shrugged. "Ghulam said he saw a big nobleman go in to visit the prince. He challenged him, he said, shouting terrible things. Ghulam came running home, telling us we must help the prince fight the man off, or we would not see the prince again. As if the prince did not have his own guards to deal with such things."

Hasan. It had to be him.

"Did your boy see what happened to the palace?" Aladdin asked eagerly.

Rasul shook his head. "His mother had already made the evening meal. He stayed home to eat, like a good boy." He reflected for a moment, then added, "I hope the prince had guards. He pays better than the noblemen of this city. I would be disappointed if we don't see him again."

Berk clapped Aladdin on the shoulder. "Aladdin's the one we didn't think we'd see again. When he went off with that Gwandoya, we thought he'd be as doomed as the rest of them. Especially after Gwandoya came back without him, trying to get more of us to work for him. Yet here he is, safe and well. What sort of work did that madman want you to do, Aladdin? Was it as dangerous as we thought?"

Aladdin managed a smile. "Treasure hunting in the desert. So dangerous, when I got trapped, he left me for dead. I barely made it back. Whatever you do, don't agree to work for him. I was lucky to make it out alive from that place."

Berk nodded gravely. "I told you not to. None of us is that crazy. Although…I haven't seen him for the last couple of days. Have any of you?" The other men shook their heads. "Huh. Maybe he has a new employee to go treasure hunting for him. Hey, did you find anything?"

If he told the truth, every man here would head out into the desert to their deaths. Aladdin forced out a laugh. "Nothing but an old, tarnished lamp."

"Pity. We could all do with a change in fortune." Berk sighed. "Ah, well. When the prince leaves, make sure you're around. We'll tell him to hire you, too."

Aladdin thanked Berk, farewelled his friends, and headed home.

His mother was waiting for him. "What happened?" she demanded. "I heard some guards arrested you and took you to the palace!

I told you, only evil could come of messing with princesses and djinn. Djinn would try to trick the Sultan himself out of his crown, just for the fun of it. Or make his palace invisible. Or..."

That's how Hasan had done it. He'd somehow learned of the djinn that lived in the lamp, and enslaved him to his will. If the servant of the lamp could make a palace appear in a night, then surely he could make it disappear just as easily. He'd probably tried to keep Maram for himself.

Aladdin found his mother staring at him, as though expecting a reply. "You are wiser than I will ever be, Maman," he said warmly. He dug into his purse for his few remaining coins. "How about buying us a meal fit for a sultan tonight? I saw some new, exotic fruits in the bazaar this morning."

She looked slightly mollified. Wrapping her veil around her hair and face, she bade him farewell and headed out.

Aladdin let out a breath he hadn't known he'd been holding. "Kaveh, I need your help," he said.

The dejected djinn appeared beside him. "Before you ask, no, I can't bring your palace back, and as long as the other djinn has her, I can't bring your princess back, either. He's far more powerful than me."

Aladdin digested his words for a long moment before he said, "But you know where Maram and the palace are?"

Kaveh nodded. "In Gwandoya's homeland, deep in the savannah."

"Is Maram all right?" If she was, then nothing else mattered.

"I do not know."

"Take me to her," Aladdin said.

Kaveh threw his hands up in the air. "I told you, I am not as powerful as he is! Before he became a djinn, he was a powerful enchanter. One who knew portal magic and all manner of spells I have only heard of. I open doors and make things invisible. Even if I could get you there, what then? I am no match for the servant of the lamp. He will defeat me, and you, and then what will become of your princess?"

"Better to die than to stay here and do nothing. If we cannot reach her by magical means, there must be another way. I have a month to find her and bring her home, or I will die at the hands of the Sultan's executioner. Better to die trying to save her. And if I do, I ask only one more thing of you: deliver my head to the Sultan, with my humblest apologies for my failure."

Kaveh stared at him. "If that is your wish, master."

"It is."

Thirty-One

"Once again, I must remind you, Princess. Your husband is dead, and I am the only man you will ever see again. Will you finally accept me as your new husband?" Gwandoya asked.

Maram shook her head. "I cannot marry as long as I am in mourning. It is not seemly for me to take a new husband so soon."

"Who is there to know, or care? We are alone here!" Gwandoya snapped.

"As long as my late husband's shade haunts me, unable to find peace in the place where he was murdered, I cannot think to replace him."

Gwandoya jumped to his feet. "A pox on your husband's shade. Would that he were still alive, so that I might kill him more slowly, for he is such a thorn in my side that he deserves pain in equal measure!" He gestured for Amani. "I have had enough. Send me back to the city."

Gwandoya departed through the portal, leaving Maram alone with Amani. She sagged against the djinn. "Each time I see him, I dislike him more, and I hated the man on sight. When will he give up?"

Amani shook his head. "He is crazy in ways that few men are. He is not the sort to give up easily, or at all. The question you should be asking is: what will that madman do when he finally loses patience with you? I have no desire to harm you, but I am the slave of the lamp. Should he order me to kill you, I'm not sure I could disobey him. And your mother's shade would never forgive me."

"My mother is not dead."

Amani's mouth dropped open. "Briska

lives?"

Maram had never seen a man look as hungry as Amani did now. "She does. All my life, I was told that she'd been executed, as had you, but it turns out my father couldn't bring himself to kill her. He loved her too, you know. She is enslaved to something, just as you are, though I know not what or where. Only that she lives."

"One day, I wish to be free to find her."

Tears filled her eyes. "I hope one day you find her, too. You deserve to be happy."

"Your father would not think so."

"He will when I tell him how you have protected me here. If it weren't for you, I should have gone mad on that first day, or been eaten by a lion. It is four weeks since I arrived here, and you have never allowed me to lose hope that one day I might go home." Maram stared at him fiercely. "When I see my father again, I will demand that he release you from slavery."

Amani's smile seemed pitying. "He cannot, Princess. It takes magic to break a magical binding."

She refused to be put off. "Then I will make him summon an enchanter powerful enough to break it for him. If I have to endure another day here alone – "

"But you are not alone, Princess. Not any more. Open the gates and see."

Maram followed Amani to the entrance hall, where he threw open the doors and pointed. "Look out over the grass," he said.

In the darkness, she could see very little, but there did seem to be a faint glow, growing larger as she watched. Maram squinted. There appeared to be two figures, each carrying a torch. "Who are they?"

Amani's enigmatic smile told her nothing. "Wait and see."

It took an eternity for the two men to cross the flat plain to the gates. Maram didn't dare go out to meet them – in the weeks she'd been here, wild animals had picked Hasan's bones clean, and the bleached bones outside the gate were a warning of what the lions would do to her if she tried to leave.

The night breeze plucked at her veil, chilling Maram, but she simply folded her arms across her breasts and hugged what warmth she had left. If she went back into the palace for a shawl, the visitors might disappear, never to be seen again.

Finally, the figure came close enough for Maram to discern details. One man, not two, and he was cloaked against the cold, carrying a torch to light his way.

"What's that?" a familiar voice asked, lifting his torch to illuminate what remained of Hasan.

Maram's heart leaped for joy. "It was Hasan," she said, stepping forward out of the shadows. "They killed him and gave his body to the lions." She could feel tears threatening to fall. "I closed the doors, but I could still hear the bones cracking while they ate him. I have never been so alone as I am here. Then he comes at night and tries to seduce me – me! After I saw him kill Hasan!"

Aladdin set his torch in the bracket by the gate and ascended the steps. "You are safe now," he said, wrapping his arms around Maram. "I swear it."

Maram couldn't help it. Safe in his arms, she wept. For the senseless slaughter, the frustration of her own captivity, and most of all, for how much she'd missed this man.

"Everything will be all right. Tonight, we shall rest here, and on the morrow, I shall take you home," Aladdin soothed.

Amani cleared his throat. "You may go where you will, but the princess cannot leave."

A sob escaped from Maram, and the tears fell faster. "Please don't leave me, Aladdin. I cannot bear to be alone here again."

"I won't leave without you."

Never had the sensation of someone stroking her hair felt so exquisite.

"My master will return tomorrow night, and if he finds you, he will command me to kill you like Hasan, there," Amani said.

"But I am the master of the lamp," Aladdin said.

"Not any more," Amani said. "Gwandoya is my master now. And unlike you, he keeps the lamp safe on his person at all times, not in some alcove where anyone could see and steal it."

"But who would steal an old lamp?"

Amani sounded disapproving. "Anyone who knows its true worth. To have a powerful sorcerer like me at their command is something many would kill for."

"Gwandoya has already killed many men to get his hands on that lamp, and I was nearly one of them. There is no telling what he will do with such power." Aladdin sounded determined. "We must get it back."

"Nothing will make him surrender something so precious while he lives."

Maram raised her head and wiped her eyes. "Then Gwandoya must die. I won't let him kill Aladdin."

"Princess…" both men began.

She held up a hand to silence them. "I know I am not a fighter. I am a diplomat. But I have other weapons, and I'll be damned if I let him win. Tomorrow Gwandoya will die, and then I will get to go home. Are you with me?"

It took several hours and all Maram's powers of persuasion to get Aladdin and Amani to agree to her plan, but they did. The moon had reached its zenith, turning the jewelled garden into a sparkly paradise, as Amani took the hint and left her alone with Aladdin.

There were no tears when they came together this time, only kisses and increasingly urgent caresses. "Make love to me," Maram begged. She, who had never begged a man for anything in her life.

"When we are safely home and wed," Aladdin promised, stealing her breath with another kiss.

"Now!" she insisted. "Tomorrow anything could happen. Either of us could die, or he might escape with the lamp and leave us here, stranded. Tomorrow is uncertain, but I need to spend tonight in your arms."

She expected him to argue more, but all he said was, "As you wish, Princess."

Hardly daring to believe her luck, Maram led him to her bedchamber, where she eagerly peeled off her clothes. She turned, wanting to feast her eyes on Aladdin's body before she touched him. She had waited a long time for this.

"Why aren't you undressed?" she asked. Stepping forward, she seized the hem of his tunic. "Here, let me help you."

Gently, he pried her hands off his clothes. "No, Princess. I made you a promise and I intend to keep it. I swore I would set you free from your slavery, and I will. Your body is not a plaything for men to use for their own pleasure. You are the most beautiful woman I have ever seen and you deserve more, far more, than I can ever give. I love you, and I will take whatever pleasure you are willing to give me when you are free. Which you will never be, until we are wed."

"But you said…"

He gathered her up in his arms and carried her to the bed. Then he lay beside her, pulling her body against his, wrapping one arm around her breasts while his other hand rested on her belly. "I will hold you in my arms, like I said, and for now, I will be content."

She squirmed. "And if I am not? What about what I want?" She seized his hand from her belly and guided it between her thighs. "I want you, Aladdin. I am wet with anticipation, wanting the pleasure I will only feel when you are inside me."

His free arm tightened around her breasts. "Are you sure?" His voice was hoarse in her ear.

"Of course."

The words had barely left her lips before his fingers speared deep inside her, stroking all the right spots to make her gasp.

"More?"

"Oh yes!"

He hooked his leg around hers, anchoring her more firmly to his body as his fingers worked what could only be described as magic. One perfectly-placed circle of his thumb tipped her over the edge, sobbing his name.

He kissed the back of her neck. "Are you satisfied now, Princess?"

"Never!" she declared, then squeaked as his

fingers moved within her once more, stroking passion-inflamed flesh to another irresistible climax. She bucked, but he held her firmly in his arms, intent on her pleasure, even as he ignored his own growing arousal digging into her back. "You want me. I can feel it."

He laughed softly. "I don't just want you. I love you, and I desire you so much it hurts. But the only pleasure I will take in your bed tonight is yours." Again, his fingers stroked her, finding her most intimate places and making them sing.

Until…until…

"Aladdin, oh, how I love you!" she screamed.

Thirty-Two

"Something has changed. You are not as dejected as you were yesterday," Gwandoya greeted Maram, eyeing her with suspicion.

No woman could be dejected after a night experiencing the magic Aladdin could work with his fingers. The thought of what he might do with the rest of his body and hers was more than a little distracting. Not to mention frustrating, for he refused to give her more yet. That's why she'd spent the day leafing through the scrolls and books among her mother's things, looking for more information on djinn enslavement. After all, her mother had been a witch, too, with powers as limited as Maram's own.

"I miss having a man in my bed," she said honestly. "I have decided it is time to look to the future, and what you can give me. I have no maidservants here, and I have not had a new gown in weeks!"

Gwandoya's eyebrows rose, but as she spoke more fervently about maids and gowns, the suspicion in his expression slipped away. The man almost smiled.

He clapped his hands. "This calls for a betrothal feast. Bring us plenty of food and wine, for we will need it while we discuss our wedding."

Amani bowed and disappeared. Off to get what Gwandoya had asked for, no doubt. And what she had asked for, too.

Maram braced herself for what would be the biggest negotiation of her life, as she and Gwandoya argued the terms of a marriage she had no intention of entering into. Servants and jewels, palaces and gowns – for Gwandoya boasted that Amani could build her a palace anywhere she wanted, made of anything she pleased.

In the middle of Maram's lengthy deliberation of whether to have a stone castle far in the north, surrounded by blackberry hedges, or a palace like this one overlooking the sea, Amani brought a jug of wine.

"The finest vintage from the Sultan's own vineyards, which have lain in his cellar for more than a century," Amani announced, pouring cups for them both.

Maram's eyes lit up. "Ooh, is this the wine I told you about?"

Amani bowed. "Yes, Princess, it is."

She sipped, and scrunched up her face. The opium tasted as bitter as she had expected. "It does have a bite to it. Keeping it in a cellar for a century must do that, I suppose. But there is no better wine to toast our union with." She lifted her cup. "To our health and happiness, my lord."

Gwandoya preened, probably at the

unearned title. He lifted his own cup. "To our health and happiness indeed." He drained his cup, then smacked his lips appreciatively. "'Tis strong stuff. Too strong for a woman, especially one who is about to become my obedient wife and bear my sons." He snatched up her cup and drained that, too, before commanding Amani to pour more for himself alone. "We shall start tonight."

Maram stared at him in shock. His calculating eyes regarded her over the rim of his cup as he gulped more wine, daring her to object. Obedience had been one of the things she'd traded for…something. If it meant he drank more of the drugged wine, then she would not argue. "Yes, my lord," she said, ducking her head in fake submission.

An idea struck her. "I have the perfect idea for my wedding gown. I would like seven layers of silk…" She described in excruciating detail one of the gowns she'd seen on the Queen of Beacon Isle, changing her mind about the colour only to return to the original shade as she saw Gwandoya's eyelids drooping.

Sleep, you mad bastard, she thought, pasting a smile on her face as she began a long debate about the merits of the exquisitely detailed painted shoes in Kasmirus compared to the silk slippers found in the bazaars closer to home.

"A good embroiderer can do just an intricate design with thread as a painter can with pigment, but there are few painters in Kasmirus who are talented enough any more. The royal family has a pair of christening shoes that have been in their family for generations, the most beautiful pair I have ever seen…"

Gwandoya's head flopped forward into a bowl of the bugs he liked so much.

"My lord?" she enquired. "Gwandoya?" She called his name several times, before gesturing for Amani to check him. She had no intention of touching him.

Amani eased Gwandoya's face out of the bowl and laid him on the floor. "He sleeps, but he still draws breath," Amani reported.

May heaven forgive her, but she had not been able to bring herself to kill the man, even with poison. Maram breathed out a sigh of relief. "Bring me the lamp."

Amani folded his arms across his chest and shook his head. "I cannot." His tone softened. "A new master of the lamp must take it from the old. I cannot choose who I serve."

"Fine." She rose and leaned over Gwandoya's sleeping form. The detestable man let out a loud snore. She reached into his tunic and pulled it from the grimy pocket where he kept it. Maram cradled the lamp in her clean hand while wiping the tainted one down the side of his tunic. Time to see if the old books were right.

A cloud of smoke surrounded Amani as he swelled to his full height, the impressive bulk of a djinn greeting his new master for the first time. "What is your wish, mistress?" he boomed.

"Take me, and everyone and everything inside this palace, back home where we belong." Remembering the first time, when she'd hit her head, she added, "As smoothly as possible, please, so that no one feels a thing."

"As you wish, mistress."

She felt the movement, little more than the sway of a ship at sea, before a slight bump told her they had arrived. A peep out the window revealed the shadow of buildings as someone carrying a torch ambled down the street. Maram was home.

"What else do you wish, mistress?"

"I wish to be free to marry the one I love, to be no man's slave any more."

Amani looked pained. "Princess, I cannot…"

Maram lifted her dagger from the table and sliced it across her hand. "I know. But I can. Blood of the betrayed that binds this djinn, my father's blood that runs in my veins, too, will set us both free." She seized the lamp in her bleeding hand, smearing the stuff over the blackened brass. "I am no man's mistress!"

Aladdin appeared. "Maram, no…"

She tossed the lamp at his feet. "Yes." She turned to Amani. "You are free. Find her, free her, and be happy."

Tears filled Amani's eyes, as, man-sized

once more, he bowed at Maram's feet. "As you command, Princess. When I find her, I will tell her that you have found happiness, too. If you ever have need of me, you have only to call, and I will be there to grant your wish." He touched her hand, and she felt the cut heal as though it had never been. Only then did Amani rise and incline his head to Aladdin. "Enjoy your palace. Consider it my wedding gift to the princess. But if you ever hurt her…know you will incur the enmity of the most powerful enchanter in the world. A man with no master. Not any more." He stuck a finger in his mouth, withdrew it, then traced a circle in the air. A portal opened, and he stepped through and was gone.

"Why did you do that? He was a traitor! The enslavement was his punishment for crimes even we do not know!" Aladdin's wild eyes reminded Maram of Gwandoya.

"I know. His only crime was to love my mother, and win her love in return. Neither of us deserves to be a slave, serving a master who might use us for ill." She took his hand.

"Please understand."

Aladdin swallowed. "I admit I do not, but there is very little about you I do understand. You are a great mystery to me, Princess Maram, but one I intend to spend my whole life studying. As long as your father doesn't kill me first."

"Why would my father kill my husband to be?"

"He gave me a month to bring you and this palace back, or he would cut off my head. Tomorrow is the last day of my month."

Maram folded her arms. "Then we will see the Sultan now, and sort this out. Next week is our wedding, and I want you alive."

Aladdin laughed. "I want you every bit as much as you want me, Princess. As you wish it, so must it be. To the Sultan's palace we go."

Thirty-Three

Sleepy servants showed Aladdin and Maram to an audience chamber, promising to tell the Sultan of their arrival. Time ticked by with no sign of the Sultan, as Maram dozed in Aladdin's arms and he found he didn't mind being kept waiting. No matter how many times Aladdin told himself he wasn't worthy of any princess, let alone Maram, the rightness of her body against his was undeniable. And the way her body had responded to him last night…she genuinely wanted him. Him,

Aladdin the humble spinner's son, briefly the master of a lamp and its djinn, but now…now he was just a man in love, waiting to beg the Sultan to spare his life so that he might marry the man's favourite daughter.

The first rays of sunlight entered the audience chamber before the Sultan marched in, his brow furrowed with annoyance. "What kind of man wants to be beheaded before I break my fast? If you weren't going to be executed today anyway, I would think up a suitable punishment for waking your Sultan too early."

Aladdin's first instinct was to prostrate himself at the Sultan's feet, but that would mean waking Maram, so he did not move. Instead, he said softly, "I know of no man who wishes to lose his head before you break your fast, Your Majesty. But I did not dare sleep until I had reported to you, as I promised." He stroked Maram's hair. "The princess made no such promise, though, so perhaps we should let her rest."

The Sultan's eyes widened. "You brought

her back? Is she hurt?"

"Not that I can tell, but she was kidnapped by a madman and held captive for weeks. There is no telling what he did to her."

"Where is the madman now?" the Sultan demanded.

"In the dining hall of my palace, unconscious. Your Majesty is welcome to him," Aladdin said.

The Sultan ordered two guards to bring Gwandoya back, then sat across from Aladdin and stared at him for a moment before he said, "For saving her, I would offer you her hand in marriage, if I had not already promised it to you."

Much though Aladdin would have liked to be the hero, he knew he didn't deserve the title. "She saved herself. She drugged her kidnapper's wine. The only reason she didn't do it earlier was because she did not think she could escape until I arrived. Your daughter is an amazing woman, and while I have no idea how I have managed to win her affection, I know I am the luckiest man alive."

"Indeed you are. She is everything a man could wish for, but will never attain." The Sultan sighed. "Just like her mother."

Aladdin longed to ask for the Sultan to say more, but as the silence stretched between them, he could not bring himself to do so.

"Your Majesty, the man you wanted."

The guards unceremoniously dumped Gwandoya on the floor.

"Wake him," the Sultan commanded grimly.

The guards tried shaking him, slapping him, then throwing a bucket of water over the man, but still Gwandoya did not wake. Then one of the guards bent over him and pressed a hand to Gwandoya's chest, over his heart. After a moment, the guard shook his head.

"He's gone, Your Majesty."

"What do you mean?" the Sultan asked.

"He's dead."

Maram stirred. "Serves him right for stealing my wine." She eyed Gwandoya's corpse. "Far too easy a death for the man who kidnapped me and killed Hasan. Throw his body into the gutter, to be devoured by stray dogs. It is no better than he deserves."

The Sultan sagged in relief at the sound of her voice. "Whatever you wish, Maram. We will postpone this wedding until you are well, and you shall have your apartments here so that my guards can keep you from further harm."

"No." Maram struggled to sit up, then aimed a glare at her father. "I will live in the palace my husband gave me, with him, and I will marry him on the morrow. Anyone who seeks to steal Aladdin from me again will suffer a worse fate than him." She pointed at Gwandoya.

The Sultan looked taken aback. Then, slowly, he said, "Whatever you wish."

Thirty-Four

Maram had attended many feasts in her life, but she never wanted one to finish as much as her wedding feast. Courtiers gushing over her dress, fawning over Aladdin, or exclaiming over delicacies they had never tasted before barely registered in her thoughts, for all that occupied her mind was the man beside her.

Finally, the Sultan commanded the guests to form a triumphal arch for the departing couple, and she and Aladdin were allowed to leave. She ran beside him as though her feet had wings, through the arch and all the way home. Guards stood at the gates now, a gift from her father, but she had eyes for only one man. A man whose hand she held tight in her own as she led him to the best bedchamber, a room she had not entered until now.

An enormous bed occupied most of it, piled with enough pillows and coverlets to sleep a small harem, for it was a bed fit for a king. Fit for her pretend prince and her, certainly.

She paused only long enough to kiss Aladdin deeply before she started shedding her clothes, not stopping until the layers of silk and linen lay on the floor. She lifted her chin. "Now, you must make love to me," she said.

He laughed. "As my princess commands."

She shook her head. "I am not a princess any more. Not truly. I am your wife, and nothing more." She'd never felt so free.

Finally, he tugged his tunic over his head and left it with her clothes. "You are everything to me. A princess, a queen...a woman to worship. I would do anything for you, princess or no."

She smiled. "Then lie down."

Her eyes drank in every inch of his naked body as he stretched out on the bed, his head pillowed on his folded arms as he stared straight back at her. Her husband was no soft courtier, or over-muscled knight. No, he was lean and hard, with no extra flesh or muscle that a man did not need.

"I can't make love to you while I am here and you are over there," he said, beckoning. "Come here, my beautiful wife, so that I can show you just how much I love you."

She grinned and crawled across the bed, stalking like a lioness. "Two nights ago you had your turn. Now it is mine." With practised ease and considerable pleasure, she straddled him, guiding him inside her until he filled her completely. "Oh yes. This is what I've longed for. All those nights, I dreamed…"

"As did I." His hands curved around her hips, cupping her bottom, as he drove deeper inside her.

They moved together in perfect harmony, two parts of one glorious being, not stopping the first time she screamed his name, but when she felt her second climax building, he slowed.

"I cannot resist you any longer, Maram. I must...I must..." His words dissolved into a groan of pure pleasure as she clenched around him, catapulting her own body into another longed-for climax.

When she caught her breath, she finished for him: "We must do this every night we are together, for as long as we live."

Aladdin laughed, stroking his fingers across her breast. "You are stealing my wishes, just as you have stolen my heart."

She kissed him, long and hard. "Granting them, more like. With Amani gone, all you have is me."

The silver ring on his finger caught her nipple, sending a jolt through her. "You are all I ever need. I have nothing left to wish for."

She rose. "I wish for a bath. Will you join me in the bathhouse?"

"Only if you will grant a wish there that I have longed for since the day I met you."

Making love to Aladdin in the water. Maram

shivered in delicious anticipation. "Now who's stealing wishes?"

He lifted her in his arms and carried her to the bathhouse, and Maram sighed blissfully, knowing there was nowhere else she would rather be, and truly nothing else she could wish for.

Melt:
Snow Queen
Retold

DEMELZA CARLTON

A tale in the Romance a Medieval Fairy Tale series

One

"Make way for the Sultan!"

Briska's heart stopped for a moment, before it started again, beating faster than before. No one noticed, for such a reaction was normal. Every woman in the king's harem undoubtedly experienced the same stuttering of her heart, because for every minor wife and concubine, a night in the Sultan's bed was a path to power, prestige, or perhaps a pretty present. Maybe even pleasure, if the Sultan liked the girl enough.

Not for Briska, though. It was fear, not anticipation, that quickened her heartbeat. For the Sultana had no need for more power or prestige, and her dowry had been such that it eclipsed the Sultan's own fortune, so she wanted for nothing gold could buy.

"Where is my queen?"

Briska allowed herself to smile, as her fear evaporated. Only one man called her that, in this land of strange titles and stranger customs.

"She is in her apartments, Your Majesty," one of the other girls said. "I will fetch her for you."

"No need. I know the way."

Briska smiled even more broadly. She carefully closed the door to her daughter's chamber, so that little Maram would not be woken by any sounds they made, before heading to the arched entrance to her apartments to greet her visitor.

He stepped inside, and she inclined her head. "Majesty."

He closed the doors behind him, shutting out the curious horde, before he lifted his head. Gone was the regal mien he wore for everyone else – he grinned fiercely and his face transformed from the cold monarch into the passionate lover she wished she could spend every moment with. "My queen."

She threw herself at him, her lips warming from his kiss as her body moulded to his, a prelude to a more intimate union once they managed to get their clothes off.

He tasted of wine and spices, kissing her as though he wished to consume the moment and make it a part of him forever. Then his teeth grazed her lip, drawing blood.

Briska gasped, her desire transforming into a spell that engulfed them both. He just laughed, as though he'd intended this all along.

He licked his bleeding lip – he'd bitten himself, too – and his magic came into play, far more powerful than her own. Her clothes vanished, and an enchanted breeze wafted across her skin, caressing her like the skilled lover who stood before her. The man who commanded the very air itself.

"I am yours," she whispered, letting the air currents lift her and carry her to the bed.

He stood at the end, surveying her, his eyes dark with desire. "Mine to worship," he said, kneeling on the bed between her legs.

The next breeze to caress her came from his parted lips, whispering inside her of all the magic he could work with merely his mouth.

And then words failed her, for the language they shared was one of touch and pleasure, until they both lay, satisfied and exhausted, in each other's arms.

"Mine to love," he said, pressing his lips to her breast.

"And I love you, Amani, as I have never loved any man before, nor will I, no matter what the future holds."

He drew in a sharp breath. "Not even...?"

Briska shook her head, smiling. "No, not even him. No one makes my body and soul sing as you do. Love has a magic all its own, more powerful even than yours."

He laughed softly. "The most powerful sorcerer in the world, a slave to love. And I would not have it any other way. But even a sorcerer must sleep, which I will not do in any bed I share with you, so I must leave you, my queen." He kissed her lips, the soft brush of goodbye, before he rose from the bed and cocked his head, listening. "Does the harem never sleep? It sounds noisier out there than when I arrived!"

Briska pulled on a robe, wishing she had the magic to be able to dress and undress at will, like he did. But she would never possess his power. "Perhaps one of the concubines has gone into labour. A few of the pregnant ones are close to their time. Heaven only knows why babies choose to arrive in the middle of the night. Why, even Maram – "

"Make way for the Sultan!"

For the second time that night, Briska's heart stopped with fear. A fear she would not give in to, as she drew herself up with all the fortitude of the queen she was. "Go!" she hissed, giving Amani a push. "Magic yourself invisible or – "

Too late. The doors flew open, and the Sultan stood beneath the arch, his stoic face revealing nothing but the cold fury of a man who knew no mercy.

Two

"For the Sultan's wife to bestow her attentions on any man but the Sultan himself is treason," the guard thundered. "Do you know the penalty for treason?"

That's the moment Briska changed from regal queen to pitiful heap, as she collapsed on the floor. "No," she whispered, staring not at the guard, but at Amani.

He met her eyes and said the words that should have given her all the courage she needed to stand strong once more. "I love you. My love for you shines brighter than the very stars in the sky, and it always will."

Instead, Briska burst into tears.

Armoured guards seized Amani's arms, dragging him out of the harem. Whispering women clung to each other, watching wide-eyed as he passed.

The Sultan had women aplenty – why did he need Briska? He could have just divorced her, freeing her from a marriage neither of them wanted, so that she might love the man she did want, but the Sultan was too selfish for that.

Accusing her of treason said he intended to execute her. Fire erupted in Amani's breast. Amani would not allow it. Was he not the most powerful enchanter in the world? He would save her even from the stupid Sultan. Her fool of a husband.

"Unhand me," he ordered the guards.

At least, that's what he means to say, but the moment he opened his mouth, one of them stuffed a wad of cloth in, then tied a second piece of cloth around his mouth so he could not speak.

Or bite his lip to draw blood to fuel his spells.

The most powerful enchanter in the world, rendered impotent by a rag that smelled…probably even tasted…of camel dung and sweat.

Then someone hit him over the head, and he knew nothing.

Three

"Leave us," the Sultan commanded. He waited until they were alone in the room before he held out a hand. "For heaven's sake, Briska, take it, and get up."

Unwillingly, she grasped his hand – colder and harder than Amani's ever were – and rose to her feet. "What do you want?" she asked coldly. He'd make it clear since Maram's birth that he wanted nothing else from her.

"The truth." He surveyed the room, as though looking for a suitable throne from which to deliver justice, but Briska's apartments were a place of leisure. If he wanted to sit, he could sit on one of the floor cushions. That would seat him lower than her. He sighed. "The guards tell me they saw a man who looked like me enter the harem several hours ago. But the midwife didn't see him, as she was busy with the mother of my son, so she sent a messenger to my quarters, telling me about the boy's birth. So when a second Sultan appeared…the guards knew there was something amiss. Tell me the truth. Did he come to you as me? Did you think…?" There was a yearning in his eyes, the like of which Briska had not seen for years.

Perhaps the fool still felt something for her, after all. A fool who had just ordered the death of the man she loved.

"The moment the doors closed, he revealed himself as the only man I could ever love," Briska snapped, feeling a spark of satisfaction as the hope in his eyes died. "Even without magic, he's ten times the lover you ever were. I begged him, many times, to do away with you and take your place as Sultan, so that I could be his wife in truth, but he was too honourable to break his oath to you. And now he will die at your hands, not because he was a traitor, but because he was too loyal."

His shoulders slumped. "If you say he tricked you, I could still save you, Briska. Nothing will save him, but you…"

She shook her head. "I would rather die with him, than live forever as your wife, knowing I will never see him again. Summon your executioner and take off my head, like I know you want to." She tried to make the words sound brave and forceful, pushing them out as a shield to hide the yawning pit of despair where her heart had once beat for joy. Never again. "You want the truth? I tricked him. Cast a spell on him, so he would fall in love with me. If anyone's a traitor, it's me, not him. Take me. Arrest me, and let him go." Hope blossomed within her. If she could save Amani…

The Sultan laughed. "Even if it were true, I cannot do it. If I let a traitor go unpunished, it will only embolden others. No, he will die a traitor's death, but you…I don't want to see you die, Briska. He must…but you can still live."

"I will not betray the man I love," Briska returned.

The Sultan sighed. "Very well." He raised his voice. "Send in the courtesan!"

Then he began to mutter under his breath. The words sounded like the ones she'd prayed to hear more times than she could count, but…why now?

The door cracked open and a woman sidled inside, then flung herself face-first on the floor. "Your Majesty."

His regal mask had returned. "Rise."

The courtesan – for that was what she was – sprang to her feet with more grace than Briska expected. Her face was veiled as though she'd come from outside the palace, but the gossamer thin silk hid nothing, allowing anyone to glimpse her golden skin and perfect curves through her translucent clothing. Why, Briska could see her peaked nipples clearly through the cloth.

The Sultan did not seem to care. "This is the enchantress, who confessed her treachery. She used magic to commit treason against me." He pointed at Briska, not even deigning to look at her any more. "I respectfully submit her to the justice of your people."

Your people. Panic flooded through Briska and she bit her lip, desperately trying to cast a portal that would take her to safety. Away from the fate worse than death that awaited her if she stayed.

The courtesan merely smiled and waved her hand, freezing Briska so she could no longer move. "Her magic is weak, this enchantress. One wonders how she thought she could succeed in her betrayal."

Now Briska wanted to tell the truth — that she hadn't bespelled Amani at all, until she knew his love for her was as strong as hers for him. It was no crime to increase a desire they already shared. But her mouth was closed, and she could not open it. Could not even sink her teeth into her lip for another drop of blood to cast a spell, any spell, that might help her.

A servant came in, carrying a mirror, which she set on the table, before she bowed and retreated.

The courtesan placed a ringed hand on the

mirror's surface. "Now we may start. Your Majesty, a drop of blood?"

She drew a dagger from her belt and held it out, point-first, to the Sultan. He touched his finger to the tip, leaving a bead of royal blood.

She swiped her ring across her hand, leaving a shallow cut behind. The ring's jewel seemed to glow red through the layer of blood coating it.

"Kneel," the courtesan commanded, and Briska was forced to obey. "Now lift your chin."

Briska held her breath as the dagger came closer and closer, ready to slash her bared throat. The courtesan's gleeful smile was the last thing she'd see. Better than a lifetime of slavery as a queen or a…

The dagger pricked her, just above her collarbone, then retreated.

NO! Briska screamed in her head, but she didn't make a sound. She couldn't.

The courtesan touched her blood-dipped dagger to the ring, then leaned on the table. "By the blood of the ruler you betrayed, I bind you in servitude, djinn. By your own blood, the blood of a traitor, I bind you in servitude, djinn. And by my own blood, the blood of the judge who names you guilty of crimes against your ruler, I bind you in servitude, djinn."

Tears sprang to Briska's eyes and fell, unchecked, for she could not even blink them away. The courtesan had turned her into a djinn, a slave, forced to obey her master for eternity.

"Do you want her?" the courtesan asked the Sultan.

He shook his head. "As my Sultana, by my side, I would have given her anything. Now, she is nothing to me." And he said the words Briska had wanted to hear for so long, but now it was too late. "I divorce you, Briska." Three times he said it, until the marriage was void. He looked at the courtesan. "I beg you, take her away from here, and do whatever you want with her. I never want to see her again. See to it, Mistress Kun."

Briska couldn't even exclaim her horror. Slave to a courtesan? She couldn't imagine a worse fate. Having to share a bed with the clumsy Sultan had been bad enough, but a courtesan took dozens of lovers. If she commanded Briska to give herself to a man, any man, as a djinn she could not refuse. She would have to endure…

The courtesan lifted the mirror, so Briska could see the misty surface. Blood marred the frame where the courtesan had touched it, but the surface gleamed in the lamplight. "Look closely, for you will need this in my service," the courtesan said. "You may move now."

The force holding Briska upright vanished as quickly as it had come, flopping her forward in a deep bow. "How may I serve you, Mistress?" The words were out of her mouth before Briska could stop them.

The courtesan smiled. "Oh, you will be of great use to me."

"I am not very skilled at entertaining men, Mistress," Briska said. "Or at magic. The only man I ever seduced against his will just divorced me." Oh, how she wished she could have done things differently on her wedding night. He'd sworn not to consummate their marriage until she was willing, but she'd cast spell after spell at him until she forced him to take her maidenhead. A clumsy, painful encounter that she'd endured every night until she knew she carried Maram.

Maram. What would happen to her now?

"My daughter. Maram," Briska choked out. "What will he do with her?"

The courtesan stared at her. "You mean the Sultan? Is she his?"

"Of course. Amani did not come to court until after she was born."

The courtesan said, "Then the girl belongs to the Sultan. She will stay, but we must go."

"Where?"

Mistress Kun smiled. "Wherever I command you to."

"I am not very skilled – " Briska began again.

"Then you will learn to become so. Oh, not at entertaining men. No, you're going to do some matchmaking for me. Up in the Southern Isles, a daft name for such a northerly place, if ever I heard one."

"I have never…"

Mistress Kun snapped her fingers. "Silence! Bring the mirror, and come with me." She

opened a portal and stepped through.
Briska had no choice but to follow.

"It's time to meet your first match," Kun said.

Briska blinked, staring at her mistress's image in the glass. The mirror sat on a natural shelf on the cave wall, as though the gingerbread-like rock had been baked by ancient hands in readiness for this day. Perhaps it had. Who knew?

Kun's face faded, to be replaced by a vision of a beach with two bodies on it. Two wet bodies, that looked like the waves had brought them reluctantly to shore but longed to reclaim them, licking at them tentatively before swallowing them forever.

"You must do everything in your power to bring these two together. The fate of a kingdom rests on this match," Kun said. "And so does yours, for if you serve me well, you may yet win your freedom."

The mirror clouded over again, shrouded in thick mist like the island outside, most days. Not today, though – today the rain poured from the sky without cease, soaking Briska to the skin as she dashed toward the beach. And the bodies.

Well, she couldn't match dead bodies, so they had to be still alive. Or her task would be over before it began. Briska wasn't sure what happened to slaves who failed to obey orders, but she knew it couldn't be good.

The mirror had showed the truth – a boy and a girl lay on the beach, in danger of being dragged out to sea if she left them there.

Briska headed for the boy first, for if she could wake him, perhaps he could carry the girl to the shelter of the cave.

But no amount of shaking or shouting roused him, so Briska dug her hands into the folds of his sodden tunic, and proceeded to drag him up the beach, out of reach of the waves. The wet weight of him nearly pulled her arms from their sockets, he was so heavy, but she managed to drag him about a yard before she had to stop to catch her breath. One yard….two…three…until she had him above the high tide mark.

Her arms hung by her sides, feeling heavier than the boy had, but Briska still had the girl to save. At least the girl would be lighter than her husband-to-be.

If the waves didn't get her first.

Briska hurried down the beach, gasping as a wave broke against her knees, sending freezing water swirling around her legs. She grabbed the girl, fighting the sucking sea as the wave retreated, until she emerged, victorious, on the wet sand.

By all that was holy, how could the girl be heavier than her husband-to-be? Her thick skirts dragged along the sand, catching on rocks and doing their best to hinder Briska as she heaved the girl up onto the rocks beside the boy.

If ever she needed magic to help her, it was now, but all Briska wanted to do was lie down beside the pair and rest for a week. But between her chattering teeth and trembling limbs, the freezing wind and her wet clothes, she knew she had to get inside…and so did these two.

Briska's hand drifted down to the dagger at her waist – a bone-handled thing with a stone blade so shiny it resembled green glass. She'd found it in the cave, echoing faintly of magic long since cast, so she'd claimed for her own. Briska ran her finger along the wicked edge. Blood mixed with salt water on her skin, and she tried not to hiss in pain as she turned her attention inward…to the magic that rarely came even when she called. A portal, she needed a portal to take her to the cave.

Briska traced a circle in the air, over and over, but nothing appeared. She fell to her knees and wept, but still her hand circled, blood dripping down her arm and staining her sleeve. Finally, she gave up. It seemed her enslavement had extinguished whatever little magic she controlled.

Time to do this the hard way.

When her task was finished, then she could rest.

Briska seized the boy, and began dragging him home.

He gave a strangled shout and struggled free.

Briska cried out and dropped him. His head clunked against the stone and he went limp, out cold once more.

Oh, by all that was holy…if she hadn't panicked, he might have woken and carried himself up to the cave. Maybe even the girl, too. Now she'd have to do all the work herself.

Swearing softly, Briska resumed her labour. Cursed by love and doomed to serve until she made the match Mistress Kun wanted. If only the Sultan could see her now.

The girl woke first, despite the fever in her blood that sent wisps of steam rising from her clothes until they dried.

Briska approached the girl cautiously, knowing the lattice screen between them would offer her some protection if the girl lashed out. For who knew how these barbarians would react? What she'd seen of crusaders at home had demonstrated they had little honour, and these two looked no different.

"How are you feeling?" Briska asked softly,

but the girl didn't seem to hear her.

The girl grimaced as she sat up, holding her head as if it hurt.

Briska was no healer, but she could prepare tisanes for pain and fever. She slipped away to find some herbs to help the girl.

The girl's voice called her back with a question Briska could not quite make out. Yet when Briska returned, the girl's attention was on the cave furnishings…and her mistress's mirror.

A mirror in a place so backward they didn't know how to make glass, let alone a mirror.

The girl's eyes turned to Briska, full of knowing. "Let us out. I must go home." The barbarian girl drew herself up to her full height – a head higher than Briska – and stared down for all the world like she was a queen herself.

A slave she might be, but Briska did not have to obey this order. And she could do queenly better than this girl. "We all want to go home, but not everyone gets what they want. The sea wanted to take you from the beach where I found you, but I rescued you from the waves and brought you here. I must keep you two together. The mirror insists." Briska stepped out of the shadows, letting the mirror's misty glow light up her face as she tried to appear every bit the queen she once was. "Who are you?"

The girl shivered, her courage fleeing with her fever. "I am Gretel." She pointed at the unconscious boy. "That's my brother, Hansel." She kept speaking, but Briska didn't hear the words.

Brother and sister? Kun couldn't mean her to make an incestuous match like this one. Perhaps she intended to keep her here in exile, unable to make the match.

"Who are you?" the girl demanded.

Briska eyed her with dislike. "Once a queen, now a slave, loved by two men, one of whom is now dead and the other is dead to me. I am Briska, now queen of a rock that boasts little more than fearless deer and this horrible stuff called snow."

Forever cursed to be queen of this rock.

"You must let us go," Gretel insisted.

"I must do nothing of the sort." The words came out of Briska's mouth automatically, but even as she pressed her lips together to stem the flow, still the words repeated in her head. She must serve her mistress.

Then what of the mirror? Did she have to serve the mirror, too, or could it be wrong?

Haltingly, Briska continued, "The mirror says...the mirror says you must be together. But if you are brother and sister, as you say...then I am cursed!" The cursed queen of this rock, forever. "Bah, I should have known escape was an illusion." She tried to imitate Kun's superior tone: "You shall not leave here until you break the curse!"

Tears sprang to her eyes, and Briska hurried away, before Gretel could see her weakness.

Six

Briska waited for the girl to go back to sleep before she dared to use the mirror to contact Mistress Kun again. Even then, she took the mirror outside to use it out of sight of the pair.

"What is it?" Kun asked in irritation. Though Briska could not see below the woman's shoulders, she could see enough to know she'd roused the woman from bed. Briska would wager Kun had been pulled from a lover's arms instead of a dream, for Kun was too alert to be newly woken.

"You have made a mistake. They are not a

suitable match at all, but brother and sister. Hansel and Gretel are their names. Mistress, to make these two fall in love would be an abomination." Briska stuck her head inside and eyed the sleeping pair on the other side of the lattice, another of Kun's gifts. Kun had provided her with a modest bed, cooking utensils and a book to instruct her in using them and the spices from home, though djinn didn't need food, sleep or warmth. She had to appear like a normal human to these northern barbarians, apparently. As if a queen, albeit an exiled one, was anything close to normal. "I will not make this match!"

Kun's eyes flashed. "You serve me, and I order you to make this match. Do you hear me, djinn?"

"Yes, Mistress," came out Briska's mouth, unbidden. Before her tongue could betray her again, she hissed, "I hear you, but I will not!"

Pain erupted in her head, like nothing she'd ever known before.

"Welcome to your enslavement. As long as you refuse to obey, the pain will worsen. Obey me, and it will fade as if it had never existed.

Make the match," Kun said.

Blinded by pain, pressing her head to the stone floor in a desperate attempt to alleviate the agony screaming from one ear to the other, Briska was barely aware of the mirror returning to mist once more before she lost her senses to the darkness.

Seven

Shouting dragged Briska back to consciousness – the boy this time: Hansel. Her head only throbbed now, as though she'd drunk too much wine, but it was enough to make the shouting excruciating.

"Silence, boy!" she said, biting her lip and wishing she could cast some sort of spell to at least quieten him. But her magic was good for only one thing, and she refused to cast a seduction spell over the brother or the sister.

So she was forced to endure the sound of his voice as he cajoled her endlessly to let the two of them go.

Nothing he could offer her would be worth the knowledge that she'd be responsible for the abomination of an incestuous union.

Then he said words that held their own magic: "I shall build you a palace fit for a queen."

Grudgingly, Briska conceded, but only if the boy vowed never to share his sister's bed.

He didn't even hesitate.

The moment the promise left his lips, it seemed that the throbbing in Briska's head lessened. She had no idea why, but she wasn't going to question that now.

If the boy built her a palace, he would be too busy to have time to spend with his sister.

Eight

Briska's headache faded some days, only to rage with a vengeance the next, as Hansel sawed and hammered and built what the barbarian boy called a palace. The mirror flashed pictures of the pair, sometimes as they were at that moment, and sometimes locked in a lovers' embrace, as if to taunt her. But if Briska so much as thought her defiance at allowing such an abomination to happen, it was like Kun had buried a dagger in her head.

Briska took to carrying her dagger around with her everywhere, the cold stone a measure of welcome relief when her head pounded too hard to bear. She just had to lay the flat of the blade across her forehead and the pain receded.

A grunting, scuffling sound summoned her back to the cave, and Briska feared some strange creature had invaded her home. But what she saw was far worse – the mirror showed the pair naked, writhing in ecstasy in some cave that looked nothing like this one.

Briska's gaze darted to the lattice, but the girl was nowhere in sight. How had she escaped?

Briska drew her dagger. "It will not happen! Incest is against nature!" Not even the blade was enough to block out the agonising stab of pain behind her eyes. She fell to the floor, the knife slipping out of her fingers. She had to stop this. She had to. Her hands closed around the knife hilt, and Briska fought to find the strength to stand. "Better to kill them than let him defile her so. Now, before it is too late!"

She headed out of the cave, scanning the island for the entrance to the other cave, the one hiding the pair from her.

Pounding from the roof of the timber cottage drew her attention. The boy perched on the roof, whistling as he hammered one of the wooden roof tiles into place. He was fully clothed. There was no sign of the girl, either.

Briska stood watching him, not sure what to make of it. Had the mirror showed her a lie? Or had she imagined the image? No, surely not. She hadn't imagined the sounds they made. She'd never seen a couple so rapt in one another as they twined together. Not even with Amani had she ever been so…abandoned to everything but him.

Lost in thought, it took her a moment to realise the boy had climbed down, and now stood before her, holding the door open.

Hansel bowed extravagantly. "Your new palace, Your Majesty."

Some palace, but perhaps this cottage was a palace to these barbarians. Briska accepted his invitation, and made to step inside the house.

Gretel screamed something, then came running. She was fully clothed, too.

An invisible force slammed into Briska, throwing her against the door and holding her there. Magic. It had to be. Magic so powerful there was nothing Briska could do against it. She scraped her hand along the blade, desperately trying to cast a portal, but she could not even lift her arms against the force holding her in place. No portal, no escape...

"Don't you dare touch him, you bitch!" Gretel roared. Flames erupted from her hand, formed into a ball, then flew toward Briska.

Helpless to stop the missile, Briska was forced to watch as the ball of fire arced up, then down again. She prayed it would miss her, landing harmlessly on the ground.

The ball landed a foot in front of her, then bounced. This time, it landed on the toe of her boot.

Briska screamed and ran.

Too late. Her boots had caught fire, and a wall of flames surrounding her, allowing her no escape.

Unless she could cast a portal.

Blood dripped down her fingers, and Briska raised a shaking hand to trace a circle in the air, an archway through which she could pass. Pass, and live. Or burn and die.

Briska closed her eyes and wished.

Nine

When Amani woke, he was afraid someone had stuffed him into a chest and closed the lid. Or a coffin. They'd neglected to tie his hands, though, so it would be but the work of a moment to take off his gag, and cast a spell to make them rue the day they'd been born.

He tried to lift his arms, but they were squeezed so tightly between his body and the walls of his prison, he could not get even one hand free.

Wait…did he smell lamp oil? They couldn't burn him alive. Only barbarians did that.

He tried shouting through his gag, floundering in his coffin – it had to be a coffin, if they were going to burn him – but no one answered.

He heard the scrape of something rasping along the outside of his prison.

Amani tried shouting again.

It felt like a giant hand seized him, feet first, dragging him through a narrow opening that wasn't wide enough for his body. Tighter…tighter…crushing him…squeezing him into an impossibly narrow space where he couldn't breathe, couldn't feel anything but pain and pressure, couldn't even scream…

And then he was out, exploding into a cloud as the pressure was gone.

It took a moment before feeling returned to his arms and legs, and he was surprised to find his ribs didn't hurt despite definitely being crushed only moments before. Magic. It had to be.

But his hands were free now, free to untie his gag so he could spit out the foul-tasting cloth. The cloud around him cleared and he saw a man.

Not just any man. The Sultan, Briska's husband.

With a snarl, Amani opened his mouth to hurl every insult he knew at the man.

But what came out of his mouth was: "How may I serve you, Master?"

Amani tried to curse, but he only repeated the same words again. Furious beyond reason, he tried to strike the man, only to feel his body bow in deep respect for the man he hated.

He fought it, but his back bent anyway. The only bit of him he managed to keep from bowing was his head. He met the Sultan's gaze with all the fury he could muster.

"I don't want you to serve me at all. I never want to see your face again. Not after you stole her from me," the Sultan said.

"She was never yours!" Amani gasped out, before his own lips silenced him.

"But if not for you, she might have been, in time," the Sultan said. "Which is why I can't bear the sight of you."

Only now did Amani see that the Sultan held a lamp in his hands, a common thing of tarnished brass.

"So you may serve me by returning to the prison from whence you came, and sinking to the bottom of the ocean, where I will never have to look upon your traitorous face again," the Sultan said. He lifted the lamp high, then dropped it into the well. "I said go, servant of the lamp, and trouble me no more."

Amani didn't understand.

And then…he did.

His body crossed the paving stones in three strides, then dived into the well, head first, following the lamp. Amani hit the water, his strangled shout turning to bubbles in the blackness as he sought the lamp, compelled to follow. It glowed blue in the darkness, floating along in the current instead of sinking, calling for him to follow.

Not knowing why, he swam to catch up, stretching his hand out to grab the lamp. Only…his hand shrank, slipping inside the spout of the lamp, followed by his arm, until the narrow hole swallowed him up, scream and all.

Ten

Briska stamped out of her boots, but the blazing leather had already set the floor alight. Swearing, she bit down hard and fought to cast the only spell that could save her. The circle of blue light flared and died, once, twice…but on the third time it seemed to stay, wavering a little, but enough. She stepped through the portal, which collapsed behind her. She peeled off her singed stockings, to find her feet red and blistered with burns. She stuck her feet in the water bucket, moaning as the icy water numbed the pain.

The mirror unclouded for a moment and a face appeared. "Well done," Mistress Kun said.

"What do you mean, well done? That brother and sister almost killed me!" Briska snapped. This matchmaking thing was a lot harder than she'd thought. And incest…no, that hadn't been part of the bargain.

The woman laughed. "Brother and sister? You are too easily persuaded. That's what got you into this mess in the first place, but I will help you. This pair are matched, and so you will move onto your next quest. Your new assignment is in the icy north, I'm afraid. You will need warmer things."

Ice and snow? Perfect for burned feet.

Briska lifted her arms. "I am ready when you are, Mistress." The last word came hard for a woman who had once been a queen, but she had little choice now. Slavery to the mirror and its mistress was all her life held now.

A portal opened before her, and Briska stepped through. The mirror, her chest of belongings, and her precious sack of spices landed in the snow behind her.

Another day, another couple. Though she

shook her head when she thought of Hansel and Gretel. That pair would not have an easy time of it, she was certain. She might have made a match of them, however unwillingly, but they had a lot of work for even a hope of happily ever after.

Her mistress's face appeared in the mirror. "Next, you must match Kai and Gerda," she said.

Briska sighed as she saw the picture of the pair. At least these two had clothes on, unlike the fornicating brother and sister. Thank the heavens for small mercies. And snow to cool her feet.

From queen of a kingdom to queen of the snow, Briska's work was never done.

But first, she would need a place to live, for her new palace was gone. And all the ice and snow gave her an idea…

<h1 style="text-align:center">Eleven</h1>

Briska took a deep breath and then exhaled on the mirror. When the condensation from her breath faded, Mistress Kun's face appeared. "Mistress, I can't help but feel this is terribly wrong. I drove my sleigh through town, as you commanded, and just as you said, I stopped when the reindeer could go no further, and found a boy near frozen in his own sled, hooked onto my sleigh runners."

"Is he there with you now?" Mistress Kun asked eagerly.

Briska frowned at the boy, as still as a

corpse in his icy bed. "Yes," she said slowly. "But I should really take him home, for his family must surely miss him. I've put him into an enchanted sleep, which helps preserve him a little in this icy cold, but I'm not sure how long I can keep him that way, or whether it will do untold harm to do so. He's cold to the touch, barely draws breath…"

Kun waved her hand airily. "If you tried to take him home, he would undoubtedly freeze to death anyway. He has no family, no one who cares, except the girl he was trying to impress when he fastened his sled to your sleigh. Once she starts to miss his company, she will come to claim him. But if you do not, she will not yet care…and you will have to find another way to make this match."

Briska wrung her hands. "But if anything happens to him…I can't make a match if the boy's dead. And it's a dangerous journey up the mountain alone. All sorts of things might happen to the girl before she gets here."

Kun laughed. "The girl will not be alone, for she'll have plenty of help. You're not on that lonely rock any more, with nothing but deer.

You just concentrate on keeping the boy there, ready for when she arrives."

"But…"

"That is an order."

Briska slumped. "As you wish, Mistress."

"If you tire of watching him, then perhaps you can make a new match while you wait. Lubos and Molina, a prince and a miller's daughter…"

Briska stared at the unlikely pair, wondering what could attract a prince to some common peasant. Oh, she was pretty, she supposed, but not unless she stretched out naked before him, at precisely the moment when he fancied a roll in the hay…

Men. So predictable. She would have this pair so tightly entwined with one another not even the king himself could break them apart. And before Kai woke, too.

"Yes, Mistress. I will match them, too."

"Good. Watch out for Rumpelstiltskin, though, for he will try to stop you at every turn."

Briska opened her mouth to ask for more information, but it was too late. The mirror's surface returned to a reflection of the icy walls of the palace. Only then did Briska curse the day she'd ever agreed to become a djinn. A prince and a peasant, some man with a strange name, plus this frozen boy and a girl intent on rescuing him…Briska could feel it in her bones: neither match would not turn out well for her, at all.

Twelve

Daily, Briska asked her mistress about the progress of the girl who was to save the increasingly pale boy in her palace.

"She is travelling down the river by boat."

"She has been captured by a witch."

"She seeks word of him from flowers."

"Some crows have taken her under their wing."

"She is at the royal palace, sleeping in the prince's bed."

Each answer seemed worse than the last.

"If she has become a prince's mistress, then

surely she will not want the boy. May I send him home?" Briska asked, reaching out to touch the boy.

"Of course not. She merely sleeps in his bed. The prince has a wife of his own, and shares her bed. The girl mistook the prince for her match, the boy you hold, and you must keep him still, for she will come for him. She will be along shortly, for she will soon meet the reindeer who pulled your sleigh, and the beast will bring her to you."

Then the mirror clouded again, before reflecting the wall.

Briska should have felt relieved, knowing the match would be made soon, but she couldn't shake off an awful feeling of foreboding. After all, that Hansel and Gretel pair had seemed like such a simple match to make, and they'd nearly killed her.

Curse that Gretel girl for hiding her powers. What kind of witch did such a thing? Why, the girl deserved to be a djinn for misusing her powers so. It was only a matter of time before she came to the attention of her king, and what monarch would want a fire witch free in his kingdom?

The sooner the better, really, for if the girl found out Briska had survived the blaze…Briska shivered, and not from cold.

And here she was, waiting for what had to be another witch to arrive, for Gerda must have some magic in order to speak to plants and animals.

Dread settled in Briska's belly, like she'd swallowed a stone. She had to wake the boy, and take him home. No, take him home, then wake him.

A portal. She needed to cast a portal, the kind of magical doorway that would let her travel from here to his home.

Briska bit her lip, praying she could cast it this time. She traced a circle with her hand, then another, and another…

Over and over, she sank her teeth into her lip, until all she could taste was blood, but the portal never opened. Briska fell to her knees, defeated, and let her tears fall. Only they tinkled as they hit the icy floor, frozen the moment they left her face.

With the temperature dropping, both she

and the boy would need more blankets. If they could not leave, then they must endure…and wait for the inevitable.

Thirteen

The moment Briska saw the reindeer outside, she looked for a place to hide. But where did one hide, when every wall of her palace was made of crystalline ice, so clear you could see through them?

So she left the boy in the chamber with her mirror, and hid in the farthest corner of the palace from him. For hours she huddled in her corner, waiting for the couple to leave.

Finally, when it was dark enough outside for the aurora to be seen, she crept from her hiding spot. The light played across the walls, spinning and fracturing and reforming around her, but Briska ignored it. She would use the mirror to contact her mistress and tell her the match was made, and then –

Something crashed into the back of her head, sending her tumbling to the floor. Briska's hands scrabbled for purchase on the frozen floor, but she found none. The best she could do was to turn herself over to face her attacker.

"That's the witch who bespelled me," the boy said, pointing.

The girl hefted an icicle in her hand, a deadly point as long as her forearm. "What did she do to you?"

Briska scrambled back, skidding on the ice until her back met the wall. "I didn't do anything. I didn't, I swear!"

"She cast some spell on my sled so I couldn't unfasten it from her sleigh, and I couldn't get off, either. Then she cast some other spell on me so I couldn't move, and dragged me here to freeze to death. There's no other food here. She must mean to eat me!"

"No, I – "

The girl advanced. "We can't let her live. If she planned to kill and eat you…how many others has she murdered already?"

"Please – "

The boy stretched out his hand. "I should strike the blow, not you, Gerda. After all, it was me she meant to kill."

Gerda held the icicle out of his reach. "Get your own and we'll do it together. I'll watch her, and make sure she doesn't try anything." She turned her glare on Briska.

For the second time, Briska found herself facing a witch who wanted to kill her. Why hadn't she been gifted with more than a whisper of magic power? The only spell she knew she could cast would only make her situation here worse, for the one thing this girl desired most was Briska's death, and Briska could only heighten that desire, not change it.

"Please, I mean you no harm. Just take your friend and go," Briska pleaded.

But Gerda was deaf to her pleas.

The boy returned, carrying an icicle as thick as his arm and easily a yard long.

Briska's voice died. She could only look

from one to the other, begging with her eyes.

"On three," the girl said grimly.

"One, two…three!"

Briska screamed as two ice spears drove into her body. Something warm gushed down her back and she dimly realised that one of the spikes had gone right through her.

She slid to the floor, her vision fading.

The last thing she saw was the boy and girl, lifting the mirror between them to smash it on the floor, before they walked out of the palace, hand in hand.

Briska's last thought was that at least she'd made the match right before she died. Mistress Kun couldn't fault her on that.

Fourteen

Rasping again. Amani tried to shout for whoever it was to stop, but the only sound was a gurgle, for there was nothing but water in his cramped quarters. How he was still alive, he did not know.

Then the horrible feeling of being squeezed and crushed came again, before Amani drew in the most beautiful breath of air his lungs had ever tasted.

"How may I serve you, Master?" he boomed, ready to reward whoever had freed him from his tiny prison.

"It talked! The lamp smoke talked!"

Amani found himself facing two shabbily dressed camel drivers, one of whom must have dropped the lamp when he fell backwards in surprise. The two men ran away.

Amani sighed. He allowed himself the luxury of looking around. He was no longer in the Sultan's palace, judging by the desert dunes on all sides of the tiny spring. Definitely outside the city gates. He had no idea how much time had passed. A day, at least, for the sun was sinking and it had been night time when he was last forced into his prison.

He nudged the lamp with his foot. Such a tiny thing, but he could see the magic twining around it, and him, biding them together. Imprisoned in a common, tarnished lamp. The Sultan had truly intended to insult him. And he'd succeeded, curse him.

"Who are you?" an imperious voice demanded.

Amani looked up. The voice belonged to someone dressed as richly as the Sultan, or Amani himself.

"I am Amani, the most powerful sorcerer in

all the world," Amani said grandly. Hope swelled in his chest at the realisation that he hadn't been forced to bow to the man. Was he somehow free?

"He came out of this, Your Highness!" one of the camel drivers said, seizing the lamp. He shook the sand off it, then presented it to the well-dressed man.

"What was a powerful sorcerer doing inside a lamp?" the well-dressed man asked.

"I was imprisoned inside it for my crimes, Master," Amani said, hating the words that he could not stop himself from saying. "I am the slave of the lamp, ready to obey your every wish."

"Hmm." The well-dressed man eyed him thoughtfully. "I have no need of another slave, but if you are telling the truth about being a powerful sorcerer, perhaps I might find some use for you. Rejoice, for you now serve Prince Philemon of Tasnim!"

Tasnim, the mysterious underground city that owed its wealth to its water wells, deep under the desert, that travellers paid a great deal to drink from. In better circumstances,

Amani might have offered his services to the Prince of Tasnim. But he could not rejoice, no matter how strong the order. Some magic was beyond even Amani.

For without Briska, life could hold no joy.

So he said, "Yes, Master," and waited. For what, he did not know.

Fifteen

Briska blinked her eyes open, barely believing she could. "Is this paradise?" she asked.

"Heavens, no. If paradise were this cold, even the virtuous souls would have revolted by now. I'm sure it's as fitting as fire is for hell. Hardly a reward."

"Mistress," Briska managed to say as Kun's face came into view. "Why am I not dead?"

"Don't look to me for miracles. You're a djinn. You can't die. No matter how many holes that ungrateful pair punched into you."

Briska coughed, then doubled over in agony

as the movement set fire to her chest. She reached to touch her torso, feeling for the holes that were no longer there. "How?"

"I pulled them out. Then your body simply healed, like djinn do. Enslavement isn't all bad when it includes immortality." Kun shrugged. "It's supposed to be a punishment, prolonging the period of servitude. You don't age and you don't die. Some djinn have lived for centuries."

Centuries of this? "Better to die outright than to suffer it over and over again."

Kun regarded her. "You are allowed to use your magic to defend yourself, you know."

"My magic is not strong enough for that."

"After the fire and now this, I wonder what use your magic is at all." Kun hung the mirror back on the wall, which appeared to have never been broken. "Perhaps I should have just left you here, impaled on ice."

Briska moistened her lips. "Thank you for saving me, Mistress," she said. "If you give me another chance, another couple, maybe…but not a witch. Djinn or not, I do not think I can survive another spell."

Kun laughed. "Who do you think you are

matchmaking, if not witches? Someone must see that another generation of magic users is born, and tend the bloodlines. Every match you make is for a witch."

Briska shrank against the floor, wishing she could sink right through it. "Then help me hide from them, Mistress," she begged. "I will make the match, cast what spells I can to help love blossom between whoever you command, but please hide me from them. If there was some way I could stay here, far from harm, and still bespell them…"

"Perhaps there is," Kun said, stroking the mirror. "But you must promise to match every couple I send you, without protest. There shall be no repeat of the Hansel and Gretel affair."

Briska shook her head, then winced. "No, Mistress. I shall match every couple." That Gretel girl still gave her the shivers. "Is there any way you can hide me from Gretel, too?"

"I shall cast a spell on the mirror, allowing you to use it to not only see the couple you are to match, but cast spells through the glass, too. And I shall hide this palace, so that no magic may find it. All you must do is stay within its walls, and you may hide from the world. And I will not have to come here to save you again."

Briska lay back, breathing a sigh of relief. "Thank you, Mistress."

Some time passed before Kun said, "There. It is done. On the morrow, I will send you a new couple to match. Take care that you do not let all the ice up here freeze your heart, so you can't even cast your feeble love spell."

Without waiting for an answer, the enchantress cast a blinding blue portal and vanished.

Only then did Briska dare to breathe again. Her heart had frozen the day Amani died, and nothing would touch it, ever again.

And love spells? No one could cast those, not even the most powerful enchantress, for love had a magic of its own that overpowered all other spells. No, she worked with lust, and seduction. She could seduce a man to her bed in a moment, or stoke a spark of lust into a raging inferno. If that Hansel and Gretel hadn't been brother and sister, she'd have matched them the moment they woke in their prison. As for Gerda and Kai…

Briska swore she'd do better next time. And if she was safe in her icy citadel, far from the reach of any vengeful witch, Kun would never have the excuse to call her spells feeble again.

Sixteen

"Enough," Briska commanded, and the writhing, naked bodies in the mirror turned to reflected blue. Now she was done with them, no one would pry Snow White away from her prince.

She pressed her hands against the icy wall, then against her flaming cheeks, attempting to cool them. The glassy walls were weeping, it felt so hot in here, almost as though the steamy scene between Snow White and her match had heated up the palace, too.

If Briska had Amani here right now, she

would…

She closed her eyes, feeling the icy chill invade her heart again. She didn't need to look to know the palace had frozen into its usual crystalline splendour, showing no sign of the recent melt.

Mistress Kun would be pleased at her success, she was sure of it.

If only Briska could feel some measure of satisfaction in it, but she felt nothing. While passion raged between Snow White and her prince, her heart was empty.

There was no one left to love.

Even her daughter had been torn from her.

If she could only see Maram again…

Briska stretched a hand toward the mirror, wishing with every bit of her being that she might glimpse the girl again.

But Maram was too young for matchmaking. She was barely old enough to play with the dolls Amani had bought for her.

The mirror surface rippled, clouded, then cleared.

Briska's breath caught in her throat.

Maram crouched in the garden, unnoticed in

the dark. Light and laughter floated from the harem halls, but Maram only hugged her dolls tighter to her chest. What was the girl doing, awake so late? Had no one put her to bed, as they should?

Women passed her, taking no notice of the child.

Briska bit her lip, sending a spell through the aether to the harem. She let it expand like mist, until it had touched every woman present.

"Where is Maram?" murmured one, then another, until the whole harem started searching for the little girl.

It was a concubine who found her, a girl Briska remembered because she'd borne the Sultan a daughter not long after Briska had birthed Maram. What was her name again? N-something. Naheed, that was it.

Briska dug her teeth deeper into her lip, and sent out the most powerful seduction spell she'd ever cast. Not at Naheed but at the little girl in her arms.

A chorus of coos from the women standing around Naheed told her the spell had worked.

"Yes, love my daughter for me," Briska said. "He might have removed me from her life, but she will not go unloved. Every one of you will hold her as dear as your own child."

She watched greedily as Naheed hugged the girl tightly, carrying her to bed. Briska would have given anything to hold Maram in her own arms, and perhaps one day she would, but in the meantime…she would at least watch.

As long as her mistress never found out.

For Kun must never know.

Briska took one last, longing look at Maram, before wiping the picture from the mirror. She would tell Mistress Kun about her success with Snow White in the morning, and accept her next assignment. One day, the matchmaking would end, and Kun would release her to go home to her daughter. One day.

However long it took, however many matches she had to make, Briska swore she would win her freedom.

For Maram.

Seventeen

A dragon. A huge, fire-breathing, sword-crushing dragon. Briska stared in awe, hardly daring to believe her own eyes. Giants, unicorns…she thought she'd seen everything with this couple, but she hadn't expected to actually see a dragon.

It should have been simple, but she'd learned by now that no witch's mind was simple. George had needed barely a nudge from her magic to fall madly in love with Melitta, but the cool, collected maiden didn't seem to experience passion of any kind.

And when she did…Briska had thrown the spell so hastily she'd been responsible for breaking three beds before she realised the lust in Melitta the mindreader's mind was from someone else's thoughts, every time. She'd almost gotten them killed once, when the lust had belonged to a giant. But lust came in many forms, and a man maddened by battle lust became a liability.

So she'd followed their journey, day after day, hoping to find that tiny spark in the girl's mind she could fan into a flame.

If the dragon didn't burn everything into ash first. Disgusting, destructive beast. His lust for killing hung like a black cloud over its head, almost obscuring it from sight. A cunning creature, but if she could bespell him so that his battle lust outweighed his reason…her pair might have a chance…

She watched in horror as the battle raged, fire and smoke obscuring all, until a scream rose up that could only have come from Melitta.

Briska hunted desperately for the girl, but even the mirror could not find her among the flames. George had disappeared, too. If the dragon had killed him…or both of them…Briska had failed.

She slumped against the wall. She'd never hold Maram in her arms again.

The mirror had gone awfully quiet, aside from the crackle of flames. Too quiet for a battle.

"Marry me."

Briska jumped to her feet, hardly daring to breathe. Had she heard correctly?

When George kissed Melitta, Briska pumped her fist and cheered so loud icicles fell from the ceiling, but she didn't care. Her couple were alive and kissing and…she bit her lip, shooting a spell their way. Alive and kissing and Melitta had every intention of dragging George to bed with her that very night. If she didn't throw him down into the ashes and tear his clothes off then and there…

"Another happy couple, and a dead dragon to boot. There's nothing feeble about that, Mistress," Briska said.

For the first time in she couldn't remember how long, she felt a grim sense of satisfaction.

It was gone before she could grasp it, but it was there, nonetheless.

Perhaps she could win her freedom. After beating a dragon…anything was possible.

Eighteen

If anything was possible, then she could make
the mirror show him, Briska told herself for
the dozenth time. No, surely the hundredth.
But this time was different. This time she
reached out to touch the mirror as she
breathed on the glass. And wished, more than
anything, to see Amani.

The mirror fogged, like always, and Briska
held her breath, not daring to take her eyes
from it. Her heart pattered in her chest, almost
as fast as her footsteps would sound as she ran
to Amani, if she could see him again. Touch

him again.

The fog cleared, but the picture was blurred. Blurred by her own tears at the thought of seeing him again. Tears of joy, Briska told herself, blinking them away before they froze.

Somewhere…blue. The rush of water, like when she'd ducked her head under the surface in the bathhouse while her servants were filling the bath. The slight tink of metal hitting stone, like one of them had bumped the bucket against the side of the bath. But not the hollow ring of an empty bucket – whatever the metal thing was, it was full of water.

Her heart leaped. If he was in a bath, he certainly couldn't be dead. As soon as the mirror cleared, she would see his fine form, and…

The mirror surface shimmered, and Briska closed her eyes, taking a deep breath before she dared look.

At what turned out to be her own, disappointing reflection.

No Amani. No bath. Just her own pale face, in front of the palace wall of blue ice.

Had she just witnessed his death? Had they

drowned him?

Her legs refused to hold her any more. She fell to her knees and wept, not caring if her tears froze this time, for each tiny crystal drop would only reflect the ice silencing her heart.

Nineteen

Days passed, each the same as the last. She would spend weeks making a match, and only then would she permit herself another glimpse of Maram. Most days, she managed to resist temptation, but the very darkest days were made darker still by her failed attempts to see Amani in the mirror.

She told herself every story she could think of – he was a powerful enchanter, unlike herself, and he could easily shield himself from spies, even those with magic mirrors at their disposal. He could have any one of a number of reasons for remaining hidden. But in her heart she knew the truth, for Mistress Kun had already told her: the mirror could only find the living, not the dead.

If Amani did not appear in the mirror, then his heart no longer beat for her, for the Sultan had surely silenced it forever.

On those dark nights, she would weep until she fell asleep, only to wake with her face a glittering mask of ice crystals from her tears.

Once the queen of a desert kingdom, now she was only the queen of snow and ice.

And her subjects…the latest couple were a stubborn pair whose affection for one another was clear, but who let duty and family get in the way. She longed to slap some sense into both of them, but she dared not leave her palace.

He was a warrior, a general who had killed more men than she could count. Prince Rudolf, whose luck in battle was legendary. Luck. Huh. It was all her, turning aside weapons at the last moment or bespelling his opponents. She could not match him with Portia if he died in battle.

And Portia…oh, she was as stubborn as he was. An uncrowned queen from the same islands as Hansel and Gretel, surrounded by a bodyguard of young men who would have turned any normal girl's head.

If she could get the two in a room together, it would be easy – she'd have them in each other's arms within the hour. But they were miles from one another, separated by not one but two armies, and an unforgiving ocean.

It might be years before they met again, and Briska could match them properly.

So she cheated. Every night, after making sure the pair lived through another day apart, she spent an hour watching Maram.

Maram slept near Naheed and her daughter Anahita, and the two girls were never far apart. When Naheed died, it was Maram who comforted her sister, and took care of the other girl, for the lowly daughter of a concubine was beneath the wives' notice.

Every night Briska watched her, she'd strengthened the spells on Maram until the girl's own magical ability surfaced, stronger than Briska's own. Maram was no enchantress, but her seduction spells were more powerful than even those cast by Mistress Kun.

No woman in the harem was immune to her charms, and nor was the girl's father. It placed her in a unique position. On the one hand, she was easily her father's favourite, but on the other, she was his daughter, and she would never be a rival for her father's nightly attentions with the wives and concubines. Thus, the women trusted her. She knew every secret they dared confide in no one else, and more than once she'd shared them with her father without ever betraying her source. Oh, not everything – just matters that might affect the wider court, and not mere harem matters. She'd inherited her father's talent for politics, something Briska didn't understand.

All in all, Briska was proud of her daughter. The girl was growing up into a most satisfactory princess.

Then Rudolf crossed the ocean, and went to war in Portia's territory. It was a good thing Briska did not need to eat or sleep, because keeping that pair alive while she waited for them to get close enough for love to spark took every moment of her days and nights. If it wasn't one, it was the other.

She wanted to scream at Portia that queens did not need to take up a bow in their own defence – that was what she had guards for! – but the chief of her guards was that horrible Hansel who'd almost been the death of her, so Briska didn't dare make her presence known. If Portia was anything like Gretel, who had also taken up the fight beside Rudolf…a barbaric people, arming their women, instead of keeping them safe.

Once she was done with these two, she vowed wearily, she would ask Mistress Kun for a simpler match to make. Love between a pair who fate had thrown together, or turning enemies into lovers, perhaps.

Finally, a night came where both Portia and Rudolf found a safe place to sleep, and Briska dared to direct the mirror's surface away from them to something other than those cursed Southern Isles.

For a moment, she considered searching for Amani, but decided against it. She wanted to see her daughter, for she hadn't seen the girl in weeks.

She took a deep breath, exhaling on the glass, then waited for Maram's face to appear.

Briska found Maram in tears, crying quietly into her pillow. Where was Anahita? Normally the other girl would be comforting her, but Maram was alone.

Briska cast a quick seduction spell over Maram, as she did every time she saw the girl, then breathed on the mirror again, willing it to show her Anahita. The girl hadn't looked ill the last time she saw her, but accidents could happen anywhere.

Come to think of it, she hadn't seen the two together for some time. If the girl was dead...

The fog on the mirror faded, and Briska held her breath as she peered into the picture it showed.

Briska's mouth dropped open, and wouldn't close. She wanted to look away, but her own horror transfixed her.

No one deserved such a fate.

Twenty

Amani squirmed, trying to find a comfortable position in the cramped lamp, but it was no use. Whatever magic held him prisoner in the piece of worthless metal wouldn't let him move. Not until someone rubbed the tarnished brass, when he would once again be sucked out the spout to do something stupid.

Like create a lake in the desert, where one shouldn't be.

He cursed his master silently, for such were the terms of his enslavement that he could not say the words aloud. Even if the Prince of

Tasnim was all of the things he couldn't say.

It wasn't Amani's fault the idiot had ordered him to make that lake. Princes didn't care if whole underground rivers had to be shifted to grant their wishes. Bedrock cracked…the desert would be forever changed by what he'd done. So when the prince had whined that he wanted everything changed back, Amani had taken great pleasure in informing the idiot that it was impossible. Not even the most powerful sorcerer in the world could force the river to flow backward.

Which was probably why he was stuck in the lamp again, with no way out until someone summoned him. He'd lost track of the days, he'd been in here so long. How did you count days when everything was dark, anyway? He had not eaten or drunk a thing, and sleep eluded him, yet these things no longer seemed to matter.

Djinn had no need of sustenance or sleep. They served, and they waited, until they served again. Slavery. On an immortal timescale.

And the longer he sat in this lamp, the more he longed for freedom. Even servitude would be a release from this lamp.

But he'd probably need a new master to do that. That new enchantress hadn't liked Prince Philemon much. Whatever curse she'd cast on him, he hoped it made the prince as uncomfortable as Amani himself. And unable to wish for any more stupid things.

Amani sighed. The next man who released him from his prison, he'd make the man the master of untold riches.

As long as he wasn't some puffed-up prince like Philemon.

Twenty-One

"Do you know what you have done?" Mistress Kun demanded, her eyes flashing even through the mirror.

Briska lifted her head from the cradle of her arms. "I cast too strong a lust spell on him. I know. I was trying to fix it or reverse it or something when he…when he…" Raped the poor girl. Briska couldn't say the words, knowing she was responsible for the brutal violation of the young enchantress. She buried her head in her hands. "The match is doomed now."

"Worse than that. You cast your spell on the wrong brother!" Kun snapped.

"What?"

"You cast the spell on Thorn, the older brother, when Zuleika is destined for Vardan, the younger one!"

"There's two brothers?" Briska didn't believe it. "Two identical brothers? But there is only the one in the palace..."

Kun made an impatient noise in her throat. "Of course there are. And they are not identical, just similar in appearance. The other is the new Master of Beacon Isle, a powerful post his fool brother let him have without realising the consequences. Now that he does, he'd planned to send your enchantress to carry a curse to his younger brother, but your misplaced spell made him change his mind and decide to keep her instead!"

"Perhaps I can reverse the spell. If he becomes indifferent to her, he might change his mind once more and send her anyway..." Briska ventured.

"It's too late for that. Your bird has flown far from Thorn and his kingdom. That enchantress might be young and just coming into her powers, but she can cast portals like she's been working magic all her life." Kun sniffed. "Unlike some people I could name. And why weren't you watching? You should have seen her leave and done something to stop her!"

Briska gritted her teeth. "I could not watch the king rape that poor girl. Not when I couldn't stop him. She's the same age as my own daughter…and what if her father decides to marry her to someone like that? She is a princess, and a suitable wife for a king…" She trailed off before she revealed her secret – that she watched Maram through the mirror most nights. "As long as I am distracted with worrying about my daughter's future, I will likely continue to make similar mistakes to the one I have with Zuleika and…what was the boy's name? Vardan?" Briska's breath caught in her throat. "What if Zuleika comes after me, blaming me for what Thorn did to her?"

"How many seduction spells have you cast?" Kun asked, but she didn't give Briska time to answer before she continued, "And how many of the men you have cast them on turned into beasts like that one and forced the girl?"

"Just him," Briska said, "but that doesn't absolve me. That girl suffered because – "

"Because you cast a lust spell on a complete arsehole," Kun finished for her. "The girl suffered, true, but she will have her revenge. A fitting one, for he will lose his throne to his greatest fear – his brother, or his brother's heirs. She was clever, too – she managed to curse him without committing treason, because he activated the curse. She will not become a djinn."

"But what if she comes here? She is far more powerful than I will ever be. And it's still my fault!" Briska said.

Kun waved away her worries. "She does not know of your involvement, and she is on the other side of the world now, helping some warrior woman with her magic shoes. She has put the matter out of her mind, and so should you. Even if she did not, she would not find you through the shields here. As long as you continue to make the matches I command, you shall be safe. What about that couple in the

Southern Isles?"

"Blissfully in love with one another," Briska said bitterly. "No spell required. After all those years of trouble, keeping them alive, I'm not sure even magic would have stopped those two once they were reunited."

"Really?" Kun looked delighted. "Even I didn't think you could manage to make that match. Well done. Such good service begs a reward. What would you ask of me?"

"Let me visit my daughter, and speak to her father about what marriage he has in mind for her," Briska said. And persuade him not to let her marry at all. Better for Maram to be celibate than suffer the same fate as Anahita.

Kun shook her head. "I cannot. He does not wish to see you ever again."

"Then ask for her to be your apprentice," Briska said. "If she is a courtesan, she will never marry, and if you train her, she will still be able to make alliances for him. Just not marriage alliances."

"You would sentence your daughter to a life without love?" Kun asked.

"There is little love in a political marriage,

either, without a spell to bring the pair together," Briska countered. "Better that she becomes a courtesan, allowed to take the lovers she chooses, than to be forced into a marriage she does not want, where to love a man – any man – would be treason. That is a life without love. I would not wish my fate on her."

Kun inclined her head. "Very well. Princess Maram shall be a courtesan. If she has inherited your gift for seduction magic, she could well become the best the world has ever seen."

"My daughter has no magic. Mine is so weak, and her father…if her father had been an enchanter, perhaps it would be different." If her father had been Amani…but that could never be. Briska swallowed, then dared to ask, "Is there anyone this mirror cannot show? Can I see my daughter? Or…anyone else?" She didn't trust her voice to stay steady if she said his name. The pain was too raw still.

"The mirror will show you anyone living. If you wish, once your work is done, you may use it to see your daughter."

Briska let out a breath she hadn't known she was holding. "Thank you, Mistress. It would be wonderful to see her again." Then Kun's other words sank in. "By living, you mean…if the mirror will not show someone, then they must be…"

"Dead," Kun finished for her. "Dead and buried, where no magic can touch them. Any other questions?"

"No. I…thank you for taking such care of my daughter. I will watch you eagerly," Briska said.

"And while I am training her…"

"I will fix the mess I made with Zuleika."

"No, not yet. Give the girl some time to recover from her ordeal or she will reject the brother. Instead…how about a pair of starcrossed lovers, childhood friends whose families are feuding? Jael and Halvard could do with some magical assistance." Kun waved her hand, and her reflection was replaced by a picture of a pair Briska had not seen before.

"As you command, Mistress," Briska said, bowing. "And thank you," she added softly.

As long as Kun kept Maram safe from

having a husband like Anahita's, or that horrible King Thorn, Briska would do whatever her mistress asked.

Twenty-Two

"She's a girl!" Briska wanted to scream at the conceited prince. Anyone with eyes could see Mai was no man. She moved with a dancer's grace, the slight swing of her hips betraying her on every step, but the illusion spell that made her look like a man blinded them all, especially the stupid prince. Too busy looking for his next opponent in the sparring ring, he'd barely spared a glance for the girl who Kun and her cursed mirror had declared were the man's perfect match.

He called the boys ladies, sneering around

the circle, and they all hung their heads, not wishing to fight him. All but her, because, by all that was holy, she was a lady, smaller than any of them. Still he did not see it.

A small maiden with a wooden sword, standing up to the bully prince who was easily twice her size. She showed no fear, no emotion at all, as she faced him.

Briska had watched him beat boy after boy, but she didn't want to watch him beat the girl. "She's a girl!" she repeated, as she cast seduction spell after seduction spell at him, but the only thing he lusted for was battle, and he charged at the girl, murder in his eyes.

She barely moved, but it was enough to take her out of his way and send him sprawling. The only bit of her out of place from his passing was her shoe, which the prince had evidently carried away with him in his charge. A magic shoe, glowing faintly purple with power.

Prince Yi did not see the magic, not even when he pocketed the shoe.

The more Briska watched the pair, the less she thought the prince deserved her. Mai moved like a hunting cat...or a hawk...or a snake...her sword darting out like an extension of her arm to block the prince's blows again and again until she tapped him on the chest.

The prince wheezed and doubled over, backing away. Evidently it had been more than a tap, or it had touched some vital part of him.

Seizing her chance, Briska cast a spell at the girl, hoping to inspire her affection, so that she would step forward and offer to nurse the prince back to health. Then, surely...

The clack of wood on wood echoed off the ice walls behind her, and Briska held her breath. Instead of offering to help the prince, the girl had continued to battle him. What manner of people were these two, whose only lust was for playing with swords?

She swore softly as she watched them battle on until the prince landed in the dirt a second time. There was passion between the two, definitely, but it was something more akin to hatred than love. For the moment, at least, she mused as an older man broke up the bout. As long as there was passion, she could work with these two. After helping the Big Bad Wolf catch the third Little Pig, matching a prince with a girl who lost her shoe would be easy.

Twenty-Three

When the prince finally returned Mai's shoes and asked her to become his wife, after no small effort on the part of Briska and even Zuleika, Briska allowed herself the luxury of another peep at Maram.

Her daughter looked much like Briska herself, for her enchanted servitude had kept Briska unchanging on the outside while she aged imperceptibly inside. Yet the years had aged Maram, too. Travelling to foreign courts and bewitching foreigners with her beauty and wit, all the while brokering trade agreements for the Sultan had turned the girl into a woman more worldly-wise than Briska would ever be.

The courts Briska observed in secret, casting spells through the mirror while she stayed safe in her palace of ice...Maram marched into with her head held high, the unchallenged mistress of all she surveyed. When she departed, she carried many new jewels and other precious gifts, most of which she sold or traded away at her next port of call. After one trading expedition, her wealth was more than her mother's dowry, making her the wealthiest woman in the Sultan's kingdom. Richer than the Sultan himself, Briska suspected, until the trade agreements Maram negotiated began to bear fruit. Maram would have made a formidable queen, and more than one foreign prince had offered for her hand, courtesan or no.

But no matter how eligible the offer, she had declined them all. Briska thought it was because none of them had yet managed to touch her heart. Because for all she'd inherited her father's political acumen, Maram was definitely her mother's daughter. It would take an extraordinary man to capture Maram's heart, though the girl would leave a trail of broken hearts behind her.

While her mother made matches between two people, Maram united entire nations. She had a courage Briska would never possess. Briska prayed that Maram would never need to know the violence that had driven Briska into hiding.

But today, as Briska watched the girl shrug out of her clothes in the old bathhouse by the city gates, she was struck by the deep sadness that seemed to surround Maram, a dark pool far deeper than the water she stepped into. For all her conquests, happiness eluded Maram, too, much as it had her mother. Was Maram destined to spend her life alone, in the midst of so many, yet untouched?

But she wasn't alone in the bathhouse, Briska noticed – a shadow lurked in the linen room, the shadow of a man, she was certain of it.

The mirror obeyed her order to focus on the man, to see which of her suitors was spying on Maram, and whether he meant her ill. But this man was no suitor Briska had ever seen before. His patched, worn clothes made him appear little more than a common beggar, until Briska recognised the make of them. A fashion from decades past, only ever crafted in silk, but worn so threadbare now she couldn't discern any of the original sheen. A nobleman or a merchant, fallen upon hard times…did he blame Maram for his misfortunes, and seek revenge?

Briska sent a spell through the glass, fanning the flame of his existing passions. If it was Maram he wanted, then he would make himself known to her instead of hiding. If it was revenge…better that he reveal himself now that her servants were alert for her call for aid.

The man edged out of the shadows and into the light, but only to where he could see Maram better.

Not a man at all. He was barely more than a boy, his father's cast-off clothes hanging off his thin frame, but the way he stared at Maram was like a man dying of thirst regarding a cup of wine. Infinite longing.

Briska reached through the mirror and sent a stack of towels tumbling off the shelf. The boy never heard it, for he was too intent on Maram, but Maram's head snapped up, as she became aware that she wasn't alone.

She summoned him, using the same honeyed tones she might try on one of her suitors. Unlike those other men, he crept out of hiding and prostrated himself before her.

Briska would have called for her attendants to take the boy away, knowing that the boy deserved death for invading the Sultana's privacy. But Maram, for all her regal airs, was not a virtuous queen.

She called for food to be brought, enough for two, claiming the man as a lover to her servants, though she'd only met him. She even honoured him by serving him with her own hands, something Briska had not even done for the Sultan himself.

The boy – Aladdin, he'd said his name was – was nothing and no one, yet Maram treated him like her equal. She offered him food, drink…and then she did the unthinkable. She offered him her hand, and he took it.

A look passed between them, for the most fleeting moment, but Briska caught it, for she knew it well. In that touch and in that glance, two hearts had connected. If only other matches could be made so easily.

Briska sent a seduction spell at the boy, the strongest she could muster, and instead of stepping closer to Maram, he bowed his head. Swearing softly, she cast a second spell, this time aiming squarely for Maram.

Love could spark, but sometimes it needed more to fan it into a proper, enduring flame.

"Kiss me," Maram said. What should have been a command came out as a desperate plea.

Quietly, Briska retreated, willing the mirror to return to mist, so that her daughter might enjoy the boy's heartfelt kiss in peace and privacy.

For the first time in more than a decade, Briska wanted to weep for joy. A man had touched her daughter's heart. One who might be able to give her the love she deserved. Love Maram might return.

Her heart considerably lighter, Briska lay back on her bed of ice, secure in the knowledge that while her own heart was frozen, at least her daughter's future would be happy.

Twenty-Four

Another day, another master…or the same one in a different guise, but it mattered little. One master was the same as another, issuing orders and expecting miracles. Amani braced himself for being sucked through the spout again. The discomfort had become one of the least demeaning parts of his servitude.

He placed a private bet with himself that this new idiot would ask for all the riches in the world before the day was over. He'd lost the wager when it was Philemon, who'd turned out to be too much of a fool to think of asking for such a thing. So this one would have to be truly stupid to do worse than Philemon.

"I am the servant of the lamp. What do you wish of me?" Amani said grandly. He'd found he could vary the words if he wished, as long as he said something suitable when greeting a new master. If he began before the magical compulsion hit him, he could even make himself sound impressive, retaining some of his former glory, instead of presenting himself as a cringing, servile mouse.

He found himself facing a peasant woman. One who backed away from him in terror, clutching the lamp in her clawed fingers.

She tripped and knocked herself unconscious, which brought a ragged boy to her aid. Now both of them were ignoring him.

So much for making a grand entrance. Amani sighed. "I said: what do you wish of me?"

The boy – nay, a man, though a young one, turned angry eyes on Amani. "You frightened my mother and now she is hurt."

Amani opened his mouth to say it was her own silly fault, releasing a djinn she had no idea what to do with.

But her dutiful son snatched up the lamp, and continued, "I wish you would fix the mess you have made." His expression challenged Amani to refuse. Almost as if he knew the horrible headache that would ensue if he did.

It had been many years since Amani had healed someone, but he did his best for the woman. When he had stopped her head from bleeding, he turned his attention back to the man. His new master, for the man's hands were firmly wrapped around the lamp as though he knew what power he possessed.

Grudgingly, Amani said, "What else do you wish of me?"

He would not blame the boy for asking for riches. Living in this hovel, a bag of gold might change his life.

But the boy surprised him again. "Answers. What are you?"

"I am the servant of the lamp, and my master is whoever holds it in his hands."

The boy nodded, as though he already knew this. "So you are a djinn?"

"Yes."

"You can perform magic? What sort of magic can you do?"

The boy had met djinn or enchanters before. He must have, for only people who knew magic well knew an enchanter's powers were strong in some areas and weak in others. If Amani had been able to render himself invisible, he would never have been caught with Briska and he wouldn't be in this mess. But there was no point thinking of that now — he had a new master to impress with the considerable powers he did have.

Amani swelled until his head touched the ceiling. "I can make you the richest man alive. Transport you to the farthest reaches of the Earth and back again in the blink of an eye. Build you a palace so magnificent even the Sultan will beg to see inside."

The boy was going to ask for riches. Amani could almost see it running through his mind. "What would you wish me to do first, Master?" Amani asked.

The boy considered the question for a long, long time. Finally, he said, "I am hungry. Bring me something to eat."

Amani stared at him. He offered him the world, and the boy wanted a snack? Though Amani had to admit he'd seen more meat on some skeletons. Perhaps the boy was wiser than he gave him credit for.

He bowed and left, determined to bring the boy a meal fit for a king. Amani grinned. Why, he'd bring him a meal fit for a Sultan, taken from the Sultan's own table. He could spare it.

<h1 style="text-align:center;">Twenty-Five</h1>

Even in his lamp, Amani heard the name of Briska's daughter, Maram. He pressed his ear to the spout and tried to listen harder. How could this peasant boy know Princess Maram?

At first, Amani wanted to laugh at the irony of it all. It appeared his new master – Aladdin, his name was – had chanced to meet the princess in a bathhouse, and he'd fallen in love with the girl, much as Amani had fallen for her mother. Unlike Amani, though, Aladdin planned to marry the girl.

The Sultan would never let his precious

daughter marry some starving peasant boy. Amani owed it to Briska's memory not to let the girl fall into the wrong hands. Yet as he listened…it seemed the boy truly loved Maram. Whether Maram felt the same was another matter, though.

So much for asking for riches. The boy was about to ask for a love spell, and Amani had never been so happy at his own shortcomings. Even if he could cast such a thing, he could not cast one on Maram.

Amani emerged from the lamp, pre-empting the summons from Aladdin. He took a deep breath, ready to refuse the boy's command so firmly he never asked again.

Aladdin met Amani's gaze squarely, and asked for a palace.

Amani suppressed a snort. If it wasn't love spells, it was riches, always.

But as Aladdin detailed what were quite modest requirements, as far as palaces go, it dawned on Amani that he wanted the palace for Maram, and Maram alone, for Maram was marrying someone else.

Amani stared at Aladdin in wonder. How

could he be so calm, knowing the woman he adored would be another man's wife? What kind of man wasn't willing to fight for the woman he loved?

Amani hadn't stood by idly. No, he'd fought for her love and won it and…

…landed himself in his current predicament.

Perhaps there were better ways to go about winning a woman's heart, and her hand. For Maram was not married yet. And Amani owed it to Briska to see her daughter happy in marriage, as Briska herself had never been.

Amani bowed low before departing. He would build Maram a palace better than anything the Sultan had ever seen, and he would do everything in his power to find out where the girl's desires lay, and see that she had the husband her heart wished for. Whether it was the man she was going to marry or Aladdin or some foreign prince, it mattered not. He would grant the girl this one wish, for her late mother's sake. For she did not deserve her mother's unhappy fate.

Twenty-Six

It worked out better than Amani could have hoped. Briska lived, and her daughter would live happily ever after. Sure, Amani was still a slave, but he was happier than he could have hoped for. If he had to serve someone, Maram's new husband was hardly a bad choice, for he was a good man. If Amani told Aladdin how much Maram missed her mother, Aladdin might even order him to find Briska. One day, perhaps.

Lost in his daydream at what might be, Amani should have paid attention to Maram, who now stood with the lamp in her hand. His mistress.

Maram's eyes glowed, just like her mother's had when she attempted magic. But the power flowing through Maram was far more than Briska had ever commanded.

"Blood of the betrayed that binds this djinn, my father's blood that runs in my veins, too, will set us both free." Maram placed her bleeding hand on the lamp, smearing the stuff over the blackened brass. She turned her glowing eyes on Amani and threw the now useless lamp on the floor. "You are free. Find her, free her, and be happy."

It felt like waking up from a dream, a dream he'd believed was real. The fog lifted from Amani's brain, allowing him to think clearly for the first time in too long.

How could he possibly have considered himself happy, serving some peasant boy? Sure, the boy had honour and a good heart, and he'd won the heart of Briska's daughter, too, but that didn't give him the power to command the most powerful sorcerer in the world.

Amani considered the order Maram had given him, but he no longer felt a compulsion to obey. He truly was free. Free of his prison, free from slavery, but he would never be free of his debt to Maram.

So for the first time in his life, he willingly abased himself before someone.

"As you command, Princess. When I find her, I will tell her that you have found happiness, too. If you ever have need of me, you have only to call, and I will be there to grant your wish." He touched her hand, healing the cut she'd made to free him. Only then did Amani rise and incline his head to Aladdin, the man a moment ago he would have willingly served. "Enjoy your palace. Consider it my wedding gift to the princess. But if you ever hurt her…know you will incur the enmity of the most powerful enchanter in the world. A man with no master. Not any more." He bit his finger until it bled, then traced a circle in the air. The portal opened, as he knew it would, and Amani stepped through.

Twenty-Seven

Amani stepped out of the portal and sank up to his knees in sand. In his absence, the desert and the thick stone walls had kept his home secure, but he hadn't counted on the desert itself invading his castle. Perhaps because this was a war his servants had fought while he lived here, but now they were gone.

It mattered not. When he returned here with Briska to make the desert castle her home, she would help him choose suitable servants. In the meantime…Amani closed his eyes, summoning a magical sandstorm to blast his palace clean.

He surveyed the tiles, laid at the command of one of his royal ancestors. The same one who had ordered the mosaics and frescoes on every wall and domed ceiling, from which he'd taken his inspiration for Maram's palace. Modern art, created for one of these new religions that had invaded the region, could not compare to this. Four hundred years it had stood, and it would outlast these religious fanatics, he was certain of it.

And these ancestral walls would witness his triumph as he found the woman he loved, and brought her home.

Amani ensconced himself on the floor of the entrance hall, beneath the frescoes of his ancestors hunting, and closed his eyes to begin his own quest.

He bit his lip, tasting blood, then cast a searching spell, letting it spiral out over the desert, looking for his lost love.

He concentrated on Briska's beloved face, breathing deep and steady to keep his focus. The spell must find her. Over sand and water, mountains and plains, forests and fields, army camps and cities, his spell flew, searching for what he did not find.

But Amani would not give up. She lived – Maram would not lie to him about something so important. Unless the Sultan had lied to her, too…

Fury built as Amani's spell swept around the globe, finding nothing but emptiness.

Amani opened his eyes. Nothing could hide her from one of his search spells. Nothing. For who was more powerful than him? Only death could outmatch him. If death had taken Briska…

Then the world was no longer a place he wished to live in, either. But first he would exact his revenge on the man who had driven his beloved to her death.

Amani leapt to his feet, slashed open a portal, and strode through.

Twenty-Eight

Amani almost skidded on the tiles, he moved so fast, but he merely slowed to regain his balance before marching on. "Where is she?" he demanded.

The Sultan had aged twenty years and swelled as round as the world he wanted to rule, but somewhere in there was the bastard Briska had married before he enslaved them both. So much for the virile young leader, hungry for power and wealth, who had thrown Amani's lamp into a well. Now he'd eaten so many perfumed jellies he'd turned into one.

"Where is Briska?" Amani repeated, louder this time, as the quivering wreck of a man cringed away.

"I don't know!" the Sultan shouted back, his eyes bulging. He opened his mouth again, undoubtedly to shout for his guards.

Amani grinned. A wave of his hand slammed the doors shut, shrouding them in a bubble from which no sound could escape. "No one can hear us, and I will not leave until you tell me what you've done with her."

The Sultan's mouth opened and closed, like a dying fish. Amani had a brilliant idea.

"If you don't tell me where she is right now, I shall turn you into a fish, and I will sit here and watch you suffocate to death, drowning in air like you tried to drown me in that well." Amani seated himself on a bench and folded his arms.

The Sultan blinked, his fear fading. "Amani?"

Amani inclined his head. "The very same."

"You haven't changed a bit. You look just as you did the day you betrayed me." The Sultan jumped to his feet. "And as your master, I command you to open the doors, and get out of my sight!"

Amani grinned. "Ah, but didn't you hear? I am not a djinn any more. I have no master, for I am free, and my powers are greater than they have ever been. And it is you who betrayed her, for I know she begged you for a divorce so that she might marry me. You loved her money too much to release her, and look at all it has bought you!" He waved his hands at the palace walls, which he was happy to see were still inferior to Maram's mosaics.

"My wise rule, and my trade agreements have won me this wealth. Not some wife's paltry dowry," the Sultan snapped.

"You mean trade agreements won by the lovely Princess Maram, don't you? You whored Briska's daughter out to foreign princes while you sat here like a fat spider in his web, waiting for her to bring rich prizes to you!"

"How dare you insult my daughter!" the Sultan roared.

Amani flashed a mirthless smile. "I know the lovely princess well. You would have given her to that piece of carrion, Hasan. If not for me, she would not have lived long enough to marry her beloved Aladdin. I know everything she has endured, and you will pay for that, too. But first, you will tell me where you have hidden her mother, or I will make Hasan's fate seem like a paradise filled with houris."

The Sultan paled. "I do not know!"

"Tell me!"

"I do not know!" the Sultan shouted. "Much like you, I could not bear to look upon her. The enchantress who bound her took Briska into her service."

"Where?"

"Somewhere far to the north, where it is cold and snow falls from the skies, or so she said. But that was years ago! She could be anywhere now!"

An enchantress powerful enough to hide Briska from him? Not possible.

"Who is this enchantress?" Amani demanded.

"Mistress Kun, the courtesan."

Amani burst out laughing. "The contortionist, you mean? Your left testicle has more magic than Mistress Kun. Why, every man at court has had her, one way or another. Tell me the truth, old man, or I'll set your hairy balls on fire."

The Sultan glowered. "The woman may be free with her affections, but her magic was powerful enough to bind you, and Briska. Who do you think enslaved you to that tarnished lamp?"

Common gossip in court had held that her youthful appearance and sexual prowess were through magical means, but then, most of the court considered owls and broken mirrors bad luck, too. They were a superstitious lot.

"If this is true, then she may have more to answer for than you do." Including how a lowly courtesan had managed to hide her powers from him, Amani thought but didn't say. "Tell me where she is and I will let you live."

"I don't know that, either. She left my court some time ago. Maram may know, for she trained with her, but I do not." The Sultan threw his arms up to shield himself. "Don't hurt me! I am telling you everything I know!"

Which wasn't much, but it was something,

at least. Amani narrowed his eyes. "Divorce her, and I will let you live."

"I already have. Before she was bound as a djinn. Because it is not fitting for a sultan to be married to a slave." The Sultan sniffed.

"And what of her dowry?" Amani asked.

"Slaves cannot own property. I have it still."

And he'd profited mightily from it, Amani didn't doubt. He lifted his chin. "See that you have it ready for her when I return. For I shall free her, and when I do, she will return to claim what is hers. Down to the smallest copper coin." He'd endured two decades of slavery because this man refused to divorce a wife who did not love him. A little payback was called for. "And if you think to withhold any of it, I will make sure you die an agonising death. After I tell Princess Maram's husband everything about her past." Not that there was much Aladdin did not know, but the Sultan wouldn't know that. He still believed Aladdin was a prince, after all.

The Sultan paled. "None of this is Maram's fault. Leave her out of it."

Amani grinned. "That's up to you, old man."

He cast a portal, and departed.

Twenty-Nine

When he'd finished an evening meal lifted from the Sultan's kitchens on his way out of the palace, Amani sat in his own hall and attempted another search spell.

He sent the spell north, questing wherever he found snow, not for the courtesan, but for Briska. But no matter how hard he looked, still he could not find her.

So he turned his attention to the courtesan, Mistress Kun. A woman who'd managed to hide her magic from him, keep him from finding Briska and, the biggest insult of all, she'd bound him to that brass lamp.

He paced the length of his hall and back again, sensing the spell seeking through the northern snow for the courtesan. It should not take so long. Why, he'd never taken more than a moment to find anyone, no matter where in the world they were. To take so long…to fail twice! Why, it was unheard of. Had his enslavement dulled his powers, perhaps?

Amani broke off the search and stormed outside. From the courtyard, he could see the dry riverbed from which his castle drew its water in the wintertime. Winter was a while off yet, but there were autumn storms brewing in the Middle Sea that would suit his purposes perfectly. Finding a storm was harder than finding a person – if he could not even fill the water tanks at home, then his time tied to the lamp truly had weakened him.

His magic slowed as it hit a patch of moist air, closer than he'd expected. Amani took a deep breath. Now all he had to do was summon a strong enough breeze to blow it over to that low pressure system and keep them together long enough for the storm to make landfall here instead of one of the countries further north.

Holding the storm system together took most of his focus, and what he had left he pushed into steering the behemoth to where he wanted it. For hours, he battled the beast, or perhaps it was only moments – Amani did not know. But as the storm hit the wall of heat rising from the desert sands, Amani knew he had succeeded. He eased back from the roiling mass of clouds, content to watch nature take its course as the clouds dropped their deluge before fleeing over the mountains in defeat.

Rain filled the streams, turning every depression into a rivulet, tumbling headlong toward the river. Amani felt the water like blood rushing through his veins, spreading its cold fingers across the land. The desert bloomed and all manner of beasts surfaced from the sand to slake their thirst.

But still Amani waited, for the flood had not yet reached his home.

The river began to run, a trickle at first, before it became a steady stream. A distant roar heralded the rushing surge that swept all before it. Waves licked hungrily at the high walls of his castle, but the magic-reinforced stone kept it at bay. He waited for the first wash to take the silt and debris out to sea before he opened the aqueducts, allowing the cleaner water to flow through the pipework into his holding tanks.

When he brought Briska here, to his home, she would have a better bathhouse than her daughter's. All he had to do was find her, or the courtesan who had stolen her away.

No common courtesan would keep him from the woman he loved, Amani swore, as he sent out another searching spell, secure in the knowledge that his powers were stronger than ever.

Thirty

Amani stood on the road outside Maram's gates, wishing he did not have to be here. But he dared not portal into her home without an invitation, especially not when he intended to be even deeper in her debt before the day was out.

A debt he would make that worthless courtesan pay, when he had her in his grasp.

Amani had taken the time to bathe and dress appropriately for visiting a prince, as that's what everyone believed Aladdin to be, and Amani had no intention of changing that.

He'd worked too hard to build Aladdin's reputation as a prince to destroy it now.

The guards stopped him at the gate, but politely, as befit someone of his stature. "Your name and your business, master, so that we may announce your arrival to the prince."

"I am the sorcerer, Lord Amani, and I wish to congratulate the prince and his new bride on their nuptials," Amani said smoothly. Now she was married, he could not visit Maram without her husband present. Never mind that she was an ex-courtesan and he'd lived alone with her for weeks without any impropriety…as though he'd do any such thing with Briska's daughter!

One of the guards headed into the house, before returning to escort Amani inside.

Maram rose to welcome him into her sitting room, where he'd spent many pleasant hours conversing with her while they were trapped on the savannah, but Aladdin stood by the wall, looking as awkward as ever in such fine surroundings. A good man and a merchant's son, but no prince. And yet, of all the masters Amani had been forced to serve, Aladdin was the only one he was willing to share a cup of wine with, without poisoning the contents.

Aladdin ducked his head in a brief bow. "It is lovely to see you again so soon, Lord Amani. Forgive me, but I am on my way to see my mother, who I hope to persuade to take up residence here, at Maram's request. I'm sure my wife will entertain you in my absence." He moved to depart.

"You're leaving us alone?" Amani blurted out. Did the boy not know what this would do to his wife's reputation?

"We both know this palace belongs to Maram, and she is well able to entertain any visitor she pleases in her home," Aladdin said with a smile. He rubbed his thumb across a ring on his finger in a gesture that seemed completely unconscious, but Amani knew better, for he recognised the ring. The weak djinn who was bound to it was no match for Amani in most things, but his combination of invisibility and unusual physical strength still made him a formidable protector for Princess Maram. And an unseen chaperone, who would tell Aladdin everything that had passed between them in Aladdin's absence.

Maram sighed. "He has no idea. I've never met a man who cared less for his reputation. Amani, if you'd be kind enough to help him travel to his mother's unseen…"

Amani opened a portal, and gestured for Aladdin to enter. Aladdin departed, and Amani waited for the portal to close completely before he said, "He might be gone, but it was not my intention to keep any part of our discussion a secret from your husband. Perhaps another time…" He gritted his teeth. He didn't want to come back. He needed her help now.

"I keep no secrets from Aladdin, but there are some things I think he does not wish to know," Maram said softly. "Like how to free djinn, for example." She beckoned a servant forward and accepted a cloth-wrapped parcel from the girl. Maram then held it out to Amani. "I had the lamp polished. It's not gold, but…I thought you might like to keep it. And…inside it, you will find something that may help you in your quest. Something…you will need, but that your pride will not allow you to ask for. There are other ways to free djinn, but they require several sorcerers working in cooperation and the results can be unpredictable. This way is better."

Amani swallowed, then held his breath as he unwrapped the lamp and forced himself to lift the lid. The lamp was stuffed with what appeared to be a roll of fine linen, but inside the linen was a glass vial of some dark liquid. He held it up to the light, and his gut clenched as the liquid glowed red.

"I cannot accept this." The words burst from him unbidden. This was royal blood, the same as that which ran in her father's veins and her own. With this, he could curse the Sultan's entire bloodline.

"Then why did you come, if not for more of my blood to free her?" Maram's dark eyes, so much like her mother's, were wide with curiosity.

"I cannot find her," he confessed. "She is a djinn, bound to serve whatever master holds her in thrall, just as I was. And she serves Mistress Kun, who I cannot find, either."

Maram drew in a sharp breath. "Kun? The

courtesan? No, she can only cast seduction magic, like me. The occasional small blessing or curse, like she did for Vardan. She couldn't possibly be powerful enough to hide from you. Why, Mother always said you were the most powerful sorcerer in the world!"

Amani grunted. "I am, or I was. But there are some forms of magic I cannot perform, and cloaking, invisibility, is one of them. And she has done something that hides herself and your mother from me. Please…is there anything she said, in passing, perhaps, that might help me locate her, and maybe your mother, too?"

Maram spread her arms wide. "She is a courtesan, the kind who travels for both business and pleasure. She could be anywhere in the world. The last place I saw her was Beacon Isle, before I met my husband. But if you wish to get a message to her…there is a city on a swamp, a republic, like the one in the ancient legends, with a port that is a favourite among crusaders. She keeps a palace on one of the islands in the floating city."

"She's from a floating crusader city?" Even

Amani didn't believe it.

Maram smiled faintly. "No, she has a house there, is all. She was born in the Kunlun Mountains, far to the east, where the horse people war with the middle kingdom, and no one truly wins, or so she says. There are magical peach trees in the mountains where she was born, so powerful that one bite of the fruit can grant you immortality, or so it is said. What I do know is that I have known her for most of my life, and she has not aged a day. Perhaps immortality is possible, after all. The floating city…while I have not been there myself, I have heard many crusaders speak of it. It is no myth."

"I have heard she is in the far north, where it snows."

"Perhaps. Who can say? I last saw her at Beacon Isle, in the northern seas. There are tales of places further north where the ground is made of ice, ice that never melts." Maram laid a hand on Amani's wrist. "I do not know where Mistress Kun is, but if I were to go searching for her, I would go first to the floating palace and leave a message, telling her you wish to find her. For me. And you will take the lamp and the vial, because I ask only one thing of you: that you find my mother, free her, and bring her home to me."

"Princess…"

Maram clasped her hands before her. "If the most powerful sorcerer in the world cannot find her, then I fear she is lost forever. Please, Amani. If you love her…if you ever loved her…"

Amani dropped to one knee. "I have never loved any woman as I love Briska, and I will never love another. I will find her, and I shall free her, and I shall bring her here to show her the wonderful woman her daughter has become. This I swear."

"Ah, men and their oaths. Actions speak louder than words, Amani. Go find her!"

He rose, bowed, and left, with the lamp tucked firmly under his arm.

Thirty-One

Amani stayed in the floating city long enough to determine that it was indeed real, and built on poles thrust deep into the swamp. It smelled like the river at the end of the spring, too, when the water dried up and formed shallow, stagnant ponds that would make a man so sick he'd die if he drank from them.

Kun the courtesan kept a house there, and Amani left a message with her servants, but they had no idea when she might return. He gathered it had been some time since they'd seen their mistress, and Amani didn't blame her. He never stayed home when it smelled like the river had died. Instead, he'd travelled during that part of the year, including the summer he'd paid a visit to the Sultan's court and first glimpsed Briska. The woman had mesmerised him with her eyes alone. Almost like magic, and yet it was not.

Once he left the city, though, he found himself with two choices. Either he could follow the silk road east, or the crusaders' way north. He cared little for silk and less for horse people, whatever those might be, but he was curious to see what had inspired the religious zealots in their crusade, so he headed north, as it had been some time since he'd last seen snow.

But every city he stopped at…no one had ever heard of a courtesan named Kun. The more prosperous cities had heard of Princess Maram, though, and they sang her praises. When he mentioned he was on a quest for her, doors opened as they never had before. A powerful sorcerer they looked upon with suspicion, but Princess Maram's envoy was beyond reproach.

By the time he reached the ports along the northern sea, Amani had all but given up asking for Kun. It was as though the woman had never existed, which he knew couldn't be true.

Weary beyond belief, he took a room in an inn in Kasmirus that had an enormous skull mounted above a sign that proclaimed it was the Dragon's Head, for some famous dragonslayer had once slept there. And left the beast's head behind.

He claimed a table near the roaring fire in the crowded taproom, for the winter in those parts was biting cold at the best of times. He refused the ale and asked for some wine, but these northern barbarians had never heard of grapes, so their wine tasted more of raw spirit than the fruit it was brewed from. Perhaps they needed the liquid warmth, with the air so cold. He sipped it slowly, letting the stuff warm all the way down to his toes before calling for another.

A black-haired barmaid brought it, dumping his drink on the table before sitting across from him, unasked.

Amani waved her away. "I'm in no need of company tonight. Better sell your affections elsewhere."

She raised her head and met his eyes as she took a deep draught from his cup. "A slave cannot afford such things, anyway."

He laughed. "Your mind must be addled! Me, a slave? Take care, girl, for I am a lord with a castle back home."

"You are a slave, because I bound you, and only I can break the bond between you and the lamp. Who do you serve?" she demanded.

Amani met her gaze squarely. "Most times, I serve myself, but right now, I have the honour of doing a small favour for Princess Maram."

Surprise flickered in her eyes for a moment, so quickly Amani might have imagined it, but he knew he had not.

"What message do you bring from Her Highness?" she asked.

Amani took a careful sip of his drink, wiped his mouth, then said, "Not so much a message as a request. She wants to see her mother."

Mistress Kun smiled, for the girl could be no one else, though she looked a decade younger than Amani remembered her. "And she sent you. She always was a clever girl. Because no one wants to find Briska more than you do. Did her father give her the lamp, or did she find it on her own? Ah, it does not matter, not truly. The real question is: what are you willing to offer me for the information you want?"

For Briska? "Anything," Amani answered.

Thirty-Two

And that's how he'd ended up back in the desert, where this whole mess started. Well, perhaps not quite the same place, for Briska's bed was cold and empty, but now he stood at the blocked-off entrance to an underground city. A city with no people inside and, he discovered as he used magic to shift the enormous entrance stone, stale air that said no one had been there for some time.

For a moment, he feared that the treasure he sought would be long gone, but the glitter of gold beside the entrance caught his eye.

Several statues were lined up along the wall, all life-sized. If anyone intended to steal something, these would be the first items he'd take, yet here they were, untouched.

With increasing hope in his step, Amani headed into the tunnel.

As he'd moved away from the city gates, the air had grown fresher, fed by the ventilation shafts in the ceiling that ran deep into the earth, but the dust on the ground had also become deeper, muffling his footsteps. A closer look revealed it was fine sand and not dust, undoubtedly carried down the air shafts by the swirling sandstorms outside.

Aside from the dust, the place had been left in a surprisingly orderly state, as though the city residents intended to return, but had been prevented from doing so. Bad air hadn't driven them out, the usual culprit in underground places, and the place hadn't been sacked, so…what else could it be?

He approached one of the numerous wells around the city, and peered in. He should have been greeted by the drip and rush of the underground aquifer, but all he heard was silence. Amani bit his lip and sent his magic questing after the water.

The well was dry, and so was the next, though the cavern where the water should have been was deep enough to hold more water than a city of this size could ever need. He followed the twisting cavern, carved by the ancient, underground river, until he found the natural stone dam that had once kept the enormous reservoir secure beneath the city. No more – the rock was cracked all the way across, and the water had followed its natural course, down to a natural depression where it leaped to the surface in a bubbling spring. A spring so new there were no trees around it yet, though a clump of tiny date palms huddled together in solidarity, proclaiming their intention of claiming this waterhole as their own.

He knew the waterhole – it was Philemon's folly. Which made this city…Tasnim. A city guarded by the djinn who served Aladdin. A djinn who had no liking for Amani.

Amani swore softly. If Kun had intended to humiliate him, she'd chosen her quest well. His lamp prison had been stored in the treasure rooms here for a time, at the command of another, younger and comelier enchantress than Kun. If Philemon had owned an enchanted object that negated all magic in its vicinity, rendering an enchanter like himself powerless, it would be in his deepest treasury, where Amani's lamp had been. For what better way to protect his other priceless treasures than with a powerful magic object?

After an hour of walking and still he hadn't reached the bottom of the tunnels, Amani waved his magical light source to a halt and summoned a waterskin to quench his thirst, for there was no other drinkable water in the city.

Finally, he arrived at the city's treasury, and a stone door heavier than the rest stood in his way. He used magic to shift it aside, then sent his magical ball of light inside first, as a matter of caution. If a magic-nullifying artefact lay inside, he would rather lose his light source than all of his powers at once.

Yet the light glowed serenely as it bobbed across the room, so Amani followed it. There was less dust on the floor here — fewer air shafts, most likely — but there were gold coins strewn around, as though someone had tried to take some with them and not cared if they dropped a few.

The scattered coins grew more numerous, the deeper he ventured into the treasury, until he reached a sort of altar, with an open chest before it. Whatever had once graced the altar was now gone, leaving only a circle in the dust to show it had ever existed.

Amani was willing to wager that whatever had sat there was the item he wanted. Without it, Kun would never tell him where to find Briska.

Then again, she hadn't known what it looked like, just what effect it had.

Amani took a moment to contemplate his options. Perhaps he could provide the courtesan with a magic dampening device after all.

<h1 style="text-align:center">Thirty-Three</h1>

Right. This time, he thought he had it.

Amani set the lamp down in the sand, then backed up against the outer wall, as far as he could get away from it while still in his castle compound.

If this worked, he could meet Kun before nightfall, and have Briska in his arms before morning.

If it didn't...

He sighed. If it didn't, then he would have to seek out some even more ancient scrolls in the hope that he'd find the spell he needed, for he'd scoured through every spell he had.

Amani took a deep breath, and bit his lip. A flame-trail flickered across the sand, headed for the lamp. It touched the wick, and the lamp flared to life, flames dancing a little in the breeze. At almost the same moment, the trail extinguished itself, leaving nothing but wispy smoke and a line of scorched sand to mark its passage.

So far, so good.

Amani conjured a ball of light, like the one he'd used to light his way in Tasnim. He lobbed the ball at the lamp.

The ball arced up, reaching the peak of its flight, before it began to fall. Then it winked out. Gone.

Amani measured the distance with his eyes. That had to be…twenty feet, at least. Hard to tell at that height.

He conjured another ball and sent it skimming along the sand. It vanished sooner than he expected. Not twenty feet at all – more like thirty.

So the spell had a radius thirty feet wide…but did it stretch up thirty feet, too?

Amani used magic to scoop up some sand, then floated it to a point fifty feet above the lamp. Then, he let it sink, foot by foot, until it was just above thirty feet. So far, so good.

Another foot. Fine. Another. A third…

The sand dropped, and no spell he cast at it could touch it. He was powerless to do anything but watch as the sand buried the lamp, extinguishing it.

He sent a magical breeze toward the lamp to blow the sand away. It took some concentration to ensure he'd scoured away all the sand, leaving the lamp as shiny as it had looked when Maram handed it to him.

It looked nothing like the tarnished piece of trash it had been when he'd been trapped in it. If Amani himself scarcely recognised his prison, Kun would surely not know the difference. As long as it negated all magic within thirty feet of it, she would not care what it was.

He squinted at the sun. It was perhaps not too late to portal to the northern town where Kun had insisted they meet once he'd found what she wanted.

Just the thought of having Briska in his arms again…tonight, even…

Amani opened a portal, pausing only to conjure warm clothes for himself as he stepped from desert sands to deep snow.

Thirty-Four

Kasmirus was a tropical paradise compared to this place, Amani fumed as he tried to move closer to the fire without actually sitting in the flames. This inn's fire was larger than the one in the Dragon's Head, but the very air seemed to drink the warmth from it before it reached him. He'd downed two drinks, enough to stop him from shivering, but it did little to slow the creeping numbness in his fingers and toes. If Kun didn't turn up soon, he'd head home and return on the morrow. He had no intention of trying to sleep in this frozen nightmare of a place.

He signalled to the innkeeper for another drink. If Kun had not arrived by the time Amani had drained his cup, he would depart.

A cloaked figure came into the taproom, almost bent double under the weight of snow on her cloak. And it was a woman, so ancient-looking Amani wondered how she could still be alive. The innkeeper took her cloak with reverence, and the taproom fell silent.

Beneath her cloak, the crone wore a gown that was more suitable for the desert than a blizzard, yet she did not seem to feel the cold. She made her laborious way across the room to Amani's table. The nearest place to the fire.

He debated whether to offer his seat to the old woman, but she made up her mind before he did. She perched on the bench across from him and patted the table, indicating for the innkeeper to set her drink down.

Amani rose, then bowed. "I must beg your forgiveness, revered grandmother, but I am waiting for someone. I will move to another table."

"And what makes you think I'll let you?"

The crone lifted her head, and Amani found himself staring into Kun's unwrinkled eyes. She pressed a finger to her lips. "I hope you brought what I asked for. If you've dragged me out into a blizzard to beg and make excuses, I will turn you into one of those squirrel things so prized for their fur hereabouts. Vair, I think they are called."

Amani had no idea what a squirrel was, but he did know he didn't wish to become one. "Mistress Kun." He ducked his head and returned to his seat. "I believe I've found the object you wanted."

He pulled the lamp from the pouch at his waist and set it on the table.

Kun squinted at it, then tapped it. "It looks like an ordinary lamp. Aren't you sleeping in its twin these days?" She cackled with laughter, sounding like a crone.

"I will not rest until I have found Briska," Amani snapped.

Kun grinned. "Is the compulsion to obey getting painful for you? So much for being a powerful sorcerer, when you're rendered useless by a little headache." She lowered her voice to a whisper. "And it will only get worse. If this isn't what I asked for, you will fail in your quest."

So she knew about the skull-splitting headaches djinn suffered when they resisted their masters. A malady he would suffer from no more, though she did not know that.

"You asked for a magical object that can dampen any magic around it. This lamp does precisely that – at a radius of thirty feet," Amani said.

Kun snorted. "Do I look like a fool to you? If this was anything more than a common lamp, you would see me as I truly am. None of this white hair." She waved her hand at the white tresses that crowned her youthful face.

"It needs to be lit," Amani said, conjuring a handful of flames. He held the flames to the lamp wick until the oil caught.

Kun gasped.

So did Amani.

Before him sat a teenage girl, wearing a short tunic so thin it was almost transparent, leaving none of her skeletal body to the imagination. The only ornament she still wore was a ring that sat loosely on her finger, giving off a red light that shimmered across her skin, as though setting the very blood in her veins aglow. Magic of some kind, he guessed.

"And I thought all those muscles were an illusion. No wonder you seduced the queen so easily," the girl snapped. Her eyes betrayed her – they belonged to no child. "You should show your true form to young Maram. She will keep you close to home, no tiresome quests, and make you serve her in the bedchamber instead. She is a gifted courtesan, as capable of giving pleasure as she is at receiving it. You will come to enjoy it, I am sure."

The very thought of lying with Maram – Briska's daughter, no less! – disgusted Amani, and he made no attempt to hide it.

"Enough," he said. "You have what you asked for. Now, tell me where she is."

Kun wagged an admonishing finger at him. "Oh no. You have not told me how to control this thing yet."

"When the lamp is lit, the spell is active. When you extinguish the flame..." Amani dipped his fingers in his drink, then used the dripping digits to pinch the wick out. "When the light is out, magic may be used again." He waved his hand and his torso was once again covered by a thick fur vest.

In the blink of an eye, Kun had changed, too. The poor peasant girl was gone, replaced by the curvy courtesan he'd once bedded. She pursed her lips, as if to beg for a kiss. "You must think me a fool, Amani. This is not the treasure I asked for, but a poor imitation you have conjured to trick me. Does the disgraced queen mean so little to you, that you won't even go on a simple quest to save her?"

"I would do anything for her!" Amani protested.

A wide, predatory smile showed too much of Kun's perfect teeth. "Pledge yourself to me. Become my bed slave, and when I decide you have atoned for trying to trick me, perhaps I will tell you where to find the woman. If you still want her, once you have had me." She fluttered her eyelashes. Once, long ago, the slight movement had fanned his desire into a raging blaze. Now, he could only see the starving child who'd been seated across from him only moments before.

"No. You have what you asked for, I swear it. Now tell me where she is!" Amani roared, rising to his feet.

People were staring, but Kun paid them no heed. She was a crone once more, even more frail-looking than before. She raised her hand to wave, the ring on her finger seeming to glow red in the firelight. "Farewell, sorcerer, and good luck finding your snow queen without my help. When you are ready to offer me what I want, then I will help you."

She marched across the room, pausing only to pull on her cloak, before sweeping out of the door into the whirling snow.

Amani swore, then called for another drink. He'd need it if he intended to go outside into the snow to cast a portal home. At least he still had…

He stared at the table, but the lamp was gone.

The bitch had distracted him, somehow, and stolen it, taking with her his only chance of finding Briska.

The innkeeper brought his drink. Amani

drained it, then ordered another. He may as well drink himself senseless, for he was the biggest fool the world had ever seen. And poor Briska would pay the price for his stupidity, once again.

He deserved to lose her.

Thirty-Five

"How fares Zuleika, and her prince?"

Briska blinked. Kun's face filled the mirror, and she'd asked a question. Haltingly, Briska begged her to repeat it.

When she had, Briska answered, "As well as to be expected. She is warming to him, and I think it will only be a matter of time before they give in to their mutual attraction."

"Good, good. You have done well. I have a reward for you."

This was unusual. "Thank you?" Briska ventured.

Kun continued, "You asked for my protection from magic while you are here in your citadel. At great personal cost, I have procured such a spell for you. Here." She held out a brass lamp, and Briska hurried to take it from her.

It wasn't until Briska's fingers touched the glass that she realised how silly she'd been. Spells passed through the mirror, but a solid object could not, surely. Yet her hands closed around metal, and she now held the lamp in her hands, while Kun's were empty.

"Once lit, the lamp will extinguish all magic around it. But when the lamp goes out, your protection goes with it, and you must light it again." Kun peered into the mirror. "If you place is within ten yards of the entrance to your palace, no one will be able to bring magic inside or cast a spell anywhere near you."

"But only when it is lit," Briska corrected. "Right now, it does nothing." She stared back at Kun. "I'd best keep it away from the mirror, then, for if the lamp removes magic, it will surely turn this back into an ordinary mirror."

Kun laughed. "I doubt it. The magic

enchanting that mirror is more powerful than any living spellcaster could produce. The little lamp will not harm the mirror, or its magic. But the mirror is more than ten yards from your gates, so if you place the lamp at the entrance, you will have nothing to worry about."

"Yes, Mistress." The words that came out of Briska's mouth were the last thing she wanted to say. She had plenty to worry about, not least of which was this new, strange artefact that Kun was only giving her now. Did that mean the current couple she was trying to matchmake would attack her, and it would be worse than Hansel, Gretel, Gerda and Kai combined?

But two decades of servitude had resigned Briska to her fate. Amani was dead and gone, and Maram was surely happy with her devoted lover. Briska's ex-husband surely had plenty of other wives and concubines and perhaps even a new queen to keep him amused. Anyone who knew her had surely forgotten her by now. Except Kun, who never failed to bring another assignment, a new couple to match.

Briska had given up any hope of freedom, for the more successful she was, the more couples Kun gave her.

Nevertheless, she thanked Kun again before the woman disappeared from the mirror, and Briska returned to the delicate task of transforming a warming friendship into something more. If only the girl would forget the incident with the man's brother...

Thirty-Six

"Another!" Amani slurred, waving his hand aimlessly. He couldn't recall how many of these potent jugs of wine he'd drunk, but as long as he could still think, he would drink. For wine was harder and harder to get in his homeland, with that new religion that said you shouldn't drink the stuff.

"How much more do you think you'll need, friend?" the innkeeper asked. He spread his arms. "The taproom is closed, and everyone else has gone to bed. I will go soon, too, and I would advise you to do the same."

"There is only one bed I want, and it belongs to the queen in her snowy citadel," Amani announced. "But I will never find her, so I must drink to forget. More wine!"

The innkeeper sighed. "Her bed is cold as ice, my friend, and best forgotten." He set a second cup on the table, then filled first Amani's and then its companion. He lifted his cup in a toast. "To forgetting."

Amani raised his cup in salute, then downed the contents, ready to bring oblivion.

Thirty-Seven

Briska didn't take her eyes off the pair. She'd matched enough couples to know this was the crucial night. She was no seer, so she didn't know the precise moment, but they were both humming with so much…potential for love, something important would happen tonight, and she would ensure it was the right something.

She watched them eat without even a twinge of hunger, unable to remember how long it had been since she'd last eaten. Years, maybe.

He asked the girl to dance, then stood up

with her, to Briska's surprise. Oh, commoners sometimes danced with the opposite sex, but nobility like this pair were not unlike her people – the ladies danced together, and the men just watched.

Ah, it surprised Zuleika, too – but it made her smile, so that was all right. And it gave the pair an excuse to link hands, which certainly helped. The room raged with lust – the townspeople might be invisible to anyone else, but Briska saw them clearly. The musicians caught the mood and changed the tune, so that the dancers broke from their long chain into pairs.

Vardan's spirits soared as he took the enchantress in his arms. He needed no help from Briska at all, for his feelings for Zuleika had proceeded far beyond lust.

But nothing more could happen in this crowded room. Vardan was the ruler of these people, and while he was certain of his own feelings, he was unsure of hers. A ruler would not want to lose face before his people.

Briska blinked. No, it wasn't about losing face at all. He cared what his people thought about her, if she rejected him. How strange. A ruler loved by his people.

So the push must come from Zuleika, not Vardan.

Zuleika's tongue darted out, moistening her lips, and it gave Briska an idea.

She concentrated, intensifying the girl's thirst just as one of the servants brought a tray of drinks into the hall. There. She had the pair close to the door, and if they chatted for long enough, one of them would…yes!

Vardan took her hand and led her out.

Briska leaned forward, so her nose almost touched the glass, as she watched them go to…a library? A peculiar place for a tryst, but there was no accounting for some people's taste.

Sure enough, this pair were soon distracted by a hand mirror, their lust fading fast.

Not if Briska had any say in the matter, she resolved grimly, hitting them both with a seduction spell. "Resist that, I dare you," she muttered.

She gave them ten seconds, but it only took them six before they kissed. Briska knew her job well. She allowed herself a silent victory cheer.

A scream pierced the silence, so loud it shook an icicle free from the ceiling to crash into the floor behind Briska.

Briska cursed. What had she done this time?

Had Zuleika heard her? Seen her? Somehow known Briska was there?

All colour drained from Briska's face. If she knew this was Briska's second mistake…if she could pin the blame for Thorn on her…

Briska watched with mounting dread as she saw Zuleika flee from the other brother, knowing her flight would end in her casting a portal to take her far away. Far from Beacon Isle, but to where?

Here. Where Briska was no match for the powerful young enchantress.

Briska fell to her knees. She was doomed. The enchantress would destroy her, and rightly so.

Briska's eyes fell on the lamp. Kun's mysterious gift.

She could scarcely conjure a spark any more, so it took some time with the tinder box before a trembling flame sat atop the lamp wick.

Briska breathed a sigh of relief. She was safe, for no magic could touch her here, and the girl's portal would never reach this eyrie.

Thirty-Eight

"Sleeping on tables is not a wise thing to do. What was Kai thinking? My fool of a husband should have offered you a bed," a woman grumbled, far too loud for Amani's liking.

He lifted his head from his distinctly uncomfortable pillow, glad for the dimness of the taproom. "I was not sleeping. I was merely resting my pounding head for a moment," Amani announced. He reached into his pocket, plucked out a coin and tossed it on the table. "For some quiet while I rest it a little more."

She laughed. "You'll get no quiet here. Last

night's blizzard has blown itself out, and as soon as the old men of the village have nagged their sons into shovelling a path, they will be gossiping about whatever war they fought in that everyone else has forgotten, it was so long ago."

"I need to find the queen. In her icy castle…and her icy bed." So much for forgetting. He hadn't drunk enough, after all. "No. What I need is more wine."

"What you need is breakfast and some water, for you are not right in the head. The Snow Queen has been dead these fifteen years and more."

Amani shook his head. "No, that can't be possible. She lives, I am certain of it." Maram wouldn't have lied. Not to him. Djinn couldn't die.

The innkeeper's wife folded her arms across her chest. "I stabbed the bitch myself. She kidnapped Kai, and nearly killed him."

Briska? Kidnap some innkeeper? Why?

But Amani knew the answer. He'd been a slave himself, forced to obey every stupid order he was given. She'd done it because someone had ordered her to.

"Even if she'd somehow survived being stabbed in the heart, she'd still need to eat. And no one's seen her come down from her mountain since the day she kidnapped Kai," the woman said firmly. "She's dead and she deserved it."

Punishing a slave for her master's crimes? Despicable. If this woman had truly tried to kill Briska, then Briska deserved justice. But first he had to find her.

"Which mountain? Where?" he demanded.

She narrowed her eyes. "You're a bigger fool than my husband, if you plan to go up there in winter. You'll die for certain, for no one will venture up the mountain until the snow melts in spring."

Amani seized her shoulders. "Tell me, and I will let you live." He should not be offering this woman her life, not when it was already forfeit for her attempt to murder Briska. Then again, he was no king or lawmaker, and meting out justice was not his job.

She thrust out a hand and pointed. "Step through the door and you'll see it. Look for the frozen waterfall, and it's perched on the crags above it. Impossible to reach, even in summer, unless you have a witch to help you. If you go up there, the shepherds will bring your body back for burial come spring." Tears formed in her eyes. "If she had not taken Kai, I would not have gone up there. As it was…we almost didn't make it back. My family would have mourned us both. If you go up there, think of the family who will come here searching for you. Who will die on the mountain for you?"

Amani released her. "No one will die for me. I have no family left. She is all the family I ever wanted, and…" He blinked, forcing back what could only be tears. He would not cry in front of this strange, violent woman. "I must go after her, for she is all I have left."

"Wait until spring. Maybe I could show you the path I took…"

Amani shook his head. "She has waited long enough. So have I." He rounded the table and headed for the door.

Without even a backward glance toward the innkeeper's wife, Amani headed out into the snow. His breath froze in his throat, but he strode on, not even pausing as he conjured one layer of fur and then another over his winter clothes. When he reached the outskirts of the village and could be certain there was no one watching, he cast a portal to take him to the top of the glittering waterfall. Mere ice and stone would not keep him from Briska. Not now he was so close.

Thirty-Nine

Amani landed in snow, tumbling head over heels in a headlong flight he could not seem to stop until he hit something that knocked the breath from his lungs. If the snow hadn't been so deep, the fall would have killed him. As it was…he winced as he felt what had to be one, maybe even two cracked ribs.

He rose painfully to his feet, scanning the snow for something, anything. His portal, or the icy spires he'd glimpsed from the valley, but he saw neither. In a world of moonlit white beneath a still dark predawn sky, at least there was sound. His boots crunched through the snow, as the wind whistled off the rocks. And there was a dull roaring sound, just at the edge of hearing.

The waterfall!

Just like the floodwaters filling the river outside his castle, only vertical instead of horizontal.

He followed the sound of water, wishing with all his might that it would lead him to Briska. If he didn't find her here, he didn't know what he'd do. Where else he could search. How did you find one woman in a whole world of people? A woman who couldn't be found by magical means…

Amani's head spun, as though he'd run too fast, but he couldn't seem to catch his breath. The aftereffects of wine had never made him feel like this before.

And cold! Where had his furs gone? And his shirt? He must have lost them in the snow somewhere. At least his ribs hurt less in the cold. There was that, he told himself, as he trudged on, wrapping his arms around himself in a fruitless attempt to keep warm. He tried to conjure a cloak, a blanket, anything to keep him warm, but whatever had stolen his breath had stolen his magic, too.

What in all that was holy could do such a thing? If it was Kun, he would kill her. No magic necessary. He'd wrap his hands around her throat and squeeze until she stopped breathing. Nothing would get between him and Briska ever again.

Amani blinked. Was that...glass? He dragged his numb feet up to the wall and pressed his hand to it. No, not glass. Ice, stealing his remaining body heat as he tried and failed to pull his palm from the wall. Then he managed to get his other hand stuck, and Amani knew he was in trouble.

His whole body was numb. Death would come to claim him soon. At least he would meet his fate standing, for he could not lie down in the snow with both hands stuck to a wall.

He waited for the memories to come, the last thing he would ever see, to distract him as he passed into the next world.

As if on command, the best came first.

Briska walked into view, as perfect as the first time he'd seen her. A marble statue come to life.

Yet this wasn't a memory. It couldn't be. For there it was.

Nestled in her hands was a lamp. His lamp.

Forty

Briska stared at the flickering flame, wondering if something so tiny could truly protect her from the enchantress. She didn't dare look in the mirror again, just in case the girl saw her.

It took her a long moment to remember all of Kun's instructions about the lamp. Not only did she need to light it, but it had a limited range – in order to stop anyone from entering the palace, the lamp needed to be near the gates.

Her heart froze in her chest. What if her forgetfulness had allowed someone to enter the palace already? Even now, the girl could be inside, creeping up on her.

Briska cradled the lamp in her hands, holding it close to her chest as she took it to the entrance hall. She hunched her shoulders over it, hating the feeling that she was being watched.

She set the lamp in the middle of the entrance hall, where it looked as out of place as a child's discarded shoe.

While she'd been distracted, the sky had begun to lighten, building up to dawn, and now she could see the valley spread out before her, through the thin, transparent walls. A view she rarely looked at any more, for what was there to look at when everything was covered with snow? Even the waterfall was frozen.

She fancied she heard someone say her name, but a quick glance at the gates told her there was no one out there.

In here, then, she thought with a shiver. Briska edged closer to the lamp, until her boots almost touched it. She turned slowly in a circle, scanning the room with all her normal senses. Even if the enchantress was invisible, she still had to breathe.

Twice she circled, and still she did not find the girl. But there were marks on the wall, marring her view of the waterfall. Briska stepped closer to investigate.

Why, they looked like handprints, two of them, and a thin trail of blood frozen to the wall leading down. Quite macabre, really. If the girl thought to frighten her…

Briska held her hand up to the print. No woman had made these. A large man, maybe, or a bear might have. But white bears did not climb so high, away from the sea and their source of sustenance.

Whoever had left them wouldn't have survived long up here. But she would have to go outside and clean them off, or stare at them every time she looked to the waterfall.

She opened the gates and stepped out, careful to keep to the path that now lay buried under a layer of ice and snow. One wrong step would bury her for good – or at least until Kun came looking for her.

Snow had piled up beneath the handprints, perfectly placed for her to stand on so she could reach the marks. Ugh, the blood was worse than she'd thought, smeared down the wall in two wide, pink streaks. Briska set one boot on the drift, testing her footing before putting all her weight on it.

The drift groaned, not unlike a bear.

Briska backed away, darting a glance behind her to make sure the gate wasn't too far away. Once she rounded the corner of the palace, she'd run. Before the bear could rise.

It groaned again, and flung out a paw. No, not a paw. A bloody hand, tinted blue. It was a man in the snowdrift, and if she didn't do something, he'd be a dead man.

Taking a deep breath, Briska forced herself back the way she'd come. She thrust her gloved hands into the snow and grasped the man's shoulder. Brushing away the snow, she found his head, and used all her strength to roll him over, so she could see his face. If it was Vardan, she'd have no choice but to save him. But if it was that fool boy from the village, back again…

With a mighty heave and a groan of her own, Briska managed to turn the man face-up.

His eyes drifted open and the dreamiest smile lit his face. "My queen," he croaked. "Finally, I have found you."

Briska's heart stopped. She couldn't even draw breath. It couldn't be. He couldn't be. The Sultan had executed him more than twenty years ago, and she'd looked for him in the mirror every day since. Yet he didn't appear to have aged a day since she last saw him.

"Amani?"

But his eyes had closed again, and his face was turning as blue as his fingers. She had to get him inside, and warm. She hadn't found him after all this time just to lose him again to a bit of snow.

Briska hooked her arms under his armpits and began to haul him home.

Forty-One

Briska managed to get Amani onto the bed once occupied by that young fool, Kai, but she had no idea how to help him. She needed to warm him, or send him into an enchanted sleep like Kai until she could heal him, but her magic refused to cooperate. No matter what spell she tried, she couldn't conjure so much as a spark.

She would have to do things the mundane way, she guessed.

Briska bundled up every blanket and item of clothing she had, and tucked them around

Amani, hoping to preserve what body warmth he still had. Next, she headed outside to find the woodpile, buried under the snow. She couldn't remember the last time she'd built a fire, so she had to dig deep before she found the topmost logs.

She carried them inside, then went back for more, until she had a healthy pyre piled up in the fire pit. She lit it from the lamp, but the tinder caught too slowly, smoking sulkily instead of blazing into eager life. Swearing, Briska opened the lamp and tipped the oil onto the wood. Then the fire caught, licking at kindling and logs alike as it greedily drank the oil.

Briska dropped the lamp on the floor, for it was useless now.

What else did ordinary people use to heal someone who'd come this close to freezing?

A fire, warm clothes and blankets, and conserving their body heat. Or sharing it.

Briska slipped out of her clothes, then slid into bed beside Amani. His skin was cold to the touch – even colder than hers! – but she rubbed against him, trying to share what little warmth she had. A good lust spell would come in really handy right now. Not that she needed it. Just touching him again was enough to kindle her desire. It had been more than twenty years since she'd last touched him, but she remembered every line, every ridge of muscle, like it was yesterday.

She covered his face with kisses, then bit her lip to cast a lust spell. Knowing it would not work, but wishing with all her might to feel his hands on her body one last time.

She kissed and caressed him, her own skin afire at the contact with the man she loved. Against her belly, she felt part of him stirring, though the rest of his body did not. Her fingers strayed lower, stroking him harder until she could bear it no longer.

She climbed atop him, easing the length of him inside her until she could hold no more. Then she began to rock her hips against him, just as she used to do when they were lovers.

Once, he would stare up at her in wonder, his hands moving to cup her breasts, his lips murmuring endearments before he kissed her, moving within her in a blissful harmony that would bring them the most glorious release.

But now...

Briska blinked away tears, wishing for what could never be again.

Behind her, unnoticed, the lamp's light went out.

Forty-Two

Amani debated whether he was dreaming, or if he'd died and attained paradise, for there was no way Briska could be truly sitting astride him, riding him hard in the pursuit of her own pleasure, as she sent him inexorably to his own glorious peak.

He reached up to cup those glorious breasts, bouncing as she rocked. But there was blood on his hands, and the dimly remembered pain of tearing his palms free of the ice. But blood could cast magic. He sent a powerful healing spell through his body, gritting his teeth against the pain as his ribs knitted together and his hands became whole once more. Only then did he place reverent hands on Briska's hips, wanting to touch her to see if she was real.

Her eyes flew open. "Amani?"

He managed a smile. "You mistook me for some other lover? My queen, you wound me."

"I have no other lover. Never. Not in all this time…"

He rose up, so that he might kiss her lips while still driving deep inside her. Bliss, the like of which he never thought he'd feel again.

"Then you have been neglected for too long. It will take me weeks to make up for my absence. I will make you never want to leave your bed, my queen. For I know I have no wish to leave it." He thrust gently, changing the angle until she gasped. He fixed his gaze on her face as he pushed her to heights of pleasure no one else could reach, and was rewarded by the sound of her screaming his name. At last.

His pleasure could wait. For Briska was and forever would be his queen, and nothing mattered more than bringing a smile to her face, a sigh to her lips, and an enormous, shuddering orgasm that engulfed her completely.

Forty-Three

Briska cried out again, her voice hoarse for the first time in too long. And still Amani played her body until it sang, just for him. She'd lost count of the number of times he'd carried her to that lofty peak of pleasure that made her scream, for once he'd reached it, he started again, just as lovingly as the first time.

"Stop fucking that man!"

Kun's icy tone cut through Briska's pleasure, freezing her in place.

"Now pick up that lamp, and hold it in your hands. He is the slave of the lamp, and as long as you are holding it, you are his mistress. Hold it in your hands and order him to throw himself off the nearest cliff!"

Briska winced as Amani slid out of her, wishing she could disobey the order, but even the thought of trying made her head pound. Blindly, she groped for the lamp.

"Go ahead. You're too late for that," Amani said. He rose from the bed, so that both Briska and Kun could see his naked magnificence, and folded his arms across his chest.

Briska touched the lamp, now cold from lying unlit on the floor for so long, and cradled it in her hands. She didn't want to do this. She didn't. Yet her mouth opened and the words came out anyway, followed by a sob.

And the sound of smashing glass.

Blood trickled down the surface of the mirror, tinting Kun's horrified face red.

"Blood of the betrayed that binds this djinn, set her free!" Amani commanded.

All of a sudden, a weight lifted off Briska, as though she'd been carrying a heavy load that had almost crushed her. The fog in her head – fog she'd scarcely noticed until now – cleared, and she became aware of just how cold she was, standing naked in a palace made of ice.

"NO!" Kun screamed.

"Yes," Amani replied. He flicked his fingers at her. "Now, you will leave us alone, for if I ever see you again, you will not live to see the next day."

Amid a storm of cursing, Kun vanished from the mirror.

"Did you kill the Sultan?" Briska asked, wrapping her arms around herself to try and stay warm. But the very thought of Amani – the man she loved – killing anyone, chilled her heart.

"No, of course not. That blood came from Maram."

"You killed my daughter?" Briska shrieked. She sank her teeth into her lip, determined to curse Amani into oblivion for hurting Maram, but nothing happened. "What is wrong with me?" She rushed at Amani and pummelled him with her fists. "What have you done to me? To her?"

He grasped her wrists and gently pushed her back. "I've made love to you, to the best of my ability. And I have done nothing to Princess Maram that she did not ask for."

Briska snatched up the lamp again. This time, she said the words of her own free will. "I order you to go jump off a cliff and never touch me again."

Instead of obeying, Amani laughed. "If it is your wish, I will not touch you. Because it is your wish. I am no longer a slave, and I have your daughter to thank for it. So do you, for she gave me the vial of her blood and commanded me to use it to free you. Until she told me, I had no idea that you still lived. The moment I was free, I did everything within my power to find you. Now I have…and you are free. No more orders, ever. Least of all from that whore, Kun."

Briska took this all in, looking for a lie, yet knowing she wouldn't find one. His words explained everything, and they even made sense. All except one thing. "But why isn't my magic working?"

His brow furrowed. "I do not know. If you permit me to touch you, perhaps I can find out."

Briska stepped into the circle of his outstretched arms, and breathed a sigh of relief as his warmth engulfed her.

He stood silent for a long moment, before he finally said, "Your magic is working fine. If anything, it's stronger than it ever was. This castle is absolutely humming with it. Every inch of ice and snow, obedient to your command, woven into a protection spell so powerful no one could see through it. Not even to search for you."

"But Kun said…she said she cast the spell. I didn't. I know I didn't. I would have remembered…"

"For a spell of this strength, it would have taken a lot of blood. No wonder she managed to hide you from me for so long. If she cast the initial spell, then used your blood to enhance it…but the amount of blood this would have taken…I don't know how you survived, my queen. Unless she took a little at a time, every day…"

The truth dawned on Briska so suddenly she gasped. She had not thought so quickly in years. "Gerda. When she and the boy stabbed me, I feared I would bleed to death. The floor was awash…and when I awoke it was gone. Kun saved me, or so I thought." She grimaced. "How do I break the spell so that it no longer uses up all my magic?"

"Just let it go," Amani said.

"Let it go?" she asked doubtfully. Breaking spells was usually far more complex than that.

Amani's arms closed around her, his voice a sultry whisper in her ear. "Feel the spell, just as you feel this." His lips kissed her neck, sending a flood of warmth deep into her body. "Then release it."

It was hard to focus, when all she wanted to do was return his kisses and caresses with a few of her own, but Briska did her best. Reaching deep within her to the magic in her blood, she found the spell, a delicate web of threads that radiated out of her and into every facet of the castle. Now she could feel the magic pulsing through the walls of the palace, keeping the world out. No more.

Briska severed the connection.

Magic boiled through her veins, like a flood unleashed on a dry river bed. She bit her lip, and cast the barest whisper of a lust spell.

The power of it swirled around her, more powerful than any blizzard. Swirled around both of them, as desire darkened Amani's eyes.

"My queen, I'm taking you home. My castle is yours, and right now, we need a bed, or my desire will melt this castle the moment I kiss you," he said roughly, tracing a circle in the air.

Lifting Briska in his arms, Amani stepped through the portal, from icy mountain to searing desert. No, not just the desert. A castle in the desert, and he was already carrying her inside.

Briska laughed. Inside, the castle was bare, but she had magic to spare. She conjured a bed, big enough to fit a sultan and a dozen concubines, then squealed as Amani tossed her on top of the silk cushions.

He fell to his knees on the end of the bed. "Permit me to love you, my queen. Every day for the rest of my life. Be my wife, and I shall worship you every night for as long as I live."

"Yes," she whispered as Amani took her in his arms, sliding between her legs and deep within her. "Yes!" And she melted under his touch, just the way she wanted. She was the snow queen no more.

Forty-Four

Kun stepped out of her portal, pulling her cloak more closely around her thin frame. There was no sign of the accursed couple, or the magic that had once protected this icy palace from the elements. Already the wall beside the waterfall had collapsed into the river, letting snow into the chambers where Briska had hidden from the world for so long.

Kun sighed. She would never find another matchmaker as talented as Briska. The girl had a gift for finding precisely the right moment to cast her spell, weaving the couples together so closely they never even suspected. She would have liked to keep the girl for longer, for her work was nowhere near done, but that damned enchanter had ruined everything. She still didn't know how he'd managed to free himself from servitude, or to free Briska, but it served him right. He'd thrown away immortality to rut like rabbits with the little matchmaker queen. So stupid. But so were most men, when they thought with their pricks. Centuries had passed, but men never changed.

She stepped into the palace, trudging through the blown snow, until she reached the mirror. A thin layer of blood crusted the glass, but that could be cleaned off. She would take the mirror back to her palace in the floating city, where it belonged. It had served her purpose, and so had Briska.

She'd pushed Molina and Lubos together, ensuring they produced a child, and she'd even dealt with that dreadful scion of House Rumpelstiltskin. And with Briska doing all the matchmaking, she'd left Kun free to tend to the training of Molina's daughter, and to do it properly.

Grasping the mirror, Kun stepped back through the portal. She would return it to her palace later, when Molina's daughter was asleep.

"Good day, Mother," Rapunzel said.

Not that the girl knew she was Molina's daughter, of course.

Kun smiled. "It is, isn't it? The future looks quite rosy, now I have you."

Rapunzel looked puzzled, but still she smiled. "Yes, Mother."

Yes, the future looked rosy indeed, though it could darken as much as Kun desired, for now she had Rapunzel, she could weave whatever fate she wanted.

About the Author

Demelza Carlton has always loved the ocean, but on her first snorkelling trip she found she was afraid of fish.

She has since swum with sea lions, sharks and sea cucumbers and stood on spray drenched cliffs over a seething sea as a seven-metre cyclonic swell surged in, shattering a shipwreck below.

Demelza now lives in Perth, Western Australia, the shark attack capital of the world.

The *Ocean's Gift* series was her first foray into fiction, followed by her suspense thriller *Nightmares* trilogy. She swears the *Mel Goes to Hell* series ambushed her on a crowded train and wouldn't leave her alone.

Want to know more? You can follow Demelza on Facebook, Twitter, YouTube or her website, Demelza Carlton's Place at:

www.demelzacarlton.com

www.ingramcontent.com/pod-product-compliance
Lightning Source LLC
Chambersburg PA
CBHW070331170726
48291CD00001D/19